# Critical Error

by

## Murray McDonald

First Published by Kennedy Mack publishing

**Critical Error**

ISBN 978-0-9574871-4-7

Copyright © Murray McDonald 2013

# Part One

# Chapter 1

**Fajr Hotel**
**Ahwaz, Iran**
**September 1st 2007**

Finally, thought Sam, as a hand clamped over his mouth and the cold steel of the blade pressed into his throat, he was getting somewhere.

"You ask too many questions, my friend!" offered the knifeman. His foul breath hung heavily as he pinned Sam to the small bed.

The Arab use of the word 'friend' was not lost on Sam. He had heard them come for him, clumsy, poorly trained. About the only thing they had got right was the timing. At 4.00 a.m., Sam would have been in a deep sleep had he not expected his visitors.

Sam tried to answer but the hand remained clamped over his mouth.

"Let him speak," came a different voice from the doorway, calm and authoritative.

The boss, thought Sam.

The knifeman removed his hand from Sam's mouth but pushed the blade harder against his neck.

"Just trying to find my girlfriend," choked Sam as the knife pressed on his Adam's apple. "She went missing about a week ago," he struggled but persevered. "Perhaps you can help me."

"Perhaps," offered the boss. "Can you describe her?"

The knifeman barely contained a laugh as the boss teased Sam. The hold on the knife relaxed slightly, allowing Sam to speak more freely.

"About five seven, dark hair, cute, oh and she had a CNN van and a cameraman with her. Hard to miss really."

"Piercing green eyes, dimples in her cheeks, a tattoo on her left wrist and far too young for you?" offered the boss.

Sam nodded, although he didn't quite agree with the too young jibe. He was only ten years older than her.

"Nope, don't know her," concluded the boss. "Now, who the fuck are you?" The calm friendly tone had gone. The joking was over and they were down to business. The knifeman pressed the knife harder once more. A small trickle of blood ran down Sam's neck.

Sam had no intention of telling the boss who he was. At least, not who he really was. As far as anyone in Iran knew, Sam was the boyfriend of the missing CNN journalist, kidnapped a week earlier from the streets of Tehran. She and her cameraman had quite literally vanished. No terrorist group had claimed responsibility nor had anyone demanded a ransom. With the trail cold and the Iranians blocking every request by the US to help, Sam Baker, one of the CIA's top operatives, had gone in as the grieving boyfriend, desperate to find his loved one.

After two days of searching, the CNN van was discovered near the city of Ahwaz, not far from the Persian Gulf. Sam immediately turned his attention to the streets of Ahwaz, showing the photo of his girlfriend to anyone who would look and listen. The photo showed the pair enjoying a meal with friends. The photo was fake but the CIA forgers defied anyone to prove it. It was one of their finest forgeries and showed the American couple enjoying a meal with Sam's supposed uncle, the President of the United States.

As the knife cut into his skin, Sam couldn't help but smile at how well the photo had worked. Ahwaz was surrounded by secret terrorist training camps and the likelihood of the CNN team being taken by terrorists had jumped tenfold as news spread that they were in the region. The subtlety of the link to the President had been key. Sam had touted his picture around the city and it had worked. The mention of the journalist's tattoo was just the confirmation Sam needed. He had his men. Sam hid the small .22 caliber pistol he had pointed at the knifeman from beneath the covers.

Three hours and a bone churning ride on the floor of a pickup truck later, Sam was being led into a small barracks building. Neither the boss nor the knifeman had uttered a word since they had bundled Sam through the hotel's main lobby in nothing more than his boxers and a vest.

Sam had counted four guards as they drove into the compound. Knifeman and Bossman made six. A further two stood guard inside the barracks. Eight men that he could account for. At least half again would be resting. A minimum of twelve in total, a little more than he had expected. Actually, it was about eight more than he had expected. Standing in a pair of boxer shorts and a vest, things couldn't get much worse.

"Who the fuck is this?!" screamed the female journalist at the sight of Sam in his underwear.

Sam smiled at his 'girlfriend's' loss of memory and at how much worse the situation had just become.

"Don't be silly, Honey, it's me!" he said, his eyes begging her to realize he was on her side. Bossman nodded to Knifeman and the knife was once again at Sam's throat.

Sam noticed that the journalist and cameraman were unshackled, free to roam around the small barracks. Not exactly what he had anticipated. Not good either. A bond had been struck between captor and hostage. A bond they were unlikely to break for a stranger in his underwear. Sam prayed she would play along, recognizing a fellow American's accent.

Sam's 'girlfriend' backed away. "I have no idea who this man is!" she said definitively.

Bossman began to speak rapidly in his native tongue. Whatever he was saying, Knifeman didn't like it and the blade grew tighter across Sam's neck.

Sam dropped his chin despondently and shifted onto his right foot. The movement caused a slight separation between blade and skin but enough to ensure Sam's survival. Plan A was dead. Plan B was Sam's only option. He just had to work out what that was. Sam swung his hand up and grabbed Knifeman's hand in a vice-like grip just as the heel of his left foot crushed down into Knifeman's foot. Sam snapped his head back like a wrecking ball and smashed Knifeman's nose to a pulp. The combination of actions had all been thought through precisely and executed to perfection, all in the blink of an eye. Knifeman dropped to the ground, immobile. Sam grabbed the knife and spun across the floor grabbing Bossman as he moved and placed the knife carefully across the not so cocky boss' throat. Plan B was going to have to go with the flow.

The two guards at the door of the barracks had reacted to Sam's move but Sam was too quick. The knife was at their boss' throat before either could raise their weapon and get a shot.

"Holy shit!" exclaimed the journalist. Her cameraman grabbed her and tried to keep her calm.

"OK, now nobody needs to die here," said Sam. "I just want to take these nice people back to their families."

Neither of the terrorists dropped their weapons.

The journalist burst into tears, gesticulating wildly at Sam. She looked furious at his rescuing her.

"They can't let us go before 9.30 a.m.!" cried out the cameraman, still struggling to contain the increasingly hysterical journalist.

"Sorry?" asked Sam, incredulous at the suggestion, that after 9.30 a.m., they could quite simply walk out of the door.

"They have no intention of harming us," explained the cameraman. "That's why she's panicking. You've put our lives in danger, not saved them!"

"This is not fucking Disneyland! Wake up guys!" shouted Sam. "We're in fucking downtown central Terroristville! I don't know which nutters they represent but trust me, they only mean us harm!"

"We…" the boss began but was interrupted by the journalist.

"…they are the Izz ad-Din al-Qassam Brigades." She choked back tears as she spoke. "Palestinian fighters. They have given us an exclusive to release when we leave here which, up until you arrived, was about an hour from now!" she added angrily.

Sam couldn't help but ask. "Why an hour from now? Why not now? Why not yesterday?"

4

"Because today, in less than an hour, we will bring the Israelis to their knees," promised the boss proudly.

While Sam was distracted by the journalist and the boss talking, the two guards worked their way closer, silently closing the gap between themselves and Sam. Sam, of course, knew exactly what they were doing and had hoped they would do exactly that.

He had heard enough and the angles were now perfect. Without a moment's hesitation or warning, Sam drew the knife across the terrorist leader's throat almost decapitating him and killing him instantly. The action caught everybody by surprise and as the guards began to compute what had just happened, Sam was already dispatching the knife towards the guard to his right whilst kicking the dead weight of the boss into the guard on his left.

As one guard died with a knife embedded in his chest, the other was coping with the almost headless corpse of his boss as it crashed into him. The head lolled wildly as both the guard and the boss crashed to the floor. Before they even hit the floor, Sam was on them to help ensure the guard's skull cracked as he powered it into the floor.

The gruesomeness of the scene left the cameraman with little hope of quelling the journalist's screams, ensuring the rest of the camp would be ready and waiting for them.

"In an hour, they would have let us go!" shouted the cameraman, furious at what had just happened.

"We have to warn Israel," replied Sam, firmly and simply. He grabbed the guard's gun and checked the magazine.

"How many terrorists?" demanded Sam as he ran to the window.

"There were eleven," stammered the cameraman. "I suppose there are seven now…"

One better than he had anticipated. Maybe the day was looking up.

The door crashed open and two guards ran in. Their weapons were drawn but not having heard any shots, they had not known what to expect. Sam didn't hesitate and shot them both as they entered the room.

"Five left," corrected the cameraman.

With the first shots fired, no more guards would be running blindly into the room.

"Wait here!" commanded Sam as he opened a back door and disappeared.

Sam had no intention of becoming a sitting duck and instead was going on the offensive.

By the time the five guards were in position to launch an assault on the barracks, it was too late. Sam was behind them. As they charged, he simply picked them off. These were men who strapped bombs to themselves and blew up women and children. Sam had no compunction about shooting them in the back, front, head or balls. The only good terrorist, as far as he was concerned, was a dead one.

As he walked back into the barracks it was a very different scene. The journalist rushed across the room and hugged him like a long lost friend. The cameraman tried his best to join in but Sam was in no mood for celebrating. The clock was ticking. "I need a phone, is there one here?"

"The next building is a small office, there's one in there," offered his new best pal.

As they rushed to the next building, the journalist explained what had happened. They had been kidnapped in Tehran after inadvertently hearing one of their contacts discussing the plan to attack Israel. They didn't know what or how the attack would happen, they just knew it was massive and they knew when. September 1st 8.00 a.m.

After what felt like hours, Sam was eventually patched through to the Head of Shin Bet, Israel's security service. The phone rang and rang. Sam checked his watch, 9.31 a.m. local time, 8.01 a.m. Israeli time.

# Chapter 2

**Jerusalem, Israel**
**September 1st 2007**

As the bus drew to a stop, the excitement and trepidation of the small crowd was palpable. Rebecca Cohen's hand shook as she held on tightly to Joshua. Her body trembled as she fought back the tears. She always knew this day would come. For six years, she had waited for the day that her constant companion, her best friend and confidant would leave her side for the first time. She looked down into the eyes of her son and for the first time, she didn't see his father looking back. For six years, Joshua had been her savior, her only link to the one man she had ever truly loved. If it were not for Joshua, she would most definitely have given up. His dark eyes glistened with excitement, in just the same way as his father's had before him. A father whom Joshua would never meet. A father whom he knew about and could be proud of. A man who had died for his country, his people and his beliefs. A man Rebecca had adored and worshipped.

The tears started to flow as the door opened. Rebecca tried desperately hard to hide them. Joshua didn't like it when Mummy cried. His eyes saddened as he watched the tears run down her cheeks.

"It's OK Josh, Mummy's happy. They're tears of joy," she lied.

Joshua looked around. It seemed most of the mummies and even a few of the daddies were crying. Even some of his friends were crying. Was there something he didn't know about?

Was there something he should be scared of? No, his mother worshipped him and would never do anything that would upset or harm him. If she wanted him on the bus, it was because it was good for him. He disengaged from his mother's tightening grip, gave her a final hug, a kiss on the cheek and told her he loved her.

"I love you too, my darling," replied Rebecca as she watched her son, in his new school uniform, board the bus and run straight to the back to jump onto the backseat. Pressing his face against the window and waving wildly, he shouted 'I love you!'

As the bus began to pull away, Rebecca's tears flowed freely. She mouthed 'I love you too'. The smile on his face exploded into her retina. The initial blast of the explosion took her completely by surprise. The ball of flame engulfed the bus for what seemed like hours before the shockwave hit her. The lasting image of her son waving excitedly as his body was torn to pieces would live with her forever.

# Chapter 3

"What in the name of God was that?" shouted the Prime Minister, Chaim Goldman, as the bomb-proof room shook on its foundations.

Most of the cabinet had seen active service at some point in their lives and all instantly knew that the force of the explosion had to be massive or extremely close to have been felt so strongly in one of the most secure rooms in the country. Before anyone could respond, a second and a third shockwave hit the room in quick succession. As the doors to the Cabinet Room flew open, cabinet members drew their weapons and aimed. In the doorway, stood the Sergeant-At-Arms of the Knesset and a group of cabinet bodyguards and senior aides.

Quick to respond and before anyone was shot by accident, the Prime Minister screamed "STOP!!!"

Silence fell and order was restored.

The Prime Minister turned to the Sergeant-At-Arms, the man responsible for Knesset security.

"Avi?"

"A number of large explosions have hit the city. The Knesset is secure, Mr Prime Minister. Lockdown procedures were put in place the moment we heard the first explosion."

With each explosion, the occupants of the ultra secure room had flinched, perfectly safe but feeling the pain of each explosion. This was happening on their watch.

As the news cameras rushed across the country, the scale of the attack unfolded. The TV screens in the Cabinet Office ran the images as phones rang and updates flooded in. Every target was the same. The monstrousness of the attack was overwhelming. Two hundred buses carrying the youngest and most vulnerable members of society had been bombed. Survivors on the buses were few and far between and those who had survived were unlikely to live a normal life. Within the hour, the death-toll was already in the thousands. The overwhelming force of the explosions on each of the buses was staggering. The death-toll of passers-by began to exceed that of the bus passengers. This was a co-ordinated attack on a massive scale, even surpassing that of 9-11.

At 8.00 p.m., twelve hours after the initial explosion, the Prime Minister called the meeting to order, not that any order needed to be called. The Cabinet Room was deathly silent, despite its inflated numbers. Deputies and assistants lined the walls as the Cabinet gathered round a large conference table in the center of the room.

"David, can you please give us the update," asked the Prime Minister, turning to his Defense Minister, David Hirsch.

As the Minister of Defense got to his feet, the cabinet door opened and the President of Israel, Ehud Rabin, entered the room, nodding to the Prime Minister and looking for an empty seat against the wall.

"Please Ehud, sit next to me," offered the Prime Minister, motioning for an assistant to move a chair next to him. The President nodded his assent and took the seat next to Chaim.

As with many elected presidents who inherit prime ministers of a different political party, the two men had fought publicly for years and had split the allegiance of the Cabinet between them. However, this was a message to the Cabinet, from the two master politicians of Israel, that petty differences were to be set aside. Israel was to be united. The President nodded for David Hirsch to continue.

"This Morning was the first day of term for a new school year. At approximately 7.58 a.m., a primary school bus in Jerusalem exploded, killing everyone on board. By 8.06 a.m., over 200 bombs, all targeting primary school buses, had exploded across the country. Casualty figures are changing by the second but as of five minutes ago, the numbers stood at 4,237 confirmed dead and over 10,000 injured. Over 2,000 of those are critical. Despite the chaos, our infrastructure is holding its own. Hospitals have initiated emergency procedures and field hospitals have been erected. The armed forces are on high alert."

As the Defense Secretary paused for a moment, the room remained silent. The scale of the attack began to hit home.

After a few seconds, a quiet voice came from the head of the table.

"How?" asked the President.

"We're not entirely certain yet. The bus depots are highly secure and as such, there is no way the devices were planted before they left for the school run. The bus drivers are all security trained and armed. Suicide bombers would have been repelled and certainly would not have succeeded 200 times within ten minutes."

"So how?" asked the President in a whisper, the tone of his voice conveying his utter dismay and fury.

"It is unconfirmed but..." David paused as he thought about the horror of what he was about to say and whether it really could be true.

"Yes?" prompted the President regaining some volume.

"There is speculation that the attack was in fact by suicide bombers. Except that the bombers may have been unaware of their actions. Perhaps the term *sacrificial bombers* may be more appropriate."

David paused. He could see that some understood what he was saying but others were struggling, either because they were slow or more likely, their brains could not comprehend or refused to compute the possibility of what may have happened.

"Two hundred families have completely disappeared," he added, seeing more of those in the room piece together the evidence. "We believe they may have been planted here to commit this atrocity." He paused again as even he could not believe the words he was uttering. "Or more accurately, the bombers were raised within our own communities for the sole purpose of being sacrificed today."

"Are you seriously suggesting the bombers were children?" asked the Prime Minister.

"Yes. It looks like these were children who we believed to be our own but in fact were the sons and daughters of infiltrators, frauds, brought here as supposed Jewish immigrants, destined only to attack us and destroy us from within."

"So two hundred families posing as Jews have raised their children within our communities to carry out today's attack using their six-year-olds, packed with explosives, as bombs??!!" asked the President.

"It appears so," confirmed David, looking as though the weight of the world had collapsed on his shoulders.

With silence descending on the room again, the feint sound of raised voices could be heard through the almost sound-proof Cabinet doors.

Chaim Goldman got up and opened the door to find his Head of Security tussling with an old man. As the Cabinet watched the bizarre scene, the Prime Minister tried to separate the two men.

"Avi, get your hands off me!" shouted the old man.

"I'm sorry, Sir…" replied Avi, with the utmost deference. "But you can't…"

"Avi, it's OK," said the Prime Minister, recognizing the old man. "Ben," he said acknowledging Ben Meir, a man known to every Israeli and highly respected. He still had great influence in Israel and was the main reason Chaim and Ehud held the offices they currently held.

"What the hell are you doing?" asked the Prime Minister.

"Still showing this old bastard I can take him," he said pointing towards Avi, thirty years his junior and almost twice his size. "I need to talk to you and this was the quickest way."

"OK Ben but things are critical right now, we're just getting our heads around…"

"I understand but I need to see you, Ehud and David immediately. Whatever you're doing can wait until we've spoken."

"But Ben, we need to respond…"

Ben reached up and took hold of Chaim's shoulder and looked into his eyes. "I need to speak to you, Ehud and David, *NOW!*" he shouted. Ben Meir was not a man who took 'no' for an answer. Before Chaim could respond, Ben looked at the Cabinet and motioned for them to leave.

Despite the fact that Ben Meir had not held office for fifteen years, when he spoke, people listened. Within minutes, he had taken control of events and stood in the Cabinet Office with a Prime Minister, a President and a Defense Minister wondering what the hell had just happened. Ben picked up the phone and barked a number of instructions to whoever was on the other end. The three most powerful men in Israel simply looked on helplessly.

The room remained silent while Ben's orders were carried out. Ehud and Chaim had tried to talk but on each occasion a simple "hush" from Ben had stopped them dead.

Eventually, the door opened and four men entered the room. The Head of Mossad (the Israeli intelligence service), the Head of The Shabak (more commonly known as Shin Bet, the Internal Security Service) and Israel's two Chief Rabbis.

Chaim, Ehud and David looked at each other as the four men entered the room. The first two men were not unexpected but the two Chief Rabbis were a surprise. They all knew Ben's stance on retaliatory attacks - hit fast and hit ten times harder.

After a quick round of greetings, Ben stood up. This was his Israel and this time, they had gone too far. He reached down to his old attaché case, took out a battered old folder and placed it on the table in front of them.

"Gentlemen," he began. "Today, the terrorists have gone too far. Above all else, it is our duty to protect the children of Israel." Ben paused as he let the words reverberate around the room. "Gentlemen, what we discuss here today can never leave this room." Ben waited for nods from each of the attendees and only then pushed the folder to the center of the table.

"I give you Project Ararat."

# Chapter 4

**November 2007**

Ben Meir stood near the summit of Mount Sion, his grandson at his side. It had been two months since the explosions had shaken his country to the core. Two months of long days and interminable nights. He had once again reigned over the country he had helped build. His calls had secured the funding he needed. His calls had made men give whatever was required to their spiritual homeland. Only he could make it happen. This time, the Arabs had gone too far. It was time for Israel to be safe and secure. Its citizens would no longer worry about suicide bombers or crazy gunmen. Ben Meir was going to give the Israelis what they always wanted and what they deserved: a safe and secure homeland.

The funding and support had been the easiest to secure but it was the Rabbis that had held up the plans. It was not until the previous evening that they had finally come to him with news that agreement had been reached and the plan could go ahead. In less than two hours, the walls would start to go up. The Army and a mass conscription of civilian contractors were ready to move and at 8.00 a.m., it would begin. Israel was not just tightening her borders, she was closing them down. The twelve-foot structure would encircle the land and close Israel to the outside world. The Arabs were, without exception, to be resettled in Gaza and the West Bank. By nightfall, Jerusalem would once again be completely within Israeli control.

The Air Force was already circling the skies. The message to any disagreeing neighbors would be decisive and clear. Simply put, overwhelming might would fall upon them. Israel had been pushed too far. In two months, it had not taken vengeance upon those who had orchestrated the cowardly attack on its children but that day would change all that. Israel was going to stand tall.

Ben smiled down at his grandson, his pride and joy.

"My son, what do you see?" he asked, pointing towards Jordan.

"Hmm, nothing," replied the young boy.

"Exactly, nothing. Just miles of desert."

"Now tell me, what do you see over there?" he asked, pointing towards Israel.

"Green plants and things."

"Exactly. That's what we did, the Israelis, we made this from that. Life, we gave life to this dead land!" he exclaimed proudly, stopping himself from adding '*and they tried their best to kill it off again.*'

As the clock ticked nearer to eight a.m., Ben boarded his waiting helicopter and headed back to Jerusalem. The shit was about to hit the fan and he was not going to miss it for anything. As they touched down, he could feel the ground shake. The roar of powerful diesel engines drowned out all other noises. The mass construction army and its machines were on the move. By nightfall, Israel would be secure. Transport ships had been arriving over the last month carrying huge concrete slabs. Massive swathes of ground had been requisitioned for their storage until that day. The whole event had been shrouded in secrecy. No one outside of Israel had any idea of what was about to happen.

As Ben entered his office in the Knesset, an office usually occupied by the Prime Minister's Special Adviser, he noticed a young woman sitting next to his desk. As he turned to chastise his assistant for letting her into his personal sanctuary where God knows what could have been left for her to see, the young woman turned and smiled at her Uncle Ben. He had not seen his goddaughter for more than fifteen years but recognized her instantly. Rebecca Cohen looked exactly as her mother had at the same age, stunning.

"Rebecca," he rushed and embraced the woman who, fifteen years earlier, had cut him off, blaming him for the death of her parents.

"Uncle Ben! My God, you don't look any different! You must be... what...almost eighty?"

"You're as old as you feel," he said. "And just now, looking at you, I feel about thirty five!"

"I have missed you, you know," she said with genuine sorrow. "I was young and foolish, please forgive me."

"Not at all. I lost two great friends because of my arrogance and a loving goddaughter that I hope I can win back. I should have listened. You told me your parents were in danger and I did nothing. For that, I will be eternally sorry."

"Please don't. That's the past and now's the present. I've heard you're planning something in retaliation for the attack?"

"You hear things?" he asked suspiciously.

"Yes, I do," she replied matter-of-factly.

"You will see soon enough. Now tell me, how is that fine son of yours? I hear things too, you know. What's his name, Josh isn't it?"

Rebecca's eyes dropped and she struggled to maintain control. Josh's name had not been said out loud since the funeral, almost seven weeks earlier.

Ben was no fool and read the situation instantly. He embraced Rebecca for the second time in fifteen years. Both stood in silence as Rebecca fought to keep control of her emotions. After a minute, she stood up, resolute and forceful. "I hear you're planning some kind of retaliation?" she said again. There could be no mistaking the steel in her voice.

"Yes we are." The time for games was over.

"I want in."

"It's been what, seven years since you were active and on your last mission, your husband died," replied Ben quietly.

Rebecca did not even justify Ben with a response. She merely gave him a look that suggested he not dare keep her out.

Ben averted his eyes from Rebecca's deathly glare. Who was he to deprive Israel of one of its most talented operatives? Particularly one who was so personally motivated?

"You're in," he almost whispered, regretting it as he spoke. He knew he was placing another loved one in a situation of mortal danger. Those words were almost certainly sealing her fate. But Ben had given his heart and soul to Israel since its birth and could not deprive her of a weapon like Rebecca at a time she most needed it.

# Chapter 5

**Mexico**
**July 2008**

Sam's aim was interrupted by the vibration of his cell phone. He glanced at the screen. The name of the CIA's Director, Johnson, was flashing. The target's truck was speeding towards him. Only seconds remained to take the shot. He touched the small bluetooth earpiece and accepted the call.

"Don't shoot!" commanded Johnson as the call connected.

Sam stared down the scope, straight into the eyes of the terrorist driving the deadly truck towards America's border. His finger began to tighten on the trigger. There was no way the truck should be allowed anywhere near America.

"Do not shoot!" repeated Johnson more forcefully, having received no response.

Sam continued to track the target, keeping the crosshairs trained on the center of the targets head. The range continued to drop as the truck rushed towards him. His hilltop vantage point allowed a view straight into the truck's cabin but not for much longer as the truck would soon pass below and any chance of a shot would be lost.

"Baker! Stand down!" shouted Johnson in his ear. "Stand the fuck down!"

Sam depressed the trigger. He could feel the hammer moving back. A few more ounces and the hammer would fire into the bullet and expel the small projectile at over 3,000 ft/s into the target's brain, ending the mission.

"Baker!!!" screamed Johnson.

Sam Baker pulled up the rifle and fired in frustration, the muzzle flash startling everyone in the communications room, almost 2,000 miles away, in Langley. Sam threw his rifle to the ground and raised his finger to the MQ-1 Predator he knew was beaming images straight to his boss. Two months earlier he had received a tip. The CNN reporter he had saved in Ahwaz had overheard mention of an attack aimed at America. Learning from her previous mistakes she passed on what she had heard to Sam and had not followed it up herself. Sam had tracked down the terrorist and the weapon, desperate at every turn to stop them but always being stopped by 'management' who wanted to uncover the terrorist's contacts and command structure. Finally, he thought, he was getting the chance to stop the nonsense, only to be stopped at the last second. They were less than twenty miles from the American-Mexican border.

"Calm down!" commanded Johnson.

"Calm down?!" repeated Sam, incredulous. "You're letting a terrorist drive a nuclear bomb into America and I've got to calm down!"

"It's no longer a CIA operation and no longer your concern..."

Sam cut the connection. He was in no mood to get into the bullshit that Johnson was about to hit him with. His cell began to buzz but Sam ignored it as he packed up his kit and kick-started the motorbike for the perilous journey back down the trail to the main road. As he reached the road, he contemplated screwing them all and chasing down the truck. He could still catch it before it reached the border. He looked into the sky and knew that Johnson was watching him and was squirming at the thought that Sam may disobey him but Sam was a soldier and an order was an order. No matter how screwed up or how much he disagreed, orders had to be obeyed. He turned right, away from the border and back towards San Fernando. He could almost hear Johnson's sigh of relief.

"He's out of control."

Johnson nodded in frustration at the statement made by his second in command. Sam and he had seldom seen eye to eye and over the last two months the tension between them had become unworkable. Sam's world was black and white, right and wrong. Life wasn't that simple. He exited the room and retrieved a pre-paid cell from his coat pocket. He typed a quick text and hit 'Send'. Sam Baker was retiring.

Yuri Andriev's phone beeped. He pressed the 'Accept' button and a link appeared on the screen. He clicked it and the browser opened to reveal a map. A flashing dot moved quickly across the screen. Yuri zoomed out and the dot's progress slowed down as Yuri's own location also appeared on the screen. His target, Sam Baker, was, as promised, less than ten miles away and heading straight towards him. It was going to be a very easy fifty grand.

Yuri screwed the suppressor onto his USP.45 pistol and waited. He preferred his work to be up-close and personal. He liked to ensure that when he put a target down, they didn't get back up, as did his clients.

Yuri heard the motorbike pull into the parking lot. He checked his screen and the small dot flashed less than one hundred yards from where he stood. Yuri closed the phone and waited. The next time he'd need it would be to photograph Sam's headshot. Two holes in his forehead were all the proof the client would need to release the final payment.

***

Sam walked towards his motel room. It really was one of the worst dumps he'd ever had the displeasure to frequent. He had stayed there for over two weeks, waiting for the ship to dock and the truck to appear, only to be stood down at the last second. He had caught God knows what from the bedding. His body was covered in bites and lumps and he had an insatiable itch in his crotch. All for nothing. He was furious. The powers that be had lost it.

Sam inserted the key and opened the door to his flea pit of a room. The only up-side was that he'd not be spending another night there. He stepped into the room and froze. The door slammed closed.

Sam wasn't sure if the day could get any worse, when it did. The silencer pressing into the base of his skull was all the evidence he needed. There were two things to do in the situation. Panic and beg or accept your fate with some dignity. Sam was in no mood for either. Just as the silencer touched his skin, he moved, surprising Yuri who was used to the begging and acceptance routine.

The speed with which Sam calculated the situation and reacted, caught Yuri off-guard. By the time he pulled the trigger, Sam had already spun out of danger and his hand was already closing in on the large cylindrical silencer, while his other was forming a fist and making its way towards Yuri's shocked face.

Yuri had not lasted twenty years in the business for no reason. He regained his composure and managed to evade most of Sam's punch, knocking him only slightly off balance. As the punch landed, Yuri felt the pistol being twisted from his hand. He needed to regain the upper hand and ejected the magazine before letting go of the pistol.

As Yuri expected, Sam's energy was focused on wrestling the pistol from his hand and suddenly releasing it, sent Sam crashing into the wall as his momentum suddenly had no force to restrain it. Yuri went for his knife as Sam threw the bulletless pistol at him and dived across the bed towards his bag.

Sam grabbed the bag and rolled into the small bathroom, flicking the door closed as he crashed against the bathtub. The door closed just in time to catch the knife that Yuri had thrown, the blade protruding three inches into Sam's side of the door. Sam reached into his bag for his backup pistol. It wasn't there.

Yuri had him. He had checked the room and removed all the weapons. He had even checked the bathroom and the cistern, just in case. Sam was unarmed. Yuri picked up the pistol and re-inserted the magazine. He slammed it home, ensuring Sam heard it.

Despite the powerful .45 bullets, the only sound that could be heard was the ripping of wood as Yuri systematically pumped 9 rounds into the wall and door of the bathroom. Yuri aimed carefully at various heights and angles to ensure at least two or three hits. With no cries of pain emitted from the bathroom, Yuri had to assume he had either hit Sam in the head or missed. But, looking at the placing of his shots, that did not seem likely. He raised his foot and kicked the door open, ready to deliver the final two bullets if required.

As the door swung open, the two bullets struck. Two head shots ended the battle once and for all.

Yuri fell to the floor, no mother in the world would recognize the mess left by two bullets entering the back of the head and exiting the front. Sam looked at the small rectangular window above the bath and wondered how he had managed to squeeze through such a tiny gap. It was not surprising Yuri had ruled out the prospect and in the process had become a sitting duck.

Before he left, Sam took a photo and sent it to the last number in the phone's memory. Sam Baker had retired and Yuri Andriev had a booking on the last flight to New York and Sam was determined to make it.

# Chapter 6

**Mexican – US Border**
**Brownsville, TX**
**July 2008**

Hassan Al Husseini wiped his brow. The sweat was flowing freely as he inched his truck towards the border crossing. He, above all others, had been chosen for what he regarded to be one of the most important attacks in the history of the world. He would deliver, to the Zionist-loving scum, some of their own medicine, a taste of what their Israeli puppets had made him and his Palestinian brothers endure since Palestine was betrayed.

As he approached the customs official, he took a deep breath. He was aware that alarms at all border-crossings would be triggered at the slightest hint of a nuclear device. He had, however, been assured that the bomb was enclosed in a lead-lined casing and would not betray him or the cause. They had also assured him that the customs officials, particularly in the middle of the night, would be more interested in stopping illegal drugs and illegal immigrants than finding a nuclear bomb none of them were expecting.

Hassan had grown up in the Jabalia refugee camp, one of the most crowded places on earth. Over 90,000 people were crammed into an area less than 1.4km2. Located just 3km from the Israel/Gaza border, the conditions were a perfect breeding ground for Izz ad-Din al-Qassam Brigades, the militant wing of the Hamas group. With few or no prospects, the young men of

Jabalia were under constant threat from Israeli Defense Force raids and by the age of sixteen, Hassan had lost friends and family to Israeli aggression. With each Israeli incursion, the Brigades' numbers swelled.

Hassan had always refused approaches from the Brigades. He had a future ahead of him. Excellent language skills and a keen mind for numbers had already seen him accepted into the Islamic University of Gaza's Faculty of Engineering. His father had died young, just 41 years of age. Another symptom of the camps, life expectancy was low. With a mother and three younger siblings, the young Hassan had taken seriously the responsibility of heading the household and had planned to make something of himself and move his family out of the camps.

All that had changed one fateful night. Hassan, walking home from school, watched as the Israeli helicopter gunships swooped low over his head. The three machines swung their front-mounted 30mm cannons menacingly as they flew past. The tank-busting cannon was ridiculously powerful for a shanty town constructed of basic materials. The rocket pods hung ominously from the choppers' stubby and pointless wings. Hassan noted that their path was his path. However that was nothing unusual. The Israelis constantly offered the refugees a glimpse of their awesome war machine, a reminder that they were dominant and not to be trifled with. But this was a message that Hassan was uninterested in. For him, the Palestinian – Israeli conflict was in the past. His people had to move on, adapt and progress.

Even when the rocket pods lit up, Hassan looked on with little interest. His home was in a quiet part of the camp, well away from any of the militant strongholds. It was only when the rockets began to rain down on their targets that Hassan's breath stopped and his world ended. As the night sky lit up with a fireball of explosions, Hassan's family and his reason for living were obliterated in a cloud of bloody ash.

Hassan met with the local Brigade Commander the next morning, after burying his entire family. Within four hours, he was in a truck heading south and by evening, he was in one of Izz ad-Din al-Qassam Brigade's most secret and specialist training camps. The Brigade had big plans and Hassan was exactly the type of Palestinian their new plan called for.

As the customs official waved him through, Hassan breathed a huge sigh of relief and as instructed, he changed the destination on his GPS device from Corpus Christi to his real destination. The ETA changed from 2 hours 41 minutes to 28 hours 17 minutes. Just over a day until America would lose its iconic White House and with any luck, its President too.

***

As Hassan's truck approached the border, the Department of Energy's monitoring alarms triggered. Red flashing lights lit the room as the radioactive detectors did the only thing they were programmed to do, detect the imminent and immediate threat to the United States of America. The agent in charge of the monitoring station moved immediately to implement the procedure he had trained for all his professional life but had prayed would not be needed.

His first call was to the border guards to instruct them to close the border. His second was to NEST, the Nuclear Emergency Support Team, to deal with the nuclear threat. The next would be to the local National Guard station which would immediately implement Martial law within a controlled area and if required, conduct an evacuation up to an area determined by the size of risk estimated by the NEST team.

As he picked up the receiver to make the first call, a hand appeared on the phone's cradle, killing the call. The agent looked up into the dark sunglasses of a man who had appeared from nowhere.

"What the…?" exclaimed the DoE agent.

The man with the sunglasses flicked his badge open revealing a Defense Intelligence Agency badge. Before the agent could see the name, the leather holder flicked shut. Four soldiers had taken up station at the back of the office, their weapons drawn, as the DoE agent tried to study the badge.

"Way above your pay grade, your shift's over!" replied the DIA agent, his tone leaving no room for discussion.

As the DIA agent issued his order, the soldiers moved forward as one, making it crystal clear to the DoE agent that his shift was most definitely over. Without another word, he stood up, grabbed his jacket from the back of his chair and made a swift exit. As he exited the building, two compact black choppers sat in the small car-park, each filled with soldiers, heavily armed and dressed entirely in black. Whatever was going on, the DIA agent had been right, this was way beyond his pay grade. How he hadn't heard the choppers land, he didn't know but what he did know was that he was getting the hell out of there before the inevitable hit the fan.

The DIA agent immediately went to work. All data collated over the previous few minutes was replaced with clean data. The truck that had just crossed the border and set off every potential warning signal, no longer existed. According to the data now in the system, the truck was clean.

As the DoE agent pulled out of the car park, he failed to notice a Ford F-450 pick-up pull out from the street and follow him. Ten minutes later, as they drove past one of Brownsville's major reservoirs, the same pick-up brushed the DoE agent's car aside like a fly swat hitting a fly. The car plunged down the embankment and straight into the water. Had the door locks and windows not been tampered with, he may have survived but all eventualities had been covered.

*** 

With his job done, the DIA agent circled his finger, signaling to the soldiers it was time to move out. As they emerged from the building, the choppers powered up and once they had boarded, immediately took off. The pilots followed the road and within minutes had caught up with the truck and were following just beyond the horizon, out of sight. Their orders were to hold off until told to take the truck down.

*** 

The pick-up driver waited until the DoE agent's car had disappeared below the surface before turning and driving towards US 77N, the route he knew Hassan would take. He reached across and picked up the walkie-talkie from the passenger seat and pressed the transmit button.

"Team One, please give me your location."

"We are five miles NW of Brownsville, approximately one mile behind the target, travelling at 55mph. Team Two is 200 yards behind us. We're in position and just need the signal to take the target down," replied the DIA agent from the first helicopter.

"Excellent, please continue to shadow the target until further orders. Out," replied the pick-up driver as he pulled into the truck-stop on the outskirts of Brownsville. Wiping the dash and steering wheel down, he exited the pick-up and retrieved his standard issue Crown Victoria saloon car. He pulled out of the truck-stop and floored the accelerator. He quickly calculated his position, approximately ten miles behind the target. He pushed the speedo to 75 mph. In an hour, he would be 10 miles ahead of the target.

Up until three months earlier, he had had one master, the US government. They had trained him, trusted him and paid him well for his services. The DIA left no stone unturned during his application. They were aware of his Middle-Eastern background. His ability to speak the language and dialects of all major protagonists in the Middle-East had been one of the major reasons he had been recruited in the first place. His background and family affiliation had checked out and no risk was believed to be present. Zak was a solid and trusted member of the world's most powerful intelligence agency.

However, four months earlier, the Izz ad-Din al-Qassam Brigades had declared war, launching a catastrophic attack on Israel and everything had changed. Sleepers across the world were being unleashed. Calls were being made in the dead of night and a secret army was being awoken. Zak had received his call and listened intently. He didn't like what he was being asked to do. He didn't fully understand it, but, ultimately, he had been asked and it would be an honor to do what he could.

After forty-five minutes of driving, Zak could see Hassan's truck ahead. He knew that the helicopters were up there somewhere but in the darkness that enveloped that part of Texas at night, he knew it was pointless even trying to spot them. The OH-6 little birds were developed to be one of the quietest and stealthiest helicopters. Even in the middle of the day, you'd struggle to spot one if the pilot didn't want you to. Pushing the accelerator, Zak shot past Hassan, stealing a glimpse as he hurtled past. The glow of the dials gave Hassan's face a ghostly glower. Zak's foot subconsciously pressed harder on the accelerator.

The lack of any ambient light and traffic made this the ideal location. Zak pressed the accelerator ~~further,~~ constantly calculating distances as he tore away from the bomb. At 115mph, Zak was gaining a mile a minute on the bomb. He had been told to be at least 5 miles away and he planned to be at least six.

"Team One, this is Team Leader, please confirm position," instructed Zak six minutes after cruising past Hassan.

"Holding at one mile out from target as instructed," replied the DIA agent.

Zak paused and checked his calculations. It had now been over six minutes since he had passed Hassan. Over six miles' distance.

"Go, I repeat go, take him down!" commanded Zak.

"On our way!" replied the DIA agent.

Zak hardly heard the agent speak. After issuing the order, he had dropped the walkie-talkie onto the passenger seat and subconsciously floored the accelerator. He removed the small transmitter from the inside of his jacket and counting to thirty, pressed the button.

***

Hassan's head began to nod. It had been a long day and the interminably straight and dark road was taking its toll. What he wouldn't give for a few hours sleep. Just even twenty minutes. The stress of the border-crossing had exhausted him and the monotonous 55 mph was more effective than counting sheep. He shook his head. He was showing weakness when he must show strength. He had been selected for this above all others. He was going to surpass those of 9/11 and he felt tired! He was ashamed of himself and slapped his face and wound down his window.

As he wound the window down a flash of movement in the side mirror caught his eye. Something had moved across behind him but with there were no lights. Hassan at first thought the darkness was playing tricks on him but as the order was given the helicopters rushed towards him. Hassan spotted them instantly and knew he had failed. The glory that should have been his would now be shame. He Hassan al Husseini had failed his people and Allah. Hassan wished he could blow the bomb and take the infidels with him but he was not given a suicide trigger.

His task was to blow up Washington and the White House, anything else would be regarded as failure. There had been some debate over the suicide trigger but previous plans had been thwarted by over eager bombers prematurely detonating devices. Hassan therefore was not given any option. A GPS locator would activate the bomb when its target was reached. Hassan punched the steering wheel. The bomb would fall into the hands of the Americans. He had failed.

As the helicopters swooped towards him, their powerful searchlights lit up his cabin. Shielding his eyes with one hand, he reached for his knife with the other. He was not going to spend his life in prison, just another Muslim failure. Hassan grabbed the knife and swung it towards his neck. He had been trained on how to slash both his jugular and carotid artery with one movement. He need not have worried. The sharpshooter in the helicopter opened fire. One carefully placed bullet tore through the cabin, killing Hassan instantly. Other well-placed bullets shredded the tires, stopping the truck almost on the spot. The Americans were not taking any chances. The truck sat motionless as the helicopters landed.

The DIA agent boarded the truck and checked Hassan for a pulse. Hassan was dead. He looked at the Satellite Navigation screen and noted the destination, Washington. He grabbed his walkie talkie just as Zak pressed the trigger and at 3.22 a.m. in Kenedy County, Texas, home to 414 Texans and over 40,000 cattle, the truck exploded and the world really did change forever.

# Chapter 7

**El Arish Hotel**
**Arish Resort**
**Egypt**
**July 2010**

It had been nearly three years since Rebecca Cohen's life, as she knew it, had ended. Josh's expression of sheer horror, as the explosion took him from her, was as clear in her mind now as it was then. Her life was meaningless, devoid of purpose. Although there had been a few moments of happiness, these were mainly linked to death, the death of anyone responsible or involved in the bombings that had killed her precious son.

As she lay on her sun lounger and soaked in the Mediterranean sunshine, the waves lapped on the pristine sands and she smiled inwardly. Her next targets had arrived, just as predicted by her last victim.

The sniveling coward had begged her for mercy, begged her to spare him and offered more information than he could deliver but Rebecca had just sneered at him. Josh hadn't had the luxury of begging for his young life, thanks to the piece of scum sniveling at her feet. She had kicked him hard in the face and, as he lay sprawled in front of her, she had shot him four times. Once in both kneecaps, just for the pain. Once in the balls because he shouldn't have any for targeting six-year-olds. And finally, once in the stomach. The pain would be intense for the last few hours of his life. Death would be inevitable but thankfully not quick. It wasn't the way of the Kidon but thankfully, they had just let her do her own thing and asked few questions. Her secondment to the Mossad Assassination Team had been arranged by her Uncle Ben. However, it soon became apparent that Rebecca was not going to be a team player. Her recklessness in the quest to avenge Josh was only going to get her or her team-mates killed but her abilities and drive were never questioned. Uncle Ben had come to her aid again, suggesting that perhaps they should just let her do her own thing. Eighteen months later and ten kills to her name, more than any other team, Rebecca was as hungry for revenge as the day she started.

It had been less than twelve hours since the sniveling scumbag had given her the details of the meeting at the El Ashir Hotel and despite her orders always to report her movements, she had on this occasion failed to report. Time was of the essence and if her information had been correct, there was a possibility that not only four commanders but the leader of Izz ad-Din al-Qassam Brigades would be present. She knew that there was no way she'd be given such a big job herself and, as no other Kidon members would work with the 'suicidal bitch', she would have been sidelined which, to her, was not an option.

Rebecca inserted the small earphones attached to what to anyone would think was an iPod but was in fact a laser listening device. She pointed the base of the device towards a beachfront table which, according to the waiter, had been reserved for a meeting. Despite the small armory of weapons at her side, Rebecca was more self-conscious of the bikini she was wearing. Purchased from the hotel lobby, it had failed to cope with her slight frame and large bosom. Normally she would mix and match sizes but with little to choose from, she had the option of bottoms that fell off or a top that struggled to contain her spectacular breasts. Much to the delight of the men in attendance, she had opted for the latter. Rebecca carefully adjusted her top again and tried to maintain her position. Despite its more open attitude than most Muslim countries, topless bathing was most definitely not acceptable in Egypt's most Northern resort.

As the afternoon wore on, Rebecca began to think that her latest victim had just been trying to bullshit her to save himself. However, just as she had fixed her top, for what felt the hundredth time, a young Arab approached the table and pulling out a seat, he sat down. His eyes fervently surveyed his surroundings and unlike every other hot blooded young male, his eyes merely scanned across Rebecca, just as they had every other sunbather. Rebecca had positioned herself well. Her feet and more importantly her listening device, pointed towards the table. Her eyes looked closed to the casual observer but were open just enough to watch the table.

The young Arab, she realized, fitted the description of Ahmed Hameed, a young man tipped as future leader of Al Qassam and possibly of Hammas itself. He waited nervously but not for long. Another two Arabs joined, one with a distinct limp and the other with a badly pock-marked face. Both fitted descriptions of Al Qassam commanders. Rebecca strained to control herself. At least another three scumbags would soon be meeting their maker.

"Assalamu Alaikum" could be heard clearly through Rebecca's headphones. 'Peace be upon you' was the standard Arab greeting followed by an embrace.

"Are we early?" asked the young Arab.

"No but The Sheikh will not show himself until we are all here," replied Pock-Mark.

Rebecca struggled not to respond visibly to the reference to 'The Sheikh', the mastermind behind all major atrocities and the most likely candidate for the nuclear explosion in Texas. Not since Osama Bin Laden, had a terrorist been as sought after as the mysterious 'Sheikh'. Initially, references to 'The Sheikh' were believed to be references to Osama. However, it soon became apparent that the two were not one and the same. The Sheikh, unlike Osama, was keen to keep his identity a secret and after five years had remained, much to the world's intelligence agencies' embarrassment, nothing more than an urban myth. Rebecca was going to confirm his existence and extinguish it, in one fell swoop.

Before she could fully consider what to do, five more men approached the table. However, only one took a seat and greeted the waiting three. Mohammed Deif, the leader of Al Qassam took his seat. The other four, his bodyguards, stationed themselves carefully, covering all angles. Rebecca heard the words again. In her mind, Pock-Mark had definitely referred to The

Sheikh and then Deif had joined them. The mysterious Sheikh was Deif? Surely that connection would have been made already. Rebecca opened her eyes a little more and found herself looking directly into the eyes of one of Deif's bodyguards who gave her an appraising wink and affirmative smile. Rebecca closed her eyes again and replayed the image in her mind. Two seats remained vacant at the table and other than greetings, conversation was negligible. They were still waiting.

Rebecca did not have long to wait. Less than a minute after Deif arrived, the pool area was swamped by a number of heavily armed and traditionally dressed Arabs who immediately took up strategic positions around the pool area. Deif's bodyguards were frisked and weapons removed by the significantly more professional and powerful force. Whoever was coming was making it very clear they were in charge. Rebecca struggled to keep her eyes closed under the scrutiny of the Arab guards. Their eyes missed nothing as they scanned continuously. Rebecca thanked God for her skimpy bikini. The eyes of the guards scanned beyond her quickly as the guards desperately tried to avoid being caught looking at the brazen woman. No matter how enthralling the view, none of the fundamentalist guards wanted their Sheikh to believe they were being tempted or weakened by a mere woman. Rebecca also posed little threat, 8 square inches of fabric and an i-pod hardly threatened 12 men with AK47s.

Rebecca heard the chair scrape and slowly lifted her eyelids a fraction. The seat directly facing her had been filled. An average-sized man faced her, head on, but unfortunately was covered, like his guards, from head to toe. His scarf was pulled across his face, allowing only his eyes to be seen. The eyes moved quickly, scanning the area and resting for a brief second on Rebecca's body, a hint of interest registering before the eyes quickly moved on.

Rebecca listened with interest as the introductions were made around the table. Her listening device was picking up every word loud and clear. Deif was apologizing profusely for the failure of his man to complete the Sheikh's American Project.

The American Project, Rebecca assumed, must have been the failed nuclear bombing of America. Of course 'failure' being detonating the bomb in the middle of nowhere in Texas rather than at the heart of Washington. However, detonating a nuclear bomb and clearing a huge swathe of Texas was hardly a failure. The Americans had replaced 9-11 with the now more infamous 1-11, the day a nuclear device changed the face of America, quite literally, forever. It had obliterated a significant proportion of American real estate and created a no-go zone to the south of the new, more Northerly, US border. It had been decided that the US would rather not have a nuclear waste zone within her borders and as a result, the land was abandoned and Corpus Christi was now the most Southerly Texan city. Nine counties had been entirely evacuated while another three had lost their southern most portions. Laredo, within Webb County, was the most northern city to be evacuated. In all, over 1.3 million Americans had been relocated from an area the size of Belgium and accommodated within the sparsely populated southern Texan states. Texas had lost just over 4% of her mass, while America had reduced her landmass by an almost negligible 0.29%. Had it not been for the predominantly Hispanic heritage of the local inhabitants, the furor over the move may have lasted longer. However, with significant relocation allowances, new cities and homes being built and jobs for all, more than a few of those affected by the blast were thanking God for their good fortune.

Rebecca reached down and patted the small bag at her side. She had come prepared for most eventualities but almost twenty heavily armed men were stretching her capabilities to the limit. Underneath her frothy literature, she could feel the steel of her weapons: two fragment grenades, a compact Sig Sauer P229 handgun, a micro Uzi sub machine gun, both with spare magazines, totaling 76 rounds and a knife. Rebecca knew she'd never live through an attack. However, between Deif and the Sheikh, she was guaranteed to avenge her son's death, a trade she was more than willing to make. She watched the guards carefully as her hand moved towards her Uzi. Nudging the beauty magazine aside, her fingers closed around the grip. Her thumb flicked the safety and she waited. One guard whose Ak47 stood poised was facing her way. All she needed was a second. One sweep of the table would take out The Al Qassam commanders and the Sheikh. Twenty-five bullets in one sweep. One second and the scum would be spending eternity in hell. She would probably join them a fraction of a second later as the sixteen bodyguards took aim. Rebecca had considered the grenade but if she didn't time it right, they may be able to toss it away and she would die in vain. It wasn't the dying that got to her, it was knowing she hadn't avenged her son. Rebecca had died the day Joshua had but it was just that they weren't quite ready to meet up yet.

Rebecca positioned her legs. She was going to have to move quickly but unthreateningly to ensure her window of opportunity was maximized. As the guard moved his head to the side, Rebecca saw her chance. Her hand began to move and the Uzi began to rise.

Rebecca's hand emerged from the bag. The guards who had watched her move, flinched as the full horror was displayed before them and more importantly their Sheikh.

Rebecca sensed the panic rise and quickly folded her magazine to hide the cover photo of the naked woman. Rebecca listened intently as the Sheikh repeated the words again that had just saved his life and doomed millions of others. I am sending you five nuclear warheads which you must use against Israel.

# Part Two

# Chapter 8

**Present day**
**September 2011**

Sam looked down and smiled as the almost empty ferry docked far below him. A throng of cars waited eagerly, hoping that there'd just be enough room to squeeze them on. Summer season was coming to a close and the island paradise that he had first ventured upon two years earlier would soon be returned to normality. The four months of mayhem were over. Well, mayhem North Haven style that was.

Sam watched as the single car leaving the ferry paused at the ferry crew before driving on towards the main street. A shiver ran down his spine. Sam couldn't take his eyes off the car. Something wasn't right.

"Sir?"

Sam ignored the voice as he followed the car with his eyes. Only when it dropped from sight, did he register the student.

"Yes Miller, what is it?"

"Sir, where to now?"

In the three years since the explosion and his retirement Sam had become a sports coach. He had initially assumed the identity of his assassin and fled, taking Yuri's seat to New York. Months of wandering aimlessly had ended the day he stumbled upon North Haven, the small island in Maine where nobody knew nor cared who or what he was. Sam had found a new life, one that made him happy, happier than he had ever thought possible.

He looked at the wheezing and gasping group that lay before him. Summer had obviously made them lazy. Before the vacation, they would have bounded up the hill with ease. He had some work to do. He should have taken them another mile or so but the car was playing on his mind. Something was wrong. He thought his past was behind him, why would they come now, he tried to think rationally, it didn't make sense, after three years there would be no reason to come for him. He considered going on but the car worried him.

"We'll head back now."

A small cheer went through the group. They had all expected the worst. Sam was tough. He hadn't produced two state cross-country champions by being soft.

"It's only half a mile, so we'll run back. Now GO!"

Sam took off on the word 'go' and left them all in his wake. At 45, he was still as fit as he had ever been. It was just the aches and pains that were more noticeable. He had always been fanatical about fitness and thanks to that, he still passed for a man ten years younger. That was perhaps the only reason the beautiful twenty-eight year-old ninth grade teacher had ever fallen for him and made him the happiest man alive with the birth of his son, Sam Junior, only ten months earlier.

Sam's breathing began to quicken, his heart rate raced, it wasn't just himself he had to worry about any more. The game had changed, if he made a mistake in the past he would pay the price but that had changed with the birth of his son. Sam quickened his pace as the vision of the car played in his mind. Something was wrong.

Sam was way ahead of the nearest student and raced past the school. He sprinted down Main Street and stopped in his tracks as he spotted the car parked opposite the town's main harbor. The Virginia plates brought back memories he had hoped to bury forever. Something was definitely wrong.

"Did you see who was driving this car?" he asked one of the local fishermen who stood nearby, forgetting the normal pleasantries.

"Good Morning, Sam. Can't say I did but I did notice some fellas hiring one of those fancy speedboats from Jim."

Without a word, Sam ran to the end of the pier, just in time to see the speedboat disappear into the distance. The blood drained from Sam's face as the realization of the danger his family faced hit him. A wave of nausea was quelled as his training kicked in, he had to be strong, he had to protect his family. Sam ran back to the small booth covered in posters advertising everything from small sailing dinghies to whale spotting cruises.

"Jim, where are they going?" Sam pointed to where the speedboat had been.

"Morning Sam, sorry no idea. They just wanted to tour the island, I think. Why?"

"How many and what did they look like?" he asked firmly.

"Four big fellas. Come to think of it, they weren't really dressed for the weather. You know that wind's a bit nippy this time of year. Is everything OK Sam? You look like you've seen a ghost."

"No, no, I'm fine. Have you got another speed boat?"

"'Fraid not, that's the only one. The rest are all up at the yard being serviced, end of season and all." Seeing the look of desperation on Sam's face, he added "I've got a small launch, only 10hp but it's faster than rowing."

"That'll do!"

Two minutes later, Sam was in the launch and turning the throttle as far as it would go. Three years earlier, Sam had stumbled across a small rundown shack on Goat Island and for the first time in almost 25 years, he had somewhere he could call home. Goat Island lay just a mile off the far end of the island and was one of the reasons Sam had maintained his fitness. Every day, he rowed to the main island and then ran the length of the island to school and back again in the evening which was a ten mile round trip. By boat from the harbor, it was seven miles and, at twelve knots, was going to take him just over half an hour. The speedboat could do twenty-five knots and already had a five-minute head start. They were going to arrive at least twenty minutes ahead of him.

The speedboat cut its engines long before it arrived at Goat Island. The four men were taking no chances as they rowed the final half-mile to the small island. They saw the tell-tale smoke sign telling them someone was home. They approached from the rear and already had their guns out and ready as they rowed the final few yards. As two stood guard, the other two pulled the small craft onto the shingle beach. The chimney of the house was just visible above the small hill that lay between the beach and the house.

Before they could secure the boat, a large golden retriever came bounding over the hill, tail wagging as it rushed towards the new visitors. Without hesitation, the first man raised a silenced pistol and as the dog bounded toward him, shot it once in the head. The dog fell silently, a look of shock on its frozen face.

"What the hell did you do that for, Alex?" whispered the second man standing guard.

"If it barked, we'd be dead. You have no fucking idea who we're dealing with, do you?" replied Alex angrily.

"I know he used to be something."

Alex just shook his head and ensuring the boat was secure, waved the other men on, fanning out as they neared the brow of the hill. On reaching the top, the view below revealed a small wooden cabin and a shadow passing by the window told them all they needed to know. He was in.

The four men took aim and unleashed a brutal wave of bullets from their assault weapons. Glass and wood splintered and shattered everywhere as the bullets tore through the flimsy wooden structure. As one magazine emptied, another was loaded, until over 400 rounds had been pumped into the small cabin. Even a mouse would have struggled to hide from the onslaught. The noise was deafening. Although, with no landmass within a mile, it was as though nothing had happened.

An eerie silence fell as each of the four guns halted. Shards of glass dropped and shattered every few seconds as the house settled into its new state. Alex was the first to move, tentatively making his way towards the front door which hung awkwardly as one hinge struggled to hold its weight. One kick sent it crashing to the ground. The small lounge was a sea of feathers, floating aimlessly as the air blew through the aerated room. He walked across the lounge and entered the kitchen at the rear of the house and spotted the young and beautiful woman sitting on the floor holding a baby in her arms, her lifeless face looking longingly into the shattered bloodied body of her child.

A scream from outside told him instantly this wasn't the only mistake they had made.

# Chapter 9

Sam's launch rounded the headland of North Haven Island and almost came to stop as he left the relative shelter of the North Haven and Vinalhaven Islands and out into the main bay. The waves battered the small launch and Sam could only pull the throttle harder in a vain attempt to close the mile and a half distance to home. After what seemed like hours, the outline of the speedboat came into view just as the deafening sound of gunfire ripped through the air. Sam twisted the throttle further. The knot in his stomach released. His worst fears had come true. They had found him.

As each shot rang out, adrenalin pumped through his veins and with each bullet, the feeling of impotence flowed through him. His wife and child needed him and he was failing them. As the launch mounted the beach next to the speedboat, the gunfire stopped and silence fell. Sam bounded out of the launch and almost stumbled over his dog, its blank eyes staring up at him. Tears streamed down his face, Sam loved three things more than life itself and Goldie was on that list. Until ten months earlier, she had been top of the list but now she sat firmly at number two.

Sam hardly missed a beat as he stormed to the top of the hill. Three men stood watching the house as another made his way towards the front door. Sam ignored the state of the house as his only focus was overcoming the men and ensuring his family were safe. He ran around the hill and approached from the rear, sprinting down the hill out of the sight of the three guards and grabbed his wood axe as he ran past his firewood stockpile.

With three heavily armed men on the other side of the house, he had only one advantage, surprise.

As the front door crashed to the ground, Sam ran round the side of the house and at full sprint, ran at the first guard, the axe swinging in a powerful arc. Sam leapt up and using all of his 6' 2" frame to maximize the force at which the axe fell, the razor sharp blade sliced through the man's neck at a forty five degree angle and removed not only his head but right arm in one fluid motion. As the axe cleared the man's torso, Sam spun round and sent the axe flying end over end into the second guard standing directly in front of the door. A short scream was instantly silenced as the axe embedded itself into the man's stunned face, killing him instantly. Sam was rolling back towards the head and right arm of the first guard and his XM8 assault rifle even before the axe had landed.

By the time the third guard had managed to react to the deaths of his colleagues, it was too late. Sam already had him in his sights and was squeezing the trigger. A three round burst ended the encounter and dropped the last guard where he stood.

Sam didn't hesitate. He ran and dived through the front door and into the lounge just as Alex rushed towards him and the butt of his gun. Alex's face hit the immovable force and stopped dead despite the momentum. His cheek and nose bore the full brunt of the collision while his body continued its forward motion, crumpled to the floor and landed at Sam's feet.

Sam stamped on Alex's right hand, crushing the bones, rendering it useless. He kicked the gun from the man's hand before walking into the kitchen and seeing his worst nightmare. The lifeless bodies of his wife and son sat awkwardly under the window. Sam turned and walked back to the last of the four men. Tears streamed down his face as the memories of his wife and son flashed through his mind.

A kick to the ribs brought the man round.

"Who sent you?"

"You know who sent us!" replied Alex who already knew he was dead.

"Who gave the order?"

"I don't know."

Sam stamped on Alex's hand, grinding it further into the floor.

"Who?"

"I don…"

Sam raised the gun and shot Alex's kneecap clean off. Alex passed out almost instantly from the intense pain but was kicked back to consciousness.

"Who?"

"I really don't know," struggled Alex through gritted teeth, the pain unbearable.

"Well you're absolutely fuck all use to me!" spat Sam as he shot the other kneecap.

Sam walked outside and taking a shovel, he began to dig, ignoring the screams from Alex. Within twenty minutes, he hit metal. Ten minutes later, he had retrieved a trunk that he had hoped he would never see again. Pulling the trunk from the hole, he loaded three of the bodies into the now empty hole and covered them with earth, carefully replacing the turf on top. Comfortable the hole wouldn't be found, he walked back to the shingle beach and retrieved Goldie and carried her back to the cabin, placing her carefully at his wife and son's sides.

Kissing them all goodbye, Sam stood up and walked out of the kitchen. He doused the cabin in petrol and with a heavy heart and vengeance in his mind, he set fire to his family and home. The final screams of Alex reverberated around the small island as the cabin burned to the ground.

Sam Baker was back and all hell was about to break loose.

# Chapter 10

**Washington D.C.**
**Hart Senate Building**

"Mr Chairman?"

The Senior Senator for Montana and current Chairman of the Senate Appropriations Committee for Defense turned in the corridor and was met by the sight of an exceedingly attractive young woman dressed from head to toe in Armani. He knew it was Armani because his wife refused to wear anything else. The tall and athletic blonde was drawing more than a few admiring glances from the Senator's aides.

"Yes, Miss?"

"Special Agent Clark, Amy Clark."

"How can I help, Agent Clark?"

Special Agent Clark took the Chairman by the elbow and led him conspiratorially away from his three aides. Looking around to check no one was listening, she turned back to the Chairman. As she did so, the Chairman noticed a small coiled cable running to her ear.

"Mr Chairman, we've received a direct threat to your life," she said calmly.

"By *we*, you mean?"

"Sorry, Secret Service."

The Chairman smiled knowingly. "I'm getting three death threats a week at the moment. What's so special about this one that it caught the SS's attention?"

"I'm not aware of the detail, Sir. I've just been instructed to place you under Secret Service protection because of a plausible threat to your life."

"I've always been told that the people we should worry about are those who don't issue threats."

"Not entirely true, Sir."

"I'm sorry, Miss Clark, but the last thing I need just now is the Secret Service surrounding me at every turn. Anyway, people will think it's a gimmick and I'm over inflating my importance before the nominations are concluded. I'm sorry but I'll have to decline the offer."

Clark turned around and looked down the corridor where another equally well dressed young man stood at the elevator, accompanied by two uniformed officers of the US Capitol Police Force and shook her head slightly. Receiving a shrug of the shoulders from the man, she turned back to the Chairman who had watched the interaction with interest.

"Now if there's nothing else, Agent Clark, I really need to get back to work," he said, checking his watch. "The Secretary of Defense is currently twiddling his thumbs waiting to give his evidence to my committee."

As the Chairman tried to move away, Agent Clark grabbed his arm firmly. The Chairman was a powerful man, both politically and physically, standing over six foot tall and despite being in his sixth decade, he was not a man people tackled lightly.

The Chairman looked at the hand on his arm, before raising his eyes to meet Agent Clark's.

"I'm sorry, Sir, but the threat is real and we've been ordered to protect you, whether you like it or not," said Agent Clark nervously.

"By whom?" boomed the Chairman, having lost patience.

"The Director."

"Well you phone that little shit and tell him I refused. And if he's got a problem with that, tell him to grow some balls and come and see me himself, instead of sending me his little bit of fluff. Now if you don't mind, please remove your hand."

Amy Clark had, since a very young age, dreamt of joining the United States Secret Service. She had dreamt many times of what would have happened had she been at Kennedy's side on that fateful afternoon and on each occasion, she had sacrificed herself for her president. Her looks, however, more befitting of the front pages of a glossy magazine, had always worked against her. People automatically assumed her promotions or postings were earned by looks rather than merit.

However, no-one had ever thrown the assertion at her so blatantly. The vision of a naked, overweight and thoroughly repugnant Director turned her stomach. Clark removed her hand from the Chairman's shoulder and slapped him firmly across the face. As her hand made contact, the realization of her actions hit home, as did the noise waves reverberating down the corridor, carrying her career with them.

Everyone in the busy corridor turned to look at the slapped face of the potential presidential candidate from Montana. The agent previously covering the elevator was already running to protect the Chairman from the woman who, rather bizarrely, had been sent to protect him. The Chairman looked at Agent Clark in stunned silence, his face stinging from the open handed slap and his mouth hanging open in complete and total surprise.

"Oh my God, I'm so sorry," stammered Clark, her eyes filling with tears.

The Chairman quickly came to his senses and looked around at the sea of stunned faces, all waiting to see his reaction.

"Excuse me, excuse me!" could be heard from the small crowd as the Secret Service agent and two police officers struggled through the crowd that had formed. Without thinking, the Chairman grabbed Clark's limp arm and ushered her into a small office, closing the door firmly behind them.

"I don't know what came over me. I mean, I can't believe I hit you. Don't worry, I'll resign immediately," said Clark pulling herself together.

A banging at the door announced the arrival of her colleague.

"Mr Chairman, Sir? Are you OK?"

The Chairman opened the door slightly. "Fine, thank you. Now if you could just clear the on-lookers, that would be greatly appreciated," he said before shutting the door again and turning back to a very embarrassed Special Agent Clark.

Rubbing his cheek, he paused before he spoke.

"Feisty little thing, aren't you? OK, you've got my attention. Why should I take this threat more seriously?"

Clark was stunned. She had fully expected a tirade from the Chairman, not a weakening of his position.

"But I hit you?" she struggled.

"You're not the first and won't be the last. Now, stop giving me the run-around and tell me why the Secret Service has its knickers in a twist over this threat."

"But lots of people witnessed me hit you? The press will be all over this. I'll have to resign."

"You'll do no such thing. I'll tell them I fully deserved it, that it was a lover's tiff. One photo of you in the press and the suggestion I was or am your lover will do wonders for my approval ratings."

"But…"

"No buts, it's fine. The fluff comment was out of order and more a reaction to that detestable director than to you. I apologize. Now cut the crap and tell me why they're worried."

"The threat came by phone, not by letter and the caller left his name and told us he had had enough of the bloody Senator from Montana. He said it was time somebody did something about the liberal piece of shit before he destroyed our great nation. He claimed to be on his way and was willing to do whatever it took to rid the country of the scumbag."

"Nothing unusual in that, is there?"

"It's not so much what he said, it's the name he used."

"What?"

"Yuri Andriev."

The Chairman's face went white with horror.

"You know him?" asked Clark, surprised.

"Yes. Very well. Who sent you here?"

"What?"

"Who sent you here?"

"I told you, the Director."

"Did he personally select you?" he asked firmly.

"No, he selected my colleague Special Agent Travis who was at the elevator."

The Chairman looked around the office. "The uniformed officers with your colleague, did you bring them with you?"

Clark considered the question. "No, they met us here. They were informed of the threat and joined us in the foyer. Why?"

The Chairman looked deep into Clark's eyes. "Can I trust you?"

"Of course, my job is to protect you," replied Clark, mystified as to where the Chairman was going with his questions.

"OK, from what you've said, my life is at risk but it's not from Yuri Andriev."

"But I've not told you who he is yet..."

"I told you, I know who he is."

"So you know he's the man who killed your brother?"

A bang on the door interrupted the conversation and was followed by "Sir, are you OK?"

"Fine thanks," replied the Chairman.

"That's Travis," said Clark referring to the voice from behind the door.

"Special Agent Clark, your sworn duty is to protect your protectee, correct?" asked the Chairman.

"Of course."

"And I am that protectee, yes?"

"Yes."

"Well, I believe the greatest threats to my life are the men on the other side of this door. You have to get me out of here and to a safe location asap."

Clark looked at him like he had completely lost his mind.

"Those men are sworn to protect you. Don't be ridiculous! As I said, the man who's making threats now was the man who killed your brother three years ago. He's a Russian assas…"

"Agent Clark," interrupted the Chairman. "You've not met my brother. There's not a man on this earth who could kill him single-handedly. Yuri Andriev is the man who tried to kill my brother. My brother's not dead. He just couldn't continue working. If my brother contacted you it's because somebody tried to kill him. That, I can assure you, is a very stupid thing to do. The men who know he's alive would not attempt that for no reason. If they tried to kill him, they want to kill me."

"I don't understand."

"Trust me, when you meet him, you'll understand. You don't mess with my brother, nor anyone he cares about. Now are you going to get me out of here or am I leaving on my own?"

# Chapter 11

Sam hit the end button and threw the cell phone he had found in the speedboat into the waters of the bay and pushed the throttle forward. He didn't look back as the last three years of his life burned fiercely behind him. Visions of his family flashed through his mind as he raced away from his past and into his history. Sam Baker had been killed for a reason and some people were going to wish he had never been reborn.

Sam knew that his own life was irrelevant. Going to the trouble of trying to kill him could mean only one thing. His brother, the illustrious Senator from Montana and according to the polls, the soon-to-be President of the United States, had unsettled some very powerful people. Although seven years younger than his famous brother, Sam had always had to watch his brother's back. Charles Baker was a talker. He fought his battles with wit and rhetoric, much to the infuriation of previous opponents who, having been humiliated, had often turned to violence. And that was when Sam stepped in, he was the fighter.

As he neared the North Haven harbor, Sam slowed the speedboat and turned towards a small jetty that lay before the entrance to the harbor and pulled up alongside. The contents of the metal trunk had been emptied and most of it repacked into a large waterproof holdall. The rest was being worn. Sam checked that nobody was watching before slipping over the side and into the cold waters of the Atlantic Ocean. It had been years since he had donned his wetsuit and was most surprised to find it still fitted. His runs to work had done the trick and kept the mid-life spread at bay. As he slowly descended into the dark waters, he flicked his legs and the huge flippers went to work propelling him through the water with ease. The old technique hadn't been lost and in no time, Sam found himself below the harbor wall and wondering how he was going to cover the distance between the water and the car park without being seen.

His plan was to take the assassins' car and make it look like the four men who had hired the speedboat had simply put it back in the wrong jetty and returned to the mainland in their car. The deaths and fire at his house would look like a murder suicide and the assassin would be laid to rest alongside his family. Something Sam would sort out in due course. For now, he had other priorities.

Sam slipped off his SCUBA tank and let it drop to the ocean floor and pulled himself up and onto an empty fishing boat tethered to the harbor. He needed a diversion. Sam carefully unhooked the boat and with the boat free from its restraints, he powered the engine and thrust the throttles forward, slipping back into the water as the propellers began to turn.

As the boat slipped out of its mooring and powered out of the harbor, chaos ensued. All eyes were suddenly focused on the runaway fishing vessel as it careened towards the outer wall of the harbor. The plan had worked perfectly. Having swum to the far end of the harbor away from the action, Sam Baker slipped out of the water and, dragging his holdall, he ran across to the car park and entered the assassins' car. The Chrysler, much to his relief, had blacked out windows and any other ferry passengers would not be able to tell that the car was three people lighter than it should have been. With only ten minutes until departure, Sam turned the key and accelerated out of the car park just as the small fishing trawler crashed into the outer wall of the harbor. Nobody would later recall the car leaving nor would they be able to confirm who was in it.

With no requirement to buy a ticket for the return journey, Sam drove onto the ferry with only two minutes to spare. Killing the engine, he sat back and with the doors locked, he closed his eyes. Sleep was going to be precious and thanks to his previous training, was something he could do at will and under any circumstance. Ninety minutes later and for the first time in three years, Sam Baker was back on mainland USA. And he was a man on a mission. Search, rescue and destroy. Find his brother, get him to a safe location and then systematically eliminate the enemy. This time, it was personal.

# Chapter 12

Senator Baker walked across to the window and looked out across Constitution Avenue to the United States Supreme Court. He was one of the most powerful men in the country, in the heart of the seat of government and had never felt so vulnerable in all his life. He was surrounded by thousands of law enforcement officers sworn to protect him but didn't know who he could trust. Even trusting the young agent in front of him was a calculated risk and he knew would elicit more than a little flak from Sam, should he live to see him. The thought of Sam flashing through his mind prompted him into action.

"Agent Clark, we need to get going."

"How? The door and corridor are covered by three men who you think have been sent to kill you!"

"Exactly, so how are we going to get out of here?"

Clark surveyed the small room. The only other exit was the window and it was a two floor drop to the ground below which ruled it out. She turned back to the door, it was their only exit.

"I don't know."

The door was banged again. "Agent Clark, I have to ask you to step out of the room!"

"Agent Travis, everything's fine, just give us a minute," shouted Senator Baker, quietly locking the door as he spoke.

"Sir, I'm sorry but I must ask you to come out immediately. I believe your life is at risk," added Travis rattling the door as he tried to open it.

"Agent Clark has informed me of that. Just give us a minute!" shouted back the Senator angrily.

"Sir, please unlock the door, it's imperative that I speak with you privately," replied Travis in a more even tone.

"I'll bet," said the Senator under his breath, before shouting again. "Agent Travis, will you please just give me a minute! I'm in a locked office with one of your agents and you're guarding the door. I'm perfectly safe at the moment."

"That's the problem, Sir. I'm not sure that you are."

Senator Baker's head spun from the door to Clark, his eyes wide with horror. The realization that he had been suckered in by believing the beautiful woman couldn't be the baddy. The door began to give as the Secret Service agents crashed into it.

Agent Clark had already drawn her weapon and had leveled it at the Senator as he turned to face her.

"Oh fuck!" he said as she pulled the trigger.

# Chapter 13

**Bethesda MD**
**Burning Tree Country Club**

The Vice President of the United States was in mid swing when the Secret Service Agent's phone rudely broke his concentration. On the 17th hole and a stroke behind the Chairman of the GOP to whom he had never lost, the VP was furious at the interruption. Phones were as unacceptable on the golf course as women were which, thanks to the Burning Tree Country Club, was never going to happen. Fines had been imposed but the ultra rich members paid them with pleasure. Even the removal of a liquor license had failed and despite their dry clubhouse, the members of the club still enjoyed their male-only haven.

"What the hell are you doing with your phone on?!" shouted the VP to the senior agent in his protective duty.

Tom Sullivan had served the VP for five of his seven years in office as VP and, of course, he knew better than to have his phone with him. "It's not mine, Sir," he answered, hiding his irritation. "It's your hotline phone. It must be an emergency," he replied calmly and handed the phone to the VP.

In seven years, the only person to have called that number was the President and even then, only once, three years earlier, after the bomb had exploded in Texas.

"Andrew Russell," answered the VP.

"I've got some bad news."

"Who is this?"

"Director Johnson, CIA."

"Ah, Allan, what's up?"

"Can you talk?"

The VP walked away from the small group that had crowded around.

"OK, I can now."

"We missed him."

The VP dropped the jovial tone. "Missed who?" he asked menacingly.

"Definitely one and maybe the other."

"What the hell does that mean?"

"I don't want to use names on this line."

"Don't be fucking ridiculous, this is the phone I'd be told the president is dead on, of course you can give me names."

"We missed the brother."

"Missed?"

"We think he took out our men. We've not been able to get in contact with them."

"Maybe they're just out of cell coverage," suggested the VP nervously.

"I don't think so. They definitely missed him."

"How can you be so sure?"

"Because Sam phoned the Secret Service."

"What?!"

"Well, he didn't give his name but just after my guys were supposed to have taken him out, a death threat was issued by Yuri Andriev against Senator Baker."

The VP almost dropped the phone. He had never agreed with the plan, it had disaster written all over it but he had been overruled.

"Jesus!...And the Senator?"

"That's the other thing, he's gone missing."

"My office. Twenty minutes!" the VP threw the cell phone angrily at Agent Sullivan. "We're leaving! NOW!"

# Chapter 14

As the door crashed open, Agent Clark fired her Sig Sauer P226. Senator Baker dived to the ground as the bullet ripped through the air, towards him. The bullet didn't deviate from its trajectory and hit its target dead center. The Senator's dive was in vain. The bullet striking Agent Travis's outstretched gun as was always intended.

"Nobody move a muscle!" screamed Agent Clark over Travis' cries of pain.

The two officers behind Travis stopped in their tracks. Clark had them cold. Neither cared to take her on, particularly when her gun was already drawn and theirs remained in their holsters.

"Travis, step aside," she demanded, before motioning to the other officers. "You two, take your weapons out, butt first, and drop them. Then move over there."

"What the hell are you doing Clark?" managed Travis through gritted teeth, the pain in his hand intense.

"Protecting the Senator, Travis."

"By shooting me?" he shouted.

"Don't be such a pussy, I shot your gun."

She turned to the other officers who were dropping their guns. "Now move over there. Senator, would you mind picking up the guns, please."

"Clark, have you gone insane? We're on your side!" argued Travis, moving over to stand next to the other agents.

"Not according to the Senator," replied Clark.

Travis turned towards the Senator questioningly.

"Don't come the innocent with me, Son," said Senator Baker angrily as he bent over to retrieve the guns.

"I haven't got the faintest idea what the hell you're talking about."

"You were sent here to kill me," replied the Senator.

The two officers, on hearing the Senator's revelation, pounced. The first dived towards the Senator and the two guns.

Clark didn't miss a beat. She drilled the diving officer through his outstretched hand, rendering it useless. The second officer paused, caught in two minds, but his hand was played. They knew he was there for duties unbecoming of an officer of the US Capitol Police Force. With Travis and the diving officer clutching their hands in agony, Clark was struggling to cover all three. She glanced at the Senator who had managed to evade the diving officer but he offered her no more suggestion than a half-hearted shrug. With her eyes averted, the second officer made his move, launching himself towards Clark.

Clark, however, was not where she was because of stupidity. She had sensed the officer was going to make his move. Her glance towards the Senator was her 'come on'. As soon as the officer had flinched, the bullet was already heading towards his kneecap.

With Travis and the two officers writhing around in agony, Clark grabbed the Senator's elbow and rushed him out of the room. Her first duty was to protect the Senator. Her second and more pressing duty was to find out exactly what the hell was going on.

# Chapter 15

A number of nervous faces greeted the entry of an obviously upset VP. As the door slammed shut behind him, he took his seat at the head of the table. Present in the room were a number of presidential appointees, all loyal to the sitting President, but even more loyal to his likely successor, his Rottweiler and surrogate son, Andrew Russell. The VP looked at the attendees with contempt.

"Well?" he asked.

Each of the three attendees sat silently.

"Don't just look at one another, somebody tell me how they're going to sort out this fucking mess???!!!!" screamed Russell, slamming the table for effect.

Between the four attendees, they commanded pretty much every member of law enforcement and the military in the country but not one dared return Russell's glare for fear he picked on them. Russell had, since the day he entered the Vice Presidents office, seven years earlier, rewritten the rulebook for Vice Presidents. He was the President's right hand man and more akin to a Chief of Staff than the normal media friendly political running mate. The President was a thinker, a grand plan dreamer, while Russell was a doer. Many had tried, during the first term, to gain the ear of the President and circumvent Russell; none had survived in politics to tell the tale. The second term had sealed Russell's power and was, as the election neared, marginalizing the lame duck President for the likely succession of Russell.

Up until just a few months earlier, everything had been running to plan. He had been the natural choice for the republican nominee in the presidential race. That was until Charles Baker had been thrown into the ring. His liberal views were winning over many of the Republicans as they fought a closely contested fight for the Republican nomination. Russell had reached out and offered Baker the VP ticket but Baker had refused, saying 'thanks but I'm going to give the big ticket a go.' In the heartland, Russell was fine but on the coasts, Baker was trouncing him. It was close and for Russell, close was too close. Baker needed to be gone. Plans were in play that Baker would never allow to continue. Too much was at stake. The very future of America and her allies required Russell to be in power.

"Jesus, will one of you useless fucks tell me what happened?"

"We're still trying to piece things together. As for Sam, we have no idea. Our men have gone off the radar. We have a satellite fly-past on Sam's property in the next few minutes and hopefully that will give us something," responded Johnson nervously. Turning to face Jim Gates, the Secretary of Homeland Security, he continued. "As for the Chairman, it seems a couple of Secret Service agents appeared and got to him before our operatives could."

With over 200,000 staff dedicated to the protection of US citizens within the US, Homeland Security was the second most powerful department within the US Government after Defense and had within its remit the United States Secret Service.

"It seems you're losing your touch, Jimmy boy," added Johnson, delighted to push the blame for at least one cock-up elsewhere.

"Our operatives have confirmed they were set upon by a secret service agent who had, believe it or not, already fired upon her colleague."

Russell turned to Gates. "Well?"

"Marx at the Service is surrounded by old guard," responded Gates shrugging his shoulders. "If he gets a threat against a potential presidential candidate, he'd have to act. What can I say other than if we'd dealt with the brother, everything would have worked perfectly. That's the problem," he added, pushing the blame firmly back into Johnson's court.

"Anyway, none of this solves the problem in hand. What are we going to do?" asked Russell.

"Gentlemen," Henry Preston's voice boomed across the room. The Director of National Intelligence was an imposing figure with an even more imposing voice. Glasses vibrated as his bass note tones resonated through the room. As he scrolled through his Blackberry, he continued. "Before we came into the room, I instructed each of the sixteen agencies within my control to leave no stone unturned in their search for Charles Baker. The cover story is that he has been taken against his will and is being held hostage, by a team of international assassins. Any sighting is to be reported to Homeland Security and will be dealt with at the highest level. That is, by us. A news blackout has been imposed, so you won't hear anything. We've suggested Al Qaeda to ensure no reporter interferes. The Patriot Act is a truly wonderful thing. I have asked each department for half-hour updates."

With every law enforcement and intelligence agency within the US reporting into him, Preston commanded a staggering force.

"It seems the fly-past has occurred and a detailed scan has been carried out on Sam Baker's property. It's not good gentlemen. In fact, far worse than any of us could have imagined." Preston paused as he scrolled through the rest of the information on his Blackberry.

"Preston?" urged Russell.

"Sorry, a lot of techno gobbledygook, basically through various scans, X-ray, infra red etc... they've been able to locate a grave with three bodies and in the remnants of a charred cabin, three other remains."

"Six remains. We only sent four guys," interrupted Johnson.

"Hmm, this is where it gets a bit messy. In the cabin, two of the remains are adults but the third was an infant and from the comparisons, it looks as though it was just a baby."

The room went silent as all four computed the information. Taking out a trained operative or even an innocent adult was one thing but a baby was not something even these four would take lightly.

"Oh and a dog," added Preston. "They found the remains of a dog."

"And they're definitely all dead?" asked Gates, a distinct tremble in his voice giving away his feelings.

"I'm afraid so. The satellite can detect a heartbeat and all seven bodies are definitely deceased."

"So it would appear we've killed his partner, wife or whatever, his child and his dog. And to his credit, he has already dealt with the imbeciles we sent to deal with him and him alone." Russell's voice rose with every word. He turned to Johnson.

"We agreed to take out the brother because you said it would solve a bigger problem in the long term."

Johnson opened his mouth to interrupt Russell but a deadly look from Russell made it clear that would not be a good move.

"So far, going after the brother has resulted in two innocent deaths and the failure of the assassination of Charles Baker. It has been a total and complete disaster. Explain to me again why I listened to you?"

Johnson composed himself before he replied, Russell was not a man known for his patience. Whatever Johnson was about to say would potentially be the difference between him remaining in post or having to spend the next week looking over his back and around every corner, wondering how they were going to kill him. He had fucked up but he still believed taking Sam out was imperative; four highly trained killers were testament to that.

"Because you have to trust me when I say you want Sam Baker dead."

"And why would that be?" asked Russell.

"Because if he were alive, he would not rest until he found his brother's killers and eliminated each and every person involved. Including the four of us in here."

"I am the Vice President of the United States of America and soon to be the President. We are talking about one man here. Get a grip Allan. What's the big deal?"

"Because if I wanted to assassinate the President of the United States, he'd be the one man I'd turn to, to get the job done."

The words hung in the air as each of the men digested exactly how highly the Director of the CIA regarded Sam Baker.

A rather less indignant Russell eventually spoke.

"So why the hell didn't you send a better team to deal with him, four amateurs to kill an assassin, are you mad?"

"Of course not, I sent four ex-Special forces killers. They weren't amateurs, anything but. That's exactly why we needed to take him out!"

Before Russell could respond, his phone rang.

"Russell," he announced as he answered the phone.

Gates, Johnson and Preston sat and watched as Russell's demeanor instantly changed to that of a chastised child. After what seemed a lifetime, Russell spoke.

"Yes, Sir," he replied and replaced the handset.

Visibly shaken, he turned to his audience. "Guys, I cannot emphasize enough how imperative it is that we find and eliminate the Bakers."

All were interrupted by a knock at the door as Russell's assistant entered the room.

"Sir, sorry to interrupt but I have the President holding on line 2. I just realized you had finished the other call."

All three attendees looked at each other in shock, the question clear in each other's faces. The VP had just called someone 'Sir'. They had all assumed he had been talking to the President, the only person the Vice President was ever likely to call 'Sir'. Who in the hell was pulling the strings and who were they working for?

# Chapter 16

"Taxi!" shouted Senator Charles Baker for the first time in many years. Agent Clark did what she did best. She watched and surveyed everything and every person in sight. So far, it seemed they had evaded whatever the hell was going on. Although it did seem apparent that the Senator's life was in danger, it was not from Yuri Andriev. Travis, it appeared from the indignation in his face, was on their side but the Senator had been clear he trusted nobody but Clark and even then, Clark didn't fully believe him.

As the taxi stopped at their side, Clark gave the driver a once over before allowing the Senator to enter the vehicle.

"OK, where to?" she asked turning to Baker.

"BWI, train station," announced Baker. As the driver pulled away, he smiled. Baltimore Washington International train station was a thirty mile run and outside the city limits. That would be a hefty bill and from the passengers' attire, he knew they were good for it.

"What the hell for?"

"Sam has a plan. Actually, Sam has a plan for everything. Anyway, if he gave me a warning or if ever I were in danger, he planned a route for me. In fact, sorry, do you have a cell phone?"

Clark reached into her pocket and handed Baker her phone. Without so much as a thank you, Baker flicked the cell through the open window of the cab, quickly followed by his own.

Clark could only turn and watch as her cell, with five years of stored numbers, disintegrated under the tires of the car behind. It wasn't the loss of the phone that upset her, it was forgetting to back up the memory of all her contacts that was really pissing her off.

"Anything else they could use to track us?" asked Baker, ignoring Clark's look of horror over the loss of her phone.

"Not sure if they can track my radio communicator," she answered realizing she had to get back to the job in hand.

"Well, now is not the time to risk it, Get it off and out the window please."

As Clark disposed of her radio communicator, Baker sat back and tried to remember all the steps Sam had talked him through many years earlier. It had all seemed like nonsense at the time but Sam had made Charles repeat every step twice as he had talked him through his escape route. He had argued how ridiculous it was. He was a Senior Senator and was going to be Head of the Defense Committee, not the President. Sam had cautioned that it was for exactly that reason that he was talking him through the plan. He had emphasized more than once that Charles had no idea what he was getting himself into by accepting the Chairmanship. He was going to be playing with people whose life was war and where contracts were measured in billions of dollars and hundreds of thousands of jobs. These were not people you wanted to upset and as Chairman for the United States Senate Subcommittee for Defense Appropriations, you were going to upset a few people, no matter what you did. Sam needed to disappear for a while but only if Charles would take him seriously. They had argued long and hard over Sam's decision to retire. Charles wanted him to come to Washington and talk about the explosion but Sam had had enough. Also, if Charles was going to be Chairman, he had to go. Sam had been called before the committee on a number of occasions and felt any future appearance could do nothing but embarrass his brother.

With the decision made, Charles had repeated the plan twice. Once Sam was happy he had taken it on board, he had left. That had been over three years earlier and Charles had not spoken to, nor seen him since. But the plan, just as Sam had intended, had remained with Charles ever since. Don't use Union Station, it's too obvious, use BWI, it's big, busy and they'd never expect it. If you went there, they'd watch the airport, not the train station. Dump any cell phone or communication device. Don't use any credit cards, use cash only. Always have $500 cash on you at all times. This is your emergency fund and don't, for God's sake, have five $100 bills. People remember big bills, have a mixture. Once you're at BWI rail station, buy a ticket to New York City. You're not going all the way but if anyone does remember your purchase, it will be a ticket to New York and whatever you do, buy a coach seat. Get off at Newark Airport and go straight to the Howard Johnson at the Airport and check in under the name Tim Wilkinson. If I've contacted you, I'll meet you there. If not, and you need me, call 555-1349-911 the first chance you get from a public phone booth. It's an answering service. Just say 'sorry, wrong number' and hang up and I will get to Newark asap.

Although it had been three years since their conversation, Charles had not forgotten even the slightest detail. If Sam said jump, despite being the older and more stately brother, Charles would have asked how high. Sam never did anything without reason.

As the taxi driver unashamedly asked for $94 dollars, Clark climbed out and surveyed the area. All was clear and Baker grudgingly settled up with a small tip, another of Sam's points, don't not tip and don't over tip, people remember both. $100 dollars lighter, he exited the cab and walked into the terminal. One concern remained. The woman sworn to defend his life was not featured in Sam's plan. Charles took an executive decision. She stayed.

"OK, we need to get a couple of tickets to NYC. Probably best you buy them," suggested Baker, handing over a pile of twenties.

Clark walked towards the ticket counter. "Oh and better get coach!" he added with a smile. It had been a very long time since Senator Charles Baker had travelled Coach.

# Chapter 17

As Johnson exited the room, he hit the speed dial button on his cell and connected to his ops center.

"Where are we?" he barked as the call was answered.

Recognizing the boss' voice, the senior operator wasted no time on pleasantries.

"The satellites have picked up six dead bodies…"

"I know all that thanks to Preston. Where are we on finding the target?" he interrupted brusquely. Preston's telling the VP information his team had been responsible for had really pissed him off.

"The call to the Secret Service was made over two hours ago. We've had three satellite sweeps on North Haven in that time and it seems the target has probably taken our operatives' car as it's not been found on the island. Which means two things. One, we can track him. And two, more importantly, he had to use the ferry. That takes over ninety minutes and the one he's on is due to land shortly."

"What assets do we have locally?"

"Nothing, I'm afraid. Our closest assets are in Boston, just under 200 miles away. However, I have managed to acquire a General Atomics Avenger unmanned combat air vehicle. It's still in development but I am told has performed exceptionally in testing and our guys are extremely keen to utilize it in a live environment.

"What have you told them?" Johnson was well aware of the Avenger's capabilities. It was one tool he couldn't wait to get in to the field. The jet powered stealthy reconnaissance vehicle could fly faster, higher, further and carry far more ordinance than her predecessors, the Predator and the Reaper.

"That we are tracking an Al Qaeda cell which we believe is targeting Seabrook Nuclear reactor in New Hampshire and or Pilgrim Nuclear reactor in Massachusetts. Both reactors are within 40 miles of Boston and as such they were happy to assist. The Avenger was operating out of the 174th air wing at Syracuse New York. They were trialing it alongside the Reaper. The Avenger is armed with hellfire missiles and will be on station when Baker's ferry docks."

"Excellent and the Senator?"

"Sorry Sir, dropped off the radar. We have nothing on him nor the Secret Service Agent. We have them on camera running from the Hart building shortly after the shots were fired. We lose them as they run into the road. We're grabbing all CCTV images from the vicinity. As soon as we've got something, I'll let you know."

Johnson knew that Sam would ultimately lead them to the Senator but to let him go when they had an opportunity to take him out relatively easily, made his decision. The Senator was an amateur and would slip up. Sam wasn't and wouldn't. They had the drop on him and that was exactly what they would do, drop the hellfire missiles on him asap.

"Keep looking for the Senator but take Sam out as soon as you get a clear shot and by clear, I mean minimize civilian casualties. We've had enough collateral damage for one day. I'm heading to you now, so should be with you in about 45 minutes. First chance you get, take him out."

"Yes Sir."

Johnson began to relax, dealing with the loose end that was Sam Baker had been a long overdue issue. Of course they could have disposed of the Senator without touching Sam. It had been a calculated risk to throw Sam into the mire but Sam knew things about Johnson that nobody should know. Johnson had seen his opportunity and he had taken it. It was just a shame that the idiots he had selected hadn't. Mind you, he thought, they certainly paid for that in spades, quite literally. Johnson knew Sam Baker was a risk, almost certainly because there were only two people who knew he was alive. One was his brother and the other was him. Johnson, therefore, would be top of Sam's hit list, not a place anyone would want to be but with 20,000 employees in the CIA, Sam would have to go some to get near him, never mind the six hellfire missiles 10,000 feet above Sam with his name on them.

***

Sam had been out of the game for three years, not something he was overly concerned about. His training regime was as tough if not tougher than it had ever been. He was as fit now as he had been twenty years earlier. He did, however, have one nagging doubt about the previous three years - how far had technology travelled and how far behind had he fallen? Three years earlier he knew every conceivable way to track a human being but things had moved on. He looked again at the sat nav system in the car. Three years ago, he would have been confident it wasn't an issue but could it be tracked now? The system was pulling information from somewhere and if it was getting it, it was giving it. He had to dump the car quickly.

They already knew where his starting point was, Rockland Maine. There was no need to give them anymore of a head-start than that. The local airport was out. Once in the air, he would be a sitting target and trackable. The train would be no better Slow and few or no escape routes would favor only his hunters. That left sticking with the roads and with over 400 miles to travel, speed was of the essence. As he pulled off the ferry, he could feel the roar of the Chrysler's engine. It certainly had the power he needed. T, the 6.1l hemi engine produced 425 bhp and could propel the car to almost 180mph. Rockland was a cul-de-sac. He had no choice but to go for it.

The Virginia plates gave Sam some comfort; whoever had sent the men to kill him did not have local help. He knew they'd be onto him but Virginia was 800 miles away and it would take at least a few hours for them to regroup and get assets on scene and in that car, he could be in Newark in three hours, traffic allowing.

# Chapter 18

## Five miles south of Gaza City

The sun's dying embers slipped below the horizon as darkness fell. Candles in the deserted beach shack threw a wavering dimness on proceedings. Mohammed Deif entered the shack and instantly killed off the conversation. His three lieutenants were already in attendance. All four had spent the best part of the day ensuring no tails had tracked them to their remote venue.

It had been a terrible few years for Al Qassam. The retribution by Israel on all groups for the attack on her children had been devastating. Over 80% of the brigade had been captured, tortured and killed. However, the majority of those had been in the previous year. It was no secret that Israel was aware of the nuclear devices the Sheikh had offered Al Qassam. The Sheikh's spies had uncovered that truth shortly after their meeting a year earlier. Somehow, the Israelis had listened into the whole meeting and knew the plan; the force with which they had responded was overwhelming. The retribution for her children paled into insignificance compared to what the Israelis had unleashed. All non Jews had been expelled instantly from Israel, even Jerusalem; the holy city had been cleansed of all non Jews. The uproar and protest at the Israeli action around the globe was muted by the evidence of the Palestinians' nuclear ambitions. Her twelve foot walls, erected almost four years earlier, had created the world's first truly closed state.

Mohammed and his commanders had managed to evade the Israelis through the most primitive actions. Like Osama Bin Laden, they had turned their back on all electrical and electronic equipment. Cell phones, telephones, computers, anything that required an electrical pulse had been ditched and replaced by pen and paper. The meeting that was about to take place had been months in preparation and would see the culmination of Al Qassam's planning. The Sheikh would hand over the codes that would turn the nuclear warheads from dull pieces of metal into the most lethal devices ever created by man.

Mohammed smiled as he considered the Israelis' actions. The building of the walls, the expulsion of all non-Jews. None of it had done anything for the safety of her people. The five warheads lay within the Jewish state. It had taken months to infiltrate the Israeli defenses and secure safe passage for the five weapons but it had been done. The five warheads were being slowly positioned, ready to unleash their awesome force and tip the scales towards a Palestinian victory. Palestine would be reborn.

The Sheikh's small inflatable, its engine hardly registering a decibel, slipped noiselessly ashore. Unlike their previous meeting, he had only one guard. This was not a public meeting and only he and the Al Qassam commanders were in attendance.

As the Sheikh took his seat and greetings and blessings to Allah were exchanged, the Sheikh quickly brought the meeting to order.

"Is everything on course? Have you selected the targets?"

"Yes, Sheikh, all of the warheads are in Israel and we are in the process of placing them at the targets we've selected. We will destroy the Jews once and for all."

"Show me!" commanded the Sheikh.

Mohammed pulled out a map from a bag and spread it across the table. Of course the map was pre 1947 and was of Palestine. However, the locations of the five weapons were marked in detail. One in Jaffa, the Arab name for Tel Aviv. Two in Haifa, Israel's major seaport. One in Eilat, her jewel in the Arabian Sea and one in Rishon leZion, Israel's fourth largest city.

"As you will see, all five weapons are to be placed within Israel, as per your stipulation."

"But two in Haifa? And none in Jerusalem?" asked the Sheikh looking at the detail on the map.

Mohammed was well prepared for the question. "Haifa is the seaport and lifeblood of Israel. If we destroy that not only psychologically but physically we will break the Zionist back. She needs her seaport more than ever since the walls went up. As for Jerusalem and as a Muslim, I'm sure I do not need to explain why not."

"Of course not," agreed the Sheikh quickly. "But I would have thought two bombs in Tel Aviv would have had more effect than two in Haifa."

"My Sheikh, they are your weapons and only because of you do we have this opportunity. If you believe we are wrong, please, we will move one from Haifa to Tel Aviv."

"Mohammed, my friend, please, this is your struggle. You have lived it your whole life. I should not question your plan. You are right, they are my weapons but it is your plan my friend," the Sheikh reached into his pocket and handed Deif a small piece of paper. "Allahu Akbar, my friend. They are now your weapons. These codes will trigger the devices. I'd advise being at least 10 miles from each of them when they go off. Any idea of when you'll be ready?"

"Let's just say we are going to give the Jews a Yom Kippur to remember!"

The Sheikh did not reply other than to nod his head in approval. Yom Kippur was only two weeks away. After a year in the making, their plan was finally coming to fruition. With a shake of hands, the Sheikh stood and exited the shack. Not until he was out of sight did Deif feel comfortable beginning the second part of their meeting. The true destination for the fifth weapon. Haifa was home to two weapons and Mohammed had not lied when he had assured the Sheikh that all weapons were in Israel. However as he had said, Haifa was the largest port in Israel and as such was home to many ships, one of which was carrying a decidedly more deadly cargo than her manifest suggested.

# Chapter 19

As the train pulled away from the platform, Senator Charles Baker pushed himself back into his seat and relaxed for the first time since they had left the Hart building. For Secret Service Agent Amy Clark, the last thing on her mind was relaxation. She was now in a public location with her protectee who was not only the target of an assassination plot but was also one of the most recognizable faces in US politics. You couldn't be considered one of two front runners for the top job and not be. Every other day, the Senator's face was emblazoned across newsstands and every hour, at least one of the news channels would be doing something that would extol the virtues or pronounce their contempt for him, depending on their loyalties. Clark had insisted they take the last rear facing double seat in the carriageway, the Senator by the window while Clark took the aisle seat, offering a clear view back down the carriage. Clark's eyes continually scanned for threats in a carriage full of passengers.

Clark looked at the Senator as the train began to pick up speed. If he hadn't been a politician, she was in no doubt he would have been a movie star. He reminded her of Gregory Peck in his later movies. Whatever the case, he was instantly recognizable. From his immaculately styled hair and impeccable dress sense, he turned heads wherever he went. She reached across and much to her surprise, met little resistance when she began to remove his tie and undid his top button. A little more resistance was met when she ran her hand through his hair and slightly ruffled his coiffure.

"I'm sorry, Sir, but let's not try to give them the exact image you portray day in day out and at least try to look a little less presidential candidate," she offered as an excuse for her actions.

"Sorry, of course," he agreed, embarrassed for not thinking it himself and ruffled his hair significantly more than Clark had dared. "Is that better?" he asked proudly, showing Clark the results of his efforts.

"Uncanny, Sir, a complete transformation," she lied. His coiffure was not for moving. Years of perfection were not going to be overcome with a quick rub. However, it was amazing how just removing the tie and undoing the top button had helped.

"Thank you, said the Senator as he relaxed back into his seat. With twenty years under his belt in politics, Senator Baker had no illusions that Clark was simply humoring him in an attempt to ensure he remained calm. "So, come on, we've got two and a half hours to kill until Newark. Tell me about yourself, why the Secret Service?"

Clark watched the other passengers as she answered. "Nothing really to tell. For as long as I can remember, I wanted to be a Secret Service Agent," she said, attempting to kill the discussion.

"That's it? No family connections, you know, my dad was in the service, my uncle..."

"Nope. What about yourself, why President?"

Baker laughed as Clark asked the question half heartedly. Her mind was almost entirely focused on the rest of the carriage and ensuring her protectee stayed alive.

"Agent Clark, please relax, nobody knows we're on this train. Look around us, none of the other passengers even know we're here." Baker lifted his hand as Clark attempted to interrupt. "In just over two hours, we will need to be alert but for now, please relax. We're in no danger just now but if I know my brother, there is going to be plenty around soon enough to keep you amply amused."

Baker noticed a slight, almost negligible flinch as Clark appeared to relax. "So, come on, why the Service?" he tried again.

"Seriously, it's all I ever wanted to do, no great story. I remember the assassination attempt on President Reagan and watching the agents protecting him. That was it. From then on, nothing else would suffice."

Baker looked more closely at Agent Clark. "You must have been a baby when that happened."

"Eight," replied Clark.

Ever the mathematical genius, Baker quickly calculated Clark's age to be at least five years over his outside guess. She was a stunning specimen of a woman. In her late thirties, her face showed no signs of her advancing years. She had flawless skin, wrinkle free and only wore light make-up. Her blond hair was tied tightly back and flowed down her perfectly cut Armani suit which did nothing but emphasize the lithe and firm body underneath.

"Married?" he asked

"Are you flirting with me Senator?" asked Clark as she appraised Baker's lingering stare.

"Sorry, no not at all," he blushed. "Admiring, yes, flirting, no. I'm not ashamed to act my age nor behave my age. I'm old enough to be your father, well just," he added quickly.

"So what about you, Senator, why politics and why President?" asked Clark, changing the subject to avoid any further embarrassment.

Senator Baker paused as he considered the question, a question she had heard him answer numerous times before on countless news interviews.

"Politics because I felt I could make a difference. The Presidency because I have no choice, I have to make a difference," he answered from the heart.

"I've not heard you say it like that before?"

"That's because you've only ever heard me in public before. The Vice President was almost guaranteed the Presidency at the next election and I just can't allow them to continue with what they've been doing to our country for the last eight years. They're systematically tearing our democracy apart. Another eight years under Russell would effectively kill the United States as a democratic nation."

"You make him sound like some sort of dictator. I've met him once, he was charming."

"You, my dear, are a very attractive and unthreatening young woman, I am not in the least surprised you found him to be anything but charming. But let me assure you, once the doors are closed and the private Andrew Russell comes out, there's no colder soul than that ruthless little shit."

Silence fell between them as they digested the possibility of the ruthless Russell being the man who had targeted Baker and his brother. Surely not, Baker told himself, but the more the thought played on his mind, the more sense it began to make.

"You don't think?" Agent Clark broke the silence and paused, the thought too horrific to verbalize.

"I'm thinking the same bloody thing," replied Baker. "Russell!"

# Chapter 20

Sam gunned the 425 horses as he exited the ferry and had no intention of letting up until he reached Newark. The car rocketed out of Rockland as Sam considered the route, back roads or main roads. US Route 1 ran through Rockland and would connect him to I95 but that was the most obvious route and would leave Sam seriously exposed for over 50 miles. The back roads, cutting North to pick up the I95 to the North of Rockland, offered a less obvious solution but this meant his journey time would be extended by almost an hour. An hour Sam ventured he didn't have. So US 1 it was. With no obvious tails being picked up as he sped through Rockland, he felt comfortable that he had at least a couple of hours before he'd have anything to really worry about.

With his route selected, Sam's mind began to fall back to Goat Island and the family and life that had been wrenched from him. Sam Junior, Goldie and Jane, his wife, slaughtered. Sam knew he should stay focused but the picture of his wife and child torn apart wouldn't leave him. The adrenalin rush that had helped him overcome the attackers and got him to the mainland was wearing off and the cold light of day was hitting home; he was alone again. During his working life, Sam had remained single. His life had never been one to share. His new life had been though. Sam punched the steering wheel in anger. The resulting horn blast snapped him back. He had to leave Sam Junior, Jane and Goldie behind, not forever, but at least until he had avenged their deaths. He had to remain focused. Every single person who had had a hand in their deaths had to pay and to ensure that, Sam had to keep his mind focused.

First and foremost, Sam had to get to his brother and see just who it was he had pissed off this time. Charles had a habit of taking things too far and neither realizing nor taking account of what or who he was up against. In Montana, it had been an Albanian gang who had been prosperously running a prostitution and drug ring before the Senator had waded in. Little did he know how close he had come to being at the end of a three man hit team, sent by the Albanian ganglord. Sam had taken care of the hit team and the ganglord quietly and in such a fashion that nobody would ever again consider something so stupid, certainly not in Montana. But Montana had been a small stage. Charles was now playing with the big boys and obviously Charles had continued to push people way over the edge.

Sam considered the possibilities. Top of the list would be defense contractors. If Charles had taken issue with one, as Chairman of the Appropriations Committee, the impact could have been massive, involving billions of dollars and hundreds of thousands of jobs. Next were the usual whack jobs, white supremacist groups, Nazis, terrorists etc... but none of them would have known about Sam or his family.

Before he could consider anymore, Sam reached the junction with US Route 1 and the 131, his turning should he wish to use the less obvious circuitous route. He paused at the junction before making a final decision. He floored the accelerator and pushed out of Thomaston and on down the US Route 1. Time was of the essence.

***

The Avenger looked down on the junction and the clear open countryside ahead. From Rockland to Thomaston, the road had been lined with buildings and homes. After Thomaston, the road cleared and offered little or no cover for Baker, not that he even had hint he needed it. The Avenger was locked on and silently following its target's every move from over 25,000 feet above him.

"Sir, we're moving towards open road. The target has remained on US Route 1. Target is locked and weapons are hot."

Johnson listened as the operator fed him the update. If only Sam had made the turn. It was going to be tricky to time a missile strike and minimize collateral damage. After all, he had promised the Vice President exactly that. However, Sam was a tricky bastard and Johnson knew better than anyone, the first chance they had, may be the only chance. So with little concern for collateral, he barked his orders.

"Fire the first clear shot you get. Just don't hit a bloody school bus. We clear?"

"Yes Sir," barked the operator.

The operator looked towards his screen which really wasn't any different from an arcade game. His target was clearly visible in the middle of the screen and in the top left, he had a range of weapons to select from. However, in this instance, only the AGM114 showed any ammunition. AGM-114 were hellfire missiles, small and extremely accurate laser guided missiles. More than capable of destroying a car and certainly more appropriate than the other far more powerful laser guided bombs compatible with the Avenger. The operator zoomed out and keeping the target dead center, he began to note the area around the target. Release of the weapon to impact would be in the region of 20 seconds. The target's speed was varying between 50 and 110 mph. Although traffic was light, the variables were mind-blowing. Minimizing collateral was almost impossible, other than if the road were totally clear for a couple of miles around the target which, looking at the flow of traffic, was highly unlikely.

At least the schools were still in he thought, looking at his watch. With a long straight ahead of him and little traffic, the target accelerated again and pushed over 100 mph. Of course, the Avenger had no issue with the target's speed, nor would the missile which could fly 10 times faster. The issue was that the distance travelled by the target from release to impact doubled. The operator considered his boss' final words and hit 'Fire' – there were no school buses anywhere near!

The missile dropped from its bay and immediately ignited its rocket, dropping and accelerating to its maximum speed of 1.3 Mach, almost 1,000 mph. The laser designator was firmly fixed on the roof of the car. The operator's view switched from the Avenger to the nose mounted camera on the weapon, a small distance to target tracked down the meters to impact. Switching back to the Avengers view, the operator looked at the road ahead, it was looking good, the only vehicle visible in the distance that was likely to fall within the impact zone was a lone truck. Taking Sam Baker out with just one innocent victim would be a seriously good result.

***

Sam looked at the long straight ahead and floored the accelerator. The Hemi engine reacted immediately and the car powered to over 100 mph. The early afternoon traffic was light and Sam looked at the clock and wished he could keep up the 120 mph pace he was now setting but there was no way the route would remain this quiet. The I 95 was a main trunk route that fed Boston and New York. However, he would make hay while the sun shone and depressed the accelerator even further, sending another surge to the drive train, increasing the speed to almost 140 mph. Covering over two miles per minute, Sam needed all his wits about him. Cars coming towards him would close at over 200 mph and he could quite easily run into the back of dawdlers travelling in his direction. One such dawdler was dead ahead, having just pulled out from a small side road. Sam was closing fast, travelling at little over 45 mph, Sam guessed the driver of the ageing pick-up was probably in his seventies and was certain would be wearing some sort of head wear. Slow drivers had one thing in common, they always wore a hat, well in Sam's experience anyway. Sam edged out to see beyond the pick-up and pulled back in sharply. A large truck was bearing down on him. In the blink of an eye, Sam had to make the call, slow and pull in behind the dawdler or accelerate and hopefully just miss the oncoming truck. It would be tight and he would have to be careful. The 300 was fast but only in a straight line. Agility was certainly not its strong point. The road ahead narrowed and disappeared into a wooded area. Being stuck behind the slow moving car was not an option, so Sam floored the accelerator and for the first time, did not feel the surge of the 425 horses. At 140 mph, the car was already pushing towards its limits. Acceleration was now harder to come by. Sam flinched as he noticed the truck bearing towards him. It was going to be closer than he thought.

In fact, he may not make it but at the last second, he shot past the pick-up and pulled in ahead of it. Unable not to look, Sam smiled as the old boy with a Stetson who threw him a disapproving look.

That was the last thing he saw before the explosion threw his car clear across the road.

*** 

"Direct hit, Sir," announced the operator as he watched the center of the screen blossom into a fiery red rose indicating impact.

"Whoa!!! Holy shit!" he followed quickly as the initial blossom bloomed and filled the whole screen.

"What?" asked Johnson looking across at the operator's open mouth. "What the hell just happened?" he asked impatiently as the operator tried to comprehend what had just happened.

"I think, I'm not sure, but that truck may have been a fuel tanker of some type because there was a massive secondary explosion. It certainly wasn't the hellfire that did that." He pointed to a massive hole in the ground where the road had been.

"And Baker?"

"No way he survived that. Look, there's just a hole where the truck, a pick up and his car were."

"Excellent and we can cover the explosion as a tanker accident. Couldn't be better, well done. Now get that Avenger out of there before all hell breaks loose and the place is crawling with cops, firemen, news crews and God knows what else.

# Chapter 21

"No, that's absurd," suggested Charles Baker as he considered the possibility that Russell would have perpetrated such an action.

"Yes, you're right," agreed Agent Clark shaking her head. "So tell me about this brother of yours?" she asked keen to change the subject.

"Sam? Well, I've not seen him in almost three years," Baker pondered, considering a question he'd not been asked in many years. "He's seven years younger than me. I may be older, have the education and position but he's the brains in the family."

Clark turned to look at one of the most powerful men in America who was renowned for his intellect and considered the revelation that the younger brother was the brighter of the two.

"I'm not talking here about knowledge you pick up reading books, I'm talking about raw intelligence, the type that makes you compute and see things faster and quicker than anyone else. Solving problems, seeing solutions, that's what Sam does, he solves problems and avoids creating more problems in the process."

Sorry, I'm not really following you. What kind of problems do you mean?"

"Sam never started fights but he was always the guy that finished them. He joined the air force to see the world and trained as a pilot but after a crash killed his navigator and almost himself, he retrained and became a Pararescueman, a PJ as they're called."

"Never heard of them. A P what?"

"Pararescue Jumper, they're trained to go into enemy territory and rescue downed pilots and servicemen. One of them saved his life after his plane went down. He doesn't talk about it much but this guy impressed him so much he gave up flying and joined the PJs."

"OK, he rescues people, so why the hell was a Russian assassin trying to kill him?"

"He did rescue people but you have to understand my brother. He never does anything by half. PJs go into battle zones to rescue people. They're trained for just about any eventuality and are considered members of the special forces. They fight their way to wherever they have to get to. Sam joined the forces during the cold war. There weren't many battle zones that US troops were going into but training opportunities were aplenty. He signed up for just about every course he could. He learnt to scuba with the SEALs, he completed combat courses with Delta Force commandos, he tracked and observed with Marine recon, he was like a sponge. He was even signing up for training courses with the Allies, the SBS, SAS in the UK, jungle training with the Ghurkhas. You name it, he did it. Before he knew it, he was on secret ops deep in the heart of Afghanistan, helping the CIA fight their secret war against the Russians. When shit hit the fan and Special Forces or the CIA needed assistance, it was Sam that would go in to rescue their guys."

"Can't believe I've never heard of these guys."

"Only those in the military really know about them. They're the original unsung heroes. Mind you, if you're a PJ and you walk into a bar with servicemen, you'll never buy a drink. Because every guy in there knows that you're the guy that's gonna get them out when everybody else has given up."

"I just don't get how rescuing people in Afghanistan leads to being targeted by an assassin 20 years later."

"Ah, well. It turned out that after a few years of rescuing their people from God alone knows what, Sam made a bit of a name for himself. He was the guy everybody wanted backing them up. If you were in trouble and needed help, Sam Baker was the guy you wanted. Whoever was in charge of the CIA's Special Operations Group at the time began to take a keen interest. Sam's name kept popping up in reports, injured agents owing their life to the Pararescue guy who had appeared from nowhere, popped a couple of Russians and then carried them to a safe extraction point. Sam's additional training it seemed had really paid off. Particularly in Afghanistan, his time with the Ghurkhas in jungles and mountains had made Sam quite a specialist. Anyway, Sam was nearing the end of his tour when he received a call-out. An agent was injured deep in the heart of Russian occupied country. Sam was dropped as close as the helicopter dared and then proceeded on foot for the final few miles. He came across the camp where the agent was supposed to be and found it empty. He tracked the trail in the darkness, deep into the mountains and by this time was over three miles behind enemy lines. He found the new camp, took out six Russians and reported back to the extraction point, devastated to report that the injured agent had simply disappeared. He was no longer at the camp and Sam could only assume had been killed at some point and discarded off a cliff face, as there was absolutely no sign of any further tracks leading to anywhere else."

"Oh God that's awful, I can only imagine what they would have done to the agent."

"Don't worry, there was no agent. As Sam finished his report to his officer, a man walked into the room and dismissed Sam's officer with a flick of the head. Sam was then face to face with, his words "the coldest bastard I have ever met in my life, I swear to God the temperature dropped when he entered the room." He informed Sam that there was no agent, the Russians were a Spetsnaz team that had always managed to evade the CIA and Mujahedeen and had been causing untold havoc. Of course Sam took one look at the smug look on the guy's face and shot a punch straight to his chin. The guy never saw it coming and was knocked to the floor. He never retaliated, he just stood up and welcomed Sam to the CIA's Special Operations Group, handing Sam a letter signed by the President asking Sam to move across as his skills would save far more lives if he were the one leading the operation, rather than the one mopping up. Sam could not refuse a request from his President and so spent the rest of the war doing what he does best."

"Saving people's lives?" asked a confused Clark.

"No," the Senator said shaking his head. "Ending them!"

"Oh!"

"Sam worked for the CIA up until three years ago. Right up until the nuclear bomb exploded in Texas."

Clark read between the lines. "Was he there?"

The Senator looked around the carriage, delaying any answer as he pondered what he should tell Clark. He decided on the truth.

"Sam was there. Sam was the guy who could have saved the day. Sam was the guy that was told not to shoot the terrorist four hours before he detonated the bomb."

Clark just stared at the Senator. The revelation that the government could have stopped the atrocity left her speechless.

"Sam had tracked the terrorists for months. He had many opportunities to kill them but every time, he was stopped by his bosses. They wanted to know where the target of the attack was. It was the one thing nobody could uncover."

"But I thought it was Washington."

"That's the story but Sam says not a chance. The terrorists knew the bomb would set off every alarm we've got. That bomb was not ever going to get near Washington. Sam told everybody that they had to be stopped before they got to America but they just ignored him."

"Oh my God. So what did he do?"

"After he was stood down, an assassin tried to kill him and very nearly did. Sam's not sure who hired him, it could have been the terrorists or any number of people. Andriev was a gun for hire. Anyway, after everything that had happened, Sam decided to quit. He sent a picture of himself looking dead to the assassin's contact, burnt Andriev's body and left his own ID next to it. The Mexicans didn't waste time checking. They just declared the body as Sam Baker and as nobody local claimed him, they buried it in a pauper's grave. Sam used Andriev's tickets and travelled back to the US."

"My God," Clark could hardly believe what she was hearing, "So, what did he do then?" she prompted, keen to hear everything.

"We talked, he told me what had happened and that he would be going away. He'd contact me when he could. In the meantime, he gave me instructions on what to do if I needed him. The bomb going off hit him hard. He wandered for a while before he found North Haven and settled down. He was happy for the first time in a long time."

"Until today?"

"Until today," repeated Baker, "I've not seen Sam for over three years. Not since he saved the CNN journalists, just before the bombings in Israel…"

Clark turned to look at Baker as his voice dropped. She was expecting to see a tear in his eye but instead saw a look of horror.

"What's wrong?" she asked, looking down the carriage towards where the Senator was staring blankly.

"I've just shivered all over, it's like somebody walked over my grave," he said quietly. "Something very bad has just happened."

# Part Three

# Chapter 22

**London**

Rebecca tapped on the door gently. "Room Service!" she announced.

"Can you come back please, I'm not quite ready," responded the guest.

Rebecca Cohen smiled. He certainly wasn't ready for what he was about to receive and nor would he ever be.

She inserted the master key borrowed from the front desk and began to enter as if not having heard the guest. Footsteps came rushing towards the door as it opened.

"Sorry, I said I'm not ready." Irritation replaced the guest's jovial tone.

As the door opened fully, Rebecca was faced with the limping Izz al Qassam Brigade Commander she had seen over a year earlier. He, of course, did not recognize the woman in front of him as she was fully dressed. Although he did recognize that she wasn't wearing the correct attire for a cleaner. She wore black trousers, a black top and more worryingly on a hot day, a pair of gloves.

As he stepped towards the door in an attempt to shut it, she lifted her arm and fired. The small darts flew towards the Palestinian, catching him in the chest. Over 50,000 volts pulsed through his body, sending him crashing to the floor. Rebecca closed the door behind her and placed the Taser X3 on the small table before manhandling the Palestinian towards the bed.

"Come on, wake up!" urged Rebecca.

The man looked at Rebecca as his eyes opened. He remembered going to open the door and then nothing. He looked down and saw he was naked. He tried to move but his arms and legs were secured to the four corners of the bed frame. He tried to speak but his mouth was stuffed full of what felt like a sock.

Rebecca smiled as the fear in his eyes grew and the realization of the situation sank in.

"My name is Rebecca Cohen," announced Rebecca. Her voice almost sang as she savored the helplessness of the terrorist scum's situation. "And you, my friend, are going to tell me everything you know."

The man shook his head wildly in protest at the thought of telling her anything. The realization that it was a Jew bitch that he was lying naked in front of replaced fear with anger.

"Before you make up your mind, there are a few things you should be aware of." Rebecca stared coldly into the young Palestinian's eyes as she spoke. "Firstly, this is not going to end well for you. You are going to die and secondly, you are going to tell me everything you know before you do."

Rebecca could see from the arrogance in the man's eyes that he thought she was very mistaken. It was always the same, she thought. This foolish misconception that they couldn't be broken. Everyone could be broken and much quicker than they ever imagined.

She almost pitied him, almost. She looked into his eyes and made him an offer while removing a small scalpel blade from a belt around her waist, a belt that held many other tools.

"If you talk now and I believe you are telling me the truth, you will meet your 72 virgins intact."

The subtlety of her threat was not missed. The Palestinian's fear returned instantly. The bravado dropped as his eyes fell towards his crotch. However, he shook his head. He was a proud and strong Palestinian.

Rebecca shook her head. It was such a shame, the naivety of these men. Of course, this would not be easy, being in a busy London hotel added to the complexity of the situation. Noise was going to be a problem. His screams would have to be contained.

Rebecca turned on the TV, selected a radio station and turned up the volume to almost the highest setting.

She moved the scalpel to within a few millimeters of the Palestinian's manhood and watched his eyes for any hint that he may forego the pain and suffering. The defiance in his eyes suggested not. She shook her head and started cutting. The screams were almost entirely muffled by the boxer shorts in his mouth, anything else was nicely covered by the music.

It took just over ten minutes and the loss of one testicle for the man to tell Rebecca everything he had ever known. His name was Rafik Azzam and, as she had thought, he was a deputy to Mohammed Deif. She listened without emotion as he talked of the plan to deliver a blow to both Israel and America. Some details he knew, others he did not. He was in London to make a final payment to a third party. A ship had been fitted specially for the American bomb but he did not know where the ship was, its name or what the special fitting was. He didn't know who he paid the money to, other than he sounded Russian. Finally and under the threat of losing his manhood entirely, he divulged the timescale for the attacks.

Happy that there was nothing left he could tell her, she fulfilled her first promise. She placed a small .22 caliber pistol against Rafik's head and pulled the trigger. She turned off the TV, left the room, placed the 'Do Not Disturb' sign on the door and made a call to the Mossad office in London. There was a mess to clean up. Her next call was to Ben.

As she waited to be put through to Ben, she thought back over the last year. It had been the shortest year of her life. The more time she needed to track down the nukes, the less she seemed to have. After the revelation a year earlier, she had informed Ben of the Sheikh's plan before announcing to him that she would go deep. Ben had not even had the chance to discuss it with her. She had ended the call and to all intents and purposes disappeared into an abyss. Ben had tried desperately to find her but to no avail. Six months earlier, he had all but written her off as dead.

As he ended the call with the Prime Minister, he picked up the waiting call.

"Ben Meir!"

"Uncle Ben," she began.

"Rebecca, my dear!" he exclaimed, loud enough for the top floor of the Knesset to hear.

"My God, Ben you're going to burst my ear drum," she said smiling. She could hear the smile in his voice.

"Where are you? You must come in," ordered Ben, gushing and overjoyed to hear her voice again.

Rebecca remained motionless. "I'm sorry Ben but time is not on our side. The nukes will be detonated on Yom Kippur, just two weeks from now!"

Ben sighed.

"I know," he said slowly.

"You know," repeated Rebecca. "What are you doing? Holding meetings? We have to evacuate major cities, high profile targets. We can't let them win," she argued.

"We can't and we won't, please, what do you know?" he asked again.

Rebecca remained silent. Just because she had gone deep, did not mean she was not aware of the intel Mossad had and didn't have. She knew Mossad was not aware of the two week deadline.

Ben read the silence and filled in some detail.

"We've tracked all five weapons to their locations and have teams watching them. It's all in hand. We're waiting for the right moment to take them down. The weapons need to be armed. At the moment, the weapons are safe. When they come to arm them, we will take them down. Everything is in order."

"Thank God," exclaimed an extremely relieved Rebecca. A year of worry evaporated in an instant.

"But how? How did you find them?" As the worry subsided, reasoning took the initiative.

"Let's just say I have my sources," replied the old master, tapping his nose. "I've not lost it yet, you know. Now tell me, where have you been?"

"All over, I'm in London right now but mainly in the camps." Rebecca was referring to the many Palestinian refugee camps, the breeding ground for the terrorists. "I got a break and discovered one of the Al Qassam Brigade commanders was going to be in London. I tracked him down to a hotel in Paddington."

Rebecca had been one of their most successful deep cover agents. Her skin tone and facial features blended perfectly with the Palestinians. It was amazing how a change of clothes, altered make-up and hair could transform Rebecca from Jew to Palestinian freedom fighter, to French heiress, to Italian beauty and in fact with her linguistic talents and natural Mediterranean beauty could pass off from being from anywhere she wished.

"I just finished interrogating him. I can't believe you already knew but thank God Haifa, Tel Aviv, Jaffa and Rishon le Zion will be saved."

Ben knew better than to ask what she had done with the Palestinian.

"Don't worry, we have them under constant watch. As soon as they come to arm the weapons, we'll pounce."

"And the American city?"

Ben wasn't sure he had heard her correctly. "Sorry, what did you say?"

"The American city, which one is it?"

"What American city are you talking about? There are five nukes and we've accounted for all five."

Rebecca counted out the cities on her hand. "Haifa, Tel Aviv, Jaffa and Rishon leZion, that's four."

"But there are two in Haifa?" panicked Ben, beginning to realize a massive error might have been made.

"There were but one was destined for America. They want to make amends for missing Washington last time. All I know is that it's not Washington they're targeting."

Ben's face turned white as he lifted his other phone. "Get me the Unit's Commander." The unit was the nickname for Sayeret Matkal, Israeli Special Forces, modeled on the British SAS and was the elite force within the Israeli Defense Forces.

After a brief wait, Daniel Rosenberg was on the line.

"When was the last time we had eyes on the weapons?" barked Ben with no preamble and catching Daniel off-guard.

"Hmm..."

"Don't hmm me man, tell me when did we last physically see the weapons?"

"If you're meaning the nuclear devices, well we've been watching them for the last few days and nobody has been near them."

"Check the Haifa ones now and call me back. I want physical checks of their presence immediately. Call me back," ordered Ben not waiting for Daniel to confirm the order.

Hearing the end of the other call, Rebecca continued. "But what if I'm wrong, you may tip them to the fact we're watching them?"

"It's a risk we have to take. The weapons are Israeli, stolen from us. If they go off anywhere but on our soil, all hell will break loose and we could end up losing our nuclear mandate."

"Jesus, do you ever think of anything but Israel Ben?, What about the millions that could be affected by the blast? No, you just move to the next step, a weakened Israel."

"That's why I'm in this office and not in any other. I'm paid to protect Israel."

Before the argument could really take hold, the other phone rang. Ben answered it immediately.

"Yes?"

"They're not there Ben," said an almost breathless Daniel.

"Shit! Check the rest?"

"We have, they're all gone, all five are unaccounted for."

"How the fuck do we lose five nuclear weapons?" he screamed, his anger welling over. A headache instantly pounded in Ben's head as the ramifications of the news began to sink in. Five nuclear weapons under their surveillance had simply vanished and if Rebecca's information was correct, at least one was bound for America, an ally they could not afford to lose.

# Chapter 23

**Mediterranean Sea, Cyprus**

Akram 'Pock-Mark' Rayyan had obtained his nick name like most who had suffered from severe acne as a teenager. However, not many dared mention it in front of him, particularly since he had become Deputy Commander and one of the most ruthless members of the Al Qassam Brigade. Akram stared across at the Cypriot coastline, the nearest he had been to his homeland for some time. The warmth of the air was a blessing from Allah after his last few weeks on the Northern coast of Russia. Severodvinsk was, even in the summer, cold and wet. Pock-Mark was not a sailor. He loved land and particularly his people's land. Palestine. Pock-Mark had been honored by their leader, Mohammed Deif, with the task of delivering the momentous blow to the American infidels. He looked again at his hand-picked team, twelve young men in their prime who would sacrifice themselves for the cause, ten sailors and two young men trained to deliver the weapon, although only one would have the honor of taking the weapon into the heart of America. It was going to be one of the hardest choices he would have to make on the mission: to whom to bestow the honor. He genuinely did not know who should go. Both men were worthy so it may even be decided by a toss of the coin. Perfect, he thought, that was the solution. Allah would choose, as only Allah would make the coin fall the right way to ensure success.

For a man who loved land, he had been at sea for what felt like months, although it really had been only 15 days.

However, the work on the cargo vessel had taken some time and thanks to Deif's paranoia, Pock-Mark had had to stay on the ship throughout the work, as had the engineers who were being paid handsomely for their efforts. Unfortunately for them, it was not handsomely enough. Pock-Mark's instructions were clear. The men had been lured to a job in St Petersburg and had then been taken by private jet to Severodvinsk in darkness. For the three weeks, they were on board a ship in a closed dry dock and had no idea where they were. After the works were completed, a celebratory drink to mark the end of the job turned into a slaughter that saw the four engineers stowed in a meat freezer. After a couple of days at sea, they were tossed overboard to feed the fish.

Pock-Mark spotted a small fishing trawler. Using his binoculars, he checked the name. It was their contact and he was exactly on time. Not that he thought that he wouldn't be. So far, everything had gone exactly as planned by Deif. The equipment required to convert the cargo vessel into one of the most lethal ships on the seas had been exactly where Deif had said it would be. The Soviet military power-base had resulted in bureaucratic disaster at the end of the cold war. The port of Archangelsk was the country's oldest seaport and had been a key military installation throughout the country's history. Deif had reckoned on a fifty fifty chance that the equipment would have survived the collapse of the old Soviet Union, mainly because no one would know what the hell it was. His only concern was scrap value but even then that would probably have been worth less than the shipping costs of transporting it from what was effectively the middle of nowhere. Pock-Mark had been sent to the warehouse on his arrival and a rather bewildered owner accepted the offer for the 'junk' that had been there as long as he could remember. The world's largest shipyard lay just 30 miles away. Having been built during World War II, it provided the ideal location for the conversion. The old Russian freighter had been a steal. Its owners were glad to be rid of it as it cost more to keep than it was worth thanks to the recession. Although it had seen better days, it had two major plusses. It was the perfect size, at around 8,000 tons, and it flew under a Russian flag. Despite being the only super power, the United States did not lock horns with the Russians readily.

Pock-Mark smiled again at what they were planning to do. It was ingenious and was going to surprise the hell out of the Americans. Even if they were aware of the impending attack, they'd be defenseless. And all thanks to an old British cartoon book.

The trawler pulled alongside and transferred the weapon which had been sneaked out of Haifa under the eyes of the Israelis. The false bottom of the containers that held the weapons had been another ingenious plan by Mohammed Deif. Deif trusted no one, not even the Sheikh. From the moment the Sheikh had offered the weapons, Deif's deception plan had begun. The storage locations for each of the weapons were carefully selected and long before they were delivered, tunnels and false floors had been prepared. When delivered, the containers were carefully placed over the secret trap doors and Deif waited. His watchers did not watch for containers, they watched for people watching the containers. It hadn't taken the Israelis long to track the weapons, their spy satellites could search for such things with ease, something Deif knew very well. However, he was also confident that once they found the weapons, they'd stop looking any further.

As the Israeli watchers got comfortable, Deif's men used their tunnels and removed the weapons from under their eyes. Pock-Mark couldn't help but smile as he thought of Deif's master plan. All five weapons were now secured in new locations, one of which was with him. As for the other four weapons, only Deif knew where they were. He believed in compartmentalization, as Deif called it. Deif read a lot of western spy thrillers. He believed it gave him an edge. Pock-Mark had tried but reading books that were fundamentally anti Muslim just didn't seem right.

Just as they had fooled the Israelis, Deif's plan would fool the Americans too. If they looked for the weapons, they'd never suspect a cargo ship. Its destination was Nuuk, Greenland and then Sao Luis, Brazil. At no point would they be within 500 miles of US soil. They would be pretty much the last ship expected of being involved in an attack.

Pock-Mark went aboard the trawler to personally thank the captain of the boat. It was a magnificent day for the cause, he reiterated, before drawing his pistol and executing him and every member of the trawler's crew. Deif's plan was to be followed to the letter. Nobody who saw the boat was to live to describe her. The plan was bigger than any individual Palestinian and any who did die would die a martyr's death. A small charge in the bows ensured the trawler sank quickly. As he re-boarded the freighter, he heard a chirp from his mobile phone. Purchased on a pay as you go contract in Cyprus, it had never been used for voice calls and never would be. The chirp simply alerted him to a new tweet that had been delivered to his account. An account that only one other person knew existed, Deif. Twitter had proved invaluable to the terrorist community. They no longer needed to send emails, SMS texts or make calls. Messages could be sent to twitter and deposited on any account that followed it. The messages were tiny and created no trail as the recipient read them through a message server. It seemed there was one method of communication from the 21st century that was untrackable.

Pock-Mark read the innocuous note about the weather in Prague. However, the true meaning was more relevant. The Israeli's knew the devices had been moved. He had one more stop to make before heading to America. Akram walked to the bridge and gave the navigator their destination. They had a couple of very important containers to pick up.

# Chapter 24

Ben joined the other five permanent members of Project Ararat. The chief Rabbis were absent as they were only involved when religious matters were to be discussed. Religion was the last thing on the minds of the President, Prime Minister, Defense Secretary, Mossad and Shin Bet's Chief. The room silenced as Ben entered.

"Gentlemen," began Ben. "I believe the state of Israel is in grave danger and I feel we have no choice but to bring forward the final stage of Project Ararat to 12 days from now."

"Bring forward?" questioned David Hirsch. "But the logistics, it's just not possible, we need another two months," he stumbled, as the impact of the change crystallized in his mind.

After David's question, the room lit up as they all tried to put their feelings across about such a monumental change of plan. Debate raged for some time but with five nuclear weapons scheduled to explode in thirteen days, there really was no alternative. Action had to be taken and Project Ararat was certainly a solution.

"OK, OK, gentlemen, please. I think we have debated the point enough," interrupted Ehud Rabin, the President of Israel. "Let's take a vote."

"Everybody for the move forward, please raise your hand."

Four hands were raised immediately and they were grudgingly followed by the final two. A unanimous decision was reached and everybody stood up to leave. There was a lot to do and less than two weeks to achieve the impossible.

Only Ben remained seated. "Gentlemen, we have one issue I believe we still need to discuss and it is rather pressing."

"Yes?" asked Chaim Goldman, the Prime Minister.

"We do have a slight issue of the Palestinians taking a nuclear weapon to the United States."

"But we have no confirmation of that, it could be just talk," argued David. "We have just one woman's word and let's face it, she's hardly stable."

Ben turned to David and spoke in a tone only Ben could get away with. "That woman has sacrificed more for this country than almost anyone I know. She's lost her parents, her son and her husband. And she doesn't sit back and mourn. No, she stands tall and fights back. She, herself, has killed more of the scum that bombed our children than any other team that was tasked with the retaliation. She originally brought us the information that alerted us to the bombs in the first place!" His voice boomed as his anger boiled over. "And you dare question her?!"

"Look, we're all edgy. It's a very trying time. Whether it's confirmed or not, we have to let the Americans know," said Ehud. " I will call the President and let him know. Is there anything else I can tell him?"

"That we have our best teams on it and we will find the bomb before it gets to them," offered the Mossad chief.

"I have sent two of my best operatives to America," added Ben turning to David and smiling. "Which includes Rebecca Cohen."

"OK, I'll tell him that Mossad is on it. I think I'll leave out your guys, Ben."

"Are you going to tell him about the threat to us?" asked Chaim.

"I have to," replied Ehud, matter-of-factly.

"You should also give him the heads up on the blackout," added Ben.

"Sorry, the blackout?" asked Ehud.

"Project Ararat, two weeks from completion. We'll have a nationwide blackout, all telecommunications are to be cut off and Martial Law imposed. All our media will be off-stream as of the end of this meeting. You can use the threat as the reason for our disappearance from the world stage. Israel is going back in time. No phones, no radio, no television, no internet. The military will keep the peace and calm on the streets. Only essential military and high level government communications will remain in place."

"Is all of this quite necessary?" asked Chaim, shaking his head. "It just seems so extreme."

"Gentlemen," Ben addressed the room. "We have taken the decision and we are nearing completion. Now is not the time to lessen our resolve. David, you have your work cut out for you. I suggest you get going."

# Chapter 25

**Observatory circle**
**Washington**
**USA**

Andrew Russell watched the CNN feed. The President had just phoned and updated him on his call from the Israeli President. The nuclear weapon was nowhere to be found on the news bulletins. In fact, there was only one story of any note: Israel had shut down. Hundreds of people were writing in discussing how telephone calls they had been having with business colleagues and loved ones had simply ended. Emails were bouncing back as if the recipients didn't exist. It was as though the whole country had just ceased to exist. Andrew grabbed his coat and headed for the door. The President had called a war cabinet and wanted Andrew in the Situation Room asap.

His cell phone buzzed in his pocket as he walked towards the waiting limo.

"Hello?" he answered.

"It's me."

Andrew recognized the voice instantly.

"We need to see you straight away."

"I'm on my way to the White House," he offered as an excuse.

"I'll see you in ten minutes, don't be late." The caller ended the call. Russell looked at his phone for a few seconds before placing it in his pocket and entering the limo.

"The White House, Sir?" enquired his driver.

"No, the Hay Adams, please." He decided the President would have to wait.

As they pulled up outside of one of Washington's most renowned hotels, Russell rushed inside and made directly for the elevators and selected the top floor. He walked, rather ironically, beyond the Presidential Suite and knocked gently on the door of the larger and grander Federal Suite.

"Come in," shouted a voice.

Russell opened the door and walked into a wall of thick cigar smoke, the Cuban stench was unmistakable. Russell was a fitness freak, teetotaler and non-smoker and couldn't help but cough to try to protect his lungs. The next breath as he walked closer was even heavier than the first. The four men that sat waiting for his arrival were some of the most reclusive and richest men in America. And to those in the know, the four most powerful. Although their names would appear on no shareholding listings, between them and their complex maze of thousands of trusts and charities, they owned majority stakes in just about every major industry in America and controlled almost every piece of news printed or broadcast in the western world. With them, Russell would be king. Without them, he was nothing.

"I can't be long gentlemen," suggested Russell as he took the last remaining seat and declined the offer of a scotch or a cigar.

"I really do worry about you Andrew," said Walter Koch, Russell's main contact with the elite group. "No alcohol or tobacco. Christ, next we'll discover you don't like pussy!"

Everybody but Russell laughed.

Russell rued the day he had ever got involved with the group. It had all been thanks to his girlfriend at Yale, Elizabeth Koch. Through her, he had met Walter. Walter's eyes had lit up on hearing the Russell family history. Their family credentials were impeccable. New England WASP's, part of the fabric of America. His family could be traced back to the Pilgrim Fathers.

Walter had informed the group of his daughter's blue eyed American beau and told them he had found their future President. Andrew's relationship with Elizabeth had been short-lived. Her father was far more interested in Andrew than she ever was. And with Andrew spending all the time at their house discussing politics with her father, it was not long before her eyes had wandered to other men who were less likely to excite her father.

Russell was introduced to the group of four and they instantly agreed with Walter. Russell was perfect, intelligent, witty, sharp, confident and most importantly for the all important female vote, he was dark and handsome, with sparkling blue eyes and dazzlingly white teeth. The cameras would love him.

From that moment on, Andrew's life had not been his own. His path was planned and at no point would it be deviated from. He had graduated top of his law class, joined the Navy, then the Boston DA's office, rocketed through the ranks as the toughest DA in town before winning his first election as Suffolk County District Attorney. From there, he won the Massachusetts State Attorney General's seat despite being a hard-line Republican. His opponent hadn't had a chance. Andrew's campaign outspent his by 10 to 1. After that, the Governor's mansion and soon after, Senator Russell was sworn in as one of the youngest Senators in US history. The press, under the control of his benefactors, was already calling him the Republican's JFK.

Initially, things had been like a whirlwind. Andrew had just kept his head down and followed the plan. It was only as he began to gain power that he realized how little he actually had. The four were always there, pulling his strings. Andrew had once joked to himself that the four were like the Four Horsemen of The Apocalypse - Conquest, War, Famine and Death. It took him a few more years to realize it wasn't a joke.

"So, where are we?" asked Koch, getting back to business. Andrew saw Walter as Conquest. He was the planner in the group and it was Walter who had picked Andrew as their man.

"Sam Baker was taken out by a missile fired from an unmanned combat vehicle in Maine. Charles Baker, I'm afraid, has gone to ground but we'll find him. I would hope that in less than twenty four hours, this issue will be closed."

"I would hope so, it's been a cluster fuck since it started. I mean how hard is it to kill two people when you know where they are and you've got pretty much the whole fucking US government behind you?" William Hathaway was the mean son of a bitch of the group. Everything was fucked up in his opinion and pretty much the only thing that was guaranteed in life was that everybody would let you down. Andrew had designated him Famine. He had more farming land than the rest put together and enough to feed the hungry of the world and Andrew truly believed he'd rather it go to waste than sell it at a loss.

Andrew stood firm. "I have personally taken charge of the operation and can assure you this will be resolved in the next 24 hours."

"I fucking well hope so," added Hathaway. "For your sake. Charles Baker will trounce you as candidate for President."

"Not to mention the damage he would do to our businesses. Christ, I think even the Democrat would be better for us. And I can't believe I just said that!" offered Lawrence Harkness. Charles Baker's hints at ending America's interference on the global stage ensured he would be the biggest loser of all. His industrial might included a massive armaments and munitions division that would be decimated by an end to America's wars. Harkness was War.

"Gentlemen, rest assured the problem is in hand. Now I really must go, the President expected me twenty minutes ago," Andrew stood up.

"Sit down! You'll go when we tell you we're finished," commanded Walter. "And not before."

Andrew sat down.

"I'm hearing rather disturbing rumors," offered a voice that Andrew hardly ever heard. James Lawson rarely attended the meetings but when he did those meetings held a special coldness that never failed to send a shiver down Andrew's spine. Lawson was Death and without doubt the most powerful man in the room. His family's wealth had been generated over the previous 150 years and under ruthless management had made fortunes throughout the recessions, wars and depressions. Only the Rothschilds' in Europe could challenge their wealth or influence but as Lawson was quick to remind people, they had had a five hundred year head-start. It had been a few years before Andrew had discovered Lawson's penchant for killing rivals, adversaries and in fact anyone that seemed at all threatened him. Not that he killed anyone himself. Lawson had people that did everything for him and of course because Lawson demanded nothing but the best. His killers were never caught nor was Lawson ever implicated, no matter how obvious it looked.

"What would they be?" asked a very nervous Russell There were certain things that Russell had kept from the group and one thing in particular, he knew would infuriate them. But he had another couple of months to work out how to break that one to the group.

"A nuclear bomb?" asked Lawson.

With some relief, Russell realized Ararat was still unknown to them. "Hmm yes, I'm supposed to be at the White House discussing this right now."

"Well, discuss away, please tell us just what in the hell is going on?"

"It seems the Israelis have discovered that a group of terrorists are heading to the US with a nuclear weapon. I'm not entirely sure how solid the evidence is but it seems we're taking the threat seriously."

"I told you," announced Lawson to the group. "These fucking Jew bankers are going to be the death of us. We need to cut the ties and let them go it alone."

Here we go, thought Russell. The Jews again. The Horsemen were not fond of the Israelis. In fact, 'hatred' was a more appropriate word. Their power and influence within the American banking and political systems infuriated them above everything else. The power of the Horsemen combined was staggering but paled into insignificance compared to the influence and power of the Israelis. One word from Israel and the Jews would do as their motherland wished. According to the Horsemen, America could be bankrupt overnight, should Israel give the command. And that was one power they promised to wipe out when they had their man at the helm.

Ararat was not Russell's only secret however. He had not known the Horsemen held supremacist views when he met them. They had kept that hidden. They had come across as Conservative, right of center but not extremists. Over the years, their facade had slipped and their true colors had become apparent. However, Russell was no angel either. He had chosen his course and he would stick to it, no matter how unsavory it might become. As much as he now detested the Horsemen, he wanted the power more. He just had to ensure that the little picture of his mother waving the swastika as Hitler walked past was never revealed to the world as it would surely end his political career. Nor to the Horsemen as the fake that it was. His mother was pictured waving the flag to ensure she could flee Nazi Germany. She was the only one of his family who had survived the Holocaust. Nazi Germany was no place for a Jewish orphan.

# Chapter 26

**Howard Johnson Hotel**
**Newark International**

"Team Two, are you in position?"

"Yes Sir, we have eyes on the rear of the building."

"Go, go, go!" repeated the commander firmly.

The four-man hit squad would attack their target from both sides. The proximity to the airport was perfect. Three hours earlier, they had been relaxing in Bermuda when the call had come through. They had been on standby and being paid $100,000 to just sit and enjoy the late summer sunshine was not a bad gig. However, the pay packet had just jumped to a cool million. They were needed in Newark as a matter of urgency. Luckily, the call had come in at 6pm and they managed to secure seats on the Cargojet scheduled service out of Bermuda bound for Newark just an hour later. Having been cleared through US customs in Bermuda, the flight was classed as domestic and as such, they would simply land and walk out of the airport without further checks. Of course, the CIA boss had ensured that their passage to Bermuda was not recorded in official records.

As the ageing Boeing 727 came in to land, the four additional loads of cargo readied themselves for disembarkation. As far as the crew of the Canadian Cargojet company were concerned, the four men were stranded Americans hitching a lift home. Little did they know that it was very convenient not to have to file a separate flight plan between Bermuda and Newark for a military jet. After the rendition flights, CIA flight-plans were under much greater scrutiny.

The plane taxied directly to the cargo area and the four passengers disembarked without so much as a thank you. The Pilot looked on as one of the four bent down at the rear wheel of a Suburban parked next to the plane's arrival gate. Shortly after, the hazard lights blinked, the men jumped into the vehicle and sped off into the night. The pilot didn't see the massive arsenal of weapons or the Sat Nav system pre-programmed to take the men to the Howard Johnson Hotel.

The leader of the group would be taking the lion's share of the money for the hit and he was no stranger to CIA wet work. Jens, South African by birth, had earned his name as a ruthless mercenary willing to work for anyone as long as the money was right. When it came to the CIA, the money was always right. The Americans knew how to pay. For the last few years, they had been his team's only paymaster. Usual haunts included Iraq, Afghanistan and Pakistan. Their main job was to take out targets too sensitive to ever be linked to the Americans. Although he had no proof that it was the CIA that was paying his way, there really was no other agency which gained as much from his work. However, this was his first job on American soil and he was determined it went without a hitch. The pay for that one target was double the normal rate and the location was certainly a lot more inviting.

"Remember the target is Tim Wilkinson, Room 216 and watch out for the woman he's with. She may be armed." He reminded his team of the instructions he had received on the voicemail.

Normally, the four would have gone in, weapons up, shooting. But this was America not a third world war zone, so they exchanged fatigues for slacks and sports jackets which, truth be told, were far better camouflage than they had ever worn. Amongst the thousands of businessmen travelling through New York, they quite literally disappeared. The clothes were not the only change in operational procedure for these men. Their weapons were rather more discreet. They were silenced, concealed and, thanks to whoever had arranged the mission, South African in origin. Each man had a BXP silenced sub machine gun, a South African version of the Uzi and a Vektor SP2 silenced pistol. It seemed no stone was left unturned to ensure that the mercenaries would not be confused for Americans.

"We're in!" Jen's ear piece alerted him to Team Two's progress.

"Excellent, take the back stairs and come up from the emergency exit. We're just coming into the lobby and will come in from the opposite end of the corridor," said Jens as though he were talking to the man next to him. As they entered the lobby, both laughed quietly and headed casually to the elevators, just two businessmen returning to their room after a meal.

***

"Sir, you're going to wear a hole in the carpet," said Clark taking the Chairman's arm and guiding him back to the small sofa in the corner of their king-sized room. The Senator had objected vehemently to the hotel's view of what constituted a King-Sized room. Even the TV was small. However, there was nothing small about the impact the screen was having on the Senator as the news network continued to play the footage of a tanker exploding in Maine.

"It's him, I know it is," he said to himself, transfixed by the burning forest in the background.

"Come on, whatever's happening doesn't involve tankers in the middle of a highway."

"You have no idea," he said shaking his head.

Their train journey had passed off without incident and a quick cab ride had taken them to the Howard Johnson where, as directed, Senator Baker had checked in as Tim Wilkinson. He used the driver's license that Sam had given him six years earlier as ID. He had offered to take two rooms but Clark had refused. She made it very clear that she would not leave his side until they could get help. It had been four hours since they had arrived and over seven hours since Sam had warned his brother.

"Something has happened to him. I'm telling you, there is no way he would take this long to get to New York. We need to reach out to someone we can trust."

"I'm sure he's fine." But Clark's protestations were wearing thin. "I think we should give him another hour." She checked her watch. "If we've not heard anything by 10pm, we'll make a move."

Senator Baker was unconvinced. If there were a person in the world you could rely on, it was Sam Baker and if he were coming, he'd have been there by then.

# Chapter 27

**Hay Adams Hotel**
**Washington**

As the door to the Federal Suite closed, the bedroom door opened and the Governor of Idaho, John Mellon, joined the Horsemen. He had listened in on the meeting and wasted no time in offering his opinion.

"The little shit's hiding something, you know," he announced to the group as he took a seat.

Mellon was unknown to Russell. He was the fifth member of the group. He also, unknown to Russell, would be his running mate on the Vice President's ticket. Mellon was the richest, most obnoxious and right wing politician in the land and had no chance of becoming President but as Russell's Vice President, he would be the proverbial heartbeat away from the seat. As much as people loved Russell, they loathed the old bastard from Texas. The young Russell would be doing a Dick Cheney, just using the old war horse as an adviser and bringing some experience to his young presidency.

Everything had been running perfectly smoothly until Senator Baker had thrown his hat in the ring. The loose cannon Baker was a vote winner and had his allies. Of course, Russell had the support of the President thanks to the Horsemen's funding support. Unfortunately, their influence over the sitting President did not extend further. He was his own man and had made it clear to them on many occasions. Russell had ingratiated himself as instructed but again his influence only went so far. They tried in vain to discredit Baker but nothing stuck, despite their control of the media. They had tried to get him to accept the Vice President's ticket, much to Mellon's objections, but the idea was just to get him off the Presidential ticket. Mellon's Vice Presidency ticket could have been resolved at a later date. Baker had flatly refused. As the numbers started to swing in his favor, it was, as ever, Lawson who had voiced the need for a permanent solution. Senator Charles Baker was in their way and had to be removed. Mellon agreed without hesitation. Russell was informed and tasked with the job. Normally, they would have dealt with it quietly but it was agreed that a strong message would be sent to all those in Russell's camp. Plus, of course, when Russell was assassinated, three months into his presidency, as was the plan, Mellon would be made President. Mellon would have something on each of Russell's team to ensure complete loyalty and compliance.

"Perfect," said Lawson as he laid out his plan to the group.

"Well, we've been assured it will be dealt within the next 24 hours," reminded Walter.

"Jesus, Walter, don't be so fucking naive. The CIA could fuck up a piss up in a brewery," said an irritable Lawson. "However, I'm confident it will be dealt with in the next twenty four hours but only because I had arranged an insurance policy for just this eventuality. A certain contractor who has worked for me on a number of occasions is on the case."

# Chapter 28

## The White House
## Situation Room

Johnson, the Director of the CIA, grabbed Russell by the elbow as they made their way into the room and guided him to a corner, away from prying eyes and ears.

"We have our target cornered."

"Excellent, where is he?"

"Our face recognition software picked him up at Newark train station as he was rather stupidly hailing a cab. Amateur. Anyway from there, we tracked the cab, discovered he was dropped off at the Howard Johnson and from the timings, found he checked in as a Tim Wilkinson. No idea where that came from but anyway, we have a team about to take him out."

"Make sure your guys don't fuck it up again," warned Russell, starting to regain his authority following his meeting with the Horsemen. "So what's the story here?" he asked looking back at the Situation Room.

"The Palestinians have got their hands on another nuke. I don't understand how careless people can be with these things. I blame the Commies personally," replied Johnson conspiratorially.

"How good is the intel?"

"We're told they're 90% certain it's real. When the Israelis give you anything over 50% it means it's serious. 90% means they bloody well know it's coming."

"Shit, any ideas where they're targeting?"

"Nope, not a clue. America is all they can give us. But I have to say we would normally have heard something ourselves. There's been no increase in chatter which we would expect when they're trying to pull off something this big. So I'm not sure they're right."

# Chapter 29

Jens nodded at his two colleagues at the far end of the corridor, the signal to move. They closed the stair door quietly and began to casually walk towards Room 216. This approach was somewhat alien to them. Normally, the approach would have been fast with guns at the ready. Unfortunately that was not an option. Armed men, guns drawn, walking down a corridor in Newark would rouse more than a little suspicion. While two moved towards the door, Jens and his sidekick kept the elevators stationery on their floor. He didn't want any passers-by stumbling into the action. One clear message had been to minimize collateral damage and by minimize they had meant none.

As they neared the door, the two assassins drew their BXP machine guns and readied themselves.

\*\*\*

"Shhh. What was that?" whispered Clark, putting her finger to her mouth and turning the TV off.

The Senator did not need to be told twice. Clark was a highly trained Secret Service agent and if he had learnt anything over the years, it was that when they said shush, you shushed.

Both listened intently. The Senator heard nothing. Clark drew her weapon and motioned for the Senator to get behind her and began to back up from the door. Her gun was trained just above the center point of the door.

"I'm sure it's nothing," whispered the Senator, more to himself than Clark.

After what seemed like an hour to the Senator but was almost instantaneous, Clark began to lower her weapon. "I think you're right, a bit jumpier than I realized, sorry."

Her stance relaxed and she stepped forward allowing the Senator at least a little breathing room. Her gun had almost made it back to her holster when all hell broke loose.

*\*\**

The two assassins took their cue from Jens. With the elevators still in position, he nodded for a second time and the two men down the corridor moved. One raised his Size 12 boot and with every ounce of his 230lbs of flesh, literally took the door off of its hinges. His colleague rushed in, the BXP quietly spewing its deadly cargo ahead of him.

*\*\**

Clark's reaction times were amongst the best in the service but a door crashing down caught her entirely by surprise. The main door had crashed to her left and not where she had been focusing her attention only a second earlier - the interconnecting door with Room 218. As the door left its hinges, bullets tore through the room, fortunately at angles that were in their favor. Standing back from the interconnecting door had meant they were up against the far wall on the other side of the room. The gunmen would have to clear a small corridor before being able to get Clark and Baker in their sights.

Clark raised her weapon and pushed the Senator behind her for the second time in as many seconds. A second weapon began to fire. Clark was cornered and was now facing significantly greater firepower. She was no fool and knew that was it. She would go down in history as one of the few Secret Service agents to have failed in their duty.

A second crash and the interconnecting door flew towards her. Jesus, she thought, these guys are serious. Whoever wants the Senator dead has covered all bases. Clark swung her pistol towards the interconnecting door. She wasn't going down without at least taking some of the bastards with her and fired three rounds, just high off center.

As the second door crashed open, the two assassins paused. That hadn't been the plan. Jens was supposed to wait. This was their kill. Jens was cover but neither wanted to take out the boss so they both stopped firing.

Unluckily for them, Jens was exactly where he was supposed to be, holding the elevators.

The rounds of a Frag-12 shotgun are particularly unpleasant and combining those with an AA-12 fully automatic shotgun with a 32 round drum magazine and a fire-rate of 300 rounds per minute meant that what was left of the two assassins could be scraped up. Ten Frag-12 rounds made it into the small corridor before the shotgun stopped firing. The highly explosive shells did exactly what the ammunition box said they would. They exploded on impact with the force of a small grenade, making mincemeat of the South Africans.

***

Just as Clark pulled the trigger, her arm was momentarily forced upwards because of a deafening shriek in her ear.

"NO!!!!!!" screamed the Senator.

Before she could make any sense of what just happened, pressure wave after pressure wave hit her as the shotgun shells hit their targets. With little or no hearing and her other senses not entirely stabilized, Clark looked at the interconnecting door and the mass that lay prostate in its doorway.

"Jesus, you shot him!" yelled the Senator, pushing past Clark.

"Stay behind me!" ordered Clark.

The Senator ignored her and rushed towards the body on the floor, pushing Clark away.

As the Senator reached the body, it moved. Clark raised her gun and aiming for the head, she pulled the trigger.

"Hi Charlie," said the body.

Clark immediately released her trigger, with 9 lbs of pressure depressed out of a 10lb trigger, she had just managed to avoid shooting dead the Senator's brother.

"Agent Clark, this is my brother Sam." The Senator struggled to hide an extremely proud grin as he introduced the two.

"We'll have time for niceties later," suggested Sam, pushing the Senator aside and getting up from the floor with an audible wince.

"Did I hit you?" asked Clark, worried she had caught him with one of her rounds aimed at the door.

"Fortunately not," he said, pointing to his left arm which hung rather limply. "This is from a rather spectacular car crash earlier. That's for later though, we need to move, these guys weren't alone."

Sam ushered them both into Room 218 and holding his AA-12 in one arm, he led them to the door of the corridor.

"Wait here," he ordered.

Clark began to protest but one look from Sam shut her up. He was in no mood for discussion.

Listening at the door, he stepped back and was clearly about to open the door when he realized he only had one working arm.

Clark was ready and waiting. Her protestation had been a realization that he would need help getting through the door with a shotgun up and ready.

They mouthed 'on three' and nodded as they counted out the three. Clark opened the door in one swift motion and Sam hurled himself into the corridor. The AA-12 was up and shooting before Jens and his colleague had a chance to react. Their focus was the carnage in the entrance hallway of Room 216. Being on his feet assured his aim. Although hindered, he was more accurate than before and with only two shells per man, the job was significantly less messy, not that either man would be having an open casket funeral.

Sam turned from the gruesome scene and pointed towards the back stairs. Clark took point, the Senator following closely behind, while Sam took up the rear. Sam reckoned that the whole incident, from the door crashing open to his final shot, had taken less than ten seconds. People were stirring from rooms and doors were beginning to crack open but no guests, as yet, had plucked up the courage to venture out into the wild yonder. Just as well, the massacre would certainly have given them something to remember.

As they flew down the stairs and moved quickly to the exit, they remained silent. None of them dared to speak. Clark moved swiftly, her pistol up, scanning the staircase ahead while listening for any noise that would give away a potential threat. However that was short-lived. The sirens had started, first one then a second and then a cacophony, too many to count, the sounds just merging into one big noise.

As Clark broke through the emergency fire door, Sam directed them to the police cruiser parked at the rear of the car park, somewhat out of place with its light blue coloring and Maine State Police decals.

"Long story," he said as he fumbled awkwardly to remove the keys from his pocket.

Clark saw her opportunity. Sam had his shotgun leveled at the emergency door they had just exited. As he fumbled hopelessly for the car keys, she stepped forward, grabbed his injured arm, pulled it up and out of its socket in one swift movement. For good measure, she then wrenched it sideways and up in one sharp movement. Sam screamed as he tried desperately to bring the shotgun to bear but Clark had him. There was no way to get to her. He could feel her breath on his neck as she twisted his useless arm and was now holding it tight against his back in a classic police arm lock. As the pain intensified, Sam's knees buckled.

The Senator looked on in horror as he watched Clark attack his brother. He had walked to the passenger door of the car and had the car between himself, Clark and Sam. As the realization that Clark had set them up hit home, he rushed towards them.

"You bitch!" he screamed, diving at Clark.

# Chapter 30

Clark released Sam as his brother dived towards her. Strengthened by the pain relief, Sam spun round and leveled his shotgun at Clark who immediately raised her arms in surrender, her pistol dropping to the floor. As both had moved away from the high flying Senator, he was left to pick himself up from the ground and, brushing himself off, he surveyed the scene. His brother still had a shotgun leveled at Clark.

"Wait a minute," he said, looking at his brother Sam. "How come you can do that?"

Sam did not take his eyes off of Clark who began to smile back at him.

"Do what?"

"You're using both hands!"

Sam looked down. His right hand held the pistol grip while his left cradled the stock, something he had been unable to do since the crash. The pain, although still present, was significantly less than it had been. He lowered the barrel and moved his left shoulder around. Although weak and painful, his arm was now usable.

"Don't mention it," said Clark as she lowered her arms and stepped towards the Senator. As she got closer to him, she raised her hand and slapped him gently across the face. "Bitch?!" she exclaimed with a smile.

"Sorry," he offered lamely in response.

Sam mouthed a 'thank-you' to Clark before telling them to get into the car and with the police lights and siren on, they pulled out of the car park.

"Can we switch the siren off now?" pleaded the Senator. The noise was deafening.

Sam checked the rear-view mirror. They had been travelling at over 80 mph for over five minutes and were well away from the Howard Johnson. He flicked the switches off.

"Thank God! Now we can talk," said Senator Baker.

Sam took another long look in the mirror and nodded.

"So what in the hell is going on?" blurted the Senator. The adrenaline rush that had kept him going for the previous few hours was wearing off.

Sam composed himself. It was the first moment of relative calm for a number of hours.

"Well?" insisted Agent Clark from the passenger seat, certain that whatever the hell was going on had something to do with the Senator's gun toting killer brother.

Sam turned to her. The tears in his eyes surprised her and killed her anger instantly. Whatever she and the Senator had been through clearly paled in comparison to what Sam had endured.

Sam turned and faced the road as he spoke.

"It started this morning. I spotted what looked like an agency car come off the ferry. Something inside me knew it was about me. I raced home but was too late. By the time I got there, they were dead. All dead."

Saying it out loud made it all the more real. It had really happened. The tears rolled down his face.

As Sam stared silently ahead, Agent Clark looked at the Senator.

"Who's dead?" asked the Senator in barely a whisper. He knew Sam had built a new life. He knew about Sam's son, Sam Junior, his only nephew. The realization that something he had done could have endangered Sam was one thing but his family had not even entered his mind.

"Sam, Julie and Goldie!" he replied coldly as the tears cascaded down his face.

"Jesus Christ!" exclaimed the Senator, falling back into his seat.

Agent Clark placed her hand on Sam's upper arm and squeezed lightly.

After a few seconds, Sam brushed his arm across his face, wiping the tears and continued.

"I killed the men, then tried to contact you but couldn't. So I called in the threat to the Secret Service and hightailed it here. On the way, I had a bit of a disagreement with a missile but managed to get through that."

"Sorry? A missile?" asked Clark.

"I assume so. I must have been doing 140 and had to swerve violently to avoid some old timer in a pick-up. As I swerved, a flash of light took out the pick-up. Had I not swerved, it would have hit me. The explosion blew my car onto its side. Then a fuel tanker exploded and the underside of my car took the full brunt of that. Had I not been in an armored agency car, I'd have been vaporized but instead, it blasted the car like a catapult about 100 yards into the woods. I must have been knocked out. The first thing I was aware of was that my left arm was messed up…"

"Your shoulder was dislocated, just very slightly. I don't think enough to cause any real damage. I'm sure it's just bruised," interrupted Clark.

"Thanks for your help, by the way, I tried to pop it in myself but it wasn't for moving. I thought I had broken something."

Sam had had his fair share of medical training, particularly as a pararescueman.

"Two years pre med!" offered Clark which elicited a rather surprised look from the Senator.

"I thought you always wanted to be in the Service?"

"You have to have a fall back," replied Clark, shrugging her shoulders.

"…Anyway…," Sam interrupted the interruption. "…I had half of Maine's emergency services at the scene of the explosion. But nobody spotted my car, so I sneaked out, grabbed what I could, borrowed this car and got to the hotel. When I got there, I spotted the team outside and with no time to get you out, I booked the room next to yours and took them by surprise. I couldn't alert you in case they were monitoring your room. So here we are."

"I am so sorry, Sam."

"It's not your fault Charlie. It's whoever wants you dead that will be sorry," promised Sam.

"I'm afraid, I have no idea who that is," replied a very troubled Senator.

"We'll find them, I can assure you."

"Oh my God, what about Beth?" panicked the Senator, realizing that if Sam's family were targeted, so might his wife.

"She's fine, I called her. She's gone to a friend's. I gave her instructions to ditch her cell phone and stay out of sight. She's safe."

"Thank God!" As soon as the Senator said it, he regretted the selfishness of it. "Sorry," he added again, although the uselessness of the word just made it sound even worse.

Sam sensed the awkwardness and turned to Clark.

"So what happened to you guys?"

Clark looked at the Senator but realized he was not in a state to talk.

"Well, I was with my partner Agent Travis when we received the call. We were stuck in traffic and gave an ETA of around ten minutes but managed to get there in five."

Senator Baker was hearing this piece of information for the first time.

"What do you mean you were in traffic?"

"What do *you* mean?" she asked, confused. "We were in our car and we were stuck in traffic, what's that got to do with anything?"

"I mean," said the Senator who had found his voice and was taking charge. "I was in the Capitol building when the threat came through. There were probably hundreds of federal agents in that building and scores of Secret Service agents." He paused to let the information sink in.

"Oh my God." The penny dropped. "They picked us because we were ten minutes away. That would give them time to deal with you. But we arrived early and if we had been even ten seconds later, those two guys posing as Capitol Police would have got to you first!"

"Yep, whoever sent you there had time to kill me and they could still say they had responded to the threat."

"But that means we're talking about people with influence at the very top of government."

"Exactly," emphasized Sam.

"Holy shit, we're screwed." Clark hit the nail on the head as each of them digested just what they were up against.

# Chapter 31

Rebecca Cohen stepped off the British Airways flight 115 from London with a new identity, Marie-Hélène Abouaf, a French citizen of Tunisian descent. Mossad had some of the best forgers in the world and creating passports at short notice for its agents had never been an issue. At least not until the debacle in Dubai where twenty six Mossad agents had been linked to the assassination of Mahmoud al-Mabhouh, all holding fake or fraudulently obtained passports. Passport officers the world over were just a little more vigilant following the incident.

It was with this in mind that Rebecca approached the immigration officer at JFK and placed her most entrancing smile upon him. As Rebecca herself would say, the male really was the weaker of the sexes. Put a beautiful woman in front of a man and he became a blubbering wreck. Pathetic. She passed through without incident and hailed a cab as she exited the terminal building into a blustery September evening. Her mission was simple. Ben had been very succinct. Find the bomb before it goes off!

As soon as she was clear of the terminal and comfortable she had not picked up a tail, she called Ben.

"I've landed."

"About time! All hell has broken loose at a hotel in Newark."

"The terrorists?"

"Not sure, multiple shootings but almost as soon as it happened, the press went quiet and intelligence agencies went ballistic."

"Our contacts?"

"Can't get in, whoever is controlling it is at a very senior level."

"Any assets I can use?"

"No, you are, as our American friends would say, off the grid. Nobody knows you are there. You have a free hand."

"Good, what's the hotel's address?"

Rebecca passed the Howard Johnson address to the cabbie and hung up on Ben. She opened her make-up bag and with a particular twist removed the bottom of the bag to reveal a lead lined bottom. Not large enough to be noticed during the scans but large enough for a few IDs and a few badges that she always found came in useful. Particularly when she needed information.

As the cab drew near the hotel, Rebecca would not have imagined a multiple shooting had taken place there within the last hour. In America, even a simple shooting would elicit a significant response, crime scene tape, strobing emergency lights, scores of law enforcement officers and numerous vans. The Howard Johnson at Newark, scene of a multiple shooting, failed to have even one police car in attendance.

Rebecca exited the cab and made directly for the entrance lobby. For all the lack of activity outside, the lobby made up for it. Grey suits were everywhere. Obviously, whatever happened here was way beyond uniform policing.

"Excuse me, Miss?" A man approached Rebecca. His jacket was open and his holstered pistol could easily be seen as he moved towards her. "I'm sorry but the hotel is full." He moved to take her arm and divert her back the way she came.

Rebecca very subtly side-stepped his hand and removed the badge she had taken from her make-up bag in the cab and showed it to the man.

"Special Agent Todd, NCT," informed Rebecca forcefully.

The man stopped and looked at the badge quizzically. "Sorry, NCT?"

"Nuclear Counter Terrorism, part of the NNSA!"

"Sorry, NNSA?"

"National Nuclear Security Administration, part of DoE."

"DOD?"

"Delta Oscar Echo, Department of Energy and you?"

"Homeland Security," he paused. Rebecca was playing him perfectly. Act confidently like you have every reason to be there and 99 times out of 100, no one will second guess you. "How exactly can I help you?" he asked.

"Just show me everything you've got and that will be fine," replied Rebecca, looking around the room for whoever was in charge.

"Just wait here," he said, waving for her to remain where she was as he walked across to the main desk and whispered in another grey suit's ear, a far older and obviously more senior agent.

Rebecca had no intention of waiting and as the two men turned from their whispering, Rebecca was at their shoulders.

"Rebecca Todd," she offered her hand to the senior agent. Confidence exuding from every pore of her body.

"Director Mark Carter," he offered automatically, shaking Rebecca's hand. "I'm sorry, I believe you're with, is it DoE?" he looked at his colleague for confirmation and received a nod.

"Yes, Nuclear Counter Terrorism. I believe there has been an incident."

"There has been a small incident, totally unrelated to either terrorism or nuclear material. So if you don't mind, Miss Todd, this is a crime scene and we are very busy," he said, nodding at his younger colleague as an instruction to remove Rebecca.

Rebecca again very subtly side-stepped the agent's attempt to take her arm.

"It's not Miss, it's Special Agent and I apologize, I was looking for the agent in charge," Rebecca again looked around the room. "Perhaps your superior?" she mused, taunting the Director.

"I can assure you, Special Agent Todd," he spat, "I am the senior agent in charge and you will not find anyone more senior other than in Washington."

"Well I would have thought that you being so senior, you might be aware that we have a severe threat level of a nuclear device in transit or already in the US. As such, I'll decide whether this incident is worthy of my interest."

Rather than go toe to toe with, he had to admit, a very attractive but arrogant little bitch, he turned and taking his cell phone from his pocket, he hit the speed dial for Henry Preston, DNI, his boss' boss.

After a very muted and it appeared one way conversation, he turned back towards Rebecca.

"It appears you're correct. There has been a warning. However, I can assure you this incident is not linked."

"You have the shooters in custody?"

"No."

"You have a positive ID of the shooters?"

"No."

"You have confirmed who the victims are?"

"No."

"So I'm sorry Director Carter, exactly how can you be so confident that this incident is not related to my investigation?" inquired Rebecca.

"We have the victims identified as South African nationals. The belief is this is to do with diamonds or drugs. So, if you don't mind we're very busy."

Rebecca smiled. This was actually proving to be fun. "South Africa you say? Well I'm afraid that changes everything." She drew her phone from her pocket and began to dial a number.

"Sorry, what are you doing?" asked Director Carter.

"Calling in the full team," replied Rebecca nonchalantly. "Oh and NEST, you know, the Nuclear Emergency Support Team who I'm sure will want an exclusion zone in place asap."

"Just wait a minute," he said trying to grab her phone. "I said South African!"

Rebecca moved her hand away firmly. "I know what you said. South Africa had a nuclear Weapons programme in the 80s and 90s." Rebecca did not add that they only had six weapons and they had been dismantled in 1989. "And I'll need you all out of here. This area is now designated hot, until NEST deem it otherwise."

Director Carter raised his hands in surrender. "OK, OK, you win the pissing contest, what do you want?"

Rebecca relented slightly and half lowered the cell phone. "I just want to check this is not linked to the nuclear threat and if not, I'll be out of your hair."

Director Carter considered the request. He didn't like it. So far, the situation was well contained. The four shooters, even if they were identifiable, were not linkable to the CIA. As for the Senator and his accomplices, they were long gone. If only she had waited another ten minutes, the clean up would have been done and they would have been long gone themselves. The thought however of a full blown nuclear incident chilled him to the bones. There was no way they'd be able to keep that quiet and quiet was how he had been told to keep it. His second salary and soon to be retirement job rested on his keeping the incident very quiet.

As Rebecca began to raise her phone, Carter could see millions of dollars disappearing from his future potential earnings and 401K.

"OK, where do you want to start?"

Rebecca smiled. Her fake badge for an agency that dealt with the stuff that everyone else wanted to avoid and her total confidence, laced with a heavy dose of BS had got her in. That and the *Sayanim* who had implanted the record for Rebecca Todd as an agent in NCT. *Sayanim* were an urban legend that happened to be true. Jews from every nation in the world knew that whenever the time came, they would be welcomed with open arms in Israel. Their spiritual homeland was always there for them, not just in spirit but in body also. As such, when their homeland called, they answered. It was one of the main reasons that the relatively small Mossad punched far beyond its weight. If Mossad needed a room in a hotel, a *Sayanim* could arrange it. A safe house in any city in the world, not a problem. A rental car with no papers, a seat on a plane, a train delayed, not a problem.

Jews throughout the world were in positions of power. Some less so than others but one did not need a very powerful position, just a well placed one. For example, the Human Resource record holder at the Department of Energy was an American born woman of many generations but she had Jewish blood that coursed through her veins. Israel was not an enemy of the US and never would be. So, adding the name of Rebecca Todd, along with a photo and a history spanning ten years' service was not only easy, as far as she was concerned, it was harmless.

After fifteen minutes of quizzing Director Carter and a few witnesses, Rebecca was 100% confident that the Newark shootings were totally unrelated to the nuclear threat. After giving this conclusion to a very happy Director Carter, Rebecca left the hotel convinced she had just uncovered something far larger and significantly more worrying than any nuclear threat.

# Chapter 32

Johnson closed his cell phone, caught the VP's eye and nodded towards the corridor. As they stepped out of the room, he spoke quietly.

"That was Carter. They have confirmed that the Senator and Agent Clark are not among the casualties at the scene."

Russell looked at Johnson in disbelief. "Are you winding me up? Is this some kind of sick joke?"

"I'm afraid not, all the casualties are ours. And from what Carter has said, it's not a pretty sight."

Russell fell against the wall. The plan to assassinate his challenger for the presidential race had been put to him as a simple but essential job. The plan had been straightforward. A threat would be made, the Senator would be taken from the Capitol building by police officers who would later be discovered to be terrorists but only after his body was found. The brother was an afterthought by Johnson. He knew that, left alive, he would not rest until his brother's killers were caught or killed.

Simple. Plus, there was the added benefit of a swing to the right in the presidential vote to ensure victory for Russell against the Democrat candidate. It had all sounded so logical and impersonal at the time. To become president, they just had to take Senator Charles Baker out of the race. However, the body count was mounting. So far as Russell could tell, there were four dead Agency staff, four dead South Africans, one dead trucker, one dead old man, the Senator's brother and sister in law, his nephew and a dog, all dead. To call it an unmitigated disaster would be a compliment.

"Cover story?" he barked.

"So far, the only public casualties are the trucker and pick-up driver in Maine. Everything else has been cleaned like it never happened. We've called in a lot of favors but as far as the world knows, all that has happened today is a fuel truck exploded on a fairly remote stretch of road."

"What the hell happens if Senator Baker just walks into a police station or, even worse, a news station?" Russell was becoming more incensed as the ramifications of what their actions would mean if they didn't get Baker.

"Not a problem, Homeland have a BOLO (be on the lookout) for Senator Baker. He has to be held incommunicado as a matter of National Security until Homeland can secure him."

"That will work?"

"Trust me, we mention National Security, people start imagining Gitmo, rendition flights to Poland, Turkey and Egypt and nobody wants that. He'll be locked in a holding cell and nobody will go near him."

"So just Homeland and CIA are involved?"

"No, the FBI are in on it too. We've got some good people there on our payroll. Trust me, we'll get this closed down by midnight."

Russell allowed himself to relax. Baker had nowhere to go.

"Wait a minute, you said the pick-up driver and trucker in Maine. You didn't say Sam Baker?"

Johnson's face flushed red. He had hoped to avoid this revelation. He knew it would not be taken well.

"Hmm, it appears the reason we missed them at Newark..."

"Don't tell me, Sam Baker!" interrupted an incensed Russell.

"It appears so. Reports suggest a third party with a shotgun helped the Senator and Secret Service agent before the three drove off in a Maine State Police cruiser."

Just as Russell thought it couldn't get any worse, his cell phone rang. Before he even looked at the caller ID, he assumed the Horsemen were about to add their grain of salt. On checking the ID, he smiled. It was an international number. Some relief from the Baker debacle.

"Mr Vice President?"

Russell took a second before he recognized the voice.

"Ben, how are you doing?" he responded to Ben Meir.

"I'm fine thanks, Andrew, which I believe is more than can be said for you!"

Russell was somewhat taken aback by the Israeli's bluntness.

"Sorry?" he replied indignantly. He had assumed, on hearing Ben's voice, that the call was about the nuke.

"I've just had a very interesting chat with one of my agents. I can only surmise that you have just recently failed to assassinate your presidential challenger."

Russell remained speechless as he looked at Johnson in horror.

Johnson mouthed to him "What's wrong?" which brought back some of Russell's composure.

"I'm sorry Ben, I have absolutely no idea what you're talking about," he replied with all the sincerity he could muster.

"Let me elaborate then." As Ben spoke, Russell pushed Johnson into an empty room and pressed the speaker button. "My agent just visited a very violent multiple shooting in Newark. The scene was being supervised by a Director Carter who I believe is the second or third most senior officer in Homeland Security. The scene was being cleaned, not investigated. And from what my agent discovered, a man fitting the description of Charles Baker was ushered out of the building just after the shooting and fled the scene avoiding the police. I'm also aware of the BOLO issued for the same Senator Charles Baker and putting two and two together and getting five, I've concluded that the biggest beneficiary of a dead Charles Baker is you."

"Ben, I'm sorry I don't know what to say other than of course this is nonsense."

"Andrew, Andrew, my dear boy. You've got it all wrong. I'm not calling to give you a hard time, I'm calling to offer you my help!"

# Chapter 33

As Johnson called Carter to confirm the details, Russell stalled.

"Exactly how can you help me do something I'm not even doing?"

"I'm not going to debate the issue Andrew. I'm offering you the assistance of one of my very best operatives."

Realizing he wasn't getting anywhere, he tried a different tack.

"Ben, somebody has just come into the room. I'll call you straight back."

Hanging up the phone, Russell turned to Johnson, whose gesticulating had become wilder with every second that had passed.

Russell waved at Johnson to hurry up with the call, patience was not his forte.

"Well?" asked Russell as Johnson ended the call.

"The only person to attend, other than Carter's people, was a ball-busting DoE agent, name of Rebecca Todd. She was there in connection with the nuclear threat we've received."

"What did she want?"

"A quick look to ensure there was no nuclear threat and she supposedly left satisfied that there wasn't one."

Russell began to wonder whether he was surrounded by complete imbeciles.

"So this DoE woman just happened to be in the neighborhood looking into a nuclear threat that me and the President have just been made aware of in the Situation Room of the White House? A threat that the Israelis themselves have made us aware of?"

"Well, when you put it like that," mused an embarrassed Johnson. "It would seem the DoE agent was an Israeli agent."

"No shit, Sherlock," replied a furious Russell.

"But Carter checked her credentials, she was legit."

"I'm sure she *was*," replied Russell as he exited the room. He was certain DoE agent Rebecca Todd had already ceased to exist on any record.

He made his way back to his office. He needed to call Ben back and quickly.

"Ben?"

"Andrew," replied Ben Meir. "How are you?"

"Worried, Ben. There are some very strange things happening."

"It would appear so, none more so however, than your little side show!" added Ben with an edge.

"Let's start with the nuclear threat. How real?"

"Very," replied Ben matter-of-factly. "But I'd rather start with your little crusade. What the hell are you doing, Andrew?" asked a less jovial Ben.

Ben Meir was an old and wise man, an exceptional strategist and one of the world's foremost politicians. But Andrew Russell was a force in his own right and the soon-to-be President of the most powerful nation in the world.

"I would suggest a change of tone, Ben," warned Russell.

"Tone, shtone," replied Ben in an even more aggravated tone. "What are you doing?"

"I have no idea what you're talking about," replied an indignant Russell.

Russell heard a click and thought Ben had hung up but before he could hang up himself, a voice he recognized came on the line. It was Johnson.

*"I don't believe so. They definitely missed him."*

It was a voice he not only recognized but was a conversation he had already had. He knew the next voice would be his.

*"How can you be so sure?"*

*"Because Sam phoned the Secret Service."*

*"What?"*

*"Well he didn't give his name but just after my guys were supposed to have taken him out, a death threat was issued by Yuri Andriev against Senator Baker."*

*"Shit!...and the Senator?"*

*"That's the other thing, he's gone missing."*

Another click signaled the end of the recording of a conversation he had had on his secure phone that morning.

"Are you still there, Andrew?" asked Ben, his smile transmitted loud and clear through the 6,000 miles of space between them.

"But how on earth?" asked Russell. He didn't know what was worse, his actions being uncovered or Mossad being able to listen into the US' most secure phone system.

"Andrew, my dear boy, I've warned you many times not to underestimate our little agency. Now, can we cut the bullshit and you tell me what you're up to."

Andrew Russell had had many difficult conversations over the years, none more so than a number he had had with the master tactician Ben Meir. However, all their previous calls were a piece of cake compared to this one.

"Hmm...," Russell didn't know where to start.

Ben interrupted before he had to. "I'm playing with you Andrew. Did you really think I didn't know about the Horsemen? Seriously, I've warned you before," he added his final point with a less than jovial tone. "Do not underestimate me. I know everything."

Andrew Russell was one of Ben Meir's most highly placed *Sayanim*. Ben knew everything about Andrew and his family. It was not long after Andrew had been recruited by Walter Koch that Andrew had been approached by Ben himself. Ben had spent hours detailing the history of Andrew's family that his mother had lost in her childhood. A number of Andrew's close family had been sacrificed in the War of Independence for The State of Israel. They were proud Jews who had fought and died for their homeland. Andrew marveled at the stories of his uncles and cousins who had helped found the country in 1948 and ultimately, he had assured Ben that whatever happened, he would help protect what they had given their lives to achieve.

From that day on, Andrew had been true to his word and when Ben had asked, Andrew had delivered. Ben knew about the Horsemen and he knew about their feelings towards Jews. Like Andrew, he was more than happy to use them and they had put Andrew Russell exactly where Ben wanted him. There was nothing like a bunch of Nazi Zionists spending their money to benefit the aims of the Jewish State to put a smile on his face.

"I'm sorry Ben, it was not my idea!" Andrew Russell knew when to admit defeat.

"I know but you should have stopped it. Ararat is bigger than any of this!"

"It has nothing to do with Ararat," protested Russell.

"Every single thing we do over the next two weeks has to do with Ararat!"

"Two weeks?" quizzed Russell.

"Yes, two weeks. The nuclear threat is not just against America. We have our own threat."

"But, two weeks, it's not possible."

"Anything is possible but we need you in power and not behind bars. I'm putting my best agent on this. Senator Baker and his brother have to be eliminated. Personally, I like the man and can't say I'm happy but Ararat is bigger than any individual."

"Does your man need help?"

"I never said it was a man and no, they will deliver what you and your agencies have failed to do."

# Chapter 34

Sam checked the mirror again. He was sure they were clear but there was something pricking at him, something was just not right.

"Are we OK?" asked Senator Baker for the tenth time.

"Yes," said Sam, shaking his head and taking his eyes off the mirror. "I'm just being paranoid, there's nothing there."

"So where to?" asked Clark, turning to check the rear view. Sam's discomfort had heightened her alertness.

"I have a safe house in Washington," said Sam matter-of-factly.

Both the Senator and Clark turned to face Sam.

Senator Baker beat Clark to the question.

"Are you mad? We've just risked our lives getting out of there!"

"Exactly," replied Sam as though it were the most obvious thing in the world. "It's the last place they'll look. Just one quick stop though," he announced as they pulled off of the New Jersey Turnpike and headed into a town called Edison.

One minute later, they were pulling into the lot of The Edison Lock-Up Storage Facility. They drove straight past the office and pulled to a stop in front of a garage-sized unit. Two minutes later, Sam had removed the combination style padlock and was backing a silver 2008 Toyota Camry from the lock-up. Clark drove the Maine police cruiser into the now empty garage.

Senator Baker climbed into the passenger seat of the Camry. Clark took the back seat.

Senator Baker kept looking around the car as though he had never seen one before.

"Something wrong?" asked Sam.

"But...but...I mean, how?"

"I think what the Senator is trying to say," picked up Clark. "Is exactly when did you arrange for the car to be here?"

"Why do you think it's a 2008 model?"

"Three years, this car has been here for three years?!" exclaimed the Senator.

"Japanese reliability. What can I say? I had it on a trickle charger which kept the battery alive. Other than that, it's as good as the day I bought it."

"What yesterday? The Senator had just checked the odometer. "Twenty miles on a three year old car?"

"Turned over first time. No wonder it's the best-selling car in America and in this color too," said Sam.

Clark smiled, she got the point. They were now driving the most common car in America and in the most common color.

As they drove down the I95, silence descended. It was the first time they had been able to relax since that morning. The full brunt of what had happened began to hit the Senator. Something he had done had led to the murder of Sam's family which had subsequently led to the death of at least two drivers in the attack against Sam. The deaths of the killers at Newark or at Sam's did not bother him in the least. They were there to kill him. He would not lose sleep over them but the others, that was a different matter entirely.

"So what happens when we get to Washington?" asked the Senator, keen to busy his mind with anything but the dead.

"I get you two safe."

"And?" prodded the Senator.

Sam didn't answer so Clark interjected.

"What then, we reach out to people we can trust?"

Sam let the question hang before answering.

"Guys, have you not figured it out yet?"

"What?" they asked in unison.

"We can't trust anyone, we're as good as dead. The President of the United States, or somebody acting within his authority, is trying to kill us. There cannot be a happy ending."

"But surely there is something we can do?" asked Clark, naive about how the truly powerful lived their lives.

"There is nothing *we* can do but *I* can do something," said Sam.

"What?"

"Make whoever started this wish they hadn't been born!"

\*\*\*

It was only when the bug's signal died that he realized something was wrong. He had been tailing them from a mile back when the signal stopped moving. The map ruled out a gas station and showed some sort of warehouse facility. He had sped up and thanked God for the female secret service agent. He had caught sight of her in the backseat of the Camry as they pulled out of what he discovered was a storage facility. He had lost the bug but not them. Well at least, not yet. He had to turn and follow them without them noticing, not something he could do easily, as he had to assume they had seen his car.

Fortunately, the street was residential. With little or no time, he pulled to a stop and got out. His driving gloves ensured no prints would be found in the abandoned car. He jogged up to the first house and rang the door bell. The Ford Focus parked in the driveway would be perfect.

The door opened to reveal a pleasant young woman with a baby in her arms. She smiled at the stranger. Edison was consistently ranked amongst the best and safest places to live in America.

"I need your car keys," the stranger announced, no preamble or pleasantries. The pistol appeared in front of the young mother's face before she had a chance to protest.

With her maternal instinct to protect her baby, she instantly nodded towards the key rack behind the door.

The silenced bullet ended her life without warning. She had not even had a chance to turn to see her baby for the last time. Her body fell backwards, the baby saved by her lifeless body hitting the hard wood floor first. The stranger heard footsteps rushing towards him. The thud of the body hitting the floor must have alerted somebody else.

"Honey, are you OK?" A voice came from deeper in the house.

The stranger waited as the young father ran towards his own death. He looked down with pity towards the soon-to-be orphaned baby. He couldn't help but think that being brought up as an orphan wasn't that bad. He had done very well and was rich beyond his wildest dreams in a line of work that was recession proof. In fact, the recession had proved particularly lucrative. Nothing pissed off a rich person more than losing money and a lot of rich people had lost a lot of money. Care homes had made him tough. The Marines had made him a killer. A psych evaluation designated him a sociopath and ended his career dishonorably. As a sniper, he was supposed to have been a little more selective over his targets. Being in the vicinity of a man with a weapon did not constitute a legitimate target in Baghdad. What had been the end of one undistinguished career was merely the beginning of a far more lucrative one; one of Lawson's' assistants had contacted him for a meeting not long after he had returned to the US. The billionaire had pulled the sniper's military file out in front of him and reading his psych evaluation had made him an offer he couldn't refuse. From that day on, he had become the billionaire's personal assassin.

The father took the round through his right eye and joined his wife. The stranger picked up the key and left. The baby could not identify him nor point out that their car was missing.

It had taken a little over forty five seconds to change cars and effectively end three lives, forty five seconds that he had to hope were not too much.

A quick burst of speed to catch up with the Toyota paid off. He could see them turning left onto US 1-S up ahead. Five seconds more and he would have missed the turn.

As he settled down to follow his targets, he thought back to the parking lot at the Howard Johnson in Newark. He had arrived just as all hell was breaking loose inside. He had spotted the Maine cruiser and had assumed that the only reason it was there was because of the brother and if they did make it out of the hotel, it was their most likely escape route. He did chastise himself for a lack of explosives and lack of rifle but Lawson had been very clear. 'Get there and get there as quick as you fucking can!' That had resulted in only one weapon being available, his pistol. He comforted himself with the fact that at least he had his silencer.

This was not like Lawson's previous targets. The sniper had become used to dispatching businessmen, lawyers, accountants or whatever unlucky son of a bitch had upset the cantankerous billionaire. Not that it took much to upset Lawson to the point he wanted to end your life. The sniper was now up against at least one well trained operative and a high profile target. The finding of the Maine cruiser had doubled the number of trained operatives and would ensure a careful approach to completing the job. With explosives and his favored rifle out and the likelihood of an all out and messy fire-fight if he tried to take them down with a pistol in the parking lot, he had no option but to track and trail.

As they approached the I-95, the sniper watched as they selected the I-95 S Trenton. They were heading somewhat surprisingly towards Washington. As the toll booths approached, he slowed down. At this time of night, the roads were quiet and the potential for being spotted increased dramatically. Washington was good. He made a call, a little more firepower was required.

# Chapter 35

**The Knesset Building**
**West Jerusalem**
**6.00 a.m. local**

Ben Meir closed the report and glared at the men in front of him. The chief of Mossad, Shin Bet and the Unit bowed their heads as if back at school and they had been called to the headmaster's office.

"You've just given me a 5,000 word report that could have been written in five, We. Don't. Have. A. Fucking. Clue."

Nobody dared point out that that was technically six words.

The chiefs of Mossad and Shin Bet both looked at Daniel Rosenberg, the head of the Unit and the man whose men were responsible for watching and losing the weapons.

Ben didn't miss the subtlety of their attempt. "Don't look at him to take the blame, you're all bloody useless. Now get out of here and find those weapons before those Arab fucks destroy us!"

As the chiefs left through a side door, Ben pressed the intercom bottom and screamed "Next!"

The day had started badly and he had no misconceptions that it was only going to get worse.

"Good morning, Mr Meir," said the head architect of the Jerusalem building project as he entered Ben's office.

"I'm not so sure you'll think it's that good a morning," offered Ben as a greeting.

The architect was responsible for a key component of Project Ararat, although of course he had no idea that was the case. As far as he was concerned, he was responsible for the building of a major new airport and a number of key government buildings. World renowned, he had dropped everything to take on the project for his spiritual homeland and holy city.

"With two months to go, everything is on target. The sun is shining on another beautiful day and I'm not sure there is anything you can say that will spoil it."

Ben looked at the architect and almost felt sorry for him.

"Well, try this," he offered, straight-faced. "You don't have two months, you have twelve days."

The architect initially laughed but on seeing Ben's face, he stopped and looked questioningly at Ben who simply nodded in return.

The Architect slumped a little in his seat.

"Well that certainly did it," he said, resigned to the enormity of the task that lay before him. "Resources?"

"Whatever I can spare but at least a thousand engineers are on their way to your sites as we speak."

Ben pressed the intercom button. "Next!" he screamed. The architect took that as his cue to leave and quietly left through the side door, contemplating exactly how to get sixty days of work completed in twelve.

Ben looked up as the next cheery "Good morning" made its naive way towards him.

This was going to be a particularly nasty one, thought Ben. Logistics for project Ararat were a nightmare already. The head of the group had argued he needed a hundred days not sixty. Now he was about to find out that he only had twelve.

Ben caught sight of the anteroom to his office. There were at least another three waiting beyond logistics and many more were scheduled to arrive throughout the morning. It really was going to be a particularly horrible day.

# Chapter 36

Rebecca had called Ben as she left the Howard Johnson. There was no link to the terrorists but the cover up of the attempt on the potential presidential candidate was not something she could ignore. The receptionist was not sure but the guy who had checked into the room 'looked like that handsome Senator, the one that could be President'. As there were only really two contenders, the Vice President and Senator Baker, Rebecca had to assume it was the latter. This revelation, combined with the obvious high level cover up by a senior member of Homeland Security, was intriguing. Two calls to contacts alerted her to even more bizarre goings on earlier in the day and before she knew it, two plus two made a mind blowing political conspiracy. Ben was as interested as she was as to what was going on and promised to get back to her. In the meantime, she was to use all her guile to find Senator Baker and report back if and when she did.

Rebecca had not been to America since the birth of Josh. However, it had been her favorite assignment. She loved America. Everything about it excited her, the vastness, the buildings, the power. The freedom to go wherever you wanted, no checkpoints, no looking over your shoulder, no worrying whether the man who looked Arab had a backpack loaded with explosives and nails or a heavy jacket to cover the explosives strapped around her waist. Freedom. She began to think how Josh would have loved America and before she knew it, the what if crept in. What if she had moved to America to raise Josh and then the why, why had she not...

Her phone rang and interrupted her thoughts. "Hi, the car is where you wanted."

It was the *Sayanim* who worked at Hertz. He had secured a car for her, off the books and completely untraceable to her. She ended the call and stepped out from behind the dumpster at the back of the Howard Johnson. The *Sayanim* had parked the car exactly as instructed; the keys would be under the wheel arch. By the time Rebecca got to the car, the *Sayanim* was already half way back to the airport terminal. He had delivered many cars in his time and had prided himself on never once bumping into any of the operatives. Deniability was key and if he didn't see them, he could deny everything about them.

As she arranged her driving position, she switched on one of the extras that most Hertz customers never knew was an option, the police scanner. The other was a Sig Sauer P228, complete with silencer, two spare mags and a box of 9mm shells. Of course, both were an option but only if you happened to work for an Israeli intelligence agency and knew a particular *Sayanim*. She knew that the Senator had escaped. What she didn't know was if anybody was in pursuit. With little or no leads, she would just have to work with what she had at her disposal which was very little. She had contacts across America and of course the *Sayanim* if required but her role was to remain under the radar which is exactly where she planned to be. She pulled out of the lot and headed in the direction the Senator was reported to have gone in, which was left! Nothing to go on would have been an understatement.

The murder of a young couple came over the scanner. It was ten miles away and from what she could glean from the radio chatter, professional and without motive. She had her lead. Rebecca input the address mentioned and accelerated towards Edison, N.J.

"Hello?" she answered her phone on the first ring.

"Hi, it's Ben," said Ben unnecessarily. "I'm sending through everything we have on Senator Charles Baker and his brother Sam."

"Brother?"

"From what we can gather, his brother has become embroiled. In any event, see what you can do. But," he emphasized. "Finding the nuclear device is the priority, OK?"

"OK."

Rebecca replaced the phone on the seat next to her and heard the tell tale ping of information being delivered. As soon as she got to Edison, she'd have a look. Something was not sitting right. Ben's interest, the timing; too many things were happening at once that had major global ramifications. Rebecca had been out of the business for six years but one thing had remained with her above all else, there was no such thing as coincidence. She also knew Ben better than he thought and she knew he was holding back. Call it female intuition, call it experience, call it whatever the hell you wanted, the whole thing stank.

The shootings in Newark were reported as happening less than 30 minutes earlier. Rebecca pushed the accelerator as far as it would go.

# Chapter 37

Mohammad Deif looked in disbelief as the small phone rang. Nobody knew the number, nor that he even had it. Its only purpose was for the sending of tweets to Pock-Mark. Even Pock-Mark didn't know the number. It could just be a wrong number, a pure fluke but something deep down told him otherwise. Deif looked around him. He was in the center of Paris, crossing the Seine. Had he been in Gaza, he wouldn't have even considered answering, the likelihood of an Apache gunship being on the other end would have been too high. However, not in Paris. Nobody was watching him, at least not that he could see.

"Hello?"

"Mohammed, my friend!"

The voice of The Sheikh chilled Deif's blood.

"My Sh…"

The Sheikh cut him off. "Let us be careful, Mohammed, we don't know who may be listening."

"Of course…" Deif caught himself just in time and managed not to repeat his earlier mistake.

"I believe you have ignored my wishes?" the Sheikh asked matter-of-factly.

Deif knew the day would come when he would have to answer to the Sheikh. He had just hoped it would be after the event and not before. He also believed the Sheikh would have been grateful as it was he who had tried the very same once before but his tone suggested otherwise.

"Am I privileged enough to know where your new destination may be?" pushed the Sheikh.

Deif remained silent. He truly believed in a need to know mentality towards information and as much as he owed the Sheikh, the Sheikh did not need to know. Deif was acting on behalf of Allah. It was Allah who had told him that he could do more for his people. It was Allah who had told him to strike the Americans as well as the Jews. The American people would not be so quick to jump to the Jews' defense after they understood the consequences of their allegiance.

"I am sorry, Allahu Akbar." Deif ended the call and tossed his only link with Akram Rayyan into the River Seine.

He turned North and headed for the Gare du Nord. Even if the Sheikh tracked him to Paris, he wouldn't be there long. His TGV train to Marseille was due to leave in 15 minutes. He had one job to take care of in Marseille before moving on to his eventual hideout, Saint Raphael, a small French resort on the Cote D'Azur. Mohammed Deif, mastermind of the downfall of the Zionist state, would spend the next two weeks relaxing in total luxury in the secluded coastal retreat of a Palestinian exile. As with every other part of his plan, nobody knew anything that they didn't need to know. As all parts of the plan were now in play, there was nothing left to do. With no word from him, the five different teams would follow their orders and detonate the devices at midnight Yom Kippur. As such, nobody needed to know where he was and nobody did. Even the Palestinian exile did not know his summer mansion would become Deif's hideout. As with most Cote D'Azur homes of the rich and famous, they sat idle for eleven months of the year. They did France in August.

# Chapter 38

If there was one thing Sam had learned from the CIA, it was the art of deceit and he had become a master. The Georgetown townhouse he approached had a shell corporation listed as its owner and anyone digging would find a number of further shell corporations behind that one. If they ever were lucky enough to reach the end of the line, they would find a small office in a remote Caribbean island with a name plaque on the door. Inside, they would find a desk, a phone and a coffee machine all owned by the same shell corporation that owned the townhouse. It really was a dead end.

Sam winced as he stretched over to the glove box. The pain in his shoulder had lessened but it would be some time before the ligaments and tendons healed. The Senator pushed Sam's attempt away and opened the glove box for him.

"Is it this?" he asked producing a small remote control with two buttons, one arrow pointing up and one down.

"Yep," replied Sam, the pain still apparent in his voice. Both Clark and the Senator had offered to drive but Sam insisted that he wanted to keep one eye ahead and one behind. The niggle that someone was following them had not gone away. He checked the mirror again. Normally, with this feeling, he would not have gone near the safehouse but he needed to get his brother out of sight. With the road clear behind, he barked his instructions.

"OK, hit the Up button!"

Sam didn't miss a beat. The garage door, two houses ahead, lifted up and he continued at speed towards the opening door.

"OK, hit the Down button!"

The Senator looked in horror at the half-raised door they were careering towards. Every instinct told him to ignore his brother. However, decades of knowing that his brother knew best resulted in blind trust and he pressed the Down button.

"What the hell are you doing?" screamed Clark from the backseat as the car turned sharply and the door stopped its upward motion, stalling briefly before beginning to close on the fast approaching car.

Both the Senator and Clark ducked as the car sped towards the narrowing gap, the screech of the tires adding to the drama and eliciting a small scream from Clark. The garage door snapped shut behind the now stationary car. A small scrape on the trunk would be testament to just how close it had been.

Sam turned to Clark. "In answer to your question, making sure nobody sees where we went."

***

The sniper followed from a discreet distance, always keeping a number of cars between himself and the Toyota. It was only when they reached the outskirts of Washington at 1 a.m. that things began to get somewhat trickier. With little traffic on the streets, he had to drive without lights and let them remain a full turn ahead at all times. It meant he had to hold well back and dart forward after they turned to ensure he didn't miss their next one. Everything had gone fine until the final turn onto Q street NW in Georgetown. He had watched from five blocks back as they had turned into the street and, as he had done many times before, he darted down 31st St NW and crawled towards the entrance to Q Street.

As his car emerged onto Q Street, he could see nothing but empty road ahead. He had Senator Baker and Agent Clark's home address and this was neither of their streets. He sped down the street and looked for taillights on any connecting streets. After two minutes of driving around, he had either lost them or they were back near Q Street. Not wanting to contemplate the former, he parked his car next to Tudor Place and began to walk along Q Street. It was 2 a.m. and very few residents would still be awake in such an affluent suburb. Homes with garages were going to be of interest. Homes with garages and signs of life would be prime suspects.

The sniper worked his way carefully down the street. As much as he wanted to find them, he didn't want them to find him first.

It was halfway down the street that he saw the movement, indiscernible to all but the most vigilant. It was the flicker of a street lamp on a face in the corner of a window. The sniper did not react. He had them. He turned and retraced his steps back to his car. He retrieved his phone from his pocket. Comfortable that the glow from the handset would not give away his position, he hit the speed dial button.

"Where are you?" he asked his young apprentice. The sniper had to resolve his weaponry issue. He had called his apprentice, a young man who had, much like the sniper, fallen foul of a poor psych evaluation. Although what was poor for some was ideal for others and the young apprentice was certainly proving himself well in the contract killing business.

"OK, you're about 45 minutes behind me, I'm…" had the moonlight not caught the tip of the blade, the Ka-bar 1222 would have sliced the snipers throat wide open.

Sam cursed as the sniper moved at the last instant causing him to catch nothing but the tiniest piece of flesh. The nick that should have been a slice didn't even produce so much as a drop of blood.

Sam had sensed being followed but hadn't been sure. As he directed Clark and his brother to the lounge, instructing them not to go near the window or put a light on, he had slipped out and taken up position in the bushes. If somebody had been following, they would need to recce the area and try to pinpoint their location. It had taken five minutes for the sniper to appear. Sam had seen enough snipers in his time. The man's use of light and shadow, steadiness and control of breathing, pretty much nailed the guy's expertise. He was good, spotting the almost imperceptible movement in the window was impressive. Clark had obviously tried to peak out of the corner of the window but the street light had reflected on her skin very briefly as she moved. Sam had watched as the sniper, having spotted the movement, immediately began to retrace his steps. Sam had followed and had had to use every ounce of his training and experience of tracking to ensure the sniper did not spot him. Sam had to know if the sniper had called in their position or whether he was making sure before he did call it in. On hearing the conversation and the fact that whoever he was calling didn't know where he was, Sam moved. He had moved silently from the bush and swung the knife in a tight arc towards the snipers throat which would ensure an instant kill and silence.

As the phone clattered and smashed to the ground, the sniper avoided the blade and was already bringing his silenced pistol to bear with his other hand. Sam was just recovering from his initial strike as the silencer closed in on his face. Like his opponent, Sam reacted quickly and as the sniper depressed the trigger, Sam's left hand burned as he pushed the barrel from his face and towards the sniper's car. Two bullets tore through the side panel and rear tire respectively. With little strength in his left hand, Sam had no option but to drop the knife and use both hands against the pistol. Seeing an opportunity, the sniper took it and delivered a massive punch to the side of Sam's head. As Sam was forced from his feet, his two-handed grip on the pistol, although weakened, was enough to wrestle the gun free from the sniper. Sam was down but with the pistol within his reach, he was most definitely not out.

The sniper surveyed the situation in an instant. Sam had the pistol, his car had a flat and his phone was useless. Live to fight another day was a motto the sniper very much lived by. So he turned and ran. He needed his apprentice and some more weapons. Therefore, he needed a phone.

Sam shook his head, The blow had been a good one and had certainly blown off the cobwebs. The pistol lay at his side and he quickly raised it in the direction the sniper had run. As with most snipers, he was quick and more importantly, silent. By the time he had him in his sights, he had vaulted the gate and was just disappearing out of sight behind the wall of Tudor Place, a five and a half acre historic house and garden in the heart of Georgetown and open to the public. Sam picked up his knife and noted the shattered cell phone. He looked at the board detailing the opening hours. The sniper would not have missed the fact that the building would be unoccupied at night and being a tourist attraction, would have public phones.

Sam sprinted after the sniper and clearing the gate, picked up his trail. As the clouds moved across the sky, the moonlight that had assisted the sniper in avoiding the knife came and went. Shadows were thrown and disappeared almost as one. Sam stopped. This time, the sniper knew he was being trailed and from what Sam had witnessed so far, this guy was very good indeed. Although he had the pistol, the sniper, if he wanted, could let Sam walk past within inches and then disarm him.

Sam stopped running and listened. His concerns were unfounded, the sniper had obviously only one concern, alerting somebody to his location. The tinkle of breaking glass from twenty yards through the undergrowth meant he was breaking into the house. Sam picked up the pace and sprinted. He could just make out the dark shape slithering through one of the small panes that led into the drawing room. Sam had always enjoyed visiting the house and grounds when stationed in Washington and loved the peace and tranquility of being transported back to a century when life was more peaceful and far easier. It was one of the main reasons he had purchased the house on Q Street. This was his favorite part of Washington.

Sam knew the public phone was located just off the main hall which was just through the Saloon. The sniper was very close to getting back up. So far, no alarm had been triggered. The system was as antiquated as the house and required a window or door to be opened to trigger it which was just the way Sam wanted it. It also meant that he didn't need to be overly careful. He had the pistol and the sniper was endangering his brother and himself. And, by association, he was guilty of the murder of his son, wife and dog. It was this realization that sent Sam charging towards the Saloon window, with its semi circular floor-to-ceiling portico window. Two spits from the pistol eased his way through as Sam jumped through the window at full pelt. The sniper, caught in the middle of the large and open Saloon room, threw his hands up in surrender; knowing that his benefactor would come to his aid, once the police became involved.

"OK, you win!" offered the sniper, standing with his hands in the air.

Sam almost laughed at the poor guy. He had misunderstood the situation very badly indeed. He must have assumed that, as his brother was a Senator, they would do the right thing.

Sam did. The first two bullets removed the sniper's kneecaps. The screams, although deafening, were contained within the old building's solid walls. Even then, the large grounds meant the nearest home was hundreds of feet away.

"You've got approximately 60 seconds to justify an extension to your miserable life!" offered Sam as he pointed the pistol at the sniper's head.

It took approximately three minutes for the sniper to tell Sam what he needed to know. Nobody knew where the sniper was, other than roughly Washington and even then, it was his apprentice who had no knowledge of who their client was nor who the target was. The client was a man called James Lawson. Sam recognized the name but didn't know where from. He confirmed the main target was Senator Charles Baker and his companions i.e. Clark and Sam. It also transpired that the sniper was unaware of and as such not involved in the attack on Sam's family. That earned him, after his three minute extension, a carefully placed bullet in the head and not the gut shot that Sam had been contemplating.

Sam couldn't cover the break-in but he could dispose of the body. A small pond in the grounds would have to suffice in the short term. Dragging a dead weight with one and a half arms was not easy but he managed and after putting the body in the pond, he found a number of large stones to lay on top. The depth and age of the pond made it unlikely that the body would be spotted, for at least a few days A quick return to the house to pick up cartridges and to wipe down visible blood stains left nothing but a break-in for the police to investigate.

The final task was to move the sniper's car. With a bullet hole and a flat tire, it would stand out in the tree-lined street of multimillion dollar properties. A six-block ride had the tire all but shredded as he pulled into the University of Georgetown Hospital. Avoiding the CCTV cameras, Sam parked next to a number of other cars and jogged back towards the townhouse.

It was time to have a serious chat with Senator Charles Baker and find out how James Lawson fitted into the picture.

# Chapter 39

## The Knesset

Ben had churned through a number of departments delivering the simple message 'you don't have sixty days, you have twelve'. All had argued it was impossible. Ben had ignored them all.

"Enter!" he shouted as the tap on the door alerted him to his next meeting.

As he looked up, expecting to see a representative from the medical team, he saw a face he did not recognize. He looked again at his diary. His secretary had inserted a name he did not recognize and added 'five minutes only' as a note.

"Good afternoon," said a rather strange little man, checking his watch. " Mr Meir, it is an honor to meet you."

"Sorry, have we met?" asked Ben, gesturing for the man to be seated. Ben could not take his eyes off the man's face. He was wearing the most ridiculous looking glasses Ben had ever seen. That, combined with his small but rotund stature, gave him the look of a mole.

"No, I can't say we have," he answered, offering nothing else.

After a moment of awkward silence, Ben spoke.

"Sorry, why are you here?"

"Because of this." The man reached down and rather clumsily produced a photo from his briefcase and laid it in front of Ben.

Ben looked at the photo and saw little more than a grainy picture from a high angle looking down on what he recognized to be the Rafah border-crossing from Gaza to Egypt.

"Where are you from?" asked Ben, still trying to assess why the little mole was in his office.

"Intelligence Group, IAF," replied the mole succinctly.

The mention of the non-Arab Affairs Department caught him off-guard, particularly as he was looking at a picture of the Rafah crossing. With everything else on his plate, the last thing he needed was something unconnected to the Arabs.

Ben was beginning to lose it. He did not have time for some emotional retard to waste his time and addressed him as evenly as he could.

"Would you mind telling me, what exactly it is I'm looking at?"

"Well, you see," the mole replied, pulling another photo from his case. "This was just," he took back the first photo from Ben's desk. "To pinpoint the location." And replaced it with the new one. "This one is a much greater resolution."

Ben rubbed his forehead as he tried to stay calm. The mole had stopped talking as he lay the second photo down. All Ben could see were a number of blurred faces. He still did not know what the hell he was supposed to be looking at.

Ben looked up from the pointless photo and stared at the mole.

The mole just stared back at him somewhat vacantly. A knock at the door and the entrance of the Commander of the IAF (Israeli Air Force) interrupted the awkward stand-off.

The Air Chief knew Ben well and could see the anger and frustration in his face. He looked at the mole who smiled back at him.

"I see you've met Harry?" he said with a smile.

"Kind of," replied Ben as evenly as his temper would allow. It was the busiest day he had had in years and he had no time to waste.

The Chief turned to Harry. "Harry, I told you to make the appointment but you were to wait for me before going in."

Harry just smiled back at his Chief.

Ben shook his head. "I'm sorry but what the hell is going on? Is he some kind of re…"

"I should explain," the Chief interrupted. "Harry is an analyst in one of our photo surveillance departments. And is an autistic savant."

Ben began to calm down. There was something wrong with 'Harry'. He understood the term 'autistic' but not 'savant'.

"Savant?"

"They have a special skill. They can be musical, scientific, artistic or any number of things. Harry here, has a photographic memory and remembers every face he has ever seen and any detail about that person that we know. Address, phone number, date of birth, anything."

Ben began to understand. He looked down at the photo again.

"So who are we looking at?"

Harry leaned forward and pointed to a face in the foreground. It was slightly blurred but revealed a middle-aged man with pale skin, something which did help single him out.

"Professor Ilya Keilson, graduate of the Moscow Engineering Physics Institute. Hero of Socialist Labor, Order of Lenin and winner of the Stalin Prize. Born November 16th 1960. He worked until 1992 in Kremlyov which changed its name to Sarov in 1995 and is the center for Russia's nuclear research program. His particular specialty is maximizing yield potential and detonation. His father was Klaus Fuchs born 29 December 1911…"

Ben held his hand up to stop Harry who was reciting all of the detail from memory.

"What use is he in Gaza?" asked Ben. "The weapons were moved to Israel months ago.".

The Air Chief looked at Ben.

"This photo was amongst a number taken some time ago. It was only by accident that Harry here spotted it. Harry's a Russian specialist and as such, doesn't cover Gaza or the West bank. He only spotted it as he walked past a desk this morning and instantly recognized the face. I'm afraid this photo is about nine months old."

Ben's mouth went dry. Nine months ago was almost exactly when they believed the Palestinians had been given the bombs.

"So this guy, Keilsen, can take a bomb and improve its yield?"

"Yep," replied Harry confidently.

"But only by so much. The mass material is key. There is a maximum. So for example, a 75kt device may be able to improve by say 20-30%, it's unlikely you could get higher than that."

Ben relaxed a little. Was a 100kt nuclear weapon really that much worse than a 75kt?

"He also specializes in trigger and detonation systems," added Harry.

"And that means?"

"He can take a device and reconfigure the trigger or design an entirely new one."

Ben's heart almost stopped.

"Ben? Ben?!" The Air Chief rushed around the desk, as Ben's face turned sheet white.

Ben held his hand up, he was still alive.

"If you wouldn't mind excusing me, I have some calls to make," he whispered in a tremble.

# Chapter 40

Sam arrived back to find Clark and his brother sound asleep on the sofas. The house remained, as per his instructions, in darkness. He grabbed a couple of blankets from a closet and placed them over the pair. Sam had purchased the house from a German diplomat who, at the end of his time in America, just wanted to take his clothes and leave. It meant that Sam was left with pretty much everything you would ever need. The German had, much to Sam's amusement, even agreed to the realtor's discount to cover the cost of removing unwanted goods. He not only got a fully furnished house, he got it for $30,000 less than an empty one.

Sam had spent less than two minutes deciding on the purchase three years earlier and since then, he had not stepped foot in the property and had no idea where anything was, let alone his own bedroom. He climbed the stairs, opened the first door and finding two twin beds, fell on the first one and was asleep by the time his head hit the pillow.

\*\*\*

By the time Rebecca reached Edison, she reckoned she was 50 minutes behind whoever had killed the couple. She fished around in the bottom of her make-up bag and pulled out another federal badge. This time, she would be FBI but with no witnesses in the house who could speak, she kept a lower profile and canvassed the neighbors. She soon had the registration and description of the woman's Ford Focus. Within five minutes, she left the scene and taking an educated guess, she headed South so as not to lose any valuable time as she worked through the leads.

Her first three calls were to *Sayanim* within America's largest cell phone networks, Verizon, Cingular/ATT and Sprint and all were asked to investigate the same occurrence. Did any of their cell phones make two calls at specific times from two locations; Rebecca gave them the gps co-ordinates for the Howard Johnson in Newark and the house in Edison and the times of the shootings with a five minute window either side. Rebecca's thinking was simple. Whoever had killed the couple were after the Senator. She did not believe for a second that the Senator had perpetrated such an atrocity. To be following the Senator the killer would have had to have followed him from Newark and whoever he was, he would have a boss or bosses to report to.

In the meantime, to keep the trail warm, she headed South, continuing on the previous direction from Newark to Edison. Without confirmation that this was the right direction, she held the speedo steady at fifty. She wasn't going to widen the gap too much in the short term, just in case.

The *Sayanim* proved their worth again. What would have taken the federal agencies weeks to uncover was relayed to Rebecca a mere 17 minutes after her call. A Sprint prepaid cell had made two relatively short calls from both locations within the time frame. Being prepaid, there were no details as to ownership and unfortunately both calls were likewise received on prepaid cell phones. So Rebecca was no further forward in who she was chasing. However, the operator not only knew where the phone had been, they knew where it was heading, or at least the direction in which it was heading, due South.

Rebecca almost doubled her speed as she hung up the phone.

It was another two hours before she received the follow-up call. The prepaid cell had stopped moving and was located in and around the Georgetown area of Washington DC. Rebecca checked the satnav. She was only 32 miles away. Two hours of high speed driving had dramatically shrunk the gap between her and the target.

By the time Rebecca pulled into Q street, Sam had already dumped the sniper's car. The sniper's phone, which Rebecca was tracking, lay in bits alongside the sniper's rotting corpse at the bottom of the pond. A phone call from the *Sayanim* confirmed the phone was no longer searching for signal, its last triangulation placed it within the grounds of Tudor Place. Rebecca had just parked on 31st NW and killed her lights as she caught a bizarre sight in her rear view mirror. It was approximately 2.30 a.m. and a man jogged across the road behind her. It wasn't a man merely running across a junction, it was a man who was jogging. Not only that, he was fully dressed. In Rebecca's experience, men out at 2.30 a.m. did many things but jogging was definitely not one of them. Rebecca was a Mossad agent and one thing Mossad instilled from day one, there was no such thing as a coincidence. If it looked out of place, then it was more than likely that it was.

Rebecca waited a few seconds before exiting the car quietly and walking back towards the Q street and 31st NW crossover. She looked tentatively in the direction of the jogging man. She watched as he entered a house further up the street. She ducked back and, checking her sat nav, she worked out which number the house was. She checked her watch, 2.43 a.m. Cell phone companies worked 24 hours in the US but legal firms did not. However, it was already 8.43 a.m. in Tel Aviv. She dialed Mossad's head quarters and was quickly connected to one of the many hackers who ensured almost instant access to records from across the world. Ten minutes later, she had the details of the person who had purchased the house some three years earlier but that led nowhere. However, the coincidences were mounting. Not many homes hid their ownership. What were the chances that the house she was researching would be purchased by an anonymous entity? Like many other coincidences that night, the chances were remote. Rebecca considered calling Ben. She was 90% certain she had the Senator in her sights but wanted to be certain. She extracted another federal badge from her bag. This time it was a Secret Service identity in the name of Rebecca Mills. She walked along 31st NW and soon turned onto Avon Lane NW. A right turn at the end, took her down to Cambridge Place NW. She hopped over the fence and dropped noiselessly into the garden of the house four along from her target. It was a three storey white house facing the Senator's hideout. Rebecca worked her way silently through the gardens before reaching the backdoor of her target property. Her next problem was gaining access without alerting the house opposite. Another call to Mossad secured an unlisted number and after a quick and alarming call to the owners, the back door opened, as instructed, in darkness. Rebecca smiled at what a woman could achieve that few men could, even with years of practice - instant trust. She displayed her badge to the property owner and continued to explain her requirement to remain out of sight and in surveillance of their neighbors. Being Secret Service, she could of course divulge little other than to emphasize it was a matter of national security and that the property owners should remain quiet about the situation.

Rebecca was offered coffee and food but refused. It was imperative that the property owners went back to bed and continued their normal routine. Rebecca took up station in a small bedroom on the third floor which directly overlooked the Senator's location. She sat down and watched. The property owners would leave for work in the morning as normal and should she need to leave, she was to simply pull the door behind her.

# Chapter 41

Sam woke up at 6.30 a.m. to the sound of a toilet flushing. He surveyed the room and instantly knew his worst nightmare wasn't a nightmare. He had lost his wife and child and was on the run with his brother.

He walked down to find his brother still lying on the sofa while Agent Clark was checking kitchen cupboards to see what had survived the three years. So far, just coffee and even then the choice was black or none at all.

"Coffee?" she offered as she turned to look at Sam in the doorway.

"Please," he said, rubbing his shoulder. The muscles had stiffened while he slept. "Is he awake?" he asked as he dipped his head towards his brother.

"Not yet," responded Clark, pouring three coffees.

Sam took two steaming mugs and headed towards his brother, kicking the sofa as he approached. "Come on, wake up!"

Senator Charles Baker sat bolt upright. "Wha, whoa, what's happening?"

"Some bastards are trying to kill you. Now wake up!" demanded Sam almost smiling. His brother had always been a heavy sleeper who, when disturbed, woke up with a start.

After a few shakes of the head and a slug of Clark's coffee, the Senator came back to life. Two more slugs and the full horror of what had happened the previous day began to hit him.

"Shit, what are we going to do?" he looked at Sam.

Sam checked his watch. 6.45 a.m. It was time to make the call he had been considering.

"I'm going to put a call into the Secretary of Defense."

Both Clark and the Senator reacted, the Senator beating Clark by a micro second. "Wait a minute! Last night you said we couldn't trust anybody!"

"I don't but a man whose life I saved probably isn't anybody. James Murphy is the single most honorable man I have ever met. I'm willing to bet my life he's got nothing to do with this. Trust me."

Clark was unconvinced. However, the Senator relaxed as he recalled the rescue of Pilot Colonel James Murphy. Murphy had been shot down over Iraq during the first Gulf War. Being the pilot of a tank busting A10 Warthog, the Iraqis had little sympathy for Murphy and had made his time with them particularly unpleasant. As it became apparent that Murphy would soon be moved to Baghdad and paraded in front of the world's press either before or during a summary execution, a rescue operation had been initiated. Over 100 miles behind enemy lines, Sam Baker was one of two pararescuemen to join the Special Forces team. The Special Forces were in the first chopper while Sam and his colleague were in a second chopper which would hold off until the Special Forces team had found Murphy. They would then swoop in and pick him up. Everything went to plan, right up until the SAM missile took out the Special Forces helicopter. The press had leaked the operation and thanks to CNN, the Iraqis knew they were coming. As the Iraqis celebrated, the pilot of the second chopper began to turn back. Sam had other ideas and with a pistol to the pilot's head, he forced him down, landing a few hundred yards from the makeshift camp. Sam jumped out and carried out the rescue mission. The confusion and chaos caused by the first helicopter's crash had given him a diversion that he used to full advantage.

His pararescue colleague had to stay in the chopper to stop the coward pilot turning tail and leaving them behind. Five minutes after landing, a very beaten up but extremely grateful Colonel James Murphy was in the air and heading home. Funnily enough, the helicopter pilot who had sworn to both Sam and his colleague that they would be court-martialed was very quiet. Even when the President had awarded him the Silver Star, he had not taken the opportunity to complain to his ultimate Commander-in-Chief about Sam's actions.

"OK, if you're sure you can trust him," said the Senator,

"I'm godfather to his first son and he sends me a card every birthday and Christmas. Trust me, he's not in on this."

Sam picked up the phone and dialed a number he had been given many years earlier. Murphy had given him the number if Sam ever needed *anything* and he had repeated 'anything' with conviction.

As the number dialed and began to ring, Sam posed a question.

"What do you know about James Lawson?" Before the Senator could respond, Sam was speaking into the phone.

"Mr Secretary?"

"Yes, I know it's Jim, Mr Secretary."

The Senator tried to listen into the call but James Lawson was all he could think about. James Lawson was the kingmaker. Nobody got anywhere without him. It was one of the biggest issues with his campaign to be president. Lawson was behind Russell. As desperate as he was to hear what the Secretary of Defense was saying, he was more desperate to know why Sam had mentioned his name.

Sam hung up.

"Well?" prodded Clark immediately.

"He's definitely not involved and is coming here to pick us up and escort Charles and myself to meet with the President."

"Holy shit!" exclaimed Clark, smiling as the tension of their current predicament began to ease.

"What about Lawson?" asked the Senator, not really having registered what had just been said. His mind was racing.

"Oh sorry, when you guys fell asleep last night, I went out and caught a guy that had followed us. Creepy little bastard."

Both looked at him in horror.

"Anyway, turns out that was who he worked for, James Lawson."

"Worked for?"

"Yeah."

"Worked, you said 'worked', in the past tense?" quizzed Clark.

"Yes, past tense, dead guys don't work," said Sam matter-of-factly, ending that point of discussion.

"James Lawson is perhaps one of the most influential men in Washington, if not *the* most influential."

"Good for him and trust me, we will soon be referring to him in the past tense too."

"That's not my point. My point is if he's involved, there is literally nobody in Washington we can go to. Nobody would be where they are if Lawson had not had a hand in it."

"What exactly did the Secretary of Defense say?" Clark's initial enthusiasm had significantly waned.

"Trust me, he knew nothing. He was absolutely stunned at what's happened."

"And you gave him this address?"

"I trust the man!" Sam ended the discussion by walking towards the window.

***

The US Secretary of Defense replaced the receiver and just stared at it. Either Sam Baker had gone mad or his country had. There was no other explanation. What Sam had described did not happen in the world's most democratic country. The United States of America was not some tin-pot dictatorship where, if you didn't like the opposition, you just took them out.

But Sam Baker was the most honorable man he had ever met. If he ever had to have somebody watch his back, Sam Baker would be top of the list every time. There was nobody more reliable and he certainly didn't sound mad.

His first call was to Fort Belvoir and the commanding officer of the 701st Military Police Group. He was not going to take any chances. The 701st was home to the US Army's Protective Services Battalion. Their role was similar to that of the Secret Service, only their protectees were military: - the Secretary of Defense, the Under Secretary of Defense and the Chairman and Vice Chairman of the Joint Chiefs, along with many other high risk individuals within the military.

His second call was to the Oval Office. Despite being only 7.00 a.m., he knew the President's private secretary would be up and taking calls. He was right and he made it clear that he would be with the President within the hour and insisted his diary be cleared as a matter of national security. Such a request by one of the President's most senior and trusted staff ensured instant compliance. Accordingly, the President's meetings were cleared between 8 and 9 a.m.

Fifteen minutes after his call to the 701st, the door bell rang. Showered and dressed, the Secretary of Defense opened the door to two fully loaded Humvees and an armored limousine, all with blue lights flashing and a total of ten men. All, as he knew from experience, were battle hardened. He checked his watch, 7.30 a.m. and with the lights and sirens, they could make Georgetown in a little over 25 minutes, even at that time of the day.

*\*\**

It had not been Vice President Russell's best night's sleep by a long way. Between the nuclear threat to America and the failure to deal with Senator Baker and his brother, it had quite possibly been one of the shittiest nights of his life. He just hoped that the ringing phone would bring some good news. So far, everything had succeeding in trumping previous disastrous news.

"Russell!" he answered.

"Mr Vice President, this is Nancy."

Russell instantly recognized the old bag who looked after the President's calendar. She loved the power and was desperate to remain in post under Russell. Not a chance, there would be a very attractive young piece of fluff adorning his office, not a miserable old dragon who had lost the ability to smile at birth.

"Hi Nancy, how can I help?"

"Well, the other day, you mentioned you'd like to be informed of anything out of the ordinary."

Nancy was staking her claim and showing she was loyal.

"Yes!"

The longer Nancy spoke, the harder he found it to breathe. This was disastrous. It took all his strength to thank Nancy before hanging up.

It was 7.20 a.m. and the Secretary of Defense was going to see the President any time between 8 and 9 a.m. as a matter of national security. Nothing new had happened overnight, of that he was sure. The Deputy Secretary of Defense was on top of everything and he was Russell's man. That could only mean one thing, Sam Baker had reached out to the man he knew was senior enough to make an impact and most importantly, knew he could trust. They all knew it was a risk but as Sam was supposed to have been the first to die, it had been ruled out as an issue.

Russell considered calling Preston but there was nothing he could do, likewise, Gates. He hit the speed dial button for the Head of the CIA. When it came down to it and you needed some real sneaky bastards, there was nobody better.

"Allan, we've got a problem," he opened.

"Already taken care of," came the very calm response.

"You don't even know what it is yet?"

"I was just about to call you. I received a call from a friend over at Fort Belvoir, a little while ago," The conspiratorial tone of his voice came over loud and clear.

"And?"

"The Secretary of Defense requested two fully loaded Humvees and his Armored limo to take him to see the President, with a pick up on the way…" Johnson paused.

Russell's frustration was growing. "You know where the pick-up is and you can beat them to it?"

"Nope, not a clue."

"So how in the hell is it sorted?"

Russell could hear the smile down the phone line. "The Humvees are loaded with my men. Eight fully armed. The Secretary will have his two normal bodyguards in his limo but that's it, the rest of the men are ours!"

Russell smiled for what seemed the first time in days as he replaced the handset.

# Chapter 42

Rebecca looked at her watch when she heard the front door close two storeys below her. It was 6.35 a.m. She watched as the property owners got into their cars and drove off. Both, she noted, had failed to do as instructed and looked back as they drove away. Fortunately, the blinds were still closed in the windows opposite. She had dozed on and off for the last few hours as it became apparent that her potential target had gone to bed.

The owners leaving had woken Rebecca from her dozing. Now fully awake, she turned her attention to the house directly opposite. She was looking for any movement and ideally just the faintest glimpse of the Senator would do. Once confirmed, she would call Ben and do whatever needed to be done.

Rebecca did not have long to wait for movement. Five minutes later, the blinds changed as a light inside the house backlit their blackness. The lines of light did nothing other than confirm that there was somebody inside. It was still forty minutes until sunrise and Rebecca predicted the blinds would stay shut until then. Why open blinds when it was still dark? She took the gamble, visited the restroom and grabbed a quick bite to eat. She did all that in semi darkness so as not to alert anybody to her presence.

By the time she was back, the third storey window had not changed. The blinds remained closed and the light on. The first wisps of sunlight began to break through and Rebecca stared intently. Even the slightest view of the Senator was all she needed. She had studied many photos sent over by Ben over the last few hours and knew many of the Senator's distinguishing features. It was 7.40 when the first movement of the blinds paid any dividends. The sun's rays had slowly multiplied until it could be said that daylight had broken. The blinds parted and a face appeared. Rebecca instinctively ducked back but the face across from her looked up and down the street, not up and across to a third storey window opposite. The face was not the Senator, most definitely not, it was a female.

***

Clark checked up and down the street and shook her head. There was still no sign of the Secretary of Defense.

"I told you, he won't be here until nearer 8.00," said Sam. "Now will you please come back here and relax," he pleaded pointing to the seat next to his brother.

"I just don't get it," said the Senator, returning to the previous conversation with Sam. "I don't understand what I have done to piss off James Lawson so much that he'd want *me* and for that matter you and your family dead?"

"You're running against his boy?" suggested Sam.

"Most of Washington are his boys. He doesn't need Russell in power that much. It has to be more than that, surely?"

"You know what they say, power corrupts and absolute power corrupts absolutely," offered Clark taking her seat next to the Senator.

"Very true," pondered the Senator.

"But what if the President is involved?" asked Clark suddenly, the thought just popping into her mind.

Both Bakers turned and looked at each other. The thought, stupidly, had not crossed their minds.

"We think Russell is. If the Vice President is, why not the President?" continued Clark, thinking out loud.

"Jesus!" exclaimed Sam. A noise at the window caught his attention and he got up to check.

"Exactly. And whether Murphy is on our side or not, if the President wants us dead, we're as good as dead," added the Senator, standing up to see what had caught his brother's attention.

"For Christ's sake, get away from the window!" Sam waved wildly at his brother to sit back down.

*\*\**

Rebecca watched as the man walked towards her, his features were similar to what she was looking for but unless the Senator had lost 30lbs, five years and had seriously manned up in the last twenty-four hours, it was somebody else. But that somebody else was certainly from the same family. She looked at the info on the Senator, compiled by Mossad and their *Sayanim*. It was at least as detailed as anything available in the US and perhaps even more so. Rebecca looked up and confirmed it. The man in front of her was Sam Baker, although her records suggested it wasn't possible. He had been dead for over three years – just about the time the house she was watching had been purchased.

It was Sam's waving behind him that had caught Rebecca's attention. She followed the hands and caught the only glimpse she needed. She withdrew her phone and made the call she had been 95% certain she could have made five hours earlier.

The call was answered instantly.

"I've found him!" said Rebecca.

"Kill him!" was the automatic response before the line went dead.

*\*\**

"Jesus, there are people trying to kill you Charles!" said Sam as he checked the street and saw the two Humvees and a limo pull to a stop at the door.

"Sorry, I wasn't thinking!"

"Well, they're here, so what are we doing? Do we trust the President or not?" asked Sam, as he watched Defense Secretary Murphy exit the limo and make his way towards the house with his two bodyguards.

Clark nodded. She did.

"Forgive me," offered the Senator. "But as you have sworn an oath to give your life for the man, I'm afraid you're ruled out of this vote of confidence."

Clark shrugged her acceptance.

The door bell rung below.

"Well?" asked Sam.

Clark walked towards the window and watched as the Humvees emptied their eight operatives, all heavily armed and obviously with no intention of anything other than storming the house.

"I'm going to change my vote," she said moving quickly from the window and drawing her pistol.

"Shit," Sam caught sight of the action below and instantly realized he had been right about one thing. He could trust the Secretary of Defense. Otherwise, he most certainly would not be standing like a lame duck with his two bodyguards ringing the doorbell.

Sam bound down the stairs, swung the door open and literally pulled the Secretary of Defense off of his feet and through the doorway, slamming the door behind him. The two bodyguards barely had time to react to the abduction of their boss before both were struck by a hail of bullets from the eight men closing in on the house.

"What the…?!!" screamed the Secretary before the bullets began thudding around him.

Sam threw the Secretary on the floor and instinctively jumped on top. As the first volley paused, Sam was up and dragging the Secretary up the staircase, grabbing his holdall as he went.

*** 

As Rebecca stepped out of the house opposite, the limo and Humvees came screaming round the bend. She pushed her silenced pistol further into her coat pocket and contemplated stepping back inside but as she had already shut the door and heard the lock click, her fate was sealed. In order to stall until they passed, Rebecca fumbled in her pocket. To any passer-by she would look just like a woman who had forgotten her phone or keys. All that changed as the scene before her unfolded. The limo stopped and the instantly recognizable Secretary of Defense, James Murphy, stepped out of the limo. The Secretary was a staunch ally of Israel and Rebecca knew he was a personal and trusted friend of Ben Meir.

With her mind racing as to what to do, the Humvees emptied and Rebecca could instantly see the eight men were in no way friendly towards the house opposite nor the Secretary of Defense.

"Shit," she muttered as she hit the speed dial button for Ben.

The first bullets struck as Ben answered.

"What is the priority, saving the Secretary of Defense James Murphy or killing the Senator?"

"Sorry?" replied Ben, somewhat caught off-guard by the question.

"Ben, you have seconds to decide, Secretary or Senator?"

Being asked to decide an eventuality that you did not conceive possible, in a fraction of a second, was not something a normal individual copes with well. Ben Meir was as long in the tooth as they came and normal was never a word that could be used to describe any part of him.

"Secretary," he answered. His mind had calculated the pros and cons in an instant. The Secretary of Defense was one of two men in the US who had helped drive Project Ararat. The Senator needed to be dealt with but that could wait. There would be no waiting if the Secretary was dead.

"OK." Rebecca killed the call and in a swift motion swapped her phone for her silenced pistol. She moved away from the door and walked towards the action.

Although it was one against eight, Rebecca had one major advantage. The men believed themselves to be the hunters and only had eyes for the house ahead of them. They obviously did not consider for a second that they would become the hunted. Rebecca could tell the men were well trained. Their movement was excellent, two forward, two covering, two forward, two covering but that meant there were two behind all the time and as Rebecca reached the side of the Humvee, she took aim and eight became six, four rounds double tap to each of the two men. The Sig had been chosen for one reason, not because it was Rebecca's favorite or it was the best tool for the job. It had simply been chosen because most federal agencies used it and as such would help Rebecca with her cover. However, as the two men dropped before her, she had to admit, it was a rather nice handgun.

***

Sam managed to drag the Secretary to the top of the stairs and had unceremoniously dumped him while he retrieved his weapons from the holdall. He grabbed a Heckler and Koch MP5 and tossed it to Clark. She obviously knew her stuff. She caught the weapon, flicked off the safety and immediately made for the window in an attempt to knock out at least some of the competition. Sam grabbed the AA-12 automatic shotgun. If the guys came through the door down below, it would be like the hotel corridor all over again. Only this time, Sam's shoulder was in much better shape. He stuffed two grenades onto his belt and his Wilson Combat Supergrade .45 handgun into the back of his trousers - it was a present from the Senator many years earlier.

With the Secretary and the Senator secured in the kitchen area, Sam made for the top of the stairs. A hail of bullets removed the lounge window and pinned Clark down. They were coming. Sam looked away from the door below him and covered his ears. If these guys were who he thought they were, he'd use it to his advantage. Almost like clockwork, the flashbang flew through the small window next to the door. Sam, despite not having witnessed one for some time, managed to maintain his wits and counting to two after the bang, swung the AA-12 barrel to his right and fired five of his explosive rounds into the space below. The screams told him all he needed to know.

"Got one!" screamed Clark from behind him.

A quick look confirmed he had killed the first two through the door. There had eight, minus Clark's, that made five.

"Three down, five to go!" he shouted across to Clark.

"Five down three to go!" replied Clark.

"Good girl," he shouted back.

"Six down, two to go" she replied quickly.

Sam was feeling the effects of the flashbang but not so much that he'd miss the sound of the MP5 firing ten yards away. OK it was quiet but he heard it.

"We've got some help and she certainly knows what she's doing!"

Sam bounded down the stairs. There was no way the men would come through the door now.

\*\*\*

Rebecca had watched as the six men had prepared to attack. The hail of bullets had taken out a side window and one of the men was preparing to toss in a flashbang. Rebecca was over forty yards away and with no cover between her and the house, any move now would be suicidal, whether they were expecting her or not. All she could do was wait for the charge and rush in behind them, hopefully in time to save the Secretary.

She turned her head as the flashbang exploded and then watched as the six men charged in, rather amateurishly she thought. Her assumption was correct and as the first rounds exploded into the charging men, those at the rear did, as one faced with overwhelming firepower would do. They ran for cover. Unfortunately, the only cover meant Rebecca could take out another one. Another double tap ensured the fastest runner would not be running anywhere. The woman in the window nailed another who was just behind her one. Which left two. They now knew they were surrounded and could do nothing but crouch either side of the doorframe. Out of range for Rebecca and out of sight for those inside.

Unless they were suicidal, their best option was to rush Rebecca. She could see it in their faces and she knew that's exactly what she would do. They also had XM8 machine guns, grenades and pistols against her Sig automatic handgun. It looked like the tables had turned and the hunted were once again the hunters. She watched helplessly as they nodded to each other and as one raised his XM8 and began to fire towards her, they didn't care if they hit her, they just wanted to pin her down so they could get to a car. Once they were nearer, then they would kill her. Rebecca had no option but to duck down behind the wheel and wait for the rounds to stop hitting.

\*\*\*

Sam reached the bottom of the stairs just as the two made their move. He dumped the AA-12 and pulled the Wilson Combat Supergrade from his pants. This was going to be up-close and personal. The shotgun was too cumbersome. The guy covering was more interested in keeping the woman's head down and so was easy work for the supergrade. Sam walked through the door and nonchalantly raised the handgun and put a round through the man's head. The .45 round almost removed the top of his head. Sam's hand didn't even stop moving. The same motion swung the gun up and as he continued through the door, he waited for the running man to realize his cover was no more. It took him longer than Sam thought. He must have covered twenty yards before his stride began to falter. At twenty yards, most handguns were still effective but the Wilson Combat Supergrade was still lethal. Unfortunately for the man, now caught in the middle, he was also within Rebecca's range. Although the Sig was nowhere near as accurate as the Wilson, it came down to the user and Rebecca was an expert shot. The twenty yards from the house also meant Clark had a shot from the window above and the MP5 was certainly more than comfortable with a range five times further.

Three highly trained gun operators, all expertly versed in how to take a man down and keep him down, trained their weapons as one. Time slowed as each of them went through a routine that was as natural as breathing. What felt like seconds to each of them could have been measured in milliseconds. The three shots from each of the weapons were almost indistinguishable, each having calculated, aimed and reacted in unison. The three bullets struck as one. The last man's body danced to its death as each shooter automatically sent a second and third bullet towards their target. Everything had happened so quickly that it was only when they stopped shooting, they realized two others had shot also.

"Eight down," shouted Sam to Clark as he looked towards the woman now standing behind the Humvee. A woman, who without a doubt, had helped save their lives.

"Hi, I'm Sam," he offered his hand as he walked towards her.

"Rebecca," she accepted his hand. "The Secretary?"

"He's fine, upstairs in the kitchen having a coffee. Do you want one?" smiled Sam. He recognized her very slight accent as he had worked many times in the middle East. Deadly and beautiful with a middle-Eastern twang. She was Mossad, without a doubt. What next, he thought as he led her into the house.

First things first, they needed to get the hell out of Washington.

# Part Four

# Chapter 43

## Port of Haifa, Israel

Saul Weisfeld had worked in the ports for over thirty years and had never seen anything like it. For the previous year, he had seen more ships dock than almost the previous thirty years put together. He checked the charts. Over 30 million tons of cargo in the last month, more than the whole of the previous year. He was working six and a half days a week and the port had employed an extra two hundred staff but were still struggling to cope. Only the previous day, the Port Director had told him that the navy was going to be sending over some help. The next few days were expected to be even busier!

Saul was worried. His wife had been moaning at him for weeks. The stores were empty and food was scarce. Electronics stores were closing due to lack of stock. Israel was struggling but the port was busier than ever. None of it made sense, except for one thing. Israel was preparing for war. With two sons and a daughter in the forces, Saul was very worried. His daughter would be fine, she was the brains and worked with the strategy department but his boys, his two beautiful boys, were both in the mechanized infantry, front line troops. The Port Director had told him not to be so daft but the lack of conviction and the worry etched on his face betrayed his lie. He too was worried. He too had children in the forces.

The phone buzzed on his desk. Another massive cargo ship had docked and needed to be unloaded and reloaded. The ships were stacking up. Capacity was being exceeded but he had to keep things moving. Saul called on his crane operator to get over to Quay Three and instructed the transport manager to get the trucks moving. He hauled himself out of his seat and looked out across the port. Every quay was filled, a sight he had rarely seen up until the previous few months. Not only that, a line of ships waited for their turn to dock. Each of the ships was piled high with containers, just as they all had been for the previous few months. But the shops were empty. It didn't make sense but then for every container that came ashore, one went onboard. So maybe it did.

Saul watched a truck drive past, its belly low to the ground under the weight of the container it was carrying. Ten minutes later, the same truck came back with a different container on its back. Saul watched as it pulled away from the checker below him. Its engine strained far less than with its previous load. In fact, it was almost as though there was no weight in there at all.

Saul watched the next few trucks and began to notice a pattern. Whatever was leaving Israel was far heavier than what was coming in. His mind started to race again. None of it made sense.

# Chapter 44

## Huntsville, Alabama

"Zak?"

"Yes. Who is this?" replied the DIA agent.

"I thought you would have recognized my voice, I know it's been a few years!"

Zak's stomach had lurched on hearing his name and had just prayed it wasn't who he feared it was. However, the more the voice spoke, the more Zak knew his worst fears were well founded. It was 'The Sheikh'.

"I can't talk just now."

"Why ever not?" asked the Sheikh.

"I'm in the office, there are other agents around," he whispered.

The Sheikh did not respond and the line went quiet. Zak visibly relaxed.

A hand on his shoulder made him jump.

"Sorry, I thought that was you," said the man as Zak turned to face the owner of the hand.

Zak froze as he looked into the face of a man he had never seen before but a voice that chilled him to the core. The Sheikh had obviously followed him. Zak was not in the office but sitting in a booth of a small roadside diner.

Zak tried to explain why he was not the office as he had said but the Sheikh waved his hand as though it were irrelevant.

Zak looked at the man whom he knew adorned governments' Most Wanted lists around the world. Although, of course, the lists showed a silhouette where a face should be. Nobody had ever even given a description, let alone a photo. Zak had expected a battle hardened, tough, bearded, Osama-like character but The Sheikh was none of these. In fact, the Sheikh would not have looked out of place adorning the front cover of GQ magazine. More Arab Prince than Arab terrorist.

"I need your help."

"Of course," replied Zak. It would not cross his mind to do anything but assist a request, particularly as he knew the request was serving his spiritual homeland.

"Come, I will explain as we drive." The Sheikh looked down at Zak's plate, his lunch was only half eaten.

Zak quickly threw his napkin across the unfinished meal but it was too late.

"I fear you have spent too much time with the Americans," said the Sheikh, shaking his head in disappointment. "Bacon?" He looked Zak in the eye and led him towards the car park, his head still shaking.

Zak felt like a five-year-old child chastised by a disappointed parent. As he walked towards the rental car, the Sheikh handed him the keys and climbed in the passenger seat. Zak was driving.

"Where to?"

"The airport, I have a plane waiting."

"But, my office, they are expecting me back."

"Well, you'd better tell them not to."

"When will I be back?"

"You'll be back when we're finished."

"How long will it take?"

"As long as it takes." The Sheikh smiled. He could keep this up for hours.

Zak got the gist and stopped asking silly questions. He called his office and told them he wouldn't be back this afternoon. He'd worry about it the next day, when, and if, that came. He was getting a very strong notion that he would never be back.

# Chapter 45

**Marseille, France.**

Mohammed loved Marseille. Although it was France's second largest city and biggest port, he never felt he was in France. Marseille people saw themselves first and foremost as Marseillais and then perhaps French. Its poor reputation, almost entirely due to the movie with Gene Hackman, 'The French Connection', was entirely unjustified. Certainly in the twenty first century, the city was almost indistinguishable from what it had been forty years earlier but the spirit, he knew, remained the same.

Deif sat on his rooftop balcony. He had booked a villa in the 7th Arrondissement, the Bompard, and thanks to its elevated position, he could observe the ships, as they plied their trade in and out of the busy port. He had been waiting two days for the ship to appear and almost cried out as his binoculars picked up the rusty freighter that was making its way between the small islands of Frioul and the Chateau D'If, made famous in Alexander Dumas' 'The Count of Monte Cristo', just in front of Marseille. He waited for the name to become visible and yes, that was it, Akram had arrived.

Mohammed made his way downstairs, boarded his scooter and taking his life in his hands, headed towards the port. Marseille drivers were almost as crazy as the roads and after avoiding a number of life threatening crashes, he thankfully dismounted the scooter and awaited his friend's arrival. The two containers that would complete the weapon lay alongside the

Quay with the two men who had spent the previous year assembling, checking and then disassembling the equipment. They had found what they needed in Malta, a relic left to rot after World War II. However, Malta was too small for their highly covert operation, so everything had been moved to France where her relatively unpopulated South offered plenty of privacy.

As the boat pulled in to dock, Akram and Deif greeted each other as brothers. This was the last stop before they made history and as the second container swung aboard, the small crew could be heard cheering. In the Captain's cabin, Deif and Akram went over the charts with the navigator. Neither really knew what they were looking at, other than the timeline, the only thing they cared about. At eighteen knots, they would be in position in eight days. They were still on time and it left them the luxury of one choice. Were they going to time it for midnight Yom Kippur in Israel or midnight, Yom Kippur in America?

"Simple," replied Deif. "Whichever causes the most casualties!"

Both laughed as they then discussed which it would be midnight or 6.00 a.m. US time.

Deif and Akram prayed together before Deif left and watched as the freighter pulled out of port and began her momentous voyage. He boarded the scooter for the last time, praying that Allah would keep him safe again and headed for the Gare de Marseille-Saint-Charles train station where his train to Saint Raphael and his well deserved break awaited him.

*** 

Had Deif learned more about Marseille than its links to the Muslim world, he may have discovered that Marseille was quite literally a melting pot of cultures and communities. It not only had one of the largest Muslim populations in Europe, it was also home to the third largest Jewish community. Almost 1 in 10 Marseillais were Jewish. Of course, they were far less visible than their Muslim neighbors and far less vocal, so this was a fact easily missed by the passing traveller.

Another traveller, however, was fully aware of this. He was a born and bred Marseillais but at the age of 18 had followed his heart and joined the military. He had flown to Israel and enlisted in the IDF. His talents as a linguist had not gone unnoticed and he was soon transferred to Mossad. Over the years, he had proved his worth and become Head of the Paris Mossad station. Had it not been for his mother's birthday and a quick trip down to see her, he would have missed the man who he instantly recognized as a person of interest to Israel. Unfortunately and slightly embarrassingly for him, he couldn't quite identify him. As the trip was a personal one, he had left his laptop at home and with nothing other than a mere visual recognition, he could do nothing more than follow the man.

He watched the man board the train bound for Nice and then once he had settled into his seat, he joined the same train. From a carriage behind, he kept an eye on Deif, careful to maintain his cover. By the time they both disembarked in Saint Raphael, he was certain Deif was not in the least suspicious nor aware that he was being followed. In fact, Deif was so brazen that the Head of the Paris Station began to think that he might be following an innocent man. Deif grabbed a taxi from the front of the station. This left the Paris Head with a dilemma. Follow and risk being spotted or wait for the taxi to drop him off and find out where he had been dropped. He elected for the latter, noting down the taxi registration. He knew he'd be back soon enough. He knew from experience that this was the only taxi rank in Saint Raphael.

He began to think he had made the wrong choice when after an hour the taxi had failed to return. Just as he was thinking the worst, it reappeared and the Paris Head, having secured a healthy sum of money from a nearby ATM, jumped in the passenger seat.

"I'm sorry, Sir but you must take the taxi at the front of the queue," protested the taxi driver.

He handed the taxi driver a €50 note. "But I really like yours!"

The taxi driver looked at the wad of €50 notes in the passenger's hand and took off to a blaze of horns from his colleagues.

After two minutes of talking to the taxi driver, it became apparent that the man he had followed was far from innocent. The taxi driver had dropped him off at one address but with no room to turn around, the taxi driver had been forced to drive further down the road before being able to complete a U-turn. When he had driven back, he saw his passenger disappearing into an entirely different property. With the address in hand, the Paris Head made a decision. Paris by train was at least five hours away but he was only thirty minutes from Nice and a ninety minute plane journey.

A little over three hours later, he was sitting in his subordinate's car at Paris Charles de Gaulle airport looking through the Wanted List of photos he had instructed he bring with him. After five photos, he found the man he had just followed and hoped to God for his career that the man was where he had left him. Mohammed Deif had been found. Well, he had been four hours earlier. The Paris Head of Station just prayed he was still there as he dialed Ben Meir's number. It was his number listed as contact, should the man be sighted.

# Chapter 46

## Naval Observatory, Washington D.C.

Andrew Russell had not slept for two nights. The Senator, his brother, the Secret Service agent and even the Secretary of Defense had vanished off the face of the earth. The attack by the CIA team at Sam Baker's house had been a debacle, all eight men dead and the targets vanishing into thin air. The President was asking questions as to the whereabouts of his Secretary of Defense and even more worryingly, the press had cottoned onto the fact that nothing had been heard of Senator Charles Baker for days. Up until his failed assassination, he was giving sound bites twice, three times a day. His office could offer them nothing more than they had not heard from him either, itself a cause for concern as to why nobody was doing anything.

It was all a total and utter disaster. He should never have agreed to it in the first place but the Horsemen had been insistent, adamant that Senator Charles Baker had to be taken out of the race. They were due to arrive shortly and he was in no state to see them. Unshaven and disheveled, he was far from presidential. He had to pull himself together or the old fuckers would be looking to replace him.

His phone rang and he looked at it with no intention of answering unless it was of national importance. He didn't want another update from the imbeciles trying to track down the targets. He recognized the number or at least the international code, 972, Israel. It must be Ben. Ben had been avoiding his calls.

"Ben?"

"Andrew, my dear boy," replied Ben.

"I've been trying to call you," said Russell almost breathlessly. His stress levels were off the chart.

"Sorry but to say I'm busy at the moment would be a monumental understatement."

"Of course," Russell was fully aware of the timeline Ben was operating to. "Did you have any luck with that little job we discussed?"

"Hmmm, yes, that little job. I'm afraid our priorities clashed at a crucial moment."

Russell was in no mood for BS. "What the hell does that mean?"

"It means, the agent who had tracked your target was in a position to carry out her orders when all hell broke loose and a very dear friend of mine and of Israel's became a potential victim."

"Shit, the house in Georgetown?"

"Yes!"

"I can assure you, no harm would have come to James. I know he's crucial to our plans and Ararat."

"Nevertheless, I could not take that risk. We're at a very crucial time for Israel. Your loyalties are split. These horsemen as you call them are a risk to our nation."

"Without them, I will not become President and Ararat may be at risk."

"Baker will not interfere with Ararat."

"But the democrats will. If any of what has happened comes to light, our party will be destroyed in the polls. You can't take that risk."

Ben remained silent. He knew Russell was right. For Ararat to work, he needed a stable government in the US. The last thing he needed was a change of politics. It was imperative that Russell, or at the very least Baker, win to keep the quid pro quo.

"Shit!"

Russell could sense a breakthrough.

"Do you know where they are?" he asked.

"Yes, but I promised my operative she would be safe."

"Give her new orders then."

"She would not accept them. She has spent two days with the Secretary and Baker and knows they're friends of Israel. She knows nothing of our plans and will not kill any non terrorists without very good cause."

"Well give me the location then."

"That, I'm afraid, is something I can't do either."

"I promise we won't harm her or the Secretary."

"Were you going to do it yourself, that may be a promise I would accept. However, you're not and so I can't take the risk. Your fellow Americans are well known for sledgehammers being used to crack nuts. The operative is my goddaughter and I will not risk somebody sending a cruise missile towards her."

"But…"

"No buts Andrew, I will sort out your mess."

Ben hung up. He had a call to make.

As Andrew replaced the silent handset, a knock on his bedroom door signaled company. His valet announced the arrival of four gentlemen.

Andrew asked him to direct them to the library while he quickly shaved and brushed his hair.

"Gentlemen," announced Andrew as he entered the library, closing the door behind him.

Three of the men looked at Walter Koch, waiting for him to respond on their behalf.

"We," the others nodded their consent. "Are very concerned of where we are."

"Gentlemen." Andrew poured himself a Scotch. He was feeling buoyed by Ben's call. If the Israelis wanted you dead, you died. Simple. "Everything is under control."

"Exactly how is everything under control?" asked James Lawson, his temper simmering. He was worried. His man had disappeared over three days earlier at a point when he was allegedly about to deal with the problem.

"I have just spoken to a contact and they're sending a team to deal with it now."

"Sending them where?"

Andrew had absolutely no idea. Ben hadn't trusted him with that information but ever the politician. "That, gentlemen, will all become clear very shortly. Now please, let's not dwell on issues that are resolved. I believe there were other issues you wanted to discuss."

Walter looked at Lawson and received an imperceptible nod. Leave it and move on.

"We have two issues. The first is the nuclear weapon that is supposedly on its way here and the second is transport."

"As for the nuclear device, there are no updates as yet but it seems this is well covered and our borders will pick up the device the second it comes anywhere near us."

"Just like Texas?" asked Lawrence Harkness, sarcastically.

"Maybe. How much did you make out of that again?" asked Lawson. They all knew that Harkness had doubled his wealth following the atrocity in Texas but it didn't stop Harkness complaining about it. He owned many of the military suppliers who had benefitted from the United States' reaction to the nuclear detonation.

"It won't happen again!" Andrew responded firmly and with conviction.

"Best cancel that new yacht you were going to buy!" joked Lawson to Harkness.

"Gentlemen, please," asked Walter looking at the two billionaires who were constantly at each other's throats. Walter knew that Lawson had made just as much out of the atrocity as Harkness and probably even more. Lawson's stock in military supply organizations had shot through the roof.

"What's even more troubling at the moment is this solar flare nonsense."

"Sorry?" Andrew was taken totally by surprise. The solar flare had been the subject of a few briefings over the last couple of days but with other things on his mind, he'd avoided them like the plague. Another was scheduled for later that day and included the President so he'd have to attend.

"Jesus, have you not been watching the news?" asked William Hathway who until then had sat quietly.

"Honestly, no. I've not had time."

"They're suggesting that in about a week from now there will be a massive solar flare. I think it's like an explosion within the sun which will cause some sort of geomagnetic storm," informed Hathaway.

Andrew just stared at the four like they were speaking Greek. He had absolutely no idea what all of it meant.

"Basically, they're talking about grounding every aircraft in the world for between three and five days!" explained Hathaway, the biggest landowner and farmer in America. To ensure top dollar, his produce was flown around the world. Grounded aircraft for three to five days would cost him tens of millions in lost revenue.

"Why the hell would they do that?" asked Andrew, stunned by the revelation and how he had missed the enormity of the problem.

"Some rubbish about magnetic field and proton storms being a risk to engines on a plane. The worry is when, and if, it hits, planes will fall out of the sky as their engines are knocked out."

"I'm sorry. This is the first I've heard of this. What do you want me to do?"

"Stop it!"

"Explosions on the sun?!" asked Andrew incredulously.

"Grounding the planes!" shouted Hathaway angrily before getting up and leading his three horsemen out of the library and the house.

Andrew Russell just stared at the four empty seats. What next, he wondered.

His phone rang. The President wanted him in the Oval Office ten minutes ago.

# Chapter 47

## Montana, USA

It had taken the best part of two days but they had made it. A slight detour on the way had increased their number by one. The Senator's wife, Beth was now safely ensconced with her husband in their master suite. The house, as Agent Clark had commented many times, was spectacular, nestling in the mountains below the Whitefish mountain ski resort, with views across the lake, framed by 7000 foot mountains that bordered Canada and offering the best skiing in Montana, as promised by the Senator. The house itself was vast. The lounge alone could fit Clark's whole apartment, as could the circular fireplace in its heart.

After the events in Washington, Sam had declared that enough was enough and they had no option but to get out of dodge. The Senator had mentioned the ski lodge, over 2,000 miles away, as a joke but Sam had instantly grabbed the idea, particularly as the Senator had explained that the lodge had been purchased the previous year by the Senator's wife's family's estate. He had assured Sam that there was no way it could be linked to them. Her estate was as tight as the Rockefellers. Once something went into it, it was like it never existed. They had spent a small fortune on alterations and upgrades and hadn't set foot in it since they had bought it. Sam wanted Charles and the Secretary of Defense safe. He wanted them secured somewhere that he could leave and not worry about them.

They had taken some convincing, particularly their newest recruit, Rebecca. She wanted to contact her HQ and arrange for a safe escort to the Israeli embassy. Sam ruled it out. He couldn't trust his own government despite having one of its most senior members under his protection, never mind a foreign one. No, they would rely on no-one else but themselves. The first plan of action was to go primitive. Rebecca and the Secretary of Defense's cell phones were ceremoniously smashed and their SIM cards discarded. They then stripped the Humvees and the eight bodies that scattered the ground of every weapon and piece of ammunition they could find. They threw it all into Sam's Toyota Camry and took off. If Rebecca's version of events was correct, nobody else had tracked them, never mind discovered what they were driving. The Camry was as anonymous as any car on the road.

They had driven non-stop, picked up a very surprised Senator's wife and settled into the lodge just as night was falling.

Clark came back into the lounge and pressed the button that closed the wall of glass that opened onto a terrace that seemed to hover above a lake below.

"Spectacular!"

Sam and Rebecca struggled to hide their smiles at the fiftieth utterance of the word 'spectacular' in the previous hour.

"Sorry," said Clark realizing she was repeating herself. "It's just…"

"Spectacular," offered Sam.

"Yes," smiled Clark. "And I am spectacularly tired so I'll bid you both good night." She tipped her head and headed towards her own spectacular room.

"How are you feeling?" asked Rebecca, looking at Sam.

"Tired," he said yawning.

"That's not what I meant," replied Rebecca, throwing a cushion at him.

During the drive, she, as had the Secretary of Defense, had heard everything that had happened. The attempts on the Senator's life and the murder of Sam's family and further attempts to stop him. Both Rebecca and the Secretary of Defense had sat dumbfounded as they listened to a story line straight from a spy thriller. None of this stuff happened in real life but here they were. Rebecca had offered little when questioned other than she worked for Mossad and was tasked with tracking down the nuclear bomb that was allegedly making its way to America. She made no mention of having being tasked with assisting with the assassination of the Senator and never would. Whoever had made an assessment that Mossad should be involved had made an error. The Senator was clearly a friend to Israel. She and Ben would have a very frank conversation about that error, although she had managed a quick chat with him during a pee break on the road. A public phone in a ladies' restroom had offered her the chance to report in and update Ben, particularly on the error in targeting the Senator. Ben had assured her this was an error and her job remained as previously, protect the Secretary and find the bomb.

Sam was silent as he thought of his wife and new born son. These were thoughts that he had managed to blank during the previous two days. A tear ran down his cheek. Rebecca watched a man, who she had come to admire as one of the strongest she had ever met, weep before her and she wept too.

"I too, lost a child," she said, letting the tears flow freely.

Over the next hour, she told Sam things she had never told another living soul. Her feelings flowed. The loss of her husband, her parents and the impact of losing her son, all came flooding out. She knew how Sam felt and the kindred spirits joined as one as each relived their worst nightmares, both as fresh as though they had just happened.

When it was time to go to bed, neither wanted to be alone and for the first time in almost nine years, Rebecca Cohen snuggled into a man as she fell asleep. Both slept soundly in each other's arms, kindred spirits healing their pain.

Sam woke up first and looked down at the young woman who lay in his arms. Her beauty was something to behold. Her dark hair cascaded down her bare back. The room was warm and the sheets had slipped off her body. The long t-shirt which had made the bed sharing so innocent when they fell asleep, lay discarded at the bottom of the bed. Sam could not help but notice how perfect her body was. Her translucent olive skin covered a perfect blemish free back and legs and there was no doubt she kept in shape. Her butt was quite frankly, as Clark would have said, spectacular. Realizing rather quickly that it was probably not the time to get aroused, he looked away and focused on Rebecca's head rather than her body. Her face lay on his right shoulder and a more beautiful face he probably had never seen. Her bone structure was European beauty. He looked away and closed his eyes. Avoiding arousal was failing again. The gentle sway of Rebecca's body became more succinct as he closed his eyes. Her breasts now bare against his bare chest heaved slightly with each breath she took. Her nipples, distinguishable from the rest of the breast, were pert and pressing into him. He felt the arousal again. He had to get up. This was wrong.

"Hmm, I see you're awake," said Rebecca before pressing her lips onto Sam's.

Sam didn't know how to respond. He was obviously aroused but it felt wrong. He had just lost his family but the tenderness in Rebecca's kiss was hard to reject and he accepted. There was no passion in their embrace or their kiss, only tenderness. Before long, Sam was on top of Rebecca and pushing inside her. Again, the wildness of raw sex between two strangers was not there. They moved almost as one, steady and slow, sharing the closeness of the moment and wanting it never to end. Both came as one, Sam exploding into Rebecca and hanging on as she struggled to contend with her own internal explosions. Afterwards, there was no awkwardness. They both held one another as lovers would after years spent in each other's arms. They shared a bond few would ever understand. They were two souls joined by grief, a grief few would ever have to bear.

"So, what now?" asked the Senator as he walked into Sam's room, spilling his coffee as he saw the two bodies entwined.

Sam pulled the sheet across Rebecca's naked body and stood up. "A shower I think," he said, guiding his brother back out of the bedroom.

"Yes, of course," he said trying to recover from spilling his coffee.

"Well that certainly killed the moment," said Rebecca as the door closed and she ducked into the en-suite bathroom, wrapped in the sheet.

Ten minutes later, both arrived in the kitchen and it was apparent that the Senator had failed to mention to the other house guests what he had seen. Sam thanked his brother with a nod and a wink. What happened between brothers stayed between brothers.

"So what's the plan?" asked the Secretary of Defense

"I want to leave you guys here with Agent Clark while I go and find out who's behind this and what's going on."

"I really should make some calls. I'm sure I can clear this up with the President. I can also have a battalion of special forces here within the hour," said the Secretary of Defense.

"To do what?"

"Protect us of course!"

"Just like your bodyguards did in Washington?" asked Clark.

"I'm sorry but there is no way we can trust anybody just now, not until we know what's going on," confirmed Sam. "I'll head back to Washington by plane and see what I can get from this Lawson guy. At least that's one lead we have to go on."

"What about me?" asked Rebecca.

The Senator looked at Sam knowingly as he waited for Sam to answer.

"Sorry, I hadn't thought about you. I just assumed you had your own orders."

"Keep the secretary alive which, if he's here and under Agent Clark's protection, seems irrelevant and secondly, track down the bomb. So I suppose I should do that."

"Fair enough, you can hitch a ride with me to the airport. Couple of hours OK for you?"

# Chapter 48

Akram 'Pock-Mark' looked up briefly as the last tip of Portugal disappeared into the murky horizon. He had dreaded the transition from the relatively calm Mediterranean Sea back to the wildness of the Atlantic Ocean. The swell below him had ensured he had been reacquainted with almost every morsel that had passed his lips in the previous two weeks. Another wave hit the boat, quickly followed by a further wave of nausea. He bent over and tried desperately to throw up. However, his stomach had been empty for some time.

"Are you OK, Sir?" asked one of his men from behind.

Quite the stupidest question he had been asked but he was in no position to answer. He could do nothing but wave the idiot away as he continued to wretch. He prayed for Allah to help him overcome the sickness. They had work to do. With everything now in place, it was imperative they not be stopped and searched. The Israelis knew about the weapons and if the Israelis knew, their allies would be alerted. That brought the US into the picture. If the US was involved, the UK would be brought in and if they were in, the Europeans would be warned. In short, once the Israelis knew, they had to assume pretty much every major intelligence and armed forces in the world would be on the look-out for the weapons and either a boat or a plane that could transport the weapon to America.

Pock-Mark had alerted his men to enact the next stage of their plan. Once they had cleared and were out of sight of landfall, a few selected containers would be moved on deck. Their outward facing panels had been painted in such a way that from a distance, they would appear to be part of the hull. The ship's structure would, to all intents and purposes, change and not by chance. From a distance, it resembled a US Navy supply ship. The movement of the containers had the added bonus of creating a wall behind which Pock-Mark's men could train. In addition, a huge tarpaulin now stretched across the top of the tallest containers, creating a vast roof over an indoor warehouse which expelled the constant drizzle and more importantly, the burning focus of American satellites.

# Chapter 49

**Oval office White House**

"Good. You're here. Take a seat, Andrew," instructed the President.

"Thank you, Mr President."

The National Security Adviser took the lead. "Gentlemen, we believe the Secretary of Defense has been kidnapped."

Russell nearly choked on the gulp of tea he had just taken. He had been assured by the CIA director that all traces of the attack in Georgetown had been covered."

"I'm sorry, did you say kidnapped?"

"Yes, he has now been out of contact since making an emergency appointment to see the President over 72 hours ago."

"72 hours? What the hell have we been doing for 72 hours?!" demanded Russell, the best form of defense was attack.

"Exactly what I said," said the President.

"We'll come back to that. So far, all we have is his limo which was found at a small airfield just south of Washington earlier this morning."

"Any sign of a struggle or a fight? I can't believe he'd go willingly."

"No, the limo is perfect, not so much as a scratch…"

The President's phone interrupted the meeting.

"Yes, send him in," instructed the President. Turning to the group, "It seems Director Johnson has some information."

The director of the CIA entered the room followed by one of his deputies whom Russell recognized as the Director of the Intelligence Department. Most definitely one of their men. He began to relax. Johnson must have worked some magic.

"Mr President," began the Director of the Intelligence Department. "As soon as we heard about the Secretary's disappearance, we checked a couple of things that hadn't previously made sense. As you are aware, the radioactive zone was declared non US territory after the accident. However, the Defense Department took ownership of the property rather than it be left ownerless and we believe it's being used by them for training purposes. However, it appears the land's now been sold but no monies have ever reached the Defense budget. Almost $250 million dollars are currently unaccounted for, as far as we can gather."

"And?"

"We have today uncovered a number of Swiss bank accounts in the name of James Murphy. To date, we have tracked just shy of $127 million dollars and are finding more every hour."

Andrew winced inwardly. He knew what Johnson was trying to do but if there was one thing you could be sure of, James Murphy was not a thief and the President would never believe it.

Johnson could see the President was unconvinced and produced a photo which he placed on the President's desk.

"This, Sir, is an agent within the Secret Service."

Russell leaned over and looked at the photo of the agent protecting Senator Baker.

"She also disappeared at approximately the same time as the Secretary."

The next few photos that were placed on the desk were masterpieces in the doctoring of photos. Had Russell not known that what was going on was a cover up, he would have sworn the compromising photos of Secretary Murphy and Clark were real.

"We believe she's influenced the Secretary and he's fled the country with her and the money. Leaving us and his wife with egg on our faces."

"Jesus, can I have a minute with Andrew please?" asked the President, putting the photos back on the desk. As always, the

Presidential request was not a question but an order. The others left the room immediately.

"Andrew, just what in the hell is going on?"

"Sorry?"

"I'm too old for all this shit, just tell me what's going on. Jim Murphy pulling that girl, don't be ridiculous, the man can't get it up and even if he did, he has other preferences which your bloody idiots out there have obviously missed. And we know the money's bullshit and you know I know the money's bullshit."

Russell shifted awkwardly in his seat. The President was right, it was all bullshit. Russell couldn't tell him the truth, he'd never accept what he had done. Despite his failings, the President believed wholeheartedly in democracy. Killing Senator Baker would be a step too far.

"I really don't know what's going on, Sir. I'm as in the dark as you are."

"Bullshit, Andrew! One last chance to come clean or I swear this will cost you the Presidency."

Andrew stood up and left the room. He was going to have to become President in the next few hours or they were all screwed.

Johnson watched as Russell came through the door. The look on his face said it all. Things had not gone well. He brushed past Johnson and whispered. "He has to go," before continuing out of the West Wing, ignoring the shouts of the President to "get back in here!"

As he stepped outside and into the gardens, he considered his options. There were none. Within the hour, the President would be calling the party and probably removing the Vice President from his position. That would mean handing the presidency to either Baker, if he survived, or the Democrats and pretty much ensure Russell's premature death at the hands of the Horsemen who were going to be monumentally pissed off.

He sat on the bench and looked out across the city that was almost his, the country that he had within his reach. All gone because of Charles Baker. If he ever did anything, he'd make sure that Baker died.

The soon-to-be former Vice President watched as a helicopter landed on the lawn. The President must have gotten fed up with the stink and decided to leave. He was probably going to meet the Party Chairman thought Russell, resigned to his fate. The Agents running towards him didn't even surprise him. The President may well have him arrested while he tried to find out what he had been up to. The helicopter was already increasing its engines and over the deafening sound, he struggled to hear the Agents informing him of his arrest.

He stood up and followed them as instructed, two behind and two in front. Jesus, what did they think he was going to do, run away?

The first agent directed him towards the West Wing and held the door for him. The first thing he noticed were the tears. Jesus Christ, a bit OTT he thought. The second agent held the next door open and directed him into the Oval Office where, no surprise, the Attorney General waited. The President really hadn't wasted any time. Not just anyone was going to read him his rights, the chief law enforcement officer of the United States was going to arrest him personally.

"Please place your right hand on the Bible and repeat after me."

Russell did what he was asked without thinking.

"I do solemnly swear that I will faithfully execute the Office of President of the United States and will to the best of my ability, preserve, protect and defend the Constitution of the United States."

Russell's mind was cart-wheeling. In the space of ten seconds, he had gone from being a political down-and-out to President. And he had no idea how! He repeated the sentence and was congratulated by the Attorney General and the two Secret Service agents still in the room.

"Would somebody mind telling me what in the hell just happened?"

"Mr President," said the agent who had come for him in the garden. "Sorry, I thought you might not have heard me. The President died from a suspected heart attack just a few minutes after your meeting. He died instantly, dead before he hit the floor, according to the doctor. He was rushed to Walter Reid but he was already dead when he left. The Attorney General was in the building and instructed us to bring you here to swear you in."

"Is Director Johnson still in the building?"

"I believe so, Sir. I believe he and the National Security Adviser were here when he died."

"I'd like to speak to him, please."

Two minutes later, Director Johnson was closing the door of the Oval Office behind him.

"Mr President," smiled the Director.

"What the hell just happened, Allan?"

"Let's just say, I'm very pleased you never touched those photos," winked the Director.

Russell thought back at the photos of Murphy and Clark that had been laid before the President. "But *you* touched them?"

"Very carefully and because I was wearing these." The Director pulled off what looked like a layer of skin from his thumb and forefinger.

"Where are the photos now?" panicked Russell. The National Security Adviser was as straight as they came and was not one of his men.

"The NSA told me to 'get them out of here' before we called anyone in. He didn't want scandalous photos linked to the President. They've already been incinerated."

"And before you ask, the toxin is untraceable. It's a naturally occurring toxin. The autopsy will show nothing but a massive heart attack, Mr President."

"But how did you know he needed to go?"

"Too many questions we couldn't answer were being asked and they were questions that could only be asked if they knew what was going on. They were onto us."

"Who?"

"That, Mr President, is not your concern. I have a feeling that those who were asking will either be silent or will be silenced."

"Thank-you, Allan."

"Not at all, Mr President. Is there anything else I can do for you?"

Russell thought back at the bench in the White House Garden.

"Please."

"Yes, Mr President?"

"Make sure that Baker dies soon."

# Chapter 50

Sam checked his disguise. The grey highlights were perfect and added at least five years to his age. The cheek and jaw implants were less noticeable but certainly altered his features and as Rebecca had promised, they ensured that any facial recognition software would not go ping when he walked past. The temporary implants, thanks to Rebecca's little make up bag of tricks, were uncomfortable but after a couple of hours, Sam could almost speak without sounding like he was, as Clark had put it so elegantly, a retard. Sam had a couple of identities in his hold-all that he had not used previously and fortunately one was a grey haired option. The implants, more to fool the cameras and computer software, did change his features but not so much that his photo wouldn't work with the less technically gifted humans who manned the departure gates.

After a thumbs up from the four they were leaving behind, Sam and Rebecca climbed into the car and headed for the local airport, Glacier Park International. Having looked at the destinations available, Rebecca had asked for clarification from her American counterparts as to why an airport with no international departures or arrivals warranted the International moniker. With no more than a shrug in response, she had booked two flights for her and Sam to New York LaGuardia leaving at 2.15pm flying via Minneapolis. Once there, they would go their separate ways. Sam would travel back to Washington by train. They had agreed Washington airports would be too risky. Meantime, Rebecca would go back to her day job and track down the bomb.

On check-in, Rebecca flashed her FBI badge and ensured she remained armed. Sam had no such trick and was feeling somewhat underdressed for whatever lay ahead. As they arrived in Minneapolis, Rebecca made a beeline for the first electronics store she could find and purchased a prepaid cell phone. She placed the new phone in its own little locker as she turbo-charged the battery for $1.00. The machine promised a full charge in 30 minutes. She gave it ten before she pulled it out and dialed Ben for any updates.

"Where the hell have you been?"

"I told you where I was. Now I'm in Minneapolis."

"I need you in France!"

"France, what the hell can I do in France?"

"I just got a call, we may have found Deif."

Rebecca's heart beat trebled as she heard the name. She was going to get another chance to avenge Joshua. She had had to let Deif go once and it wasn't going to happen again.

"I'm on my way. Where?"

"Get to Nice. I'll have somebody meet you there. Oh the Secretary, is he safe?"

"Very."

As Rebecca digested the news and looked for a sales desk to change her ticket, Sam was staring at a television screen as the news came through. The President was dead and President Russell was about to address the nation.

Now they were really screwed thought Sam, adding the former president to the list of casualties. The coincidence was just too much to take in. The stakes had just increased ten-fold. A dirty Vice President was very much easier to deal with than a dirty President.

Sam watched as the sound-bites came through, one of which was from James Lawson, industrialist and friend. He was interviewed as he entered the airport at Washington.

"Sorry, it really is terrible news. He was a wonderful man and an outstanding President. I'm sorry but I really have to catch my flight, the French President is expecting me this evening. Thank you."

Rebecca appeared with her new tickets to bid Sam farewell. Up until that very moment, she really didn't think it would be hard.

"I'm sorry, change of plans, I need to get to France," said Sam. Rebecca's mood instantly improved. The thought of a flight to Paris with nothing more than her hatred for Deif to keep her company had not been a pleasant prospect.

"I'd better go and make it two changes then. It seems we'll be accompanying each other a little further," she smiled.

# Chapter 51

President Andrew Russell made the speech of his life. He thanked his predecessor for all of his hard work and devotion to the United States and lightened the mood with some personal and witty insights into the man who had been their President for seven years. He talked of his promise to continue on with the great programme of bills and reforms that his predecessor had started and most importantly assured the country that the government was as strong as it had ever been.

He walked back from the briefing room refusing to take any questions from the press. His speech had contained everything he wanted to say at this very sad time. As he closed the door on the Oval Office, alone for the first time for many hours, he sat in the President's chair. His chair. Behind the iconic Resolute Desk, a gift from Queen Victoria to President Rutherford B. Hayes. And finally, he smiled. It was his. After decades of kissing ass and sucking up, he had made it. The highest office in the land.

A catalogue of calls he had received and was required to return was basically a list of every President and Prime Minister from around the world. They were all anxious to ensure that America was still their ally and that President Russell would only improve their relationship. One call stood out from the others. He was not a head of state or government but President Russell knew that he held just as much sway.

"Ben, how are you my friend?" asked Russell.

"Mr President."

Russell instantly noted that 'Andrew my dear boy' had been dropped.

"It's good to hear from you. How are you?" enquired Ben.

"As well as can be expected." Russell thought it best to play down his elation.

"Of course." Ben was no fool and knew exactly how President Russell was feeling. He knew him better than Russell knew himself. "I know how close you and the President were."

"Thank you, Ben."

Formalities over, Ben turned to business. "A couple of quick updates for you."

Russell was about to stop Ben in his tracks He was president and didn't get involved in detail any longer but just as he was about to speak, he thought better of it.

"OK, shoot!"

"OK." Ben could sense the reluctance. It seemed Russell was already getting a little over comfortable in his newly found position. "If you'd rather I updated somebody else, I would understand, Mr President."

Russell realized that his tone had not hidden the feeling that that was now being beneath him.

"Absolutely not. I'm sorry, it's just been a very long day."

Ben was going to have to watch Russell very carefully. He'd give him a little while to settle down but it was important that he did not forget his place and who his real friends were.

"Firstly, I'm very relieved to say that we may have a lead on the nuclear weapon heading towards America and secondly I have an address you wanted."

Russell ignored the lead and jumped straight to the address. "Baker's address?"

"Yes, my operative's no longer in the vicinity and with you being President, it removes some of the concern as regards Ararat. However, James Murphy's a friend and I'd greatly appreciate your trying to save him."

"I promise that we'll send only the best people, rest assured."

They ended the call and Russell called Johnson with the details, emphasizing that extra special care was required. It was extremely important that nobody, he emphasized, nobody, should be left breathing.

Ben made a call himself but his man wasn't picking up. He left a message and hoped he'd get it in time.

# Chapter 52

James Lawson could seriously do without having dinner with the French President but it had been planned some months earlier and Lawson was very keen to get his hands on a major French utility company. The deal was worth billions and the payback in synergies within his own organizations was being measured in months. It really was too great an opportunity to miss.

He had spent the last hour calming down John Mellon. The death of the President was as great a shock to the Horsemen as to everyone else and had certainly made their plan almost impossible. Russell would, as Mellon put it, prefer to have a tree hugging leftie lesbian than him as a running mate in the coming election. Mellon had been assured of his place as President as long as everything had run to plan. This was definitely not to plan. A conference call had been arranged with his counterparts and all five came on line as planned. He wondered at the technology. He was flying almost 600 mph and 40,000 feet in the air but could still video conference, it was beyond him.

"How's the new jet, James?" asked Koch.

"Very nice, glad I went for the 650, just a little more comfortable and certainly faster than the 550."

Harkness did not rise to the bait. He had just ordered a Gulfstream 550 himself.

"Gentlemen, what the hell are we going to do?" Mellon was in no mood for the one-up-manship bullshit.

"He obviously outflanked us. I'll give him that," offered Hathaway.

"Personally, I didn't think he had the balls," said Koch who knew him best.

"I don't think he has," suggested Lawson, the first to put any doubt as to Russell's guilt on the table.

"You don't think he did it?" asked a surprised Harkness.

"I know he didn't do it. There is no way Andrew Russell grew enough balls to take down a sitting president. Jesus, he almost wet himself over the Baker fiasco."

Silence followed as each of the attendees considered the viewpoint. It was Mellon who broke the silence.

"That, my dear friend, is exactly what we need to find out. While Russell has someone like that at his side, we'll be sidelined."

"Sidelined!" exclaimed Koch angrily.

"Absolutely." Lawson was not one of the world's richest businessmen for no reason. He read people, understood how their thought processes worked and used it to his advantage. "Trust me, you put a call into his office and I guarantee you the little shit will be too busy to see you."

"Never."

"We'll see but anyway once we find out who did it, we need to take them down and we'll get our pawn back."

"Now gentlemen, if you don't mind, I need to grab some shut-eye before I land. Good evening."

\*\*\*

Half an hour later, Ben Meir was reading through the transcript of the videoconference. He had been keeping an eye on the Horsemen for some time and had his comms team keep a close eye on anything they got up to, particularly as a group. Ben knew the whole sordid detail of their plan to make Mellon VP and ultimately President. He of course had no intention of allowing the right-wing fascist to come anywhere near the presidency. It was Mellon who would have an unfortunate accident, not Russell.

Ben had been reliving his call with Russell and it had made him very uneasy. The change in his demeanor had been obvious even over the phone. However, if what the Horsemen believed were true, it meant Russell had not turned, as Ben had thought, entirely to the dark side but it did mean that Russell probably unwittingly was going to be beholden to whoever had made him King. The Kingmaker was the person Ben worried most about and it was he that Ben would have to ensure was dealt with very soon. Otherwise, everything he had planned for Ararat could be in jeopardy.

Ben picked up the phone. He needed to know exactly how the president had died and more importantly, who was there at the time of death.

# Chapter 53

It had taken them the best part of a day to get there but at last the house lay before them. It had been over a thousand miles, by plane, car and foot, by far the hardest part. Neither of them were used to the thick mountain wilderness and would have more than a few scars to show for their efforts.

"So, at any point, are you going to tell me what we are doing here?" asked Zak, just a little frustrated at the lack of trust being shown by the Sheikh. In fact, the Sheikh had told Zak to call him Benny, it sounded Italian and would cover his middle-Eastern looks without sounding Muslim.

"Let's just say that through my contacts, it has come to my attention that in that house is the Secretary of Defense."

"And?"

"We're here to get him!"

The Sheikh removed his backpack and emptied its contents in front of them. There were two pistols, a few stun grenades, two pairs of Night Vision Goggles and a length of plastic explosives for blowing open doors.

Zak was somewhat surprised by the last few hours and couldn't help wonder out loud. "I didn't think you got involved at this level?"

"If an opportunity arises and no-one else is around, I'll do whatever needs to be done," he replied with some irritation and handed Zak one of the pistols, a pair of Night Vision Goggles and a couple of grenades.

The Sheikh was beginning to wish he had never involved Zak but with Deif sending a bomb to America, operatives were thin on the ground and he needed help. Once in position, just a few hundred yards from the house, the Sheikh ran through the plan. A few tweaks later they were ready to go. Darkness was falling and the lights were beginning to come on in the home below them.

*\*\**

A phone ringing in the house alerted Mrs Charles Baker to the unwanted visitors. The alarm company alerted them to potential intruders. Mrs Baker thanked the alarm company very much and immediately told Clark and her husband about the call. There was little they could do. They certainly couldn't call the police and their friends were miles away in Helena, the State capital.

Following the call, Clark ensured all windows and doors were locked. It could of course just be deer or wildlife knocking the contacts but she didn't think so. Coincidences were something non-professionals believed in. Somebody had found the location, it had only been a matter of time in any event.

*\*\**

Just as the Sheikh was about to give the 'go' signal, he stopped. A bright spot had appeared on the side of the house. He knew it wasn't coming from inside. It was a tiny spot almost undetectable to the human eye. In fact, it was undetectable to the human eye, he realized, as he removed the Night Vision Goggles. Where the spot should have been was nothing, no sign of any light at all. Putting the goggles back on, there it was, clear as day.

He nudged Zak and pointed to the spot. Zak took one look and knew exactly what was happening. He scanned the tree line with his goggles and picked up the contacts he knew were going to be there.

"Shit!"

"Exactly, I think we should pull back, don't you?"

"Yep!"

Both men began to crawl back, keeping their heads down and careful not to alert the others to their presence. Once at a safe distance and hopefully out of sight, they hightailed it back to their rental car parked just off the main road. They had no intention of being anywhere near the house when all hell broke loose.

***

The Avenger had proven its worth already and having lost nearly twenty good men already, CIA Director Johnson was not taking any chances. A small team of the Clandestine Service had arrived in Montana earlier in the day and made its way to the mountainside house. Their job on this occasion was simply to paint the target for the weapon which would be dispatched from the Avenger some 20,000 feet above them.

The laser designator was switched on as the Avenger came into range. Although naked to the human eye, there was no need to highlight their arrival. One minute after lighting up the target, they got the heads up that the weapon was on its way. As Ben had predicted, the Americans were using a sledgehammer to crack a nut. A GBU-24 Paveway III bomb was making its way towards the house, Two thousand pounds that would turn the cabin into matchsticks if there were any pieces left large enough to be considered useful.

The laser spotters took cover as they received warning of the bomb's imminent impact. The operator watched as the bomb glided right into the side of the house exactly where the laser told it to. A microsecond later, the house ceased to exist. A demolition team would take weeks to do what was accomplished in less than a second.

The Clandestine Team took one look at the area and devastation and left the scene. Although in the middle of nowhere, it wasn't going to be long before the locals came to see what had just woken up half the state. Their job was well and truly accomplished.

A very pleased CIA Director informed his President of a successful conclusion to the mission.

# Chapter 54

**Paris, Charles de Gaulle.**

Sam and Rebecca sailed through customs and immigration. Their false identities worked perfectly. As Rebecca pointed at the link that would take her to her internal flight to Nice, it was time to say farewell. Sam was about to say goodbye when he thought better of it. He was a United States serviceman, retired but ultimately the job being undertaken by Rebecca was to safeguard the US and, as such, he had a duty to assist. He had already discovered that James Lawson was spending the day and evening with the president, so he was going to be hanging about in any event.

"How far is Nice?"

"About 90 minutes," replied Rebecca.

"So I could be back in Paris in plenty of time for a midnight visit to Mr Lawson?"

Rebecca smiled. "I don't see why not!"

While Sam bought a ticket to accompany her to Nice, she called Ben. The news was not good. He informed her of the bombing of Baker's hideaway, assuring her that he had nothing whatsoever to do with it. He then brought her up to speed on Deif.

Rebecca watched as Sam paid for his ticket. She didn't want him to leave. For the first time in a very long time, she was enjoying someone else's company. If she told him about the bombing, he would leave immediately. She would hold off until after the job in Nice, she thought. Then she'd tell him.

"Everything OK?"

"Perfect. He's still there, a team from the Paris office have been watching him."

"What, they've not taken him in?"

"Oh no, he's mine. I made someone promise me a long time ago that I would be allowed to take this guy down."

"We'll be there by 12.30 and the last flight back is at 20.55, so you've got me for another eight hours."

"Excellent," beamed Rebecca, fighting her better judgment.

Having managed to secure his seat at the last minute, Sam was forced to sit next to a rather loud and annoying Brit who, by 11.00 a.m., was already on his fourth G and T and about whom, by the end of the flight, Sam knew pretty much everything. He was in shipping and had decided somewhat belatedly to take a last minute holiday down to Cannes. He'd been in business in Paris and just thought, sod it, what's the point. He'd spent the last month trying to find a ship that could get a shipment from China to France, anywhere in France and had failed. In the middle of a worldwide recession, he couldn't get hold of a boat. God alone knew where they all were. As far as he was aware, nobody had been able to find a ship for months, they were all at bloody sea. Of course they were at bloody sea, he had screamed as he recounted the story to Sam, they're ships, that's where they're supposed to be! Anyway, with no ships to hire he'd thought sod it, a week in the sun and I'll worry about it when I get back.

Sam was very happy to reacquaint himself with Rebecca who laughed as he recounted his ear bashing. She, on the other hand, had sat next to the most charming gentleman who had offered her a trip on his yacht if she were free over the next few days.

Sam couldn't help feeling the tiniest bit jealous as he thought Rebecca may be interested in the offer. He was very much relieved when she added the creep had given her a card after kissing her hand. She promptly produced the card and threw it in the nearest bin.

A small toot alerted Rebecca to the Paris Head who was waiting for her in a small Renault Twingo. As far as Sam was concerned, all European cars were small but the French and Italians had, it seemed, made it an art-form. Sam squeezed into the back, all six foot two of him, into a space meant for what Sam could only assume was a small child under the age of five. Rebecca introduced Sam as a colleague and left it at that. Sam noticed the demeanor of the Mossad Paris Head who would be considered very senior within Mossad. Rebecca was very obviously his senior.

The Paris Head briefed them both on the way to Deif's location, some 60km away, in a small coastal village called Anthéor. The villa was, as the Head described, rather spectacular. Set on the top of a small cliff, it was very secluded and extremely secure with only two points of entry. The main gate and a set of stairs that led up from a private beach to the main house some 50 meters up the cliff. His men had used a boat and gone as near as they dare without being spotted. An eight-foot gate protected the entry point at the beach. The whole perimeter was surrounded by a security wall topped with razor wire. Its owner was a wealthy Arab, not on any watch lists, well, until then, of course. His name was Yousif Fayyad.

"Jesus, all sounds a bit extreme."

"Actually it's fairly standard down here. Most of these villas sit empty for eleven months of the year. Burglars used to have a field day but not anymore."

"So what's the plan?" asked Sam.

"Simple, we're going to walk right up to the front door and invite ourselves in."

Sixty minutes later and after securing some handguns from the team on site, Rebecca and Sam, wearing shorts and t-shirts, did exactly that.

Rebecca rang the bell next to the gate and waited for an answer. It never came. She knew Deif was still there. She rang again and again, making it clear she wasn't leaving.

"What?" came the gruff voice in very poor French.

Rebecca had spotted the camera and knew she was being watched. "Yousif, it's me, I thought I saw you were there," she answered in perfect Palestinian Arabic.

"Yousif is not here, I am a friend," he continued to speak in French.

"A friend of Yousif, is a friend of mine! I am Noor, buzz me in. Yousif always lets us use his pool," she switched to French with an Arabic accent.

"I'm sorry, I'm busy," replied Deif, again keeping to French.

"That's OK, we'll be quiet, I promise."

"Look, I'm very sorry but I'm very busy."

"Well I'm just going to stay here until you let us in."

Sam was embarrassed at her persistence and that was despite knowing why they were there.

Deif gave in and hit the buzzer. He didn't want to attract attention and if she kept up her theatrics that was exactly what she was going to do. He didn't want to kill one of Yousif's friends; particularly one so cute but he had no choice. He had warned them but their persistence was their downfall. He could not be exposed. He'd deal with those two idiots and move to one of his alternative safe houses. Italy was just as nice this time of year, he thought. He walked towards the door and held it open slightly. The silenced pistol was hidden by the door. As soon as they got inside, he'd kill them.

She really was very beautiful he thought. Yousif was going to be very pissed off. He had always liked the ladies and could imagine this one was one of his favorites. Both laughed and joked as they neared the house. Deif actually felt quite guilty as he began to open the door to Yousif's friends who were just looking to laze by a beautiful pool.

If he had to tell you what happened next, he'd swear he had no idea. One moment he was opening the door and preparing to shoot the two as they walked in and the next, he was lying on the floor, his arm most obviously broken as the pain and angle of his elbow joint proclaimed.

It had been quite simple. As they neared the door, Rebecca had begun to remove her t-shirt, catching Deif's attention. Sam launched himself at the door and smashed through it and Deif like a tornado. Deif crashed to the floor and landed on his arm in a most unnatural position, instantly blacking out as the pain overwhelmed his nervous system.

He woke up to find his arm hanging limply and the pain searing through him. The very beautiful woman was staring at him with nothing short of absolute rage and it seemed was being restrained with some difficulty by the man. Deif was in trouble, a great deal of trouble.

# Chapter 55

**Port of Haifa, Israel**

Saul kicked off his boots and sat back in his chair. He had refused to work late. He needed to be home that evening. His daughter was coming over with their granddaughter and they had not seen nor heard from them since the blackout. All communications had now been out of action for a week. His wife normally spoke to his daughter twice a day. To say she was looking forward to the visit would have been an understatement and something Saul had been assured by his wife, in a tone that left no room for maneuver, he did not want to miss.

Saul had heard snippets from other dock workers that the blackout was not just in the Haifa area, contrary to what the police and army had informed them. Rumor was spreading that it was in fact the whole of Israel that had no communications. His daughter worked for the Intelligence Department and he was very keen to know what her take was on the situation. If anything untoward was really going on, she would know. Only that day, Saul had talked to one of the truck drivers, something the army were keen to avoid but when you've got to go to the bathroom, you've got to go! He had told Saul that Tel-Aviv was also blacked out, no phones, TV, radio, nothing. He said it was like living in the 1800s. So it was confirmed, Haifa was not on its own. If Tel-Aviv was out, the rumors about the whole country were probably true. Saul began to piece everything together. The massive increase in work at the docks, the total lack of communications across the country, the lack of food. They weren't heading for war, he thought, they were already at war! He prayed for his sons and wondered if they were even alive.

He watched and waited for the door to open but nothing. His daughter and granddaughter never arrived. They couldn't call to check where they were. They couldn't contact the hospitals or police to find out if she was OK. They just sat there and at midnight, turned out the light and went to bed. Neither slept. His wife cried into her pillow while Saul grieved for his perhaps already dead sons.

At 2.00 a.m., both were startled by a knock at the door. Saul feared the worst. His worst nightmare had come true. He rushed to the door pulling on his dressing gown and undid the dead bolt. A key turned on the other side and his daughter stood in front of him.

"Jesus, Dad, you don't need a bloody deadlock. What's the point of me having a key if you deadbolt the door?"

Saul reached out to hug his daughter but was unceremoniously shoved out of the way by his wife who, on hearing her daughter's voice careered towards her, arms outstretched. After almost squeezing the life out of her, she set about preparing her a plate of food for her "too skinny" daughter who wasn't looking after herself properly.

Satisfied that her daughter was not dying from anorexia and getting all of the news on her grand-daughter, she eventually let Saul find out the news on what was happening to the country.

"I'm afraid I know very little," she said, trying to answer her father's tirade of questions which all came down to two - what was happening and was there any news on her brothers? "Every day we go through a list of action plans, it's like some massive project. We each have very specific duties and none of us know what the others are doing but the workload is massive. I didn't get finished until gone midnight tonight and I'm due back at 6.00 a.m. It really is crazy."

"And your brothers?" prompted Saul.

"They're fine," she answered nonchalantly. She was more interested in unloading her issues. "My department's moving in the next day or so. We don't know where to yet, maybe one of those new fancy buildings in Jerusalem."

"What? The whole department?"

"Yep, in fact we're the last ones left. All five floors below us are now empty."

"It seems everyone is moving!" blurted Saul's wife.

Both looked at her. "What do you mean?" asked Saul.

"The supermarket. Every day I go. It's the only way to get food. Anyway, every day, the line is shorter and shorter. When I ask where so and so is, I just get a 'oh they moved away' but nobody ever knows where!"

Saul looked at his daughter in search of an answer but she simply shrugged her shoulders adding. "I'm stuck inside an office all day long. People are in their beds when I go to work and when I get home."

The more they talked, the more mysterious it all became. Eventually, as she was leaving, Saul returned to her brothers.

"So have you heard from your brothers?"

"Not since they went overseas!" she replied, opening the door.

"When did they go overseas?" both parents asked in unison.

"Months ago," she replied.

"No, you're mistaken," said Saul taking a note from the side table in the entrance hallway and passing it to his daughter.

She read it and looked at them in bewilderment. The note was from her brother and showed him pictured on a tank on the Israeli border. She looked at the date, it was just two weeks earlier. Saul handed her another two, likewise, showing her brothers and all dated at a time she knew they had been posted overseas.

# Chapter 56

"Rebecca, Rebecca! Calm down! You have to remain calm!" Sam held her back but it was futile, the moment he let her go, she'd go straight for Deif.

Deif it seemed had resigned himself to his fate and sat quietly in the small kitchen chair they had perched him on. A small grimace appeared as each wave of pain from his broken arm hit home.

"Just five minutes, just leave me alone with him for five minutes!" she pleaded. Ultimately she knew that the information he had was far more important than her vengeance but she could try.

Sam was watching Deif as he fought to contain Rebecca. Something was wrong. The man looked serene. In fact, almost happy. He held information that would undoubtedly ruin his plot to destroy Israel and yet he wasn't in the least annoyed or frustrated.

"Stop!" shouted Sam, shocking Rebecca into doing just that. She stopped pushing and stood still.

Sam walked towards Deif and felt the bullet whistle past him before it tore Deif's right knee cap clean off. The second he had turned his back on her, she had whipped out her gun and taken the shot. Sam turned towards her as Deif crumpled to the floor, a contented smile revealing her thoughts. She placed the gun in the rear of her shorts and folded her arms. OK, she'd behave.

Sam lifted Deif whose arm and leg were obviously causing some discomfort. He struggled to sit up straight but did as well as he could manage. He was going to die the big man, thought Sam, for which he had to give the guy some credit. He had come across a lot of hard bastards who, when the chips were down, shat themselves and cried like babies. Deif was a man who believed in his cause.

"This can be easy or even more painful than it already has been and trust me, she's just started. Where are the weapons?" asked Sam reasonably.

Deif just smiled in response. It was not the smile of a man panicking but a man smiling because he knew they'd never get it out of him. That was not an option. Everybody talked, no matter how hard or how much people thought they could tolerate pain, everybody talked and more importantly everybody in the game knew it.

Sam began to worry. Perhaps they did have the wrong guy. Maybe Deif wasn't behind it all.

He tied Deif to the chair and walked Rebecca out of the room to speak to her privately.

"Are you sure this is the guy?"

"One hundred percent. I watched him plot this thing from the start. It's definitely him."

"He's certain he's beaten us. That is not a man accepting defeat through there. That's a guy who knows we won't beat him."

Rebecca was no fool and she had picked up the same vibes. She had caught many of Deif's men and made them all talk. This was very different from any one of those.

"Let me speak to him?" offered Rebecca.

Sam shook his head. "No, it's too personal for you."

"I'll behave," she said, ignoring Sam. Ultimately, this was her operation and Sam was a bystander. She walked back towards Deif, removing a few unsavory looking implements from a kitchen drawer on the way. The corkscrew seemed to catch Deif's eye she thought and selected that first.

As she neared Deif, he smiled through the pain. "Rebecca, Rebecca Cohen I presume?"

Rebecca was taken aback at Deif knowing her name.

"I see you are surprised I know your name. Trust me, you are a very famous woman in our organization. To be honest, your beauty has been undersold. Had we known of your true beauty, we may have caught you ourselves. It makes you memorable. However, your talents and abilities I fear from my capture have certainly lived up to their reputation. To die at your hands will be an honorable death."

"Who said anything about dying?" said Rebecca, lighting a lighter and heating the end of the corkscrew.

"The man responsible for killing your son, the man responsible for you having to watch your precious Joshua be blasted."

Sam caught Rebecca as she flew at the mention of her son's name. Despite Sam's best efforts, her foot swung and caught Deif squarely on the jaw, sending him still tied to the chair across the room, emitting an ear piercing scream as his knee-capless leg crashed into the floor.

"He wants you to kill him, you fool!" screamed Sam as he put Rebecca down and straightened Deif once again.

Rebecca tried to maintain her breathing and heart rate as both were racing. She lit the lighter again and began to heat the corkscrew once more. She looked at Deif and figured which of the two was his biggest weakness, balls or eyes. It always came down to the balls and eyes with the really tough ones. She figured on the eyes. Deif liked to see the outcome of his actions, blindness for him would be his biggest weakness.

As Rebecca placed the tip of the white hot corkscrew next to his eyeball, Deif smiled. "You do not disappoint." She had found his weakness almost straight away. "You were a worthy adversary," he said moving his jaw.

Sam dived across the room, knocking Rebecca aside as he went to grab Deif's mouth but it was too late. Deif had succeeded. He had beaten them.

Rebecca tried to understand what had happened but as Sam got up, the small white bubbles foaming from Deif's breathless mouth said it all.

"Cyanide! The sneaky bastard had a cyanide pill! Shit!!!" exclaimed Sam.

"But we checked his mouth, it was empty," said an exasperated Rebecca. Their only lead and probably the only person on the planet who knew where all the weapons were lay dead at their hands.

"False tooth, how fucking cold war is that?!"

Rebecca looked down at the dead Deif who congratulated her. Cheeky bastard, she thought, kicking him in frustration. She called in the rest of the team. Hopefully they'd find something in the house that would help them. She needed some good news for Ben. This was their last hope.

# Chapter 57

President Russell welcomed the small group into his office. Henry Preston, Jim Gates and Allan Johnson had maintained a somber mood while waiting in the Oval Office's anteroom. Finally, they were called and entered the office. As the door closed behind them, Henry and Jim rushed forward to congratulate their man on becoming President. Both looked at Allan, surprised at his lack of enthusiasm for their President. Allan stepped forward and shook the President's hand. Neither Jim or Henry were aware that he had already met and congratulated their President. Jim and Henry shared a look, there was something they were missing. It had always been a cat fight with Johnson. He always wanted to be the one that pleased Russell, always wanting to be favorite and now they had their man as President, he seemed very relaxed and most comfortable. The eager to please attitude had disappeared.

"Gentlemen, at last I can relax," announced Russell, kicking his shoes off and sitting on a large sofa in front of a blazing fire.

Preston walked to the drinks cabinet. "A drink, Mr President?"

"Excellent idea. A scotch, please. No, sorry, scratch that, Champagne Henry!"

"Jim? Allan?" asked Henry, raising the bottle.

"Absolutely," replied Jim enthusiastically.

"Please," nodded Allan.

Jim and Henry shared a look as Henry poured the champagne and Jim got up to pass them around.

"The President," announced Henry, raising his glass.

Allan and Jim joined and toasted their man.

"Thank you, I couldn't have done it without you guys." Neither Jim or Henry missed the look that Allan got as the President accepted their toast. They were definitely missing something.

"Well gentlemen, down to business. I believe Allan has some news that may make our day even more special!"

"Yes I have, Sir," he beamed. "I'm pleased to announce that earlier this evening, a certain thorn in the President's side was removed once and for all!"

Jim and Henry looked at each other. Henry, as ever, took the lead. "Senator Baker?"

"The now dearly departed Senator Baker. So sad " confirmed the President.

"Fantastic!" said Henry, looking at Allan, who reported to him. The look made it clear this was something that he should have known.

"Oh there was a little collateral damage, I think that's how you guys term it." The President reached over and hit a buzzer. "Can you send in Tom, please."

"Gentlemen, you all know Tom. Thanks Honey," he added, dismissing the young secretary who had shown Tom in, a young secretary that none of the men could take their eyes off."

"You can't call her Honey, Mr President," said Jim, as the stunning young blonde closed the door behind her.

Russell laughed at the confusion. "I know, but that really is her name, fantastic eh, certainly brightens the place up!"

As the laughter died down, he resumed. "You know Tom, our excellent Deputy Secretary of Defense and a man who shares our goals in life?"

They all nodded, understanding that Tom was one of them, one of the President's men.

"Well it seems that Tom here is in line for a promotion following the tragic demise of Secretary of Defense James Murphy."

Henry and Jim quickly computed the link, the Secretary of Defense was the collateral damage. So the rumors of James

Murphy's mysterious disappearance were true, they both thought. There was a lot happening that they knew nothing about.

All congratulated the soon to be announced new Secretary of Defense.

"What are you going to say happened to James Murphy?" asked Henry, beginning to think beyond the moment.

The President looked at Allan. "Allan."

"A tragic accident, a gas explosion at Senator Baker's hunting lodge in Montana has robbed America of two wonderful statesmen, something along those lines. We're still working on it but that's the gist."

Henry did not miss the President's interaction with Allan, they had obviously been working closely on this.

"Only one thing I'd note, it was a ski lodge, not a hunting lodge. Charles Baker was no friend of the hunters so a hunting lodge may sound a little strange," offered Henry. It was all in the details and it made the point to the President that if he were getting too close to Johnson, detail was not his forte, unlike Henry.

"Why don't we just go for Senator Baker's lodge, lest we upset any skiers!" retaliated Johnson, pathetically enough that everybody just moved on.

"Have you had any thoughts about a VP?" asked Henry moving onto more important issues.

"Not yet, there are quite a few roles I want to shuffle around," replied Russell ominously.

"I would remind you, should anything happen to you just now, we'd have the Speaker of the House inaugurated as President," warned Henry. The Speaker of the House was a particularly fierce woman who ruled the House of Representatives with an iron fist and to make matters worse, was a Democrat. To say she put the fear of God into people, understated her position. The Speaker of the House was second in line in the presidential line of succession. Without a Vice President, she would be the heir apparent.

Henry could see the President hadn't considered this and the very subtle look at Johnson suggested he had not reminded the President of this point.

"Of course, but I don't want to make any knee jerk decisions. I'm sure you guys will keep me safe, at least for a few days," joked Russell.

Russell was no fool and could see Henry was a little put out. Obviously, Johnson had not kept him in the loop, something which he'd have a private word with Allan about. He didn't want Henry fully in the loop, the less people who knew about the real reason for the demise of the former President, the better. However, even from that one meeting, it was clear that Russell needed more than Johnson by his side. The hunting lodge would have been a disaster but then, from what he had heard, the lodge was far more hunting than skiing but Henry knew Charles Baker best.

"Gentlemen, can I just add that it's because of you that I sit here today and let me assure each of you, I will never forget that. You are my team and we will stick together and make this work," he said standing and walking to each of them and shaking their hands. The meeting was over and, he thought, on a positive note.

Just as he was about to ask Allan for a quick word, Henry asked to speak with him privately.

"Of course, Henry," he agreed, motioning for Allan to wait in the anteroom. Which Henry noted.

"What's up Henry?" he asked as they returned to the sofas.

"I'm a bit disappointed being out of the loop on the Baker thing."

"That's what I want a word with Allan about, it won't happen again I noticed you weren't happy and trust me, none of it was intentional."

"Thank you, Mr President," replied Henry genuinely. His next point was dependent on how the President had answered the first.

"I would like to be considered for the VP position, Mr President."

President Russell was somewhat taken aback at the declaration but considering Henry's expertise and attention to detail, he was an exceptional candidate.

"Well that sort of came in from left field, obviously I haven't had time to think about my own role, never mind the VP." Russell was struggling, he really didn't know what to say.

"Obviously you need time to think, Mr President." Henry saved him any further embarrassment. "I just wanted you to know that I'd be honored, were you to offer me the role." Henry stood up, shook the President's hand and left.

Allan entered almost immediately. President Russell got up and walked behind his desk. He explained to Allan the importance of keeping Henry in the loop. Allan looked somewhat uninterested.

"Is something wrong?" asked the President.

"No, it's just Henry's sort of irrelevant. I'm hoping you'll be making me your VP, so keeping Henry in the loop's sort of old news."

"I've not even thought about my role…" began the President.

Allan interrupted. "Of course I'm not expecting you to make your decision straight away, Mr President. It's just, after all we've been through, I thought you might consider me."

There wasn't anything Russell could pinpoint as a threat in the way Allan put his offer; his voice, his tone, his words were all perfectly friendly. It was the eyes, they gave away the soul and it was only then, at that moment, that Russell realized just how dark Allan Johnson's soul really was. He also realized, looking around the Oval Office, just how much of a hold that dark soul now had over him and he even began to consider if it was worth it.

# Chapter 58

At 7.15pm they called it quits. There was nothing, the house was empty. The backpack that Deif had when the Paris Head had followed him was there but nothing else. Other than a few clothes and a couple of books, nothing. The books had been scanned and x-rayed, no hidden compartments, no flash drives, nothing. No wonder he had smiled, he really had beaten them, thought Rebecca.

Sam came in from having checked the grounds, nothing. Deif had obviously gone there, safe in the knowledge that his plans were in motion and required no further action. Sam spotted the two books on the kitchen counter, one of which made him smile.

"Jesus, I loved these books. My uncle who lived in London used to send them over every year without fail, this and the… God, what was its name…"

"The Hotspur," offered one of the Paris Mossad men.

"That was it, every year I'd get The Victor and Charles would get The Hotspur."

Rebecca looked at Sam and the Mossad guy like they were mad, as they started to chat about a comic book from 1981 called The Victor.

After five minutes reminiscing, Sam pulled his thoughts back to the job in hand.

"I need to get to the airport," he announced, hoping somebody would realize he needed a lift.

Rebecca cottoned on and asked the Paris Head for somebody to take Sam to Nice asap.

"I'll come with you to the airport, I need a break from this place. I'll call in on the way."

As they made to leave, Sam's fellow comic enthusiast tossed him the Victor. "It's no use to us, something to read on the plane!" he offered.

"Thanks," said Sam tucking it into his small back pack.

Squeezed back into the child's seat, they made their way back to Nice. Rebecca called Ben and dropped the devastating news that Deif was a dead end. Ben had admitted the false tooth cyanide pill was very old hat and certainly not anything he had seen for a very long time.

"So what now?" he asked Rebecca.

"Don't know, back to America I guess."

Ben wasn't sure. He was thinking her talents would be better used in Israel. Four nuclear weapons in Israel were far more effective than one in America.

Ben heard Sam speaking to the driver, the American accent catching his attention.

"Who was that?" he demanded angrily.

Shit, thought Rebecca, she hadn't mentioned Sam's assistance and didn't think it was really relevant. It also didn't help that a previous assignment was the assassination of Sam's brother. She could not risk Sam overhearing the conversation. He claimed not to understand Hebrew but Rebecca claimed not to understand many languages.

"I'll call you back."

"Don't han…"

Rebecca ended the call before Ben could finish telling her not to and asked the driver to pull over for two minutes.

"Ben, sorry, I couldn't talk."

"Who's in the car?" he asked angrily. He wasn't a man people hung up on.

"Sam Baker," she replied and held the phone from her ear.

After waiting for the inevitable expletives to stop, she brought the phone back to her ear and explained what had happened.

"…it's all to do with some guy Lawson, James Lawson," she finally concluded.

Ben's brain worked like a Cray II supercomputer. The speed at which he could compute scenarios and situations and almost instantaneously come to a conclusion was staggering. Almost as soon as Rebecca had spoken, Ben had a new strategy.

"Stay with Sam Baker, assist him with whatever he needs to get to Lawson. Just be careful as to who he incriminates, we have friends in the White House."

"OK," she replied, again surprising herself at just how relieved she felt at not having to say goodbye to Sam.

Jumping back in the car, she was pleased to see the smile in Sam's eyes as she relayed the news that he was stuck with her, at least for a little while longer.

The flight to Paris left on time and during the flight, they discussed how they would proceed which, for Sam, was pretty much, get to Lawson's room, extract the information and kill him. Rebecca suggested a little more finesse which Sam considered for some time before announcing his preference for the original plan.

One problem neither of them had considered as they stepped into a significantly colder autumn evening in Paris, was that they had left pretty much the whole Mossad team in the South of France. The only people that were left in Paris were young admin girls who most certainly would not have access or the wherewithal to acquire any weapons. Sam had not expected Rebecca's assistance and had not even considered the possibility of going armed. He had a much better weapon in his arsenal, one that had fared him very well in the past - surprise. If they didn't know he was coming, it really wasn't an issue. Rebecca had been warned that Lawson went nowhere without at least four bodyguards. They would all be ex-military and almost certainly ex-special forces. Sam thought back to the sniper as she relayed this information and re-iterated his earlier point. They didn't know they were coming and that was worth more than any weapons They'd ask questions then shoot. If they knew they were coming, they'd shoot and then ask questions. Simple military rules of engagement, particularly NATO forces, don't fire unless fired upon.

As they made their way back to central Paris, Rebecca received a call. The Paris Head had tracked down Lawson's location. The Presidential Suite, Hotel Barrière Fouquet.

"Do you know it, Sam?" asked Rebecca.

"Intimately, when in Paris I wouldn't stay anywhere else," he laughed.

Rebecca looked at him, trying to ascertain if he was being serious. Israelis didn't do sarcasm well.

"Hotel Barrière Fouquet, s'il vous plait," she instructed the taxi driver.

Very nice, thought Sam, as they pulled off the Champs-Elysés onto Avenue George V. The hotel took up the whole first block and was nothing if not stunning in the darkness.

Rebecca pulled him back to the Champs-Elysés. She had spotted something that may be useful. A short walk away, Rebecca pulled him into a restaurant called La Durée. Sam looked around, it was like something out of a chintzy dream. Someone had gone wild with green aqua paint. Rebecca shoved him past the restaurant entrance and into a queue of people looking at little multi colored circles. Even more bizarrely, Sam watched as one of the staff informed an excited customer, rather firmly, that he could not take photos of whatever they were.

"What the hell are we doing?" he asked through gritted teeth. He wanted to kill James Lawson.

"Looking like tourists!" said Rebecca, likewise through gritted teeth.

Almost thirty minutes later, they eventually reached the front of the queue. Rebecca purchased a bottle of Rosé champagne and a box of mixed 'macarons'. Sam was still blissfully unaware of what they were but went along with the charade. As Sam passed over a ludicrous amount of Euros, he received a small bag in return. Rebecca seemed delighted and took the bag swiftly from him.

"OK, perfect, we look like tourists returning to the hotel," she announced with the small bag by her side. "Let's go."

They walked back to the hotel and encountered their first problem. The top floor of the hotel required a keycard to access it by lift. They exited the lift and walked back towards reception.

"Excuse me," asked Sam, putting on his best Texan drawl. All foreigners thought Texans were money men, he had explained to Rebecca, who had to agree. Any Texans she had met on her travels had all been very rich.

The reception clerk's French arrogance was unmistakable.

"Oui, monsieur?"

"What's the best suite you've got in this hotel?"

"The Presidential, monsieur."

"I'll take it."

Sam watched as the clerk took great pleasure in replying.

"I'm afraid it is taken, monsieur."

"What's the next one?"

"The Royal Suite, monsieur."

"Let me have a look," demanded Sam, making his disappointment clear.

The clerk toyed with informing the guest it was €6,000 per night but thought better of it. He had pushed him far enough and Americans did not take kindly to being called on money.

"Concierge!" he shouted.

As the concierge arrived, he was given instructions to take the gentleman and his wife to see the Royal Suite. After a quick tour of the suite, which both agreed inwardly was unbelievable, they said it was just not up to the George Cinq standard and was frankly not good enough, so they left. In the meantime, Rebecca had secured the key from the concierge's pocket and Sam had had an excellent look at Lawson's security. Two large burly men were stationed at the door. But even better, Rebecca and Sam had been spotted and assessed as just other guests.

The plan was to come back a few hours later, around 3.00 a.m., just as the guards were beginning to wane and most importantly, the receptionist and concierge had both gone home.

At 3.05 they entered the lobby and made straight for the lift. Rebecca inserted the keycard and fortunately the top floor light lit up. Sam had been concerned that keycard would have been cancelled. As the lift doors opened, the two guards jumped to attention. They had been dozing in their chairs and visibly relaxed at the sight of Sam and Rebecca, two other guests and sat back down.

"Hey guys," Sam said as he walked towards the two guards.

Sam Baker had studied many martial arts throughout his career in the military and had come to the very firm conclusion that some people could fight and others tried to fight. He could fight. Martial arts had simply honed his innate ability. As soon as the action started, time seemed to slow down for Sam. He noticed the slightest movements and could sense what his opponent was going to do almost before his opponent knew what he was going to do himself. No training in the world would give you that skill, you either had it or you didn't. And Sam had it in spades. He approached the two guards who towered over him and where some would see threat and power, Sam saw slowness and awkwardness.

The first strike was easiest, the two guards had seen no threat, Sam was at least four inches shorter and over one hundred pounds lighter than each of the guards. As Sam neared, he calculated the distance to the millimeter and struck, driving his right foot up and into the bodyguard's right testicle, as though it were a field kick from the 50 yard line. The guard crumpled. Any attempts to scream were soundless as the force of the blow drove every molecule of air out of the guard's lungs. As the first guard was crumpling to a fetal position and fighting for breath, Sam was already driving a punch towards the second guard. As his right foot touched the floor, he delivered the first hit, timed to perfection. The energy of his motion transferred from left to right foot and then powering his body forward and towards the second guard, the punch connected and it was as though every ounce of weight and momentum from his move had concentrated within the 18 square inches of his right fist and into the side of the second guard's neck. It was a stunning blow and the second guard's knees buckled instantly as the trauma of the blow triggered a protective shut down of the guard's nervous system.

As the first guard managed to catch his breath, his struggling attempts to call out were ended with a second blow. A well placed chop to the back of his neck ensured he would join the other guard in a rather deeper than normal sleep.

Rebecca had watched in awe and somewhat helplessly as Sam had, without any warning, launched the attack on the two guards. She had witnessed many fights in her time but never one so one-sided and impressive. She clapped silently in appreciation of his moves. Sam blushed at the praise and waved it away. Emptying the guards' pockets, they found two compact Walther PPS's, very thin and easy to conceal but still packing a 9mm round. Sam could only assume they were illegal. In any event, the odds had just improved significantly. They were armed and still had the element of surprise. Two down, two to go.

Rebecca finished searching the second guard and discovered one major problem. Neither guard had the room key.

The first option was to knock on the door. But there could be a code, two knocks followed by three or one knock then another two. The possibilities were endless. Rebecca looked at Sam for inspiration. He had just assumed the guards would have a key.

"Shit!"

"We'll just have to knock and hope for the best," offered Rebecca.

"Yep. Ready?"

Rebecca raised the Walter PPS and stood ready behind Sam.

"Go!"

As Sam raised his hand to knock, Rebecca suddenly remembered the keycard taken from the concierge. She grabbed Sam's arm and inserted the card, the light turned green, it was a master keycard.

Sam opened the door silently and moved into the vast lounge area. The two guards sat with their backs to the door as they sat in front of the TV. From the position of their heads hanging limply, they were obviously sound asleep. Sam crept towards them, waving Rebecca to follow. It seemed these guys were even larger than the two at the door. Sam motioned for Rebecca to slide in behind the guy to the left, while he went behind the guard to the right. He mimed what he wanted to do. Rebecca shook her head. There was no way she'd manage if the guard woke up. But Sam insisted. She shrugged her shoulders and would give it a try. Unlike Sam, she kept the Walter PPS in her hand. If he moved, she would shoot, despite Sam's protestations about not killing unless required.

Sam went first. His right arm slipped round the massive neck, locked with his left arm on the other side and he placed his left hand on the guard's head for leverage. As the guard struggled to comprehend what was happening, Sam squeezed and pulled the guard's head down. Between the slumber and the strength of Sam's hold, the guard drifted into an unconscious slumber.

Rebecca, having about half the strength of Sam, was absolutely correct in her assumption that it was a ridiculous plan for her. As her arms took grasp, the guard woke up and easily dislodged her grip. Watching his colleague collapse, the guard spun towards Sam in a vain attempt to assist. Almost certain of her failure, Rebecca was ready, she grabbed the pillow and placing it in front of her pistol fired, the bullet caught the diving guard in the one part of his body she could see above the back of the sofa, his ass, the pillow muffling the noise. He screamed as he crashed into his unconscious colleague but despite the wound, he clambered up. This time, Rebecca aimed and heeding Sam's words, shot the guard in the kneecap, eliciting an even greater scream but stopping him in his tracks.

An irate Lawson crashed through the bedroom doors to chastise his guards only to find Sam kicking the screaming guard in the head and Rebecca pointing the small pistol at him, with a finger instructing his silence which she obtained instantly.

As Sam's kick knocked the fourth and final guard unconscious, he turned and admired the sight of Lawson as he struggled to comprehend what was happening. Sam left Rebecca to watch the three as he returned to the hallway and dragged the other two guards into the suite. Curtain-tie backs made excellent ropes and before long, the four guards were trussed up so well it was going to take Houdini to undo the knots. Meanwhile, not one word had been uttered and a rather panic-stricken Lawson awaited his fate, still blissfully unaware of who had just dispatched his very capable and expensive security. Finally, as he pulled on the final knot and elicited a satisfactory "humph" from his captives, Sam turned to Lawson.

"Mr Lawson, James Lawson?"

Lawson nodded his head. There was no point denying the obvious.

"I met an employee of yours recently," said Sam menacingly. "He wasn't very nice. In fact, he wanted to kill my brother!"

Lawson looked in horror as he realized he was staring at Charles Baker's brother.

Lawson remained silent and Sam continued. "Obviously, I don't take kindly to people trying to kill my family."

Lawson, still silent, now looked at the wall rather than Sam.

"He's dead. That's how unkindly I take to people trying to kill my family."

"Fortunately for him, he had nothing to do with the death of my wife and son!"

Lawson remained impassive.

"So his death was quick, relatively painless."

Lawson twitched nervously. He knew exactly what Sam meant.

"Now, before you think all is lost, I will give you a promise. I won't kill you if you tell me everybody who's involved in trying to kill my brother."

Lawson laughed as the futility of Sam's quest hit him. He was still trying to save his brother.

Sam looked at Rebecca. Rebecca suddenly realized why Lawson was laughing. She had, because of everything that happened, forgotten to tell Sam about the bombing.

"You poor fuck, you've come all this way to save a brother who's already dead!" laughed Lawson.

The words hit Sam like a sledgehammer and he slumped onto the sofa. He looked at Rebecca who, avoiding his gaze, moved towards him and embraced him.

"Sam it's OK," she offered and smiled at Lawson, picking up the phone on the nearby table and making a call. After a second, she handed the phone to Sam.

"Hello?"

Sam instantly recognized the voice, it was his sister-in-law.

"Hi, how are you?" he asked solemnly.

"Fine, is everything OK? You sound awful."

"God, I'm so sorry, I've just heard the news."

"What news?" she asked, suddenly realizing. "Oh yes, such a shame, massive heart attack they think."

Sam was stunned at how well she was taking it and the news that he had died naturally was just as shocking. Charles was a very healthy guy.

Rebecca watched, worried as Sam's mood failed to lift.

"When did it happen?" he asked.

"Hmm, not quite sure, hold on a sec..." she shouted "Charles!"

Sam hardly heard the question about when the President had died. All he heard was that his brother was alive and well.

Senator Charles Baker took the phone and spoke at length to his brother, assuring him he was fine. They had received a call on the cell phone his wife's friend had given her when she was hiding in her friend's lodge. The lodge she had been originally hiding in was highly secure and the call they had received was of course meant for Beth's friend. Nonetheless the call from Alarm Company that there were intruders in the grounds of the other lodge had spooked them all the same.

Sam talked for a few more minutes before replacing the handset and turning to a far more subdued Lawson, who having heard the whole conversation, knew Charles Baker was very much alive and well.

Rebecca pulled Sam from the room and apologized. She had forgotten to tell him about the explosion. She had had to phone in their location but gave the house where they picked his wife up, not their new location. It seemed there were very few people they could trust. However, it seemed they thought the Senator was dead which was a bonus, she said with a smile. Sam was too elated to be angry. He walked back into the lounge and looked at his watch. It was 3.20 a.m., 9.20 p.m. in the US.

"OK, Lawson, you've got approximately ten seconds to start talking or I'm going to end your life in so much pain that you'll be begging me to kill you for the next 12 hours."

Lawson was a man who told people what to do and he scoffed at Sam's threat.

Three second later, his little finger snapped like a dead twig and he began to talk. It was probably the first time in his life he had ever felt pain, thought Sam. Even he was surprised at how quickly he talked.

Sam listened as Rebecca noted down a total of six names, four names they had never heard before, one name they both instantly recognized, one that she had been ordered to protect and one other that Sam had known from the very start had to be involved, Allan Johnson.

Sam noticed a laptop lying nearby and opened it up. A videoconferencing page was the last one to be used and it gave Sam a wonderful idea. He booted up the system and selected the names that had been given from a drop down menu. Unfortunately, only four names were available. He clicked 'conference call' and waited as the system contacted the others.

"What are you doing?" asked Rebecca, as she watched him play with the laptop.

Sam disabled the camera and watched the screen as it offered a 'waiting for attendees' note in the middle of the screen. It took about five minutes before the four faces stared back at him, obviously waiting for Lawson's face. After all, he had called them.

Sam did not disappoint them and moved the laptop in front of Lawson and enabled the camera, revealing to the other four attendees his rather disheveled and pained expression.

"James, are you OK?" asked Walter Koch.

"James!" asked John Mellon.

Lawrence Harkness moved closer to the camera, obviously having noted there was something wrong with James and taking a closer look.

"James, what's happened?" asked William Hathaway.

Sam switched on the mike and let Lawson speak.

"Sam Baker's here, his brother isn't dead!" he announced. Sam stepped into view and waved at his audience.

The four men stared back in horror.

"I just wanted to say hi and let you know that I'll be paying each and every one of you a visit very soon." Before they had a chance to respond, he raised the pistol and shot James Lawson in the stomach. A shot that he figured would not only ensure his death but would take at least a couple of hours of total and complete agony.

Sam stepped out of the camera's view and beckoned for Rebecca to follow him as he exited the suite.

"Why did you do that? We just lost the element of surprise!" she said, as they closed the door on Lawson's cries of pain.

Sam shrugged. The look on their faces and the panic they would now be experiencing was well worth it.

# Chapter 59

"Mr President, it's Walter Koch again," said Honey. "He's not going to give up, Sir."

"OK, put him through." Russell had avoided him all day but he had called incessantly for the last thirty minutes.

"For God's sake, Walter, it's 10pm. Will you please call me in the morning?" demanded the President.

"Before you say another word, look at the link I just mailed you," insisted Walter breathlessly.

Having never, in the twenty years he had known Walter, heard him in such a state, Russell obliged and clicked the link.

The live feed of the dying James Lawson shocked Russell to the core.

"Jesus?!" He hit the disconnect button on the computer.

"Sam Baker," offered Walter, by way of explanation.

"But I thought we got him with his brother?"

"We didn't because we didn't get his brother!" exclaimed Walter exasperated and panicking.

"Sorry?"

"You missed him, you idiot. And now he knows who we are and it seems pretty clear he's coming for us next."

"Shit!" Russell thought back to Johnson's warning and how if he wanted to kill the President, Sam was the man he'd get to do it.

"Exactly, we're obviously hoping you'll offer us some assistance!"

"Of course," he said quickly. "I'll get some men to you straight away, will you let Lawrence and William know?"

Walter suddenly realized there was a problem. John Mellon was also on the hit list but not on the President's radar. They'd have to cover John some other way. It was not time to admit to the plan about John Mellon becoming VP.

"Fantastic, thank you, Mr President."

"They'll be there within the hour," promised the President.

Walter realized he had not mentioned one thing. "Sorry, they're in Paris, Mr President, so the next few hours will be OK." He'd rather wait and get the best than the first few men that came to hand.

"What, James is sitting dying in Paris as we speak?"

"Yes!"

"Have you not called an ambulance or a doctor?"

"We don't know where he is, we just know he's in Paris!"

"Dear God!" Although the more he thought about it, the more he thought it couldn't happen to nicer guy. James Lawson was a particularly unpleasant man.

As President, he could probably pass the videoconference link onto the NSA and they'd track him down but he also didn't want to tie himself to Lawson's death in any way. He closed his laptop and began to worry about himself, not some old cantankerous prick that was beyond saving in any event.

He called Johnson. He had missed again and as a result, he would need to get the men to cover the remaining Horsemen. He then called the Secret Service and requested his own security be doubled. Thinking better of the request, he trebled it.

# Chapter 60

Sam and Rebecca arrived at Charles de Gaulle in plenty of time to catch the first transatlantic flight of the day, the 8.20 Air France to New York. While Rebecca went to buy two tickets, Sam wondered what had happened. The airport had taken on the look of a refugee camp. Sleeping bodies were strewn everywhere and queues seemed to stretch off in every direction. He checked his watch. It was 5.30 a.m. Rebecca returned and Sam could see she was sporting a quizzical look similar to his own.

"There's not a plane available for a week!"

"Sorry?" Sam was certain he had misheard her.

"Every single transatlantic flight is full for the next forty eight hours."

"But you said a week?"

"Yep and then there aren't any!" she said bewildered.

"What the hell do you mean there aren't any?!"

"Something about a solar flare. All planes are being grounded for the rest of the week."

"Jesus, we could take the train to London..."

"No, all flights across the world are being stopped," she interrupted, realizing she hadn't explained fully.

"I'll call Ben," she offered.

"Would that be the same Ben that gave up the address of where my sister-in-law had been hiding?"

"We don't know that for sure. Trust me, it'll be fine."

"Ben?"

"Rebecca, I'm sorry I don't have much time, I need to get to a meeting."

Rebecca quickly explained the predicament. Five minutes later, she received a call back. They had two first class seats on the American Airlines flight leaving at 11.05 a.m. to JFK.

"Excellent," announced Sam, making his way to the executive lounge. There was just enough time for a shower and a good breakfast before they boarded.

*** 

The US Secretary of Transportation had relayed Ben's request directly to the CEO of American Airlines, despite the late hour. As ever, the request was granted. Two American Airline crew were going to be spending a little more time in Paris than they had thought and two Million Miles members weren't going to get the free upgrade they had craved and was grudgingly awarded by the airline.

The conversation, despite the unsocial hour, was business-like and as it came to an end, the Secretary expected at least some reference to the upcoming grounding of the aviation industry but it never came. The Secretary of Transportation sat back in his chair and stared at the phone. For days he had sat waiting for the onslaught from the airline chiefs but it had never happened. Four or five days' grounding of all their flights had hardly elicited a squeak from them, despite the fact he knew they were being lambasted by the public at large. It just didn't make sense. The volcanic ash debacle had cost him nights of sleep as every transatlantic carrier stormed his office by mail, phone and in person. His own scientists were telling him the chance of any issues occurring as a result of a solar storm were around one in a billion but the papers and all the media were convinced it was a cataclysmic event that would bring planes down. As such, they had no option but to go with the majority and like every other air traffic control network around the world, they had to close their skies.

Was he missing something? Despite the hour, he called the CEO of American Airlines back. He had to know what was going on.

"Chris, I'm sorry to call again."

"Not at all, Mr Secretary."

"I just wondered, when the ash thing happened, you were almost camped on my doorstep."

"Yep, cost us millions!"

"But surely the solar storm is the same?"

"You're winding me up aren't you?"

"Absolutely not? Why would you say that?"

The US Secretary listened in disbelief before thanking the CEO profusely and arranging his driver to take him to the White House first thing in the morning.

\*\*\*

At 7.00 a.m., the Secretary of Transportation waited in the anteroom for the Oval Office for his President. He had been there since 6.30 a.m. and the President had been informed of his arrival.

"Come on in," he offered as he entered the office.

"Thank you, Mr President."

"I can't say I'm surprised to see you, I imagine it's chaos over at transportation," said the President offering the Secretary a seat on the sofa across from him.

"That's why I'm here, Mr President, I'm here because it's *not* chaos."

"Sorry?" Russell had lived through the ash storm and as VP with the President's ear, he had received almost as many calls as the Secretary of Transportation.

"Exactly. However, I got a call from Ben Meir this morning. He needed a couple of seats on a plane. I called the CEO of American and managed to get a couple of seats for him but at no point did the CEO moan about the solar storm. Then it hit me full on, nobody's moaning about the grounding. Well, a few from some small companies but none of the big boys, American, Delta, United, Continental, not a peep. Not one mention of lost revenue, disaster, bankruptcy, nothing. "

"None of them?" questioned Russell, having spoken to them all at least three times a day during the ash crisis. He was stunned and the ash crisis had hardly impacted America, mainly just Transatlantic flights.

"Not one. So I called him back and asked the question and you'll never guess what he said?"

"You're right I won't, so tell me!" Russell wasn't a guessing type of President.

"What did they have to moan about? Their planes were all chartered, they were going to make a killing."

"Who to?" demanded Russell, sitting up straight in shock as the news.

"Us."

"Us?"

"As far as he was aware, it was some top secret government thing and we've hired all his planes and used this Solar flare nonsense as a cover."

"What?"

"Yep and he's over the moon, reckons the profits they'll make in the next four days will sort out a number of long term issues they've had."

"I'll contact Defense and see if they know anything about it but I'm sure they would have told me!" said the President, still coming to terms with the news. Although the more he thought about it, the more one thing came to mind but there was no way that they were linked. Shutting down the world's airline industry was not within their power, surely.

The Secretary of Transportation got up and walked towards the door. His bit was done, it was the President's problem now.

"Oh, how was Ben?" The President asked as an after-thought.

"Fine, you know Ben, always in a rush"

"Where's he off to that El Al couldn't take him?"

"Oh it wasn't for him, it was two seats from Paris to New York."

Russell couldn't believe his luck, instantly making the link. One of those seats would be Sam Baker's. They had him trapped. He called Johnson. Surely even he would manage to capture an unarmed man on an aircraft.

# Chapter 61

Ben rushed into the meeting. Of all the meetings he had in his diary, that was the one that he never failed to attend and the one he prayed would deliver more than any other. The Heads of pretty much every security, police and Defense service awaited his arrival.

"Well?" he asked, repeating the same question he asked every morning and evening as these meetings took place.

"No news," was the subdued response.

There were now only five days until Yom Kippur. Five days until four nuclear weapons would devastate the land of Israel. "Any news on the American one?" he asked again, as he had for every previous meeting.

"Nothing," offered David Hirsch, the Defense Minister, without hope.

"We have every satellite the Americans have and every one of their military vessels are checking every ship they can see but nothing. Maybe it's already there."

"What about Marseille?"

"What about it?" asked Hirsch.

"Any boats leaving there bound for America?"

"We've checked them all. They were either going to Africa, staying in Europe, heading to the Far East or South America and we even checked them to make sure they were on course and they are. No boat that is on its way to America has the weapon. It must be a hoax."

"Well, if it is, the joke is on us. They'll be five explosions not four!" exclaimed Ben. "Sorry, what was that?" asked Ben not quite catching what one of the analysts had whispered to a colleague under his breath.

"Apologies, Mr Meir, I spoke out of turn," said by way of apology.

"No, please if you have information, you must share it. Please stand up and enlighten us with whatever you deem so relevant." Ben was in a particularly foul mood.

The young analyst stood up and when Hirsch spotted who Ben was picking on, he immediately tried to stop him.

"Ben, if you don't mind, I'll deal with this less publicly."

"No David, the young man has something to say!" He was not in the mood to be stopped.

"Sorry, please also give us your credentials," ordered Ben, keen to see why the young man felt it appropriate to make secret remarks.

David Hirsch sunk further in his seat. Adding the young man's credentials was just going to exacerbate the disaster.

The young man could hardly be heard as he stammered. "I work for the Defense Department in the nuclear capability team."

"Ben," interrupted David Hirsch, the young man's ultimate boss. "I really must insist you let me deal with this."

"No, carry on," ordered Ben firmly.

"My specialty is the likely scenarios and long term impact of nuclear weapons."

"Oh, OK. So I can certainly understand why you're here. Now what was so important you had to share it with your colleague but not the rest of us?" pushed Ben.

"I simply said that whether it's four or five was irrelevant. Israel's fucked either way."

Ben looked at the young analyst somewhat surprised at his tone and language.

"Sorry that was what I said, verbatim, Mr Meir, I mean no disrespect," added the analyst noting Ben's disapproval.

Ben looked at David. Nothing of this magnitude had ever been relayed to him. Israel being fucked seemed to be a fairly explicit and certainly far worse than the destruction of part of four cities that had previously been cited.

"What exactly do you mean by 'fucked' young man?" asked Ben, having calmed down and keen to hear a less edited version of the potential impact.

"With the input of Professor Ilya Kielson, the Soviet scientist, we should assume two things. The nukes are around the 100 kiloton range and will be extremely efficient. He would, I assume, also have advised the Palestinians of placement to ensure maximum damage and impact."

"Go on," prompted Ben.

"With this scenario, the projections would obliterate four major cities, wiping out pretty much all their inhabitants."

"Yes." Ben was aware of this. "But Israel is much larger than four cities, young man."

"Sorry, I'm not finished. The radiation and thermal effects would be devastating to a significantly greater area and ultimately I would anticipate that Israel, the West Bank and Gaza would pretty much be unlivable for the next fifty years. I would include a large area of our neighbors' territories in that category also."

"Jerusalem?"

"Wasteland, a radioactive nightmare!" The young analyst was on a roll.

Ben Meir, not for the first time, was hoping his heart would keep going. The stress was going to kill him. They had to find those weapons. Ararat depended on Jerusalem.

# Chapter 62

Sam thought he could get used to this as he pressed the button and for the first time in his life, actually felt comfortable aboard a plane. Two minutes after the stewardess had put out the fasten seat belt signs, he was sleeping soundly. Seven hours and almost 3,000 miles later, he woke up feeling refreshed and energized for the full day that lay ahead. The electronic map told him there was just about an hour to JFK.

He turned to Rebecca and all the pleasant thoughts that had been swirling in his mind stopped. Her face was one of sheer panic and coming from a woman who had faced what she had, he knew something was very wrong.

"What's wrong?" he asked, looking deeply into her eyes.

"I think Ben's screwed us and most certainly you," she whispered, and quickly hissed. "Don't turn around."

"You've just had a bad dream. We're in a plane, nobody can touch us up here. Nobody even knows who we are."

She shook her head firmly. "No, I haven't slept a wink. Two hours ago the man one seat behind and over to your right was called to the cockpit door and handed the phone by the stewardess. He hasn't stopped checking on us since then. So just make it look like we're talking normally, ok?"

"OK," said Sam, looking calmly into her eyes.

"I can only assume he's the Sky Marshall. He's probably been told to assist when we land."

"OK, I'm going to take a casual look, don't worry," instructed Sam as he yawned and nodded to the passenger across the aisle from him. A quick look behind confirmed Rebecca's worst thoughts. The bulge in his otherwise perfect suit trouser gave him away. The right leg snagged at the sock line, giving away the pistol that would resolve any potential hijackings.

"Yep and he's good," confirmed Sam. "Caught me looking!"

"Shit, we're screwed," said Rebecca, feeling caught in a guided missile heading straight to Sam's assassins.

Sam considered all the options which amounted to pretty much none. The cockpit door was locked and would never be opened. He could HALO and HAHO, basically parachute from inner space, either quickly or slowly but that tended to require a parachute which commercial airliners did not carry. Sam didn't want to get into the whole argument about why somebody had decided to put lifejackets on board a plane instead of parachutes. He'd argue that point when he had more time.

After thinking through the options, he was coming down on the side of Rebecca. However, Sam was not a person to get screwed. He preferred to be the screwer.

"I'm just going to nip to the restroom," he said as he kissed her on the cheek and walked the few feet to the restroom. Closing and locking the door, he waited three seconds before very carefully removing the lock. He then opened the door and charged. As expected, the Marshall had relaxed slightly, assuming Sam would be at least a couple of minutes. With the Marshall's guard down, Sam launched himself at him and stopped the Marshall's hand reaching for the gun. Sam had ended up almost sitting on the man's lap as screams echoed down the plane, Rebecca's voice piercing through them all, telling everyone to "get the fuck down!"

Meanwhile, Sam, with his right hand clamped around the Marshall right wrist and taking a number of small punches to the ribs from the Marshall's left, swung his left elbow round and crashed it into the Marshall's temple. The Marshall was dazed and his right hand relaxed. Sam grabbed the pistol just as three have a go heroes came crashing towards him.

Sam jumped and missed being washing lined by a fraction of an inch. Sam stepped back a few feet and leveled the Sig Sauer P229 at the three heroes.

"Guys, I'm on your side!" he shouted. "I've just got a few little problems I need to resolve but trust me, nobody will get hurt."

The Marshall struggled to his feet and tried to calm the other passengers down. He knew what could happen if Sam put a bullet through the skin of the plane at 37,000 ft. He was trained incessantly not to, for exactly those reasons.

"Guys, I am a Federal Marshall. I will deal with this. Please step back."

The youngest of the three was having none of it. "I've got two young babies on this plane and no Al Qaeda fucker is going to fly them into a building."

Sam turned to Rebecca. "Do I look like an Al Qaeda terrorist!" he asked.

"No," she answered honestly.

"What do you think?" Sam asked an elderly lady sitting on the left hand seat.

"Hmmm, no," she stammered, frightened out of her wits.

He could see that the young man was willing to give his own life for his children, very admirable and extremely hard to rationalize with.

"Tell him," instructed Sam to the Marshall.

The three heroes looked at the Marshall.

"Tell him what?" asked the Marshall, bemused.

"What you were told about me?"

"I'm trying to calm them down!" he pleaded.

"Exactly, tell them that I'm not a terrorist."

"I can't because that's what they told me."

"They said I'm a terrorist?" asked Sam. Somehow, that made everything even worse, to be branded a terrorist by the very country he shed blood for.

The young father was getting ready to move. Four men one gun and very little room, Sam's odds were worsening by the minute.

Rebecca moved towards the men that were now closing in on Sam. She pushed past the two at the rear and coming from behind, the young father, she delivered a devastating kick to his manhood. The young father crumpled and fell to the floor. She held her FBI badge high in the air.

"Right, you two," she barked. "Take him back to his seat before he loses the ability to have any more kids. You two then go back to your seats and you," she said, pointing to the Marshall. "Sit on the floor, right there!"

"Now everybody, just calm down!" she shouted. Somebody had taken charge who didn't have a gun and it worked.

"Now what?" she whispered back to Sam, who stood between her and the cockpit door.

Sam picked up the intercom and hit the button to speak to the flight deck.

"Captain?"

"Yes? What do you want?" he barked.

"Firstly, to promise you that absolutely no harm will come to anyone aboard this plane, as long as you do me one little favor."

"I'm sorry it's not possible," he replied firmly.

"Let me tell you what it is before you get all worked up."

"I'm sorry I will not negotiate with you. That is my final word."

Sam told him what he wanted in any event and left it for the Captain to decide.

# Chapter 63

CIA Director Allan Johnson had taken the rather unorthodox act of leading the capture of a terrorist fugitive at JFK. He had had to twist a number of arms and would be repaying favors for a number of years but he was going to end this bullshit personally. As far as he was concerned, this would pretty much seal the VP position, not that there should have been in any doubt. The evidence was all still in his hands, including a recording of President Andrew Russell, then VP, instructing him very clearly that the President had to go. However, Allan wanted the job on merit and not by using underhanded methods.

He had gotten word through to the Sky Marshall that a terrorist was on board. Although it was not expected the terrorist planned anything on the plane, he should take extreme care and under no circumstances approach him or alert him to his presence. He would be arrested at JFK. The Marshall's job was to protect the passengers, keeping them onboard when the terrorist was taken down. The flight was scheduled to arrive at Terminal 8 and Johnson had all but shut it down. The last few stragglers were disappearing as the area was cleared and flights were reassigned to other terminals.

Johnson was taking no chances. Twenty men were within the terminal with him, while another twenty surrounded the parking area below. All were dressed as airport crew and should not rouse suspicion as the plane completed its taxi and the passengers disembarked. He had him.

The tower had allocated one air traffic controller to that one flight and had, as requested, plugged the controller into the

CIA comms system. Although they could hear him, Johnson had ensured he could not hear them. Every member of Johnson's team knew exactly what was happening at any given time.

"American Heavy 45, please come left, to heading 245 and drop to 2,000 feet."

Johnson knew that meant they were just minutes from landing.

***

On board American Airlines flight 45, Sam had been praying for the Captain to do the right thing. So far, he had acceded to not radioing in what had happened on board the flight and been assured by the stewardess that Sam, as promised, had let the Sky Marshall take his seat again. No passengers were injured and no other demands were being made. Just the one favor, as requested.

As the Captain began his final procedures, Sam gave it another try. Of course, he wouldn't shoot the Sky Marshall. The Captain had obviously got his measure and realized he wasn't a cold blooded killer. Well, certainly not of innocent bystanders at least, thought Sam.

If they landed at JFK, he was dead. He had a gun but Johnson would ensure a very large welcoming committee and he knew there would be no qualms when it came to collateral. As long as Johnson got his target, collateral was exactly that, collateral.

Sam lifted the intercom again and pleaded with the Captain. He could hear the co-pilot in the background being given the instructions for final approach. On hearing the two-feet call, he gave up.

"These things I do, so that others may live," he muttered in acceptance of his fate.

"Sorry?" said the Captain.

"Nothing, just an old motto," said Sam, not wanting to repeat it. He hadn't even realized he had said it out loud.

"Just hold on a second, Mark." The captain stopped the co-pilot responding to the last call.

"Were you a PJ?"

"Yes, Sir," responded Sam automatically on hearing the Captain refer to his old unit.

"Well why in the hell didn't you say, Son? You guys pulled me out of a very tricky situation in Iraq many years ago. A slight detour is the least I could do. Take your seat, Son, this may get a little bumpy."

\*\*\*

"JFK this is American Heavy 45, we have a problem. We cannot make the turn as requested, believe we have a fault with the rudder."

"Roger that American 45, can you maneuver at all?"

"JFK, yes, can turn to right. Repeat we can move to the right."

As Johnson wondered what was going on, the tower were pulling charts and looking at options. The Air Traffic Control Director pointed wildly at the chart as the controller calmly relayed his suggestion.

"American Heavy 45, a slight right turn could land you at LaGuardia, do you think that is possible?"

"Confirm possible, as long as we get a direct landing, we will not be able to maneuver once on course."

"Of course. We're contacting LaGuardia now and informing them of the emergency."

"Thank you."

Johnson was apoplectic and was furious at himself for only having only one-way comms. He had been screaming at the tower until he realized they couldn't hear him.

"Shit! How long to get to LaGuardia?!"

"Thirty minutes by car and probably ten by helicopter but they'll shut the airport down with an emergency," responded one of the CIA hit squad.

"Mother fucker!! Let's go! They can't shoot *us* down!" he screamed at the nearest five men. His chopper was a five minute run away, ten minutes to LaGuardia, he may just make it before they began to disembark.

"American 45, I have LaGuardia, they've cleared the runway and will have you down in 5 minutes."

"Hurry!" screamed Johnson as they tore through the terminal. While one of his men briefed the helicopter pilot, he called the control tower.

The Air Traffic Director answered the call immediately.

"What gate at LaGuardia?!" screamed Johnson as he ran.

The Air Traffic Control Director didn't have a clue. He worked at JFK, although he did know American used the Central Terminal D Concourse. "I know American use the Central Terminal Concourse D..." Johnson cut him off, not letting the Air Traffic Control Director finish his sentence. Rude prick, he thought before turning his attention to the screen full of blips that had just been delayed due to American 45.

***

As the flight landed perfectly the fire trucks and ambulances chased after the 'damaged' plane. As they came to a stop, the Captain instructed the crew to abandon the aircraft. The doors swung open and the slide chutes exploded into action. The Captain exited the cockpit and shook Sam's hand.

"Best not fly American for a little while, Son," he offered as advice.

The Captain grabbed the Sky Marshall's arm as he ran to catch up with Rebecca and Sam as they jumped onto the slide.

"Son, you really don't want to piss him off. Pararescue Jumpers are the kindest men you'll ever meet, if you're on their side. But if you're not, trust me, those guys are the meanest and most vicious sons of bitches alive!"

***

Johnson's pilot had made excellent time and they arrived at LaGuardia Central Terminal just three minutes after the flight had landed. Johnson could smell them. It would have taken more than three minutes for the plane to taxi to a gate. However, after ten minutes, he began to consider there may have been a problem. He called the tower and was informed of the emergency evacuation on the runway and how, in emergency situations, it was fairly standard to get the passengers off the plane.

Had Johnson waited and listened to the Air Traffic Control Director from JFK, he would have said the same thing. Johnson was incandescent. Sam Baker had gone. With a fifteen-minute head-start, it wasn't even worth trying. Johnson rounded up his men and left. He'd have to explain another failure to the President.

Had Johnson had it his way, he'd have just shot the plane down. It was the President who had insisted on doing it that way.

# Chapter 64

Sam directed Rebecca towards the subway. Forty-five minutes later and lost to the world, they walked up and out into the afternoon sunshine in Midtown Manhattan. Sam looked around. The streets were packed and there was absolutely no chance they had been followed.

"So what next?" asked Rebecca.

"Walter Koch, John Mellon, Lawrence Harkness and William Hathaway. Take your pick."

"And the other two?" she asked, surprised he had not included Russell and Johnson.

"Saving them for last."

"Oh, OK. So where to, Genius? You warned them you were coming."

"Hmm yes, beginning to regret that a little. Heat of the moment and all that," mused Sam.

"Shall we grab a bite and have a think?" offered Rebecca.

As they stepped into the diner, her cell phone rang.

"It's Ben," she said, looking at the screen on her phone.

Sam wanted to answer and tell whoever the hell this Ben was what he thought of him but Rebecca seemed to be very close to him and had promised Ben would not have sold them out.

"Go on then, see what he's got to say!" said Sam, unable to disguise his anger.

"Hello?" She put an iciness into her voice, partly to make Sam feel better.

"Why didn't you call when you landed?" he asked sincerely.

"We were too busy running from the men with guns that were waiting for us!" she said angrily.

"What?" asked Ben, genuinely confused. "I don't understand."

"Don't you?" The accusation was loud and clear.

"I only spoke to the Transportation Secretary and he's got nothing to do with any of this, I'd vouch for him personally. Whether he's mentioned to somebody else I don't know. On your parents lives, I did not do this Rebecca." It was perhaps the most sincere she had ever heard Ben and certainly the first time he had used her parents graves to emphasize he was being truthful.

She relented and gave a thumbs-up to Sam. Ben was clear.

"I believe you Ben, how are you?"

"Rebecca I couldn't even begin to tell you how bad I am but that is not your concern, I assume you wish to find the rest of the men?"

"I think that's a no-brainer. Sam warned them he was coming."

Ben laughed, the more he heard about Sam, the more he liked him. He'd have to check his background for any Jewish ancestry, he thought. He could certainly use a man as useful as Sam Baker.

"Nice touch," said Ben. "I like it."

Rebecca was a little surprised at how much she liked the fact that Ben was impressed by Sam.

"Anyway, I've done a little digging. The men are all members of a very elite club, the Alibi Club. Tomorrow evening, they have a poker night, or at least they normally would. I'll text you the address. It's in Washington."

As Rebecca relayed the conversation she had had with Ben, Sam couldn't help but think it was a trap. A little digging? It all sounded far too good to be true and if something sounded too good to be true, it usually was.

What Sam didn't realize was that when Ben said a little digging, he was referring to over twenty years' worth of material he had built up on the Horsemen. Ever since the Horsemen had gotten their hooks into Andrew Russell, Ben had gotten his hooks into them. It was just a shame for them that they didn't realize just how big his hooks were.

# Chapter 65

Akram Rayyan looked out onto the empty ocean. They had seen the activity overhead as they ploughed towards Saint John in Newfoundland. Their Northerly course and their Russian flag had kept the Americans and her allies at bay. There were only four days to go before they would strike a blow that the Americans would never forget.

His men had just completed another exercise. The parts had been disassembled and were now being placed back in their water-tight containers. Everything was working perfectly. In fact, better than perfect. They were now down to only 28 minutes. Deif had said that even touching thirty would be superb. Akram would have loved to have told Deif but with no communications, he would just have to wait and inform him on his return, Inshallah, he added quickly. Now was not the time to forget that it was Allah's will that they were performing.

As his men came bounding towards him, he thought it was time to choose the martyr. It was only fair that a martyr should have time to prepare himself. The guessing as to who of the two would have the honor was becoming a distraction. He considered the two men's performances and, as he had predicted, it was not possible to choose on skill or ability. He would have to leave it to Allah. He took the coin from his pocket and followed his men down for lunch. One of them was about to discover his name would last for eternity and he would soon have 72 virgins by his side.

Ahmed Hameed was a child of the streets, orphaned at the age of eight and with not a soul in the world to look after him, he had fended for himself. Such a beginning to life had ensured a toughness and street-wisdom that was impossible to learn. It had to be lived.

Deif had spotted Ahmed at only fourteen. The boy had a network of vagabonds, scroungers and pickpockets at this beck and call. His network was, Deif had explained to his other Commanders, genius. He had watched the network for some time and marveled at how they knew when trouble was coming. Ahmed's boys were the first to move when there was wind of the Israelis coming. So much so that Deif began to use the movement of Ahmed's boys as a warning mechanism. If you see any of those boys scarper, he warned, you run.

After marveling at him for some time, Deif made his move and recruited the young Ahmed into his fold. It was not an easy transition. Ahmed had been the boss for his whole life and taking orders from others was not something Ahmed accepted easily. However, Deif would not accept his underlings talking down to him. So he had two options: get rid of Ahmed or promote him. The thought of a sixteen-year-old barking orders to his significant elders did not sit well with Deif but he had spotted a potential in the boy that he had never seen before and he did the unthinkable, he promoted him to Commander and gave him his own area to control. Ahmed was a huge success and even men three times his age began to follow his orders unquestioningly.

At twenty three, he was still the youngest commander within Al Qassam and with Akram and Deif overseas, he was the de facto leader in charge of Al Qassam in Gaza. His leadership would never be questioned. In fact, it was believed that Akram would step aside on Deif's death or retirement and accept Ahmed as the new leader. Akram was a right hand man, Ahmed was a leader.

Ahmed looked out across the city towards Israel. They had food aplenty, space, fresh running water. Everything they needed was just a few hundred yards away. It didn't make sense.

His people starved while they feasted. Only four days to go he thought, four days and we will have our day.

He looked down at the street vendors below as they made their way back from the twelve foot walls that the Israelis kept his people prisoner with and noticed the carts were fuller than he had ever seen them. His people would be feasting, bread and fresh produce flowed in abundance. He went down to the street and spoke to his people. The vendors had arrived at 6 a.m. as always and watched as the border gates opened and three times the number of trucks thundered through. The Israelis unloaded the food without a word and went back across the border. The gates closed and that was it.

Ahmed was troubled. He didn't know what the Israelis were up to but they didn't do anything without very good reason. Ahmed wished he could speak to Deif. He would know what was going on.

*** 

"Did you deliver the extra food?" asked Ben.

"Yes, Sir," responded the Captain who controlled the border-crossing.

"Excellent, thank you. Now remember, the same again tomorrow."

"But Mr Meir, I won't have enough food for my men."

"Your men have got fat over the years, a few days dieting won't hurt them!' He ended the call.

Four days and counting, Ben was going to try one last roll of the dice but it was going to take a few days to set up.

# Chapter 66

John Mellon had had an exceptionally comfortable night. He would have to get the details of the mattress from Walter. Mellon was staying as a house guest of Walter Koch. Walter had drawn the short straw following the call to President Russell. Mellon had moved in along with the guards supplied by a now exceptionally overstretched Special Activities Division within the CIA, courtesy of a very weary Allan Johnson. Johnson's Head of NCS, National Clandestine Services was perhaps the most unhappy man in the CIA having had to make numerous house-calls to grieving widows and children. Johnson had secured pretty much every able man in the NCS unit that had experience of carrying a gun. However, as they were pretty much all ex-special forces that experience tended to be very good or exceptional.

As the NCS chief had pointed out to his boss Johnson, whatever he was doing was putting the National Security of the US at risk. Four of the men he had lost were from the Special Operations Group, his most elite unit and were vital in the fight against terrorism. Johnson had brushed aside his concerns and ordered the men to be stationed as requested.

The homes of Walter Koch, Lawrence Harkness and William Hathaway were now surrounded and secured by some of the best trained killers in the world.

As Walter joined John for breakfast in the kitchen, both felt comfortable as the heavily armed patrol walked past the window.

"Did you sleep OK?" asked Walter half heartedly, not really caring and just asking out of politeness.

"Like a baby," replied John, with enthusiasm.

"Excellent," replied Walter, his head already buried in the newspaper. The murder of James Lawson had made it into the papers.

Walter couldn't help but be disappointed. It had taken one bullet to the stomach and a broken pinky. That was it. Lawson had spilled their names because of a broken pinky. Pathetic.

"When are you going to discuss the Vice Presidency with Russell?" asked John, with no newspaper to amuse him.

Walter folded the paper in disgust at both the story and Mellon's interruptions.

"Tonight," he offered.

"Tonight's poker night." They had already confirmed it was going ahead.

"And he's going to be invited and you're going to impress him."

"Well we both know that won't happen."

"True, but you can try."

"I meant him coming! You couldn't get him on the phone for hours. What chance will you have trying to get him to a game of poker?"

"I'll be convincing! Don't worry he'll be there," offered Walter mysteriously. "You just be on your best behavior."

# Chapter 67

Rebecca's network of *Sayanim* had come up trumps again. The hire-car was supplied with a few non Hertz extras and the drive to Washington had proved uneventful. Sam had insisted on a drive past the Alibi club and they were surprised to find it looked rather derelict and somewhat out of place. A small red brick three storey town house surrounded by seven and eight storey buildings. Not what you'd expect of a club frequented by billionaires, thought Sam. He had checked the address and it was correct. Rebecca also walked past the door and noted the sign, it was definitely the correct address.

Back at the small guesthouse where they had rented a room, Sam had done some research and the location began to make sense. There were only 50 members. Membership was only possible on the death of a member and the acceptance by the remaining 49. It was a very exclusive club and its façade was exactly that. A façade. Behind the doors would be an opulent interior. Of that, Sam was certain.

As they drove past the club that morning, everything had changed. The club was far from deserted as it had been the previous evening. It was swarming with activity. Dogs were sniffing the bins and drains, men in suits were examining every detail of the building and street and most bizarrely, remarked Rebecca, there was a man soldering a drain cover.

Sam knew exactly what it meant. His task had just got ten times harder and his list of targets had just grown by one. As they turned onto 17th street, Sam accelerated away from the area. He was going to have to be exceptionally careful.

"Jesus, they're not taking any chances," exclaimed Rebecca surprised at the scale of the operation to protect the four men.

"It's not just them. That was a presidential advance team. It seems I'll chalk five up to the good, this evening."

Rebecca considered arguing against killing the President but she knew it was pointless. The man's actions had resulted in the death of Sam's child. She knew how that felt and nothing would have stopped her wreaking her revenge. She would just have to break it to him gently that she could not play any part of it. As an agent for a foreign government, it would be considered an act of war and she could not put her country and her people in danger. However, despite all of that, she would still give Sam as much help as she could. If nothing else, that was exactly what her orders were.

# Chapter 68

At 7.30 p.m., the motorcade pulled up at Walter Koch's front door. There was one armored limo, two cars of guards, two police cars and four motorbike outriders who would ensure they never stopped moving. The journey which had never taken him less than twenty minutes, took twelve. They hardly slowed below 45mph the whole way.

"I could get used to this!" said Walter as they drew up outside of the non-descript building.

"I am getting used to it!" replied John Mellon. The thought of his own presidential motorcade was beginning to take hold again. He didn't know what Walter had on Russell but if he could get him to the club, he'd get Mellon the VP ticket and then it was just a matter of time.

As the wall of guards formed, the two men exited the limo and were ushered into the club house where Lawrence Harkness and William Hathaway already waited.

"Gentlemen, may I take your jackets?" offered a butler, before leading the four into a room where five large easy chairs sat in front of a roaring log fire. Only four drinks sat ready. A silent toast was raised by each to the empty chair.

"Poor James," offered Hathaway.

"Poor coward James, more like," suggested Walter, still angry at how easily they had been given up.

A few nods showed he wasn't the only one disappointed at how they had become the hunted.

"So when will our President join us?" asked Mellon.

"Shortly," offered Walter.

"How did you manage it? I mean, how have you got him here? You couldn't get a call returned yesterday!" asked Lawrence Harkness, mindful of Lawson's statement that their plan was ruined when Russell got the presidency without them.

"That's simple. I know Andrew Russell better than anyone. In his life, there are two things he aspires to. The first and foremost is the presidency but that my friends has a lifespan of no more than eight years. His second and perhaps to us most important and to whom we have our dearly departed friend to thank," he said raising his glass to the empty chair. "Is to become a member of the world's most powerful and exclusive club. Gentlemen," he raised his glass in the air again. "The Alibi Club!"

Smiles emitted from each of the group. Membership to the Alibi club was lifelong and the death of James Lawson had created an irresistible opportunity.

"Brilliant!" congratulated Mellon. The image of his presidential motorcade becoming clearer by the second.

***

Sam had left Rebecca behind in the room, completely understanding her dilemma. Also, if he were to be honest, it took some pressure off. Looking after himself was one thing, having to worry about somebody else at the same time was not ideal. He had spent the day preparing everything he needed. Between camping stores and DIY stores, he had secured it all.

Rebecca had, in the meantime, busied herself with tracking down potential leads for the nuclear weapon. While Sam shopped, she had hit the phones and it seemed had made some progress. While he was leaving to go to the Alibi Club, she was heading to the Palestinian Embassy, chasing a tip.

Sam had been in position for over two hours when the first limo arrived. His route into position across the rooftops had been long and circuitous. The Secret Service guys had done an excellent job, almost perfect, but fortunately for Sam, they had left the tiniest of blind spots. However, it had taken over an hour for the watcher to turn around long enough for Sam to get to it but nonetheless, it existed and Sam was in place. Moving would be a different matter entirely. The Secret Service had that well covered.

Rebecca had taken up position in the Starbucks opposite the Palestinian Embassy. Like Sam, she was just awaiting for her opportunity. It was almost eight when eventually the last light was extinguished and she had her chance. As the door was shut behind the last Palestinian, she was up and moving. Time was not on her side.

She walked up to the door and taking the key she had been given by the Head of Mossad in Washington earlier that day, she unlocked the door and entered silently. It seemed the local Mossad agents had secured a key some time ago and carried out regular checks, completely unbeknownst to the Palestinians, of what the Palestinians were up to.

Rebecca didn't find anything that looked as though it would help her find the bomb but as she finished up and left, she smiled. The journey hadn't been a complete waste of time.

As she stepped back onto the street, she wished she could help Sam more but Ben had been explicit. She was to stay well clear.

# Chapter 69

The President's motorcade waited for him. He was due to finish his last appointment at around 8.30 p.m. Thereafter, he was going to spend the evening with friends at his private club. All of course was true. The one bit that wasn't entirely true was the reference to his club. This was not yet the case. He would be a guest this evening. However he was hoping that status would change very quickly.

At 8.30 to the second, he excused himself from his, he had to admit, exceptionally dull guests and made his journey to the Alibi club. He jumped into the car and found Honey, sitting waiting for him.

"Sorry, Mister President, do you mind if we run through your schedule on the way?"

It was a very short three-minute drive to the Alibi Club and hardly seemed worthwhile. However, not one to refuse a very pretty young lady, he smiled and jumped in beside her. Before they even pulled away, Honey was undoing the President's zip and promising she would have him coming before he knew it. She lowered her head into his lap as the President rested his on the headrest, thanking God for blacked out windows, amongst many other things.

The President's announcement that morning that he was visiting the Alibi Club that same evening had caused more than a little concern amongst his Secret Service detail, particularly as the President himself had asked for security to be significantly increased just the day before, for no apparent reason, other than 'a bad feeling'.

The Alibi Club was locked down tight. Nobody was getting in or out of there. Of that they were sure. The journey to the club would be in the presidential limousine, nicknamed 'The Beast' and, immune to pretty much any form of attack. It was bullet proof, rocket proof, gas proof, fire proof. In fact just about everything proof. Unlike normal motorcades, as this was a personal trip, they had trimmed it down from the normal thirty vehicles to just four. Even that was probably overkill. Nobody knew the President was going out, never mind where he was actually going.

As the motorcade swept out of the grounds, only a small throng of tourists witnessed the cars leaving. Not one of them took any more notice than normal. Cameras clicked as they sped past. A right turn onto 17 St NW was followed two blocks later by a left onto Pennsylvania Avenue NW. One block later, they turned onto 18th St NW, a block and a half from the Alibi Club. The sixteen secret service agents prepared to jump out and escort the President into the building, surrounded by over sixty of their colleagues.

*\*\**

Rebecca had walked back across to the Starbucks café and was just finishing her coffee as the first black suburban swept past, it's blue lights flashing and clearing the road ahead. Another quickly followed.

Rebecca had seen motorcades many times before. She lifted her phone and hit the dial button twice. As it connected, she stood up and left Starbucks, not by the 18th St exit but onto H St., not missing a stride as the explosion shook the windows behind her.

The Palestinian Embassy was on the same block as the Alibi Club but around the corner on 18th St NW, rather than on I street.

*\*\**

The Secret Service agent in the third Suburban jumped as the flash of light appeared to his right directly opposite the Presidential Limousine. He knew two things from the location of the flash. It was no accident and they were very lucky. The Beast had hardly flinched as the explosion occurred. The car remained on course and unharmed. All five cars instantly accelerated as the radios broke into life.

"Lead to Cadillac One, is POTUS OK?" POTUS was the acronymic codename for the President Of The United States.

The driver and agent in the Beast, formally referred to as Cadillac One, had seen the flash like the others but had not even felt the smallest wave pressure. So it was with some confidence that they lowered the darkened glass between the President and themselves.

"Lead, Cadillac One is intact, no effects felt. I repeat no effects felt. Will double-check with POTUS."

"Return to White House." The lead agent issued the instruction to the motorcade as he awaited confirmation from Cadillac One.

As the screen descended, the agent was faced with a scene of carnage. The President lay on his side, holding his stomach. His chest and body were covered in blood while his assistant's head lolled back as blood ran from her mouth and down her chin, her white blouse crimson with blood.

"Oh my God! Lead, change of destination, Walter Reed, I repeat Walter Reed and make it quick."

# Chapter 70

Sam heard the explosion in his hideout and fought against looking. The explosion was nearby, he knew that much and he also knew it wasn't large. A diversionary type explosion, he thought. He thought back to all of Rebecca's goings on throughout the day. She didn't suddenly have something else that needed to be done, did she? She wouldn't, he thought. No, she couldn't have. She couldn't be implicated in anything to do with an action against the President. As the night air filled with the sound of sirens coming ever closer, Sam knew it was Rebecca's work. He gave it ten more minutes and rolled to his left. He could see one of the sniper positions clearly from there and unless he was staring straight back, he wouldn't be seen.

The sniper was nowhere to be seen. Sam rolled to the right, the other sniper was not there either. He rose onto his knee. They were all gone. He ventured a look down at the roof below. Six men had become two. Rebecca, he knew, had diverted the President, saving his life and robbing Sam of an opportunity. She had probably also saved his own life but that wasn't the point. He didn't know whether to be impressed or angry. He'd figure it out once he had dealt with the old men.

He looked over the lip of window at the two remaining guards. The Secret Service agents had obviously been pulled out. Not unsurprising in the circumstances. The President wouldn't be going anywhere near there for a very long time. However, the old men would have based their security requirements on the Secret Service being there. With them gone, there was probably a high probability they would make a break for it themselves. Sam realized he had to hurry.

The two guards below were not like Lawson's. The beefcakes were gone and had been replaced by real professionals but professional what? They were extremely confident in their abilities but unlike the Secret Service, they were not covering the angles. These guys were not trained defenders, they were attackers thought Sam. And just like in football, each had their own specific purpose. They would look for where they would come from themselves and concentrate their efforts there. The Secret Service never took such chances, they just covered everything.

Sam also noted a lack of intercoms. They really had expected the Secret Service to do their job for them. With the cacophony of sirens from just around the corner, Sam did not have to worry in the least about noise. Even without the silencers he had on his MP5 and Sig, he'd have been fine. He watched for a few minutes as both men wandered aimlessly from front to back of the roof, checking down below and occasionally lifting their eyes skywards towards to the taller rooftops. They really did not expect any company. They were probably moaning about having to babysit some old codgers. He watched as they came together again on their almost constant wandering. He had already perched himself ready, praying they didn't look up on that occasion. Fortunately they didn't and Sam dropped the fifteen feet and his 210 lbs onto the men below. The three of them landed in a sprawl, Sam coming off best. He had used the two men to break his fall. One, he was certain had a cracked collarbone, the other he knew had a broken leg. There was no way it would have bent that way otherwise. He almost felt sorry as he cable-tied them both, trying to make them as comfortable as possible. A fresh sock and elephant tape ensured they would also remain fairly quiet, although the guy with the funny leg was making one hell of a racket despite the gag.

Sam entered the loft space via the hatch and checking below, dropped down into the building proper. It was deceptively large and a number of doors led off the passageway. Sam tried a few and found nothing but bedrooms. He needed to go down. He made his way to the end of the corridor and peered over the balcony. Another two men stood below him, chatting inanely about football.

"Get ready to move out!" The shout from below made it clear time was running out.

The men below split. One heading up and one down. One to tell the guys on the roof and the other to prep for leaving.

Sam slipped back towards the loft hatch and noticed a small alcove just to the right of it. He pushed himself back into the space and waited as the guard moved towards him.

As the guard was halfway up the ladders, Sam stepped forward and kicked them away. The guard's legs desperately searched for some purchase in mid air like some childish cartoon. But gravity always wins and the guard crashed to the floor. It was only when he hit the ground that he realized somebody had deliberately removed the ladder. As he started to look around, Sam's right fist hit him square in the jaw. 210 lbs of pure energy connected with the very confused guard and almost raised him back into mid air. He crumpled to the ground with little or no fight left. More cable-ties and another fresh sock secured and silenced him.

Three down, at least another two left, thought Sam - the one who shouted up and the guy who went down. Sam walked down to the second floor and quickly ascertained it also was empty. His guys had to be downstairs. Time was running out.

Sam had to make a quick decision. If he wanted these guys, this was his chance and it wouldn't come again. Sam pulled out the Sig and chambering a round, he walked down the stairs as if he had every right in the world to be there.

The first guard he came across hardly gave him a second glance. Sam swung his pistol and brought it crashing into the side of his head. The guard had stupidly assumed his three colleagues above would have either stopped anyone coming in or warned them of any oncoming threats. The third option, that an intruder might get past them without warning, did not even figure in their range of potential threats. Sam had found, throughout his service, that arrogance about ability was just as dangerous as inability.

Sam heard voices to his right and walked towards them. A guard opened the door as he approached and unlike his colleague, he was obviously far less confident in his colleagues.

His UZI submachine pistol was raised immediately in response to the threat. Sam pulled the trigger on his already raised Sig and two shells ensured the guard would never pull his trigger. His lifeless body fell back into the room behind him and from the screams, it was clear that Sam had found his prey.

"Good evening, Gentlemen," he offered as he strode into the room. "I believe you've been looking for my brother and me?"

# Chapter 71

Rebecca had made it back to the guesthouse without incident. She knew that the explosion was all bang and no power, nothing more than a glorified firework. However, it had been timed to perfection and coming from the Palestinian Embassy, it would look like a bomb that had failed to explode properly. It was therefore with some concern that she watched the news and discovered the President had been rushed to Walter Reed Hospital and was undergoing emergency treatment.

The more she considered the possibility, the more ludicrous it became. The explosion was miniscule and the President was in a vehicle that would stop a direct hit from pretty much anything. It just wasn't possible.

"Ben, we have a problem." She needed to know what to do. Killing presidents was way beyond her pay grade.

"What's wrong Rebecca?" asked Ben, instantly worried by the sound of her voice.

'I think I've really screwed up," she offered.

'Why?" he asked cautiously.

"I helped Sam tonight."

"So?"

"The President was going to be there as well. As you said, I couldn't let him get to the President. So I either stopped Sam or the President. I went with my heart rather than my head and went for the President and arranged a little diversion but I may have miscalculated."

Ben began to laugh uncontrollably, to the point that Rebecca was furious.

"What??!!!" she screamed, forgetting where she was.

"I have it under very good authority," he continued to laugh. "That President Russell was almost castrated this evening. It seems his Personal Assistant is very personal and while performing an oral act in the back of his limo, your little diversion caused him to jump and her to clench her teeth. She damned near took his dick off!"

"Seriously?"

"Yep, but obviously we don't know anything about it!"

"Of course. Are they going to be OK?" she asked with genuine concern, failing to see the humor. Ultimately, she was responsible.

"They'll be fine - he just needs some stitches and a couple of teeth removed while she needs her teeth replaced, if you know what I mean?"

"Unfortunately, yes!"

"How did Sam get on with the Horsemen?" he asked, changing the subject.

"The who?"

Ben kicked himself. "The four old men?"

"You said the horsemen?"

"No I said the four men."

Rebecca could argue but she knew what she had heard. There was more to this than Ben was telling her. She dropped it but had every intention of coming back to it.

As she was about to reply, the door opened and Sam walked in, fresh as a daisy and threw her a huge smile.

"I'll call you back Ben!" She hung up and rushed across the room to hug Sam.

"Well?" she asked, eventually letting go.

"Five down, two to go!" he answered simply and without explanation.

# Chapter 72

**Walter Reed National Military Medical Centre**

President Russell insisted on leaving. He had a country to run and a few stitches weren't going to hold him back. That was part of the excuse, the other part was that the embarrassment was killing him. Every time a doctor or nurse smiled at him, he assumed they were thinking of what had caused his injury. Nancy had accepted his offer the second he had made it. Honey would be taking a role elsewhere in government and a substantial ex-gratia payment would ensure her silence for ever more. Russell was tempted to make it more air tight with a call to Johnson but she was an exceptionally beautiful young woman and so had decided against it.

Nancy sat by his side on the journey back to the White House, tut tutting at the state of his diary. It was going to take her the rest of the week to sort it out. The irony of his assistant actually running through his diary with him, following his previous car journey, was not missed as he accepted and declined a number of requests that had come in. His driver and his agent, the same ones as before, also noted the screen remained firmly down between themselves and the President.

"Saturday we have you going to Corpus Christi for the unveiling," said Nancy.

Russell didn't need to be reminded, it was down as the unveiling of a memorial, commissioned by the former President and in memory of the victims of the nuclear atrocity. It was rather ironic that it fell on the same day as a new atrocity was planned. However, it offered Russell an excuse to get out of Washington, just in case, and would give him a platform for a far bigger event. He would be naming his VP, as well as other positions.

"Best we fly down the night before, it's going to be a big day," he suggested.

Before long, they were back in the White House and CIA director Johnson was pacing the hallway as he waited for the President.

"What's wrong?" asked Russell as Johnson followed him into the Oval Office.

"Koch, Harkness, Hathaway and Mellon, that's what's wrong," he said, shutting the door.

"Christ, what now? They moaning about their babysitters?" he asked, slumping into his sofa and instantly regretting the sudden motion and impact.

"They're all dead is what's wrong!"

"Don't be ridiculous!" exclaimed Russell, not believing Johnson for a second.

"Definitely! Executed! One round through each of their foreheads. Bang, bang, bang, fucking bang." He motioned each bang with an outstretched index finger and thumb.

"Your guys were watching them!"

"While you were getting your cock sewn back on, your secret service agents left the Alibi Club and left my guys swinging in the wind with their asses hanging out. Sam Baker waltzed in, popped the guys and disappeared."

"Shit!"

"The explosion that had you jumping in the air was nothing more than a glorified firework, all bang no bluster. It was a sham, timed and placed to perfection. We did exactly what he wanted, pulled the secret service away from the Club."

"But why not get *me* at the Club? He must have known I was going if he rigged the diversion?"

"Shit, hadn't thought of that."

The President pressed his buzzer. "Nancy, get me Henry Preston and Jim Gates, please."

Five minutes later, the four were trying to work through why Sam Baker had not taken a shot at Russell.

The only conclusion any of them could come up with that made any sense was that Sam Baker did not know Russell was involved. It also meant that if he were unaware of Russell's involvement, Johnson was probably in the clear also.

"Ah, one problem. We're assuming he didn't get anything out of the four before he killed them," offered Preston.

"OK, back to plan A. I want Sam Baker dead," instructed the President.

# Chapter 73

Sam woke up with a start. Despite the hour, only 4.00 a.m., he called his brother but assured him everything was fine. They had, as ordered, not ventured outside. Cabin fever was setting in but they would be good, he assured his younger brother. They would not go out.

He looked back at the bed and the stunning figure of Rebecca. It felt wrong and he knew it was wrong. His wife and child lay dead. He hadn't even buried them properly. He knew strange things happened in times of crisis. You would do things that would otherwise not even enter your mind. Rebecca had kept him sane. She had kept his mind occupied, his thoughts alive and not with the dead. He knew he'd feel guilt and shame for what he had done but somehow it felt right as well. He stared at her sleeping figure and realized now was not the time. There would be time for mourning and recriminations later.

Sam spotted the Victor Annual in his backpack. Perfect, he needed something to occupy his mind. His mind ventured back almost 40 years as he read and followed the comic strips that told their stories of the British fighting the Germans. He smiled as one strip told the story of a spy caught behind enemy lines who managed to escape before he was interrogated and returned home. Nothing overly surprising other than the fact that the spy had a false tooth with a cyanide pill. He looked across at Rebecca to see if she was awake to tell her where Deif's idea must have come from. She was sound asleep. He'd tell her later. The next strip featured a naval convoy taking vital supplies to the Russians who were valiantly fighting the Germans on the Eastern

Front. It was real gung-ho stuff, thought Sam. The British ships fought the harshness of the seas before being set upon by German fighter bombers. Without an escort, all was lost but in good old Victor style, they pulled something out the hat and what a something, thought Sam. He stared at the little comic drawing and thought back to the false tooth. Jesus!

"Rebecca!" he shouted, no concerns if she were sleeping or not. "We need to get to my brother and the Secretary of Defense!" If Rebecca's information was correct, they had three days to stop the bomb.

# Chapter 74

The Sheikh was enjoying the warmth of the Texan sun after the biting cold of Montana. The first rays of sun, even at that time of year, radiated a wonderful and welcome heat. Zak had been an extremely reluctant passenger as they travelled towards the scene of his atrocity some years earlier. But the Sheikh had assured him on many occasions that they would not be going beyond the security wall that now protected the Southern Texas border from the wasteland beyond.

As they drove towards the small town of Bishop, the wall came into view and Zak winced at his handiwork. The wall stretched off as far as the eye could see, blocking the devastation from view. The Sheikh pulled into a small diner and joined a throng of tourists who had rather bizarrely come to look at the wall. It seemed quite the tourist destination, badges mugs and t-shirts lined the walls, all emblazoned with a mushroom cloud visible above the wall that now protected every American from the land beyond.

The tourists provided perfect cover as they joined a large group on a guided tour of the new border. There was no border-crossing. The massive steel gates that briefly interrupted the wall were firmly closed and a radiation symbol clearly warned anyone from venturing beyond. To the left and right of the gates, two large areas had been cut into the wall and it was these that the Sheikh was most interested in. Two plaques were soon to be mounted and would be unveiled by the President himself. It was anticipated that most of the Cabinet and high ranking officials of government would be in attendance and it was for that very reason that the Sheikh required Zak's assistance. On his own, he wouldn't get within a mile of the location come Saturday. With Zak and his Defense Intelligence Agency ID, he'd be able to get up close and personal.

As the site became busier, Zak and the Sheikh walked back to the diner. They saw the first trucks arrive in preparation for Saturday's event. They paused and watched as the trucks pulled off to the side and a small army of workers appeared and began unloading staging and folding chairs. If nothing else, it confirmed the event was definitely going ahead.

The Sheikh directed Zak back to their motel just twenty miles away in Corpus Christi. He excused himself and walked to the internet café and logged onto a non descript chatroom. He re-read the message a number of times. It wasn't so much what it read, it was the hidden meaning. Things had obviously taken a significant change of direction and his task had just gotten a lot harder. Fortunately, it did not alter the location, it just increased the number of targets.

# Chapter 75

Ben listened as Rebecca relayed what they had discovered in the comic book. Initially, he had scoffed at the idea, it was utterly ridiculous. But the more he thought it, the more he couldn't rule it out. He instructed his guys to widen the search. The ship did not necessarily have to be in port before midnight Yom Kippur. They could look at boats scheduled to arrive even a day later.

Ben had sat through his next meeting digesting everything Rebecca had told him over the last few days. None of it was good and more importantly, none of it was good for Israel. He excused himself from the meeting. There were less than 60 hours until midnight Yom Kippur and he had little time available. He looked at the clock, checking the time he already knew. He calculated the timings. It was quite simple. He didn't have the time but more importantly, he didn't have the time not to.

"David, what's the quickest plane we've got to get me to America?" he asked the Defense Minister.

"I'll call you straight back!"

Two minutes later, he called back. "Ben, normally one of our Gulfstreams would be as quick as we could do. Fighters just don't have the range without numerous tanker stops and by the time we get that organized you'd have been half way there in the Gulfstream."

"OK, that's normal." Ben didn't have time for explanations or pre-amble.

"Well, it seems there's an experimental American B1-R sitting at Nevatim. It's undergoing trials for long distance speed runs. It arrived a couple of days ago after doing it in five hours, half the time of the Gulfstream."

"And they'd let me hitch a ride?"

"They're keen to test it and as they go supersonic, it has to fly over sea and not land. America to here gives them about as long a straight run as you get over sea. I just need to tell them when and you're good to go."

Ben thanked God something was going in their favor.

"Fantastic David, I'll be there in four hours." Or not all, he thought, as he hung up.

Before he went anywhere, he was about to undertake the riskiest mission of his life. The Shin Bet officer greeted him as he left his office and talked him through a number of key points. The most important was that Ben must stay in full sight at all times. If at any point they feared he would be taken and interrogated, well, quite simply they could not allow that to happen. Ben was assured that the snipers targeting him would ensure a quick and painless end. How thoughtful and comforting, he thought.

As the helicopter came into land, Ben's nerves were beginning to get the better of him. It was quite the most ludicrous idea he had ever had but with less than three days to save his country, he would try anything and this was pretty much all that was left.

The small open-top jeep offered no protection. He climbed aboard and with the white flag in position, he drove towards the gates which opened as he approached them and then slammed shut behind him.

Ben Meir, for the first time in decades, was in Gaza where more than half the population would happily slit his throat and that was only because the rest were too young or too old. He drove forward and stood up for all to see the white flag fluttering behind him. Ben was hoping to meet just one person and prayed that the boldness of his arrival coming would afford him that meeting.

It didn't take long before the first armed man approached and, if Ben's contacts were correct, Ahmed Hameed would already know that Ben Meir was sitting in a jeep with a white flag.

"What do you want, old man?"

"To talk with Ahmed Hameed, in private."

"I will take you to him!" he smiled in response.

Ben almost laughed at the transparency of the offer to slaughter him. "We must meet here, for reasons I'm sure Ahmed will appreciate!"

The gunman drove off. A second gunman, more senior, insisted Ben drive further into Gaza. Ben kept a close eye on the odometer. He had been told to stay in clear view and within 0.8 of a mile of the guard tower. Any further and they would assume the worst.

Ben stopped as the gauge clicked to 0.8 and ignored the gunman's gesticulations to come further.

Ahmed had surveyed the scenes from afar. The news of one of Israel's most famous and feared men venturing into Gaza on his own with only a white flag as cover had spread like wildfire. Ahmed's network had informed him almost immediately and the news of the request to meet with him in private certainly intrigued him. If it were a trap, he could see no way out for Ben Meir. His men would cut him down with ease. Perhaps he was terminally ill and was willing to sacrifice himself for Ahmed. However, Ahmed held no illusions that his name was held in the same regard as Deif or the Sheikh. Ben Meir would not trade himself for Ahmed Hameed. Deif's plan to bring them to their knees with the nuclear weapons seemed to be the only thing that fit. Here was Ben Meir, begging on his knees. That would raise Ahmed's name alongside Deif and perhaps even the Sheikh. He instructed his best snipers to take up position. Any funny business and they were to kill the Israeli.

Ahmed jumped into a jeep and drove towards the diminutive Israeli.

Ben stood up and offered Ahmed his hand, as the two introduced each other formally.

"I do not like your snipers aiming their weapons at me, please instruct them to stand down," insisted Ahmed, refusing Ben's hand.

"My dear boy," laughed Ben. "They're not aiming at you, they have explicit instructions under no circumstance to shoot you. They're aiming at me!"

Ahmed looked at him with some confusion. The old man was mad, it was a trick.

"My government is extremely concerned that if I were to be captured, I hold some of the most secret and important information in the land. I'm too dangerous to them in your hands. I also believe you're too valuable to us dead. So trust me, if anybody's getting out of here alive, it's you. My life is in your hands."

Ahmed accepted the honesty and Ben Meir's hand.

"Now," said Ben. "Let me tell you about something called Ararat." He beckoned for Ahmed to sit, it was going to take some time.

# Chapter 76

Preston hadn't slept all night. He had become increasingly wary of Johnson's influence and closeness to the President. Johnson was not the brightest but was most possibly one of the most ruthless and ambitious people Preston had ever met. That was an exceptionally dangerous combination and he most certainly was not a man Preston ever intended to have to call 'Sir'. The President was an exceptionally bright man but unfortunately, he was also incredibly easily led. His judgment, at times, was very wanting. The old men whom he had tied himself up with were a case in point. Killing Baker had always been the wrong move but once in train, it had to be followed through. If it did ever leak, Bakergate could destroy the political system in the US.

It was therefore down to Henry Preston to rescue the President and save the American political system and in turn, he hoped, gain the Vice President's chair.

Preston, as Director of National Intelligence, oversaw sixteen of the nation's most important intelligence agencies and had literally hundreds of thousands of America's most intelligent individuals working for him. Preston had left the Oval Office the previous evening and called on his brightest and best talents. He had locked them in the room and between them, they talked through and considered all the information to date.

For obvious reasons, Preston had excluded the CIA from the session. Johnson's guys couldn't be trusted not to keep him in the loop and this was going to be Preston's baby from start to finish. Preston laid out the timeline and talked his small and elite audience through what they knew had happened to date. With two FBI agents used to working down the leads, two code breakers/hackers from the NSA, a National Reconnaissance Office analyst with access to satellite feeds both historic and real time and a Department of Justice specialist with access to every database in the land, he figured that between them, they'd get there.

It was one of NSA men who jumped on the names they had used on the Paris to New York flight as a potential for narrowing down the search area. Of course, it was unlikely that they'd ever use the names again but up until that point, the names had been clean. As suggested, they tracked the names back and one of them, Sam's, led all the way back to Glacier Park International Airport, Montana. Of course, they were no longer there but ask ourselves this, suggested the NSA code breaker. Why did they start there? Of course, that rationale, after hours of work earned a hearty laugh. However, he then pointed out that they didn't start out as just two people. Light bulbs went on around the room as the point was made. Senator Baker was probably near Glacier Park International Airport.

With a point of reference, it did not take long to track down the skiing lodge. What was a complex barrier of trust funds to a tax lawyer was a Level One line puzzle to an NSA code breaker. As morning broke, they had their location. The NRA man was instructed to get a bird over there asap and was in the process of redirecting a new KH-13 satellite to do just that. They would have visuals of the lodge any time soon. Meanwhile, Preston was on the phone to DIA and instructing a drone be put up to offer round the clock eyes on the site as the satellite would only have a specific window due to its orbit. NSA were instructed to tap into every piece of communication that went anywhere near the lodge. With eyes and ears all over the location, Preston began to consider the assault.

Having witnessed Johnson's previous failures, Preston had no intention of repeating them. Bombing was out. He wanted to know for definite that Senator Baker was out of the game. A straight through the door approach had failed as well in Washington and just succeeded in embroiling the Secretary of Defense into the mess. It was time for the professionals, Amateur

Hour was over. Preston picked up the phone and called his contact at the Human Intelligence Directorate of the DIA, similar to the NCS of the CIA in many ways, apart from one. The DIA got the pick of the crop, the CIA had to settle for the best of what was left.

Within the hour, two five-men teams were kitting up and preparing to drive their two Suburbans into the loading area on board a C130 for the trip to Montana.

Preston packed up his things, thanked his assistants and hightailed it to the National Security Council meeting. The President had increased the frequency to every eight hours as the deadline for the nuclear bomb loomed. However, with the Vice Presidency sorted, Preston would turn his attention to finding the bomb and saving the nation. It was difficult being the most intelligent guy in the room, he smiled but somebody had to do it.

# Chapter 77

Sam really wished he could just phone his brother and tell him to come to him but he couldn't. If anything happened to them, he'd never forgive himself. All it took was the tiniest slip-up at a gas station or a restroom and they'd be dead. With no option but to go get him, he had run through the routes with Rebecca. Driving was out, too long. The train, likewise. That only left airplanes which, considering everything he had done, was not going to be the easiest form of transport, nor the safest.

Rebecca made a call. It was going to get her into a lot of trouble but if it paid off, it would be fine. If not, she may be paying the state of Israel back for many years to come. Hiring private jets was not going to please the Accounts Department.

They grabbed their kit. Of course, another reason to justify the additional expense, around $25,000, was the benefit of keeping hold of their $1,200's worth of weaponry. Forty minutes later, they pulled into the parking lot of Manassas Regional Airport and avoiding any type of scanner or camera equipment, they boarded their waiting Learjet 45XR for the four-hour flight to Glacier Park. As the stewardess offered them champagne for the flight, Rebecca checked if it was an additional cost. It was. They drank water. And she added that to her list of justifications.

Just after lunch, they landed, picked up the Camry from the parking lot and drove to the Lodge.

***

The second they turned off the main road and entered the grounds of the lodge, they became targets. At least in the eyes of the Avenger's operator. The drone was stationed almost 30,000 feet above, maintaining a constant visual on the property below. It had replaced the satellite surveillance just two hours earlier and had been the same unit previously used by Johnson's team to obliterate an empty cabin. It still had almost eighteen hours left in its tanks but with the assault team due in the next two hours, it was extremely unlikely to need a replacement.

*\*\**

Sam was delighted to see his brother and quickly updated him on where they had been and how the Alibi Club may have a glut of new members joining in the near future. Once they had brought them up to speed, Sam pulled out the comic book and explained his theory to the Secretary of Defense. James studied the drawing carefully, he had heard of it but it was well before his time. However, he knew a few people in England who may be able to help. He also considered calling some of his own men but after discussion, they agreed it just wasn't worth the risk. They really did not know who they could trust, money and power talked and it seemed the President and his cronies had an abundance of both.

With leads that required a few calls to Russia, James cracked on. The comic might be correct after all. So far, things were adding up factually and had Deif searched similarly, he would have made the same links. It was all out there, as James proffered more than once. As darkness fell, James' progress slowed down. Across the world, it was the middle of the night but he carried on relentless. Numerous angry calls later and they had a breakthrough. The owner of a small shipyard in Russia had sold an item like that a few months earlier.

The owner went to get his records. He had the name of the ship somewhere. And eventually, James Murphy jumped up and down with excitement.

"I've got it! I've found the ship!"

As the others jumped up to congratulate him, Sam dived and pulled his brother and Rebecca with him to the floor.

The first bullet flew through the window and entered Secretary of Defense James Murphy's open mouth, a fraction of a second before it took the back of his head with it.

# Chapter 78

Ben Meir checked his watch as he paused for breath. He had not stopped talking for almost two hours. Ahmed Hameed sat open-mouthed before him.

"So Ahmed, my friend," offered Ben. "Do you want to be a hero?!"

As far as Ben could see, that's what it came down to. Ahmed could be a hero or a villain. The spoils in this case were very much for the hero's taking. The villain would gain nothing and could lose everything. Of course, one major hurdle had to be overcome for any of this to matter. Ahmed Hameed had to believe Ben Meir. The Palestinian terrorist would have to trust the Israeli strategist. It was a lot to ask.

Ahmed said nothing. He just looked at Ben and tried to gauge him. Ahmed Hameed prided himself on his ability to read people. That was how he had got to where he was.

"I must go now. I suppose tomorrow night, at midnight, I will have your answer," proposed Ben.

"I repeat what I have said to you many times Ben Meir. I do not have full control, everything is compartmentalized. My answer may not give you everything you want, only partially."

"Then I have wasted your time with my story. I should have sought another," offered Ben, knowing it would elicit a reaction.

Ahmed rose to the challenge. "You came to the right man, Ben Meir. You know you did. But even if I did choose to believe you and go with your plan, my network stops at the beach."

"I know, I know. Whatever happens, it has been a pleasure." Ben shook Ahmed's hand and drove back to the border gates, his head held just a little further forward than he would normally have it. But the anticipation was unwarranted. The gates slammed closed behind him.

Like Daniel, he had entered the lion's den and survived. One den down, one to go.

The short flight to Nevatim air force base took thirty minutes and the striking Rockwelll B1-R Lancer stood ready for take-off. Looking more like an over sized fighter jet than a strategic bomber, it was of a similar size to a Boeing 757 and even older. However the B1-R was almost entirely rebuilt with new engines, avionics and weapon systems. Pretty much everything but the skin was new. It was also taking on a slightly more appropriate role and was looking to become a fighter bomber with the addition of air to air weaponry. Its massive range and ability to cruise like a Concorde was going to make it a very interesting addition to the US' arsenal. In the meantime it was also going to get Ben and his two bodyguards to America before they even left.

The American Colonel welcomed Ben on board and wasted no time in kicking the engines to life and hurtling them off the runway and into the sky. They were supersonic soon after and with only his thoughts and the sound of four Pratt & Whitney P119 engines between him and America, Ben put his head back and fell asleep.

# Chapter 79

Preston waited for the Situation room to empty after the third National Security Council meeting of the day. They still were no nearer tracking the nuclear weapon and the mood of the President was deteriorating quickly. The President had been in meetings with his campaign manager prior to the NSC meeting and he had pointed out clearly and succinctly to the president that if he didn't stop the bomb it would stop his campaign dead in the water.

"Mr President, could I have a minute please?"

"Not now Henry, I need to get on," he replied picking up his papers.

"Mr President, I really think you will want to see this," replied Henry intriguingly.

Henry Preston ushered the rest of the NSC attendees from the room and closed the door, locking it for good measure, which elicited a look of surprise from the President.

"Trust me sir, you won't want to be disturbed!"

Preston hit the screen remote and the large screen ahead of the President burst into light. The grainy overview of a mountainside some 2,300 miles away quickly came into focus. The President could see the roof of a house and 10 small green blips surrounded it, five to the front and five to the rear.

Preston hit another button and the sound of men talking could be heard.

"Sniper One, I still have the shot. I repeat I still have the shot."

"Sniper One, Team Leader, confirm target, over?"

"Male mid fifties."

"Hold sniper one, we are awaiting the go command."

Preston looked towards the President as the scene before him began to make sense.

"You found him?" the President asked elated, wanting to jump up and hug Preston.

Preston nodded and indicated back towards the screen. They were waiting for him to give the go.

The president nodded vociferously, Preston pressed down the intercom button. "Team Leader you have a go, I repeat Go, Go, Go."

The President listened as Sniper One was told to fire and a few seconds later the screen flashed into life as flashbangs were thrown into the lodge.

"Target down, kill, kill, kill." Said Sniper One confirming a hit.

Two blips stayed where they were while the other eight began to converge on the house.

***

Sam had noticed a movement in the corner of his eye and reacted, Rebecca and his brother stood in front of them and he took them down with him as he dived for cover. As the back of Murphy's head exploded the house was plunged into darkness, a second later bright flashes were followed by waves of pressure as the flashbangs came from three different directions.

The front door crashed open and the main window behind them shattered as four soldiers rushed in.

Sam sucked up the flashbang and grabbed for his MP5 which lay on the side table, throwing his Sig to Rebecca as he moved. The first two men through the front door took a full magazine from the MP5 as Sam struggled to aim, he just pointed and pulled the trigger. Rebecca, like Sam in many ways remained cool under fire, as the two soldiers shot out the window and charged through under cover of the flashbang, she swung round caught the pistol that Sam had thrown and shot the two soldiers the only way she knew how, dead.

Clark was in the kitchen with Mrs Baker when the flashbangs came careening into the lodge. Clark didn't even think about her movements, instinct took over and she pulled Mrs Baker behind her and leveled her weapon at the door to the kitchen. Whoever came through it, she'd shoot and ask questions later. Unfortunately for Clark she could not cover all the windows as well as the door and certainly could not protect against the sniper one hundred yards out in a darkened wood.

*** 

"Team Leader. Two down, I repeat two down."

"Team Leader. Two down at rear also. I repeat two down."

The team leader was furious, his info was a bunch of terrorists were in the house that required to be eliminated with extreme prejudice. Terrorists in his experience did not react like that to flash bangs. Flash bangs usually allowed 2 or 3 seconds to get into a room and clear it. He was against highly trained and skilled operatives, that was not the remit. He would have never gone for a full on assault had he known.

"Team Leader, this is sniper two. I have a target, female around thirty, holding a weapon."

"Take her down."

# Chapter 80

Ben stepped off the aircraft refreshed and ready to go, despite the fact that he had lengthened the day by seven hours. The sun was just dipping behind the mountains as his car arrived to pick him up from the terminal building. It was a thirty minute drive and Ben soaked in the American air and atmosphere. He had always loved America. The openness and size was vast in comparison to Israel. As they pulled into the driveway, the darkness was complete. Only the road was lit up ahead. The massive trees which were older than the country itself, thought Ben, seemed to stretch to the stars. It was a cloudless night and the stars sparkled brightly in the deep black sky.

A series of bright flashes soon brought Ben back to earth. His bodyguards knew small explosions when they saw them. The slammed on the brakes and threw the car into Reverse. Their job was to keep Ben Meir out of danger, not drive him towards it.

"Stop!" screamed Ben.

The car ground to a halt.

"We have fellow Israelis in that house. We're helping not running!" Ben left no room for doubt in his tone. The car was thrown back into Drive and the car surged forward.

"Stop!" screamed Ben. The car skidded to a halt.

The two guards turned and looked at him.

"Perhaps a more subtle approach?" suggested Ben, opening the car door and heading into the trees in the direction of the house. His two bodyguards were by his side in an instant. One handed him a pistol before raising his Uzi and leading off quickly and silently through the woods. Flashes were followed by the sound of gun fire as they neared the clearing that led down to the house below.

***

Over two thousand miles away, it was the President that first spotted the new arrivals. He pointed to the screen.

"What's that, Henry? Looks like two beams of light, jerking about. Oh, they've just gone."

"Headlights, Mr President!"

Henry hit the transmit button. "Team Leader, you have new targets to your rear."

"You have got to be kidding me!" screamed the Team Leader in frustration. He knew there was at least a five-second delay on the video feed. What appeared now on screen was history.

"Sniper Two?"

"Sniper Two, come in? This is Team Leader."

"Team Leader, Sniper Two will not be playing anymore!" came the response.

"Shit!!" he screamed. He had not signed up for a suicide mission. "Pull out!" he screamed. He had already lost five men.

***

Ben dropped the headset and sent his men forward. He had had enough excitement for an old man and he'd just get in the way.

His two men broke cover and ran towards the house. Two soldiers in full gear ran towards them. The Israelis did not have to double-take. They shot a hail of rounds from their Uzis and cut them down without breaking stride. Rebecca heard the familiar clatter of the Uzi and grabbed Sam as the two young Israelis ran into the house.

"Shalom!" shouted Rebecca as they looked ready to fire.

"Shalom," they replied, not lowering their weapons.

Whoever they were, they meant business.

As one kept an eye on the room, the other walked back to the door and waved. A minute later, Ben Meir was being hugged by his very grateful goddaughter and being introduced to

Sam and Charles Baker. He was also learning of another old friend's demise.

# Chapter 81

Looking across the docks, Saul knew something was very wrong indeed. For the last two days, the procession of ships arriving at the port had begun to slow. It wasn't that they were moving back to almost normal levels, it was the fact that nothing was coming in. Everything seemed to be going out. The yards that had been a permanent mountain of cargo containers were almost empty. Each ship that docked left with more than it brought in and in the last few hours, nearly every ship was empty as it came into port but left bulging at the seams.

He locked up the office and looked at the board for the next day's arrivals. Nothing beyond 12.00 noon. No surprise as it was the beginning of Yom Kippur. The next day, Saturday, no arrivals. Again no surprise as it was a national holiday but beyond that, there was still nothing. Nothing, the docks were emptying and no new boats were due in. Saul Weisfield had no other skills. He had heard how hard the recession had hit around the world but up until then, they had been busier than ever. He was not going without a fight. They could, at least, have told him they were shutting the yard, he thought, as he walked towards the Port Director's office.

"Paul, what the hell is this? Could you not just tell us we were closing?!" Saul had known the Port Director personally for many, many years and threw the arrivals list on his desk.

Paul looked down at the list and suddenly realized what Saul was talking about. He knew nothing of the company closing down.

"Ah, sorry, I've just not put up the new list, there's no big conspiracy!" he offered genuinely.

"But the place is empty?"

"I'm told they're just having a big clearout."

Saul left the office a few minutes later thoroughly unconvinced. He couldn't help but notice how quiet the roads were. Perhaps it all made sense. However, when he arrived home, he found his wife packing up their house.

# Chapter 82

Ben had given the pilot two destinations. On arrival at the first, everyone except for him would disembark and he would travel alone to the second one. Ben Meir waited at the gates of the White House to be allowed in. Access, however, was not forthcoming.

"Have you told the President my name?" he asked again.

"Yes, Mr Meir, the answer I keep getting is that the President is in bed and is not to be disturbed. It is 11.30pm, you know."

Ben tried his cell phone again but President Russell was not picking up.

"Listen young man," Ben leant forward towards the guard who had kept watch on the gate for forty years and who recognized Ben very well. "Tell that little shit to let me in or I'll hold a press conference, on this lawn, right here, in five minutes."

The guard could of course do no such thing but he could call the President's office and tell them what Ben Meir had said, which he did.

Four minutes and forty seconds later, a call came back to the gate house.

"Welcome to the White House, Mr Meir," offered the guard as he opened the gate.

Ben rushed towards the Oval Office and spent the next thirty minutes telling President Andrew Russell more than a few home truths. Russell was apoplectic that anyone dared talk to him in such a manner and promptly had Ben escorted from the White House.

All in all, it had not gone well. Ben was in no position to strong-arm Russell. He needed Russell and Russell knew it. The only one piece of good news was that Russell instantly reacted to the news about the bomb. It seemed he had finally realized the threat was a genuine one.

Ben kicked himself. He could have played it far better. Russell was malleable, you just had to do it carefully. Ben's temper had not allowed any give. Seeing James Murphy's almost decapitated body had not brought out the best in him. America would have to wait. He had his own country to save.

Ben hitched a lift back to Israel on the B1-R and made it just in time for the 12.00 deadline. If the nukes hadn't been found by then, just 36 hours before Yom Kippur, evacuation plans were to be fully implemented with immediate effect.

As he walked into the meeting, he could instantly detect that the weapons had not been found. Their expressions said it all. Ben stood and wished everyone the best of luck. That would be the last full meeting. Of course, they would continue the hunt up until the very last minute but it was time to begin the full-scale evacuation of the cities as a matter of urgency.

# Chapter 83

Ahmed Hameed had spent the day mulling over the very strange meeting he had had with Ben Meir. A man whom he knew he shouldn't but couldn't help liking. The parts of Ararat he discussed were mind blowing and could, as Ben had said, make him a hero but if Ben was playing him, he'd die a zero, as many a rapper would have said. Ahmed was a new generation of Palestinian and felt sure that that was the only reason Ben had tried what he had tried. Deif or Akram would have shot him without question. It was another reason why Ahmed liked Ben, Ben got him. Something that not many of his fellow terrorists did. Ahmed looked to the future. Many of the terrorists knew nothing nor wanted anything but the violence. With nothing but Ben's word to go on, he was going to have to either trust the Jew or not. Trusting Jews was not something he had ever had to worry about before. In his world, you simply didn't.

Out of interest, he had put his network to work and it seemed Deif had done an exceptional job. Of the four weapons, Ahmed controlled one and as for the other three, nobody knew. It was looking like his chat with Ben was all going to be academic in any event.

As the day progressed, the news did not change, nobody knew. As noon struck, the sound began. A rumble in the sky that didn't stop. The noise travelled the length and breadth of the city, a constant droning rumble. Ahmed checked his watch. The timing was just as Ben had predicted. Ahmed called his deputies and gave them a message to take to their people. Find the controllers as though your very lives depended on it.

Ahmed began to believe these words were not without merit.

# Chapter 84

They woke up to the warmth of the Texan sun, welcome respite from the cold of Montana. Sam rolled over and looked out to the crystal blue waters of the Gulf of Mexico. It was amazing how the two entirely different vistas could elicit similar emotions. One was flat and blue, the other grey and looming. The small ramshackle beach lodge South East of Corpus Christi was perfect to disappear in.

Ben had insisted they travel with him. He had a plan to sort things out and he needed Charles and Sam in Corpus Christi on Saturday. He dropped them off and travelled to Washington to 'sort out' the President, with a view to a meeting with Sam and Charles on Saturday when Ben knew the President would be in the city.

Apparently, it had not gone well. The call had made it clear that they should keep their heads down. No meeting for an easing of the ways on Saturday had been arranged. However, he did have some good news. The President had reacted well to the search for the bomb.

\*\*\*

The Sheikh had watched as the small platform and arena were built. Zak's credentials had worked a treat and on seeing his DIA ID, the assumptions that the guy on the phone with him was his partner had worked perfectly. Of course, once the President was in town, there was no way the Secret Service would fall for it but by then, the Sheikh would not need Zak anymore. This was to be a lone mission.

The Sheikh could not believe how lax things were. A sheet with the list of attendees and their seating position sat at the front of the stage. A cursory glance gave him all he needed before heading back to Zak and suggesting that they keep a low profile for the next couple of days. The number of Secret Service agents was growing by the hour.

Zak drove back to their motel and they checked out. The Sheikh wanted to be even more anonymous. A couple of days at the beach, he suggested Port Aransas, would do them good.

As they drove down to the main beach road, the Sheikh sat looking for the perfect hideaway. All the agents back in Bishop had put him on edge. He wanted to disappear. He wanted to make sure he had a clear run on Saturday. They couldn't know he was coming. As his eyes swept from hotel to hotel, each looked more anonymous than the last. His eyes settled on one and he pointed Zak towards it, the Beach Lodge.

As they pulled up alongside, the beach and the gulf waters lay to their left. Zak whistled quietly to himself as he watched a stunning woman rinse the sand and salt from her body. Her head was thrown back as she let the fresh water rinse her dark hair that shone in the early morning sun. The Sheikh could not help but notice too. She was a true beauty, he thought, very Middle Eastern. Her curves were womanly, not girly like so many Americans. That was a real woman. She rubbed her face and swept her hair back, allowing Zak a look at the babe's face. He was not disappointed. The Sheikh, however was panicking. He knew he recognized the body. He had seen the face before and almost screamed for Zak to hit the gas.

A non-descript motel in the heart of Corpus Christi it was.

# Chapter 85

Only two good things had come from his conversation with Ben. Confirmation he could appoint his new Secretary of Defense and a solid lead to track down the bomb. The announcement of the Secretary of Defense's tragic death and the President's first appointee, he was delighted to see, was buried amongst the shocking news from Israel and the continuing solar flare problem which had grounded the world's airlines. The Israeli headline had shocked the world. Four nuclear weapons were believed to be imminently endangering the country that the world had heard so little from in the past months and years. A mass exodus of the cities was apparently underway but the country remained sealed and no foreign news crews were allowed in.

The President checked his watch. It would be another 24 hours before they would consider evacuations. At the moment, they didn't know if there was a bomb or if there was, where it was going other than to the US. Best guesses were Washington, New York, Chicago or LA but they simply didn't know. However, with their latest information from Ben, LA was definitely ruled out. All the others were still in play.

The President joined his National Security Council and listened as his newly appointed Secretary of Defense ran through what they had done with Ben's information. Unbeknownst to the new Secretary of Defense, not as far as his predecessor had managed to get, the previous evening, with just a phone. They were, however, now targeting a further 500 vessels that had previously been excluded as not reaching the US in time.

"Mr President, we have almost half our ocean-going Navy, some 150 vessels currently covering our Eastern seaboard, along with pretty much every aircraft whether naval, Air Force or National Guard on round the clock watch. We will catch this," assured the Secretary of Defense.

Henry Preston sat and listened and couldn't help but think of the clutter that must be caused by such a massive operation. It only needed one tiny slip and an American city would pay the ultimate price.

*\*\**

Akram Rayyan watched as his men unloaded two containers into the Canadian port of St John. He had quietened down his men as a cheer had gone up over the news of the Israelis running for cover. He knew that his men couldn't be prouder of being part of an operation that was teaching the Jews and her allies a lesson they'd never forget. He had also noted the significant increase in naval checks. The port was awash with the stories of checks even if you were going near America. He couldn't help but think somehow their plan had got out.

Deif was a genius, however, and had covered just such an eventuality. Akram's route ensured he would still be within Canadian waters when the weapon was launched. As the crane swung back on board, his men cast away and began the final leg of their momentous journey. Just to be safe, Akram instructed a trip round the North of Newfoundland. It would take longer but he had a few hours to spare and it would also mean a much calmer journey. It would also keep them even further away from the Americans while they got into position.

There would be no more drills. The next time they got ready would be for real. Akram looked at his watch. Twenty-four hours to go.

# Chapter 86

The pace at the White House was frantic. The Situation Room had become the emergency planning center as the hours clocked down. 6.00 a.m., twelve hours to potential detonation and they were no further forward. The President had to make a decision - begin the evacuation of major metropolitan centers or not. Time already had run too far to save everyone. If New York, Washington or Chicago were the targets, the death-toll was still running into the tens of thousands with the evacuation. Without that, the number was ten-fold and was if the weapon were released at approximately 2,000 feet above central Manhattan, there would be two million dead. The numbers were mind numbing.

The President's advisers were coming out of the woodwork, giving reasons to evacuate and reasons not to. However, the reasons not to were dwindling. Yes, mass hysteria would lead to deaths, There'd be looting and civil unrest and general chaos but the 2 million number was stark and staring. His political adviser was firmly of the opinion that, if it hit, he was screwed anyway and evacuating lots of cities, just in case, looked like a President who had no idea what was going on. His best option and the one he'd be able to milk for votes was finding it and then claiming they had tracked it all the way and only struck when the terrorists had made their move so as to ensure their convictions.

"Mr President, I need your answer, Sir," insisted Jim Gates, the Secretary of Homeland Security, who had his FEMA

Administrator on the phone and needed to give him the President's decision.

The President turned to Henry Preston and his Secretary of Defense. "Gentlemen, are you going to let our country be the victim of another nuclear attack?"

Obviously neither could say yes. Henry Preston answered first.

"No, Sir, we will not!" he replied adamantly followed by a "Hell no!" from the Secretary of Defense.

"Secretary Gates, you have your answer. I'm assured the weapon will not reach our country. Stand down the evacuation plans."

"Gentlemen, I suggest you pull the fingers out of your asses and find that bomb."

The President left the room. Had he not he felt sure he was going to puke, the decision he had just made was the biggest gamble of his life and more importantly, his career.

*\*\**

Senator Charles Baker had kept a close eye on the news. Nothing. They were already beyond the 12-hour countdown. 6 a.m. EST. He didn't know what it meant. Had they found the bomb and if not, why was there no news of mass evacuations? Surely they should at least attempt to minimize casualties. He called the number Ben had given him. He answered on the second ring.

"Ben, can you talk?

"Have to be quick but yes?" said Ben sounding out of breath. He shouted to somebody in the background. "Nope that cabinet first, then this one." He came back. "Sorry."

"Any news on the American bomb?"

"Nope, nothing at all, they're still looking."

"Christ, they haven't even begun evacuating!" he exclaimed angrily.

"I'll call you back."

Ben hung up and called back ten minutes later. "I've just spoken to our Ambassador. They're confident they'll find it in time."

"On what grounds?" questioned the Senator.

"Exactly," agreed Ben. "I've instructed our embassy staff to evacuate all major consulates and Israeli offices across the eastern seaboard."

"You know, Ben, I don't get it. James Murphy almost had the info to find the boat and he was calling Russia at 4am in the morning."

"Why Russia?"

"I've no idea. I just know that's where his leads led him!"

The Senator could sense that Ben hadn't heard him. Banging in the background had been followed by a couple of screams in Hebrew that he could only imagine were expletives.

"I'm sorry Charles, I need to go."

Ben hung up, not that Charles could blame him. He had a country and four bombs to worry about, not just one city and one bomb. It did, however, mean one thing. He had to track down the same lead that Murphy had and he had about 11 hours to do it in. He spied Sam lying in the sun, drying off from an early morning swim and went to join him. He briefly recounted his chat with Ben. Sam reacted similarly. James Murphy was about to get the name of the ship. How could they not have tracked the same leads as him?

Both hit their phones. The one thing they did know was that Murphy had started his calls in England. After all, the story had been about the British navy.

Sam knew some guys in the SBS, the Special Boat Service, the marine equivalent of the better-known British SAS. Most, if not all, were ex-marines and in the UK, the Royal Marines were part of the Navy - it was the closest he could get to the Navy.

It was proving slow work. Neither Sam nor Charles had the knowledge or list of contacts around the world that James Murphy had. It was going to take some time.

# Chapter 87

Ben was the last person left in the Knesset building; most had left at lunchtime to travel with their families. Ben had nobody to travel with. His only family were in America, safe in Texas. He closed his office door behind him and automatically began to lock it. He stopped himself mid turn. There was no point, the office was empty. All his papers had already gone. The building was quiet, something he had never experienced before. It wasn't a nice silence, the eeriness was unnerving.

He picked up his briefcase and walked towards the exit. One lone guard waited for him. He nodded and shut the door behind Ben. Ben didn't look back. The image of all that he had achieved in building the State of Israel was captured within that building. He didn't want to remember it dark and desolate. His memories were of life and vitality. Ben's car and driver awaited his arrival. The driver had no intention of hanging around and as soon as Ben closed the door, he pulled away. The drive to the airport initially confused Ben until he realized they were going to the new airport, a global hub for a new Jerusalem. That was the plan. Jerusalem was not meant to die. That had never been envisioned. Ararat had planned to place Jerusalem at the center of the world. The buildings that would spark a new life into one of the world's most important and ancient cities sat empty. Ben could have cried as he sped past. His driver was unaware of Ararat, unaware of the greatness it would bring to Jerusalem. His driver was only aware of the danger that was upon them, the devastation that was scheduled to arrive just three short hours away.

As they neared the airport, Ben willed his cell phone to ring. The more he willed it, the more dead it seemed. He checked the signal, it was fine. Ahmed Hameed had obviously seen the past and not the future. Ben walked through the airport. Airplanes that had never touched Israeli soil queued to ferry his people away from danger. Emirates and Qatari jets joined Singapore and Thai Jets, Qantas, All Nippon and LAN Airways. Almost every country in the world had supplied their fleets, although unknowingly, to Israel. The solar flare was a story used to ground the airlines and free up the world's jets for hire. How else could they move so many people so quickly? For months, Israeli Air Force pilots had retrained to fly the commercial aircraft of the world, Boeing 747's, 777's and every other type of Boeing, Airbuses, A380 to the A320. Every plane of any size that could be found had been leased, resurrected from mothballing and generally put to use. Over 2,000 aircraft had flown non-stop for the last two days from pretty much every strip of land capable of handling a jet.

Another ten jets were filled before the last jet pulled up to the gate. Ben and a few stragglers boarded. Many tears were shed as the plane, an EL AL Boeing 747, lifted off. It was the last plane of the night and Ben's phone still remained silent.

# Chapter 88

"I've got it!" screamed Sam.

"The name?" asked Charles hopefully.

"No, the link to Russia!"

"Oh," the disappointment was loud and clear.

"No, I know who he called, we're getting there!"

The Senator looked at the clock. There were less than three hours until midnight in Israel, 6pm EST. The time at which the bomb would go off. Even if they got the name of the boat, the chances of finding it now were almost nil.

Sam dialed the number and as he waited for an answer, he updated his brother. "It seems that the Russian Port of ArchangelSK had an RAF maintenance base. The comic book showed a British convoy heading to Russia and it seems that's where they found some old equipment. The RAF guy reckons if there's any old kit around, that's where you'd find it. After the war, things did sour a little with our Russian allies!"

The phone eventually answered. "Da?"

"Hi...?" replied Sam before being interrupted.

"Don't hang up this time! I got name you ask for," replied the Russian shipyard owner.

Sam couldn't believe his luck, the Russian thought he was James Murphy calling back.

"It's the Sergey Vazlaz. Goodnight!" The Russian hung up, it was almost midnight in ArchangelSK.

Sam turned to his brother. "The Sergey Vazlav."

"That's it? Nothing else?"

"Nope, just the name."

"Can you track ships?" asked the Senator.

"I have no idea but I know a woman who might!" Sam leaned out the window and called Rebecca in, bringing her up to speed.

"The answer is, in theory, yes. As long as they have a transponder, it's just like aircraft really, they send a signal out and tell others where they are."

Both knew about aircraft transponders. Aircraft send out a signal that air traffic controllers use to accurately plot specific aircraft positions.

"Do all boats have to have one?"

"Don't think so. I think it's just bigger boats but I'm not sure if our guys would have one transmitting."

"Oh, they will," replied Sam. "These guys have fooled everybody, they wouldn't make a simple mistake like not transponding if they have to. They'd be shining a big spotlight on themselves."

"OK, well, we just need a computer then."

"We can do it ourselves?" asked the Senator.

Rebecca was already half way out of the room as the others struggled to catch up. The manager was kindly asked if his computer could be borrowed. Faced with the three very anxious faces of Sam, Charles and Rebecca, he had little choice. He left them to his office and went for a break.

"You've done this before," stated the Senator.

"A few times," replied Rebecca with a smile as she logged onto marinetraffic.com and waited for the map to load.

"OK, I presume we want the East coast?"

"Definitely," replied Sam as a number of boxes appeared on the map next to America, each with a number in the box, signifying how many ships there were in each sector.

"Jesus, there are hundreds, it'll take us hours."

Rebecca shook her head and selected the 'Vessel' tab.

"What's the name?"

Rebecca typed in Sergey Vazlav and the details instantly appeared.

"Gulf of St Lawrence, Canada."

"Holy shit, we did it!"

"How far are they from New York?" asked Sam, suddenly realizing that was the nearest city.

"Just over six hundred miles, give or take," replied Rebecca, roughly working it out.

"Jesus, they're just about in range and they'll come in over land, not from the sea."

"I need to use your phone!" The Senator put his hand out to Rebecca. She had assured them earlier that her phone could not be traced or tracked.

Senator Charles Baker made a phone call that made his stomach churn.

"I need to speak with the President urgently!" he said as the White House picked up his call.

*\*\*\**

As they were retrieving the name of the ship, Akram Rayyan was in the process of making the information irrelevant. They had sailed into the Gulf of St Lawrence and as they approached Prince Edward Island, he had called on his men to make the preparations.

The World War Two equipment was unloaded and the scaffolding blocks were bolted onto the deck as they had been during all their previous test runs. This time was for real. The empty containers which had blocked the outside world's view were thrown overboard. They were now redundant. The scaffolding ran for sixty feet along the deck and protruded over the water below. While half the crew prepared the catapult, the other half prepared the aircraft. Two wings were removed from one container while the main body of the aircraft came from another. The Second World War fighter came to life as the wings were bolted on. The weapon had already been stored within the fuselage of the aircraft. What had been a deadly fighter in its day seventy years earlier had become the deadliest aircraft ever made seventy years later.

The Hawker Sea Hurricane had been devised as a fighter of last resort to protect the vital convoys plying the seas between America, Britain and Russia. It afforded protection to convoys against the marauding Focke-Wulf of the German Luftwaffe. The Hurricanes were flown by very brave pilots who knew there was nowhere to land once they were propelled into the sky. The Allies, without enough ships to launch aircraft, devised the catapult system, similar to the systems used on modern aircraft carriers. Rockets would fire the aircraft from standing to flight speed almost instantly.

Akram instructed the crew to lift the plane into position. They lifted the relic brought back to life after being found in Malta and guided it carefully onto the runners that now sat on top of the deck. The rocket mechanism was fixed to the base and the thumbs-up signaled around the deck. The plane was ready.

Everything that had to be said, already had been. The pilot, on seeing the thumbs-up, boarded the aircraft and immediately ignited the old but reliable Rolls Royce Merlin engine. It fired into life and warmed up. Akram instructed the ship to turn into the wind. The pins securing the plane were removed and the pilot applied 30 degree flaps and a 1/3 rudder, just as he had been taught during training. He then opened the throttle to full, pushed his head into the headrest and signaled for the rockets to be fired.

The plane surged forward under a hail of Allahu Akbar! Allahu Akbar! And dropped from the end of the rail towards the ocean.

Akram's heart sank with the plane but the power of the engine kicked and the nose pulled up and leveled before powering the plane up and away. A tear left Akram's eye as he thought of the glory that would be with them all soon. Before the old plane was out of sight, the deck structure was broken down and discarded overboard. Sergey Vazlav turned and tried to get as much distance between itself and the floating containers as possible.

# Chapter 89

"I have Senator Charles Baker for you, Mr President," offered Nancy.

Fortunately, Johnson and Preston who were currently with the President were facing away from her and she did not see the look of horror on their faces.

"OK, put him through." The President wasn't quick enough to think of anything else.

"Charles?" said the President.

"Fuck you, Russell..." that was unfortunately the best Charles Baker could come up with on hearing the President's voice. Sam waved at him wildly to calm down.

"...I've got the name and location of the freighter you need," he added quickly, before the President hung up.

The President had the phone half down when he heard the name and location. He hit the speaker button so all could hear.

"Sergey Vazlav, Gulf of Lawrence."

"Thank you, Charles," replied the President with genuine gratitude. He of course was genuine. Charles Baker had just secured Russell's re-election.

"Before you get too excited, we think they have probably launched. They're in range of New York."

"Christ!" said Russell, realizing that two million deaths was synonymous with New York.

# Chapter 90

Ahmed Hameed had talked until he was blue in the face but nobody was listening. His network had come through and he had tracked down the three other controllers. He had spent the last three hours trying to make them understand the opportunity that lay before them. Firing the devices would end nothing. Not firing them could end everything. As the time neared midnight, the men prepared to leave. They had orders to follow. Deif had been explicit. Unless he told them otherwise, the weapons should be fired.

Ahmed explained again that were Deif there, he would want them not to fire. The opportunity for a true Palestinian nation was at their fingertips. The scoffs of derision at the words of Ben Meir being believed insulted Ahmed. It was one thing to scoff at Ben Meir but these men were now scoffing at him.

He stood up and commanded silence. He gave each of them an ultimatum that, should he be wrong, they should fire their weapons immediately.

All looked at each other and nodded. If Ahmed Hameed wanted to commit suicide, that was his problem. At least two of the men fancied their chances at taking command. And if Ahmed was to be believed, Deif would not be coming back anyway.

Nods around the table gave Ahmed the go ahead. However, he was warned that he had until midnight or else the weapons would be fired.

Ahmed checked his watch. Just 15 minutes remained. Hardly time to get to the border, never mind trying to get through, he thought, as he ran towards the cars parked below. A small crowd followed him and then a convoy was soon tracing its way towards the Israeli border. Its walls loomed large, its watchtowers looming even higher. The snipers that waited for any attempt to break her defenses, watched on silently.

Ben had offered this as rock solid proof. If Ahmed didn't believe him, he should attempt to cross the border after 11pm. Ben emphasized with a smile that he would be well rewarded.

For the first time in his life, Ahmed Hameed was going to listen to the word of a Jew. He stepped down from his car and walked the final 200 yards towards the gates. He looked back and could see the men who held the fate of a nation in their hands, holding the devices that would send the signals. Their eyes were as much on Ahmed as they were on their watches. They were not going to give him a second to spare. Ahmed picked up the pace and waited for the Israeli to prove his doubts wrong.

Ahmed reached the gates, no bullets had struck him yet. He pushed on the gates and his life ended.

# Chapter 91

The President couldn't sit still. Two million dead. The number was becoming a reality as he paced his office. Before, it had just seemed like a number. He normally dealt in billions, trillions even but that was dollars not human beings. The number was massive. How could he not have ordered the evacuation? He had not only lost any chance of re-election, he had lost his soul.

Henry Preston tried to keep him calm. They still had ten minutes until midnight in Israel.

"Mr President, we still have time."

"Even if we get to the bomb now, it'll be so close it's irrelevant."

"Sir, the bomb will only detonate if it is triggered correctly. If we get to it before then, we may be OK."

Henry looked at the screen in the Situation Room. New York was literally swamped with military fighters. New Yorkers must have thought a war had started with the number of jets that were overhead. Air Force F15, F16 and F22s from as far South as South Carolina were joined by F18s from the Carriers Ronald Reagan, George H.W. Bush and Harry S Truman.

There was no way the Hurricane could evade such an overwhelming force. There was just no way. It didn't make sense and in Henry's book, things didn't not make sense. He looked again at the map and grabbed the intercom and instructed the search be widened to include Philadelphia and Washington. They couldn't find him because he was going somewhere else, figured Henry.

Captain John Fuentes had just kicked in his afterburner as he lifted his F-22 raptor off from Langley Air Force Base and was touching Mach 2 as the call came in. He was being reassigned to Philadelphia. He couldn't help but feel disappointed. The likelihood of anything happening to Philly was low compared to New York or Washington.

Almost as soon as he had pulled back the throttle, Philadelphia appeared below him. He plugged into the E-3 Sentry that was circling far overhead and looking down on the area below. Nothing. He could see nothing that shouldn't be there.

But looking down, Captain Fuentes did see what millions of dollars worth of equipment couldn't. He caught sight of a small flash of light, off to his left. It was moving slowly and it was close to the ground. Had it been on the road, he would have thought it was a fast car but there was no road there, just fields. It was certainly faster than any tractor, thought Fuentes, and it was close to the city limits.

His orders were clear. Do not, under any circumstances allow the pilot to see your approach. He powered up and over the object and pulled back, spinning in behind it. Approaching from the rear, he could see why nobody had spotted it. He was merely 50 feet off the deck and painted a green camouflage.

***

The pilot could see the cityscape ahead of him, exactly as he had practiced on the flight simulator. He checked his fuel. The needle hovered just above zero. Not really an issue, he just needed enough for the next minute or so. He powered the throttle forward and began his ascent. His target was 2,000 feet and then he'd press the button to detonate the weapon. The run had been timed to perfection. Give or take a few seconds, he had arrived bang on schedule.

His finger hovered over the firing button. "Allahu Akbar, Allahu Akbar."

***

As the clock ticked down to 17.59.50 EST, 23.59.50 in Israel, all just stared at the clock, their breaths held. Ten seconds to detonation if what they had been told was true. The President was almost climbing the wall. The tension in the Situation Room was unbearable.

\*\*\*

Captain Fuentes was caught by surprise as the bogey seemingly reacted to his presence. It accelerated and began to pull up. Fuentes followed and selected his AIM-9 Sidewinders and fired.

\*\*\*

The pilot watched as his level indicator read 1,900 feet. He caught a flash in the rear mirror that the Hurricane would use to spot enemies from the rear and saw the sidewinder as it sped towards him. He smiled. "Allahu Akbar!" as he reached for the trigger.

\*\*\*

As the clock struck 17.59.58, a scream came though the intercom system. The room jumped and the President sank to the floor.

"WOOHOO, one mother fucking bogie is down and out!" screamed Captain Fuentes into the intercom which the E-3 Sentry had fed through to the Situation Room.

Fuentes, for good measure, had fired all 480 of his 20mm cannon rounds as he had fired the sidewinder missiles. He would never know that if he hadn't, the pilot would have destroyed a city and killed almost a million people.

As the President held his head in relief, they waited for news on Israel. The clock, showing the time in Israel, struck midnight.

# Chapter 92

And his new life started, the gates swung freely. The post was deserted just as Ben said it would be. Ahmed turned to his compatriots who stared at him in disbelief. Surely not, the Jew had not been lying. Ahmed ventured further. There was nothing there. The army base that had kept them prisoners was deserted. Everything was gone. Nothing remained. This was not temporary.

Ahmed returned to the other three controllers and they debated for some time what should be done. Time dragged on. 12.05, 12.15, 12.30. The time kept ticking by as they decided what to do.

A call was made to Lebanon and the West Bank. One border-crossing was no sign of any real change. The Palestinian fighters on the Lebanese – Israeli border were reluctant to move forward. The dead-man alley was exactly that. Anyone who stepped into it died immediately. The Israeli snipers did not shoot warning shots. After some discussion, a young fighter said he would go. He, like Ahmed in the South, walked carefully and cautiously forward, fearful of the bullet that would end his life. It never came. He reached the gates that blocked the road and like Ahmed, he pushed them only to find they fell open. The crossing was deserted. Everything was gone.

The debate still raged. It could all be a trick. The call to the West Bank proved less fruitful. Jerusalem was a hive of activity, nothing appeared to have changed. The reluctant Palestinian who ventured towards the border crossing returned quickly. The border was guarded, he could see men moving around. Ahmed pushed for the man to go further.

As the man ventured further, the three controllers had reached a decision. The Israelis had tried to trick them for the last time. As they were preparing to fire, the phone rang. It was the West Bank Palestinians. Their man had ventured closer. It was not Israelis that were guarding the crossing.

# Chapter 93

The Sheikh had altered Zak's ID to show his photo and easily passed through the security perimeter. The President was due within the next hour. News had filtered out during the morning that it was likely that the President would also announce his new Vice President and if the rumor were true, it was going to be Henry Preston. The Sheikh had arranged everything he needed and was now just awaiting the arrival of his targets.

The stage was arranged across the road directly in front of the massive gates that were covered either side by huge sheets. These were the covers that would unveil the memorials. Almost two hundred seats were laid in front of a stage which itself held almost fifty seats. The audience, however, was expected to be closer to a million times that number as the world's press awaited the announcement of the new VP and an explanation as to the goings on the previous evening.

The Sheikh smiled as the first attendees began to arrive. He made his way towards the young lady that was co-ordinating the event and while talking to her, he managed to check the sheet. Nothing had changed.

***

Rebecca woke Sam up. She had just had a call from Ben and they were to meet him in Driscoll, a small town near to where the ceremony was due to take place. He didn't like it and wanted some assurances. Unfortunately, she did not have any to give.

Sam spoke at length to his brother and agreed that Clark would remain with his wife while the rest would travel to Driscoll.

***

Although they had flown down with the President on Air Force One, Preston, Johnson and Gates were part of the advance party, along with members of the Cabinet. The President liked his grand entrances and everyone would be seated and in place before he arrived.

Preston had shared a car with the others and the smile on his face suggested he would not be sharing one back. It seemed to Johnson and Gates that the rumors must have been true. However, Johnson was going to wipe the smile off Preston's face soon enough. There was only going to be one Vice President announced that day and it was going to be Allan Johnson and he had the goods to make sure it happened.

As the car pulled up to the stage, Johnson broke off from the group and made his call.

"Mr President?"

"Yes, Allan?"

"I'm hearing some very disturbing rumors."

The President knew exactly what the rumors were. "Yes, Allan and I'm afraid they're true. You've got to appreciate that it was Henry who…"

Allan's tone changed. "Killed the President for you?!"

"Allan," protested the President angrily.

"No Andrew, I have the evidence that will put us both in the frame. I suggest you change your speech and quickly." Johnson killed the call and headed back to the others with a spring in his step.

He joined them as the co-ordinator had singled the three of them out and asked them to head over to a waiting minivan. It appeared that the President wanted to arrive with them at his side. They jumped into the van and were greeted by the Secretary of Defense.

***

The President's motorcade pulled out of Corpus Christi and made its way towards Bishop. It swept along at sixty miles an hour and the President took the twenty minutes to put the final touches to his speech.

He had just had the call from Johnson when his phone rang again. He instantly answered expecting it to be Johnson again.

"How dare you!" he screamed.

"Mr President?" enquired Ben.

"Ben, I'll be with you shortly. I'll talk to you then," he needed to get off the phone and get a hold of Johnson.

"You need to meet with me now. I'm in Driscoll, in the diner on the far side of town."

"I don't have time."

"Make the time Andrew," instructed Ben.

\*\*\*

As they pulled out of Bishop, an unmarked car pulled out in front to escort them towards the President's motorcade.

"Where are we meeting?" asked Preston.

"Driscoll, Sir," replied the driver.

Preston could see the sign. Driscoll was just 3 miles ahead. He wondered if the President would take him in The Beast with him and really make a statement.

\*\*\*

As they pulled into the diner, the Secret Service began to dismount and were about to sweep the place when the President saw Ben in the window. The man sitting next to him was not a man he wanted the Secret Service to see. Despite huge protestations, he walked into the diner alone and took the seat opposite Ben Meir and Senator Charles Baker.

"Ben, Charles," he said as he sat down.

"Momentous day, Andrew," replied Ben.

President Andrew Russell did not like how Ben had dropped the 'Mr President'.

"Andrew, let's take a walk," he said, getting up from his seat. Charles Baker remained seated as instructed.

Ben walked the President out into the parking area and as both men waved away their security, they talked. At least, Ben did a lot of talking. Particularly after a minivan slowed down beside them before picking up speed and disappearing into the distance.

***

Rebecca and Sam had been instructed to stay out of sight and in the car. They were to play no part. Ben had only allowed them to come because he knew Sam wouldn't let his brother out of his sight. Ben had spent over an hour with Senator Baker before the President had arrived and as such, Rebecca and Sam were becoming increasingly restless and in Rebecca's case increasingly desperate to go to the bathroom.

After having held on as long as physically possible, she could wait no more and after securing a promise that he would not move unless the ground began to swallow him up, she jumped out of the car and ran to the restrooms at the side of the building. As she stepped back out of the restroom, feeling very refreshed, the President and Ben were arguing just a few yards in front of her. As she waved an apology for the interruption, her view was blocked by a minivan pulling in between her and them. Four men got up, as though about to disembark, only for the driver to turn and say something, after which they all sat down. Rebecca watched as the van pulled away and she could see a look of horror on the President's face that mirrored hers but for very different reasons.

As Rebecca walked back towards the car, she opened the door and slumped into her seat.

"What's wrong?" asked Sam turning to her. "You look like you've just seen a ghost!"

"I have!" she answered.

# Chapter 94

"Ladies and gentlemen, the President of the United States of America."

President Andrew Russell took the stage and looked at his audience and the people at home.

"Citizens, countrymen, people of the world. We are not here today to mark the memorial of a great disaster, we are here today to be thankful for saving a people from another. We are here to welcome and offer our support to a people who have fought to protect themselves day in and day out. Hopefully that fight is over. It will not be easy and many wounds are still to be healed but we will be there for them and I'd ask you to be there for them too." The president paused as the audience began to digest what he had just said. The murmur died and he began again.

"Behind these gates, lay a land devastated by the worst man can do. As much as we can create, we can destroy. But the land has now been made safe. Scientists and engineers have eradicated every last drop of radiation. The land is safe but we have no need for it. We discarded it so easily that we should be ashamed of ourselves. People fight and die for land and we have so much of it that we can just shut it off. Another people were threatened by a similar atrocity but they did not have land to just shun and discard. They had no land they could go to and be safe. That was until now."

The gates swung open and a sea of tents could be seen stretching off into the distance. The President and Prime Minister of Israel joined the President at the podium. He greeted them with a hug and a handshake while hardly a whisper was raised from the audience.

"Over the last few days, Israel has evacuated its citizens. It has been the largest humanitarian operation ever undertaken."

"Why the secrecy?" came a shout.

"The four nuclear weapons could have been triggered at any time. If the terrorists had caught wind of it, they may have detonated the bombs and killed millions of innocents."

"What of the holy land?" came another shout as the impact of what was being said hit home.

"Jerusalem and a large area around it has been handed to the UN. It is to become UN territory and will become the headquarters of the UN, replacing New York. It will be a neutral land from which to operate. Jerusalem and the cities around it are holy cities, not just for Judaism but Christianity and Islam also. More than half of the world's population sees these cities as some of their most holy."

Before you bombard me any further, please welcome our new neighbors. A cheer was raised as the President dropped the tarpaulins covering the plaque to reveal the Israeli flags, with 'New Israel' written underneath.

\*\*\*

Ahmed Hameed drove from one end of Palestine to the other, from Egypt to Lebanon. The area designated as the United Nations territory was substantial but not so that they couldn't see the victory in what they had achieved. They were at peace. His people were at peace. He never believed he would see the day.

Jerusalem was a free city. Anybody and everybody owned her. It was fitting for such a wonderful and holy place.

Ahmed Hameed said a prayer for Ben Meir as he accepted the thanks of his nation.

\*\*\*

As the noise began to die down, the President called for some calm.

"I have one more announcement to make. I would like to introduce you to my new Vice President, Charles Baker."

The surprise at this announcement almost exceeded that of the New Israel.

However, the audience was unaware of Ben's demonstration only minutes earlier. The President had watched in horror as his four closest advisers, Johnson, Preston, Gates and the new Secretary of Defense were paraded before him, stuck in the back of a minivan being driven to a certain death. The message had been loud and clear, Ben was calling the shots, quite literally.

The effect on the President of the President's four closest advisers being shown to him in the minivan before being driven away to a certain and painful death.

"And further, I wish to give him my support at the upcoming election to become the next President of the United States of America."

Another shock wave swept through the audience. That announcement came on the back of a promise that Sam Baker would not seek retribution. It really did help to have a scary brother.

*** 

With the announcement of the New Israel, Sam looked at Rebecca who just shook her head in amazement. She knew nothing of any of it. She was also refusing to tell him what had spooked her earlier but whatever it was, it had affected her badly.

"They can't have," she repeated quietly to herself with each announcement.

Sam looked at the field of tents and wondered how far it stretched. Five to six million people, even four to a tent, was a massive area and an unbelievable undertaking over the last few days. It was phenomenal, mused Sam, shaking his head.

"It will take them years to build a country from nothing," offered Sam, grasping the scale of what lay ahead.

"Not if I know Ben Meir," replied Rebecca, her tone far from happy. Which Sam could fully understand. She had spent her life fighting to save a country that they had been chased out of. Israel had been defeated.

Sam took her in her arms and offered his support but she remained uncharacteristically stiff.

"I'm sorry, I need to go." She left and walked towards Ben. Without looking back she walked through the gates and into New Israel.

# Epilogue

It had been two months since Yom Kippur and Sam had buried his family properly. It had been a beautiful ceremony attended by hundreds. The President had offered to come and it had taken some power of persuasion by the Vice President to stop Sam from trying to kill him for even having the audacity to consider going.

Charles had explained to Sam many times why the President was allowed to continue. They needed to maintain the government to ensure that New Israel had time to build itself into a strong and independent nation again. Sam would bide his time and promised he would not kill the President. However, he had made no such statement about not killing former President Andrew Russell. His day would come he thought.

He had bought a new house on the main island having decided against rebuilding his old house. He had thrown himself back into his work as a PE teacher and was once again racing his kids up to the top of the hill, although a far more welcome sight than normal awaited him at the top of the hill that morning. Rebecca Cohen, sat on the small mound of stones that marked the summit, a broad smile welcomed Sam to the top.

"What took you so long?" she asked.

"I didn't think I'd see you again!" he answered with a smile.

Rebecca didn't say any more. She walked across and grabbed Sam in a breath crushing embrace, much to the delight of the kids.

That next morning, Rebecca took Sam to New York and they boarded an El Al flight to New Tel Aviv. Sam couldn't believe the change. The security before check-in and boarding was no different than those for any other carrier. The flight was short and Sam had wondered what he would find when they arrived. It had only been two months and achieving the basics would still be a struggle but he vowed to do whatever he could to help.

"First time?" asked a man, seated next to Sam.

"Yep!"

"I'm Saul, first week off in years," he said, striking up a conversation. "Evacuated one day, back in a new dock the next day, unloading the same bloody stuff I loaded at the other end!" he moaned.

"New docks?" asked Sam surprised. He had never seen any docks in that old part of Texas.

"Yep, walked out the old port on Friday and walked into the new one on Sunday, not even a day off."

Sam turned to Rebecca who was on his other side and who had heard the conversation. She just shook her head.

As the flight approached the airport, Sam braced himself for the chaos of the Arrivals gate. It never came. The airport was state of the art, brand new. Sam walked through the terminal and exited into what could have been any major city in the world.

"What the hell?"

Rebecca shook her head and pressed her finger to her lips and drove Sam to the nearby beach. Sam looked around. There was not a tent to be seen anywhere. But he had followed the news and had watched the nightly reports of the refugees of New Israel as they struggled to cope with building their new nation.

"Sam, I believe you deserve to hear this but I am Israeli and my heart will always be Israel's first. I will deny it all."

Sam just nodded his head as he walked along beside her.

"The day I left you, I saw a ghost. I was not joking I did see a ghost. It was the ghost of my dead husband. A man I loved with all my heart. My son's father."

Sam nodded.

"But of course there are no such things as ghosts. I saw my husband that day. He was driving a minivan that was taking the President's advisers away."

Sam instantly liked the guy, knowing exactly what she meant by 'away'.

"Something had always bothered me. When I first discovered the nuclear weapon plot, I saw something I recognized in the terrorist called The Sheikh."

Sam nodded for her to go on.

"I recognized his eyes. They were my husband's eyes. My husband is The Sheikh."

"Your husband's a Palestinian terrorist, but wait…"

"Exactly, a Palestinian terrorist would not have killed people for Ben!" Rebecca could see the confusion in Sam's face.

Sam looked around at the infrastructure. He thought back to New Tel Aviv, the talk of the man on the plane of the new port. What he could see was years of preparation and building. The Sheikh was an Israeli plant.

"But that means…"

"Yes, every bit of this has been planned, even down to the original nuclear explosion which was actually a neutron bomb, not a nuclear bomb. Neutron bombs let off a large amount of radiation but it disappears almost immediately. Within forty-eight hours, the land was safe and construction was underway."

Rebecca slowly turned round, her arms outstretched. "I give you Project Ararat!"

Sam fell to the sand. The whole world had been fooled.

"That day I left with Ben, it all became clear. I challenged him and he couldn't deny it. He told me the plan had been drawn up many years earlier and the attack four years ago that killed all our children, including my Josh, was the trigger. Israel was not safe for her people and never would be. Enough was enough."

"Jesus," said Sam, still struggling to comprehend the enormity of it all.

"For the next two years or so, we'll play the martyrs. Nobody will challenge our right to be here after being chased from our old land. After then, we'll drop the covers and no-one will think anything of a new building here or there. It'll be old news and let's face it, our guys control most media outlets anyway. People will believe what we tell them. They'll never know we orchestrated the whole thing, they'll never know we gave the Palestinians the nuclear bombs that they chased us away with!"

"You gave them the nukes!" exclaimed Sam angrily.

"Every bit of what has happened since the attack four years ago has been part of Ararat!"

Sam shook his head, "I can't believe you gave them five nuclear weapons, what in the hell were they thinking."

"That they wouldn't work, well at least they weren't supposed to but Deif must have smelled a rat. He got a Russian nuclear scientist to re-engineer them. They would have worked better than ever."

"Jesus Christ!" the scale of the deception and Ararat was mind blowing.

"So we didn't get defeated, we have what we wanted. Peace!"

Sam suddenly realized. "What about your husband?"

Rebecca took his hand. "I met with him. He chose his country over me and his son many years ago and I realized I still only love one man. I know you may still have some grieving to do but I just want you to know that I'm here and waiting!"

Sam sat speechless. Before he could respond, Rebecca added with a smile,

"Just don't take too long about it, I'm expecting your baby."

# The End

**Please read on for an exclusive excerpt of America's Trust – available from May 31st**

# America's Trust

by

**Murray McDonald**

# Chapter 1

**Present day**
**Tuesday 30th June 2015**
**Washington D.C.**

It had been over three years since Jack had been able to walk down the street and open a bar door. The Raven Bar & Grill was just the type of place he needed: quiet, dark and grimy. The shabby exterior gave way to an even shabbier interior. This wasn't a place that was trying to look like something it wasn't. Its seventies décor was exactly that and not some hip designer's cool idea of what the seventies should have been. A line of booths filled one half of the establishment while the other was filled with a long wooden bar. Jack pulled up a stool and ordered a beer with a Scotch chaser. The barman looked at him like he knew him but poured the drinks without a word. Jack sipped the beer, his first real drink in a very long time.

In the three years since Jack's life had been no longer his own, he had lost both his wife and his purpose. Constantly under surveillance, he never had a minute to himself. Even at his wife's funeral, the shackles had not been loosened. What should have been a private occasion had been a very public event. Armed guards watched over his every move, cameras monitored his every step. He had wanted to jump in with her, go with her. He didn't want to go back. As the funeral ended, he had no choice. He had four years to serve, whether he liked it or not. That was his term. No time off for good behavior, that had been clear from the start. The federal government was a relentless beast and if it had you for four years, you gave it four years, no matter what.

Jack savored another sip. His wife had hated his penchant for dive bars but he loved the anonymity. Nobody knew him, nobody judged him. He missed her. He regretted every minute of the last few years when he had not been there for her. Her final breaths had been taken while he was hundreds of miles away. It was all his fault. Four years earlier, his actions had torn them apart. She didn't want him to do it but he had explained to her that he had to. It was a once in a lifetime opportunity. She had begged him not to. It wasn't like they needed the money. For Jack, it wasn't about the money, it was the thrill. Despite his actions, she had stood by him as a loyal wife and as the outcome was read out, she cried with him. Four years. It could have been worse. Some had served double that, but he had promised he wouldn't do it again. They had been the worst and last years of their marriage and he would never forgive himself.

He reached for his Scotch and downed it in one swift motion. It felt good. The heat of the alcohol burned the back of his throat and instantly cleared his thoughts. The TV was showing a round-up of the football and had the other six customers transfixed. Jack nodded at the barman and was rewarded with a refill. He allowed himself to relax, and began to appreciate his newfound freedom. He had walked along the street; he had entered a bar; he had ordered a drink. He was sitting enjoying the football with a bunch of guys who didn't care who he was or what he had done - all things that, for the last four years, had seemed a world away. For the first time in six months and probably in four years, he smiled, not a fake smile, not a smile for the cameras, but a genuine warm smile.

Jack was happy.

"Good whisky?" asked the drinker to his right.

"Great whisky," said Jack, raising the glass and looking at it before taking another drink. "Join me?"

"Don't mind if I do," accepted the drinker. "The name's Don."

"Jake," replied Jack. It was what his mother had called him, never wanting to name him after his father's father. He had been, she told everyone who would listen, the most unlikeable man one could ever have the displeasure of meeting. Jack's father had never once contested his mother's claim.

Jack nodded at the barman again and indicated for each of the other drinkers to be offered a Scotch. They all nodded and mumbled their appreciation and, almost as one, returned to the highlights.

"So what brings you to the Raven?" asked Don, nudging his stool nearer to Jack's.

Jack lifted his drink in answer. Don nodded acceptance and lifted his own, joining Jack in his drink.

After an hour and many Scotches too many, Jack stood up and wished his new friends goodnight. Those capable of responding mumbled a vague goodbye while Don also stood up.

"I have to head home too and face the music!" he said conspiratorially, dipping his head to the barman.

"Face the music?" asked Jack.

"Got laid off today," replied Don.

Jack had reckoned Don was mid to late fifties, around five to ten years older than himself, middle-management with a salary that allowed him few luxuries and a tough life. Jack had always been very good at reading people.

"God, I'm sorry to hear that," said Jack through the haze of alcohol. "What did you do?"

"Purchasing Manager for a government contractor, two hundred and fifty of us got canned today."

"Insignia DC?" asked Jack.

"How the hell did you know that?" asked Don, looking at Jack with some suspicion.

"It was on the news earlier, I recognized the number two hundred and fifty," said Jack, quickly covering his mistake.

Don continued to study Jack, unsure of him now. "You remind me of somebody." Don waved his drunken finger. "I just can't think who."

Jack shrugged and immediately got a response from Don. "The president! If it wasn't for your hair being thinner and wearing glasses, you could be his double!"

Jack laughed. If it weren't for the wig and the contacts he had to wear, he would have been a much more comfortable president.

# Chapter 2

"Sorry," said Don, gently punching Jack's shoulder. "You're much too nice a guy to be confused with that scumbag president."

Jack managed to hold his laughter as the words hit home. "He's not *that* bad!"

"Son of a bitch cost me my job!" snapped Don, all joviality dropping from his voice. "Transferred it to China. Fucking *China*, can you believe it?!" he muttered as he staggered off towards his home.

Jack shook his head. "I'm sure he didn't!" he called after Don, knowing he damn well hadn't. He hadn't heard anything about Insignia on the news, he remembered the contract being discussed. Insignia had the contract for printing all federal brochures and documentation. There was absolutely no way Jack wanted that work going abroad in order to save a few bucks. He had made it clear that under no circumstance was the contract to be outsourced to a foreign company. He'd be asking a few questions the following morning, but he was going have to be careful as to how he came about the information.

Jack checked his watch as Don swayed off into the distance. He had been free for over four hours. Four hours and nobody knew he was missing. In his two and a half years as president, he had hardly had four minutes to himself, let alone four hours. Of course, he was assuming nobody knew. With no Blackberry or method for anyone to contact him, they may have been turning the White House upside down to find him. Mind you, if he were missing, he had to assume there would be helicopters and police cars scouring the city. He picked up the pace as he headed south back down 16th Street, NW. There was no point ruining a good thing by being greedy on his first outing. He covered the two miles much more quickly than the outward leg. At midnight there were far fewer people around to watch and analyze.

He hung a left on K Street NW and a right onto Vermont, and as midnight signaled the start of a new day, Jack walked towards the entrance of the Dana Center. As he withdrew the key to open the security door before him, it flew open, knocking him backwards onto the street.

A man paused briefly before him, recognition registering instantly on the stranger's face as to who Jack really was. However, before Jack could say a word, the street was bathed in flashing blue lights and the scream of sirens as the street filled with police officers and FBI agents in what, to Jack, looked like full riot gear. The police rushed forward, and Jack anticipated being rushed into a car and being sped back to the White House and most likely given a severe dressing down by the Secret Service and his senior staff. However, he was brushed aside as the focus appeared to be the stranger who had almost knocked him over. The man, who Jack estimated to be in his late forties or early fifties, was thrown unceremoniously to the ground before being handcuffed and marched past Jack towards a waiting sedan. As they rushed past, a young female FBI agent holding one of the stranger's arms, brushed past Jack.

"No need to be alarmed, sir," she said. "Just a routine operation. We'll be out of your way momentarily."

Jack was frozen to the spot. Although they were the words that she would have used with the president, the way she had delivered them was exactly how she would have calmed a member of the public, which is exactly how she had seen him - a member of the public. The operation wasn't about Jack, it was about the stranger. Jack looked across as the man was being directed into the back of the sedan. The stranger caught Jack's eye and winked a wink that told Jack the stranger knew exactly who he was.

Jack continued to watch as the young female agent looked around the street and, satisfied with what she saw, circled her finger in the air. Sirens and lights instantly stopped and with one last look back towards Jack but looking straight through him, she disappeared into the sedan. No sooner had she closed the door than the car screeched away. By the time Jack looked back towards the door of the Dana Center, it was hard to believe what had just occurred. Not a police officer was in sight.

He stepped once again towards the security door and, a little more tentatively than earlier, he entered the apartment block. Checking that nobody was around, he walked towards the end of the corridor and removed another key from his pocket. This one was far older and the door in front of him was far heavier than the security door at the entrance to the building. The key turned easily, far easier than on his exit. He opened the door and entered the apartment where time had stopped over 60 years earlier. The décor was upmarket fifties. The appliances in the small kitchen were museum pieces, as was the TV set. The dust that had settled suggested, like the furniture, that Jack was in fact the first living soul to enter the apartment since its previous occupant had vacated. Jack looked again at the simple note from his predecessor.

*If you are reading this note and have come from beyond the park, enjoy the freedom it allows, I know I did! HST*

Jack instantly recognized the initials 'HST'- President Harry S. Truman, the man who had rebuilt the White House in the late forties. Obviously, his building had gone beyond the confines of the White House. Jack pulled back the rug and, lifting the hatch, he reentered the hole that led down to a subterranean tunnel. He shut the hatch and pulled the cord that ensured the rug would slip back into place. He climbed down the ladder and mounted the small bike that he had ridden what he guessed to be around a quarter of a mile from the White House. As he neared the end of the tunnel, he once again entered the coffin-sized vertical capsule and, by turning the handle at his waist, wound the small capsule up, by some hidden mechanism, back into his private office, previously his wife's dressing room.

Stepping back into the room, he noticed a small note on the floor of the capsule. He looked around the dressing room; it definitely hadn't been there when he left. He had searched every inch of the capsule when it had appeared earlier that evening. It wasn't something he had ventured into lightly. It wasn't every day that a decorative column which had stood *in situ* for the three years you had been in residence spun round and revealed itself to be an elevator of sorts. Jack had spent a long time looking at every detail and it had been with great trepidation that he ventured in and moved the lever that had lowered him to the tunnel below.

He bent down, retrieved the slip of paper, and read it.

*Mr. President, if you are reading this and have not spoken with me, they have me. I must speak to you urgently. Our country and our very way of life as Americans depends on it.*

*Find me and beware The Trust.*

*Tom Butler*

Jack's memory flashed back to the face of the man being arrested in front of him and the recognition on his face. He had known Jack was the president. It was Tom Butler he had witnessed being taken away. Tom Butler knew about Jack's escape route. Tom Butler had a key to Harry Truman's apartment. The apartment had been locked when Jack had returned. Tom Butler was a man the president wanted to talk to but Tom Butler was a man the president couldn't possibly know anything about.

Jack stepped back from the column and watched in panic as the column spun back to reveal its original and more normal decorative façade. His escape route had gone without him fully understanding how it had ever really appeared. He stepped forward in the hope that walking towards the column would elicit a response, but nothing happened. He shook his head. It wasn't that simple, otherwise his wife would have found it many years earlier. Not to mention every cleaner that had ever worked in the private apartment. He studied the column in great detail. Nothing, certainly nothing visual, suggested any hint of the hidden mechanism.

Jack crossed the small room and sat staring at the column. The alcohol had dumbed his senses, he wasn't thinking straight. He was missing something obvious. He must be.

Daylight hit him like a sledgehammer. The small room took the full brunt of the sun's early morning reveille. Jack covered his eyes desperately but the ache in his brain failed to dissipate. It wasn't the light. The memories of the previous night came flooding back. The beer and the whisky had taken their toll. He wasn't as young as he used to be and certainly wasn't used to drinking anything like the quantities that had so easily slipped down in the past.

He opened his eyes and found himself staring at the column, just as he had been when the fatigue and alcohol had ended any chance of uncovering the secret. He stood up unsteadily; the pounding in his head was going to take some getting used to. Hangovers had been a thing of the past. The President of the United States did not drink to excess and did not gamble - just two of the long list of his previous behaviors that were absolutely forbidden in his current office. *Forbidden is perhaps too strong a word*, thought Jack, *'not expected' is perhaps more accurate.* The expectation levels of a president were, to say the least, extraordinary. The expectations of a president who had lost a wife were inconceivable. He had to be strong at all times, even by her graveside. Weakness was not an option. Bollocks, it was all bollocks. His strength had never been doubted. It was exactly why he was where he was. After years of poor leadership, the country had been desperate for a strong and capable leader to take control. General Jack King, former Army chief of staff and former chairman of the Joint Chiefs of Staff, offered that in spades. Jack was exactly what the country had craved, a politician who they could believe in, a man of his word, a man who put his country and its strength above all else. The Republican nomination was secured even before Super Tuesday, with every other candidate unwilling to add to the humiliating defeats they had already suffered at the hands of the country's clear favorite.

With debt spiraling, unemployment out of control and what seemed no end to the downturn, Jack King had won the 2012 election by one of the clearest margins in modern history.

Jack was ready. His presidency was going to be one of legend, one of resolve. He was going to turn the country around in four years. In and out. That was his motto throughout his military career. Hit the problem hard and fast. He had promised his wife just that. His country had needed him and he couldn't say no. Four years was all he needed.

That was until the day of his inauguration and the revelation that was about to be bestowed on the new president, America's Trust.

# Chapter 3

**Wednesday 1st July 2015**
**Washington D.C.**

When the key turned in the lock at 4:00 a.m., Tom Butler knew he was about to die. After his arrest by the FBI, he had been marched into the local office and watched as the lead female agent had gesticulated wildly on the phone. When she had ended the obviously angry exchange, she had subsequently kicked a wastepaper basket clear across the room. "Put him in a fucking cell!" she had shouted before storming out of the building. Tom knew then he was in trouble. The tentacles of The Trust had reached far deeper than he thought possible.

The door opened to reveal two immaculately dressed men in suits, one standing well over six feet in height while the other barely cleared five feet.

"Mr. Butler?" the smaller of the two asked.

Tom feigned tiredness and nodded sluggishly, rising slowly from the narrow bench that doubled as a bed.

"How can I help you, Agent?" asked Tom stretching and yawning.

"Special Agent Wen Chan. There's been a terrible mistake but I'm pleased to say it's been resolved," smiled Chan.

"Excellent, so I'm free to go?" asked Tom, knowing it was the last thing they planned for him.

"Yes, Mr. Butler," replied the other agent.

Tom smiled. "And I suppose you're Agent John Smith!" said Tom, referencing the man's European features versus Chan's Asian heritage. Wen and Chan were the two most popular first and last names in China and the equivalent of Western society's 'John Smith'.

The American agent smiled and nodded. They knew Tom Butler would not fall for their bullshit cover story but the show wasn't for Tom Butler, the show was for the FBI.

"So what's the plan guys, get me out and offer me a lift home?"

Chan nodded.

"Airline ticket bought in my name and a look-a-like to use my passport and make the trip? I'm guessing South America or South East Asia?" added Tom, shaking his head. He knew exactly how effective the plan would be.

Smith smiled. "Quit stalling and start walking!"

"Hmm, I think I'll just hang out here, thanks."

"I would advise against that, Mr. Butler," countered Chan sinisterly.

"Or what? You'll kill me?" laughed Tom.

Chan's sinister smile didn't waver. "No, we'll simply extend our area of operation. Who knows what you may have divulged to that pretty little niece of yours?"

Tom's anger exploded and he charged across the room. Before he reached Chan, Smith's massive hands grabbed him and held him back.

"Let's just calm it down," Smith suggested to both Chan and Tom. "Creating a scene does none of us any favors."

Tom struggled against Smith's grasp but soon realized it was futile. The man was like a rock, a solid mass of muscle covered his already inflated frame.

"Stay the fuck away from her!" hissed Tom as he accepted his fate.

"All you need to do is walk out of here a happy bunny and she'll be fine, that's a promise," offered Smith in a conciliatory manner.

Tom nodded his head in acceptance and followed Chan out of the room. The sight of the three men would have raised some sniggers during the day, a real small, medium and large offering. Each stood a good head taller than the next. Tom at 6 feet had never felt taller while Chan led the way and never smaller when Smith took over as they neared the front door of the all but empty Washington field office.

"Smile for the camera!" whispered Chan as they neared the door that would lead them to the main entrance.

Tom was finding it hard enough to take his last few steps, never mind throw a smile to the inanimate cameras that followed and recorded their every move as they walked silently in a death march towards his last breath.

"Special Agent Chan!" came a shout from behind. One of the few FBI agents on duty at 4:00 a.m. stopped them all in their tracks.

Tom turned and noticed Chan's hand move slowly and carefully towards the bump on the inside of his jacket. Chan refused to look back.

"Yes?" he asked, shouting behind him towards the onrushing agent, his hand nearly touching the handgrip of his pistol.

"You left your ID card when you signed out, Mr. Butler."

Tom watched as Chan spun and in the blink of an eye, removed his hand from his pistol grip and held it out to the helpful agent who placed his ID safely in it. The movements, Butler noticed, were exceptionally fast and left the helpful agent blissfully unaware of Chan's previously deadly intent towards him.

As the agent walked away, Tom couldn't resist. "Tsk, tsk, imagine leaving your fake ID behind," he chided quietly.

"Who said it was fake?" questioned Chan so straight-faced that Tom realized he had seriously underestimated his foe.

The final door buzzed open and the coolness of the early Spring morning flooded into the vast entrance hallway. Tom looked around, desperate to scream for help but unwilling to sacrifice his niece. He knew it was likely to be an empty threat. They knew she had nothing whatsoever to do with his work but it was a threat he nonetheless took seriously. She was the only person on the planet they could have used against him. The fact they knew that was more than enough to make him take his fate with as much dignity as he could possibly muster.

He could see the car sitting waiting for them. Its engine was running and a third agent, or whatever the hell they were, was ready and waiting behind the wheel. Just a few steps and the sidewalk separated him from his imminent death. The moment he was in the car, they'd probably put a small caliber gun to his head and end it quickly. The last thing they'd want was a struggle or a fight in a confined space.

He recognized the National Building Museum directly ahead as he stepped outside. He'd never had a chance to visit but had always wanted to. Another thing to add to the quickly filling list of things he had always wished he had done. With each step, it seemed he had done less and less with his life. He tried to remain strong. He thought of the people through the ages being marched proudly to their deaths. Fighting for what they believed in, dying for their cause. *Fucking idiots*, he thought angrily while trying to remain ramrod straight and defiant to the last.

As he neared the top step, his resolve began to waver. Less than ten yards separated him from the ominous black car, its engine humming in the silence of the night while its tail lights emitted a bloody glow that cut through the early morning haze. Agent Smith stretched out and guided Tom down the stairs, his powerful hand bearing more weight than either he or Tom would acknowledge. As Smith helped Tom, Chan raced ahead and opened the rear door. There was no interior light. Great care had been taken to ensure the light had been extinguished. Another sign that Tom's fate was imminent.

As they neared the car, Smith's hand moved from near Tom's waist to his head, gently guiding it lower and lower as he maneuvered Tom into the back seat.

\*\*\*

"What the fuck do you mean he's been released?!" screamed Special Agent Jane Swanson.

She hung up in disgust and punched the steering wheel in frustration. She wasn't interested in listening to the agent's groveling bullshit of an excuse. He should have fucking well checked with her. She was a rising star but a blighted one. Her anger issues were legendary, as was her profanity. Her ability to solve cases and get her man was surpassed only by her ability to piss off every member of her team and most of the command structure. Luckily for her, she was hated slightly less than she was feared.

She had been promoted and demoted with regularity and was in a current positive trend - the promotions outweighed the demotions. There was very little doubt that her successes were all that stood between her and the unemployment queue. She was a handful and a loud one, but she was also usually the smartest and quickest in the room. Conformity was most definitely not her strong suit. A trait the FBI craved in 99% of its agents, the 1% being the acceptable tolerance of brilliance. There was no disputing Jane's brilliance; it was just whether one day her behavior would outshine it. When that day came, she and the FBI would part company, more than likely, not amicably.

She floored the accelerator and her Audi RS4 station wagon exploded to life. The 450bhp of power bit down into the four-wheel drive train and powered the family size car as though it were an Indie racecar. Jane Swanson loved the wolf in sheep's clothing and the RS4 rocketed in a matter of seconds to over 100 mph. The roads, at 4:00 a.m., were empty. She hit the switch and ignited her blue strobes just in case, and had the added security of knowing the ceramic brakes would ensure she stopped quicker than she accelerated, should the need arise.

The RS4 wasn't cheap, but with no plans for marriage or kids and an inheritance from her grandparents burning a hole in her pockets, she had taken one look and thought what the hell? If ever a car had been built for Jane, it was the RS4. They were just meant to be together.

She called the office back. The adrenaline rush from the acceleration had calmed her mood.

"Don't let them leave before I get there!" she demanded.

"They've already gone. One of the agents had left his ID and I just gave it back to them as they left the building," offered the helpful agent nervously.

"Shit!" she yelled, more in frustration than anger. "I'm heading East on G, were they pointed North or South on 4th?"

"North in a Chrysler 300," replied the agent, watching the car pull away on the CCTV system that covered every inch of the building and its perimeter. "Jesus!" screamed the agent jumping out of his seat.

*** 

Tom was forced in beside the smiling Chan, his hand resting close to the pistol that he had so nearly utilized just moments earlier. As the door shut behind him, Tom feared the worst and sucked up every piece of courage his body could muster, which was very little. The front door opened and the large frame of Smith folded itself into the cramped front seat.

No sooner had the door closed, the car began to glide away from the curb. Smith swiveled around in his seat and facing Tom, revealed a small, almost ludicrously sized pistol poking out of his right hand. Of course, in Chan's hand, the gun would have looked almost normal. In Smith's hand, the small .22 caliber pistol just looked wrong. However, at close quarters, it was an excellent kill weapon, causing only a small entry wound, no exit wound and enough power in the bullet to rattle around in the brain cavity ensuring a fairly quick and painless death. Tom knew he wouldn't even bleed much. The heart would just stop pumping and the blood would remain in situ. As clean a kill as you could get with a gun.

Tom braced himself for the bullet's impact and closed his eyes. Being thrown forward and realizing he was being thrown forward was the last thing he had expected.

# Chapter 4

"Just what in the fuck do you guys think you're playing at?!" screamed Swanson, jumping from her car. She had driven straight towards the Chrysler as it had attempted to exit 4th Street. Her ceramic brakes had been the difference between emergency braking and an emergency call out.

"What are *we* playing at?!" screamed the driver in response, rising shakily from his seat, pointing at her car just an inch from his bumper. "You nearly killed us all!"

"Don't be a fucking drama queen!" she chided, brushing past the driver towards the rear of the car and pulling open the door.

"Mr. Butler?" she asked stretching out her hand.

Tom opened his eyes for the first time and looked into the eyes of his savior. Unrestrained by a seat belt, he had hammered into the back of the front seat. He shook his head in an attempt to understand exactly what had just happened. Agent Chan, it seemed, was in a similar condition. He looked on in a daze as he also had hammered into the seat in front. However, whereas others were simply dazed, Agent Smith poured blood. His lip and nose had split due to the small .22 caliber pistol slamming into his face as his unrestrained body had also been thrown forwards in the car. The windscreen barely restrained the giant form of Smith as his outstretched hand containing the small pistol finally caught up. The irony was not lost on Tom as he began to fully understand the picture in front of him. The small weapon chosen for its lack of bloodletting had created a geyser in Smith's nose.

Tom smiled and accepted Swanson's outstretched hand.

Chan was quick to recover. "He has been released, Miss Swanson!"

"Not by me!"

"It is not your decision to make," answered Chan authoritatively.

"In which case he is free to go with you or come with me, right?" asked Swanson cuttingly. Something was amiss and she had every intention of finding out what exactly it was.

Chan grabbed Tom as Agent Swanson began to pull Tom out of the vehicle.

"Hit it!" screamed Chan.

The driver reacted quickly and began to move but with Swanson's Audi RS4 to negotiate, it wasn't the sudden acceleration that Chan had been hoping for. Swanson removed Tom with a smirk while Chan looked on in frustration as the driver eased beyond the RS4 and then hit it.

Tom and Swanson watched Chan spin around in his seat and could almost hear the screams of anger as he vented at his colleagues while watching Tom and Swanson fade into the distance.

"So, Mr. Butler," said Swanson turning to Tom. "Are you going to tell me what the fuck is going on?"

Tom shook his head, and Swanson took him by the elbow and led him back towards the FBI field office.

"I thought as much," she said despondently.

"I've been released!" Tom said, struggling gently against Swanson's grip.

"Perhaps, but I've a funny feeling I just saved your ass and for that you are going to tell me something before you go anywhere."

Tom looked at the surprisingly perceptive agent. He guessed she was mid-thirties at most, and from her confidence and the way in which she carried herself, she was an exceptionally capable one at that. She was right. He likely *would* be dead now if it were not for her instinct and, of course, her maniacal driving. He looked back towards her abandoned car, a station wagon, but a very butch looking station wagon.

"Should you not move that?" he asked, motioning his head towards her car and changing the subject.

She looked around. She wanted to get Butler back into protective custody. Her alarm bells were ringing on full alert. The streets were empty and Chan and his colleagues' Chrysler were a dot on the horizon.

"You don't mind?" she asked.

Butler shook his head and she changed direction and led him back to the Audi.

"How many kids you got?" asked Butler taking the passenger seat.

"Not married."

Butler smiled. He knew she wasn't married before he asked. "This car has a kind of family exterior but inside it's all business." He tried to move in the seat but it had devoured him with its sporty snugness. "It's so you!" he added with sincerity.

Swanson looked at him for some hint of sarcasm but Butler looked deadpan and straight ahead. She shook her head and turned the ignition key. The engine's bass-like roar announced its readiness to leap forward. Swanson eased the straining beast towards the garage entrance just a few yards ahead. The automatic doors began to rise at the click of her remote, and she looked again towards Butler and smiled. He reminded her very much of her father.

She turned the wheel sharply and floored the engine, the tires screeched and strained as the full power of the engine took them all by surprise. The car rocketed away from the FBI building and hurled its passengers across Washington.

Butler suddenly considered the prospect of a double bluff and instantly panicked.

"Have you eaten?" asked Swanson nonchalantly, taking a corner meant for 20 MPH at 60 MPH.

Butler relaxed mentally, at least as much as the G force being exerted on his body would allow. "Room service wasn't due 'til seven!"

"Excellent, I'm famished and technically you are free."

Butler was no fool; the informality and lack of prying eyes was exactly what Swanson wanted. His already excellent opinion of her increased even further. She was a very smart young woman and one that would require him to be on top of his game. The last thing he'd want on his conscience was knowing he had gotten her killed.

# Chapter 5

**20 January 2013 - President Jack King Inauguration day
Oval Office – The White House**

Jack woke up on the morning that would see a new America - an America that had spent four years in almost constant turmoil was coming to an end. He offered a new choice for America, a strong and proud America that rewarded those who worked hard and believed in the founding fathers' principles. Nobody could deny that the last president had had the unenviable task of trying to recover from the global financial crisis, but one poor decision after another had been more than the public could stomach. Change was needed and President Jack King was the man chosen for the job. It wasn't quite a landslide victory but not far from it.

It would be an uncharacteristically quiet inauguration; the twentieth fell on a Sunday and law dictated that the president must be sworn in by the twentieth. An official ceremony would be held the following day.

President King took the oath of office in a small ceremony conducted by the Chief Justice attended by his wife and senior staff. His speech, safely tucked in his inside pocket, a month in the making, would have to wait until the public ceremony the following day. It was a speech that would never see the light of day. A speech full of hope and determination to work hard, pay down the debts of a wasteful government and ensure the generations to come wouldn't have to pay for the generations in the past.

"Mr. President?"

Jack continued his discussion with the Chief Justice. He had a list of deeply unpopular laws passed by the previous incumbent to overturn as a priority and took the opportunity to discuss his plans with the Chief Justice.

"Mr. President?" asked Kenneth Lee, this time more firmly.

Jack turned, expecting to see his predecessor, but Kenneth was staring directly at him.

"Mr. President, we have a meeting scheduled."

Jack looked over his shoulder before pointing to himself questioningly, much to the amusement of those gathered in the Oval Office.

Kenneth Lee had been Jack's Chief of Staff from the moment he had entered the race. In fact, Kenneth Lee was the reason Jack King had entered the race at all.

Before Kenneth had approached Jack, he had taken an almost unheard of governor of Wyoming, America's least populous state and made him the frontrunner for the Republican nomination. Overnight, the photogenic Wyoming governor was the answer to every Republican's prayers. Swing voters loved him and with a Hispanic grandmother, another huge block of votes was in the bag. In both ability and stature, he soared above his contenders throughout the televised debates. The Republicans were back in a big way. There was little doubt in anyone's mind that he was their man. By the time November came, the race was down to three.

Jack's first meeting with Kenneth had been on a cold winter's evening. A knock at his door at 9:30 p.m. was not unheard of but certainly not common. Kenneth Lee stood before him with a look of desperation on his face. Jack recognized Kenneth instantly. Jack was a staunch Republican supporter and had been a vocal advocate of the Wyoming governor's plans to rebuild America from the ground up. Inviting him in, Jack was totally unprepared for the conversation that was to ensue.

In short, Kenneth Lee had made it abundantly clear that his country needed him to serve again, only this time in a slightly enhanced role. Two hours earlier, the governor of Wyoming had died of a massive heart attack. The announcement would be made within the next hour and with the pitiful display of the governor's Republican contenders and the rock bottom approvals for the current Democratic incumbent, it was feared the impact of the news and the lack of hope it offered would send the country spiraling into a major economic depression. A phone call from the chairman of the GOP had sealed the need for Jack to 'step up and take the reins'. The party was on the brink of meltdown, they needed somebody the country could look up to, a man of stature, a man of leadership, a man the country could respect and follow. General Jack King, former chairman of the Joint Chiefs, was their man.

His country needed him. Jack had never been found wanting when his country called. He stood up and helped the country through the mourning of a president who would never be and gave them the president they all dreamed could save them.

Kenneth Lee had been by his side from that day, an ever constant. He was a political warrior who ensured he was one step ahead and never ambushed. Money had never been an issue. Kenneth Lee had secured the largest war chest ever to be collected to fight a campaign. When more funds were needed, he doubled and trebled whatever the requirement was. Despite the election being almost a certainty from day one of Jack's nomination as the Republican candidate, Kenneth took no chances. For every dollar the Democratic incumbent spent, Kenneth spent two on Jack.

"We need to go, Mr. President," prompted Kenneth.

It was the simple act of Kenneth calling him Mr. President rather than Jack that made the realization of what he had achieved really hit home.

Jack realized then just how much his and his wife's lives were really about to change.

After a small applause from the rest of the room, Kenneth led Jack with purpose towards the Cabinet Room. An elderly gentleman, immaculately presented, awaited their arrival.

"Mr. President, may I introduce you to Mr. Warren Walker. Mr Walker, the President," said Kenneth.

He stood and bowed his head slightly, shaking hands with President King. "Delighted to meet you, Mr. President and please accept my congratulations on your superb victory."

"Thank you," replied Jack looking to Kenneth for some indication as to why they were meeting with Mr. Walker.

"I can see Kenneth has not warned you of our meeting," said Mr. Walker, correctly reading the situation.

"No he hasn't," replied Jack honestly while staring at Kenneth. He turned to face Mr. Walker.

"I asked him not to. All he knows was that it was imperative I met with you on the twentieth of January 2013. 'You' being the president of the United States, not necessarily you, Jack King, if you understand my meaning."

"Yes," replied Jack. "If I hadn't won, my opponent would be sitting here meeting with you."

"Before I begin, I must note that my instructions are to discuss this with the president of the United States only. If you choose to include your Chief of Staff that is your choice."

Jack looked back at Kenneth, his mind racing. What was the old guy going to hit him with? Was this the Area 51 alien chat or some other secret that you only became aware of when you were president?

"I didn't catch which arm of the government you represent, Mr. Walker?" asked Jack, prying for some clue.

Mr. Walker smiled warmly. "Oh, I am not from any part of the government, Mr. President."

Jack looked again at Kenneth for some clue about what was happening. Kenneth shrugged his shoulders, in an 'I don't know, your call' fashion.

"We're in this together, it's his fault I'm here!" said Jack jokingly. However, his mind continued to race, and one question was stuck in his mind.

"Actually, would you mind excusing us for a moment, Mr. Walker?"

"Not at all, Mr. President," he answered, not moving.

After an awkward second, Jack got up and motioned for Kenneth to follow him. They exited the room into Jack's PA's office.

Before Jack could ask, Kenneth was on the defensive. "No idea, I was just informed that the meeting was scheduled."

"By whom?"

"Your PA informed me it was in the diary when we came into office."

"What, we're taking meetings arranged by the previous government?!" he asked, incredulous. "How many more have they left?"

"None, this was it. We tried to clear it but it wouldn't delete. It was like it was hard wired into the system. I was sure it was a glitch until half an hour ago when I got the heads-up that your 1:00 p.m. had arrived!"

"Well I'm not going back into a meeting arranged by my predecessor," concluded Jack.

"But that's the strange thing, according to the system, it wasn't the previous government that arranged the meeting."

Jack waited for Kenneth to reveal who had, but he remained silent; it was obviously too big a deal to just tell him outright.

"So who did then?" Jack played along halfheartedly, much to Kenneth's disappointment.

"William Howard Taft. As in President Taft!" revealed Kenneth.

Jack could barely hide his incredulity that a president had allegedly arranged a meeting 100 years in the future.

"Are you mad?" he asked.

"That's not the best part, the meeting was at the request of JP Morgan, who died less than a month later."

"Bullshit! Why on earth would a meeting arranged a hundred years ago be in a modern computerized diary system?"

"I thought the same. I can only assume the meeting was noted in each of the presidents' subsequent diaries and passed onto each subsequent PA until it was computerized. Thereafter, it must have just been coded in and the code has been there ever since," Kenneth surmised, facing the door to the Cabinet office that held the answer.

"How on earth did they know it would be a Mr. Walker?" asked Jack, facing the same door, finding the weak link in Kenneth's summation.

"There's no name listed, it just states 'a representative of America's Trust'."

They looked at each other and it was clear both were desperate for more information.

Jack walked towards the door and opened it. Kenneth remained standing. He, as Mr Walker had pointed out, was not invited.

"You don't mind if Kenneth joins us do you, Mr. Walker?"

"Not at all, Mr. President, that is your choice."

As they sat down, Mr. Walker cleared his throat. Both the president and his Chief of Staff were on the edge of their seats.

"Gentlemen, how much do you know about compound interest?" began Mr. Walker. It was only thanks to their exceptional poker faces that Mr. Walker failed to notice just how underwhelmed his audience was by his question.

# Chapter 6

Butler pulled himself gingerly out of the Audi. The relief at reaching the diner in one piece was slowly sinking in. He felt as though he should bend down and kiss the sidewalk but felt the gesture, although warranted, a little melodramatic.

"You know there is a brake on the car, right?" he offered helpfully, with a soft dose of sarcasm.

Swanson didn't even justify his criticism with a response. She merely smiled politely and led the way into the diner.

"Clever name!" added Butler with yet more sarcasm. Swanson shook her head.

"You know it's a diner, so what better name than 'The Diner'?" explained Butler to the uninterested Swanson.

Swanson dismissed Butler by simply pointing towards a booth while she caught the waitress' eye. A simple two fingers raised by Swanson received a nod of understanding from the waitress, along with a warm, welcoming smile.

*Obviously a regular*, thought Butler as he took his seat. The subsequent look of disapproval from the waitress to Swanson when the waitress eyed Butler, did not go unnoticed by him.

Swanson pulled herself into the booth. "Calmed down yet?" she asked sternly.

Butler caught himself. She was right, he did have to calm down. How many people, however, had met their executioner, stared down the barrel of the gun about to kill them, only to be saved at the last second? The vision of Smith beginning to pull the trigger with a smile on his face was not one Butler would forget, nor did he ever wish to remember. He realized Swanson was staring at him, reading his every thought. She was an FBI agent trained in the art of reading every nuance, every movement and action of their suspects. He had to change the subject.

"Not a fan?" he asked, motioning towards the waitress.

Swanson looked bewildered for a second. "No, no, she's been trying to set me up for some time and you're the first guy I've ever brought here. She put two and two together and came up with about eighty seven," she laughed. A little too much Butler thought. Although who was he kidding? He was old enough to be her father. At least it had lightened the mood. She was studying him again.

"Do they have a menu?" he asked, keen to have something to do other than be under her gaze.

"Already ordered. Now are you going to tell me what the fuck is going on or not?"

"I don't know what you mean," he said unconvincingly.

"Okay, let's do it the hard way," said Swanson, noting Butler moved back slightly in his seat. "Full name?"

"Remember I've been released."

"On you go," said Swanson. She had seen the fear in Butler's eyes. She knew he was going nowhere.

"I think we both know I'm not going anywhere, although do you mind if I just nip to the restroom before we get started?" he pleaded, a little too pathetically.

Swanson wasn't quite buying Butler, something was amiss. He came across meek and mild, but his eyes told her something different.

"Fine, but don't do anything silly."

Butler got up and found the restroom. The pay phone sat next to the entrance of the restrooms just as he had hoped. He dialed the number and was pleased to hear the voice on the other end. "Six?"

"Negatori," was the slightly panicked response.

"Scatter!" he said quickly and hung up, a huge weight lifted from his shoulders. He made his way back to the booth and pulled himself in.

"Thomas Franklin Butler," he said.

Swanson noticed his change in demeanor.

"Occupation?"

"Retired."

Swanson smiled without any warmth. Butler understood.

"Retired analyst," he added with a hint of a grin.

Swanson remained silent.

"Honestly, I *was* an analyst!" he replied indignantly.

"Retired?" she questioned, unconvinced. She knew Butler was fifty-four from the APB that had been circulated for his arrest. Other than his name and age, the APB had been bereft of any other information. Fifty-four was not an age you retired willingly unless monies allowed, and from what she could see, certainly from his clothing and wristwatch, money was not overtly displayed.

"Downsized," admitted Butler reluctantly.

"From where?"

"My firm on Wall Street," replied Butler.

"So you were a financial analyst?"

"Yes," lied Butler.

Swanson did not miss the lie, the telltale movement of his eyes giving him away. Before she could challenge him, the waitress arrived with their two coffees and two of the largest mounds of pancakes Butler had ever seen. He stared at them in disbelief.

"Seriously, half that would still be far too much!" protested Butler, looking around his mound to the lithe and athletic figure of Swanson.

Swanson missed little. "I've got an extremely fast metabolism," she said in response to his quizzical look.

"I'll gain three pounds just looking at this," murmured Butler as Swanson tucked in.

She washed down her first mouthful and picked up where she had left off. "So, what was the name of your firm?"

Butler took a mouthful just as she began to speak. He took his time masticating the melt-in-your-mouth pancake, not an easy task as he desperately tried to stall long enough to work out exactly what he was going to tell Agent Swanson.

"Well?" she prompted.

"I worked for…" the sight of the Chrysler pulling to a stop at the curb stopped him in his tracks. Swanson followed his gaze out of the diner's window and calmly reached for her cell phone.

Butler's reprieve had been short lived. They knew he was with a senior FBI Agent. Whoever was pulling the strings had obviously decided this was no longer an issue and Butler's removal was worth that level of fallout. He knew Swanson was a dead woman, her intervention had sealed that. He thought he'd have time to work out a way to save her. The arrival of Chan and Smith so publicly was an extremely worrying turn of events. Such an overt display would suggest the timescales were even less than Butler had feared.

"Don't!" warned Butler. Despite the early hour, the diner had a number of patrons taking advantage of their 24/7 operation.

"Don't what?" replied Swanson angrily lifting the cell to her ear.

"Call for backup. They've already decided we're collateral, no point adding others."

Smith and Chan exited the Chrysler and took up station at the curbside. The Band-Aid on Smith's nose proudly displayed Swanson's earlier intervention.

"What in the fuck are you talking about?" Swanson was beginning to get seriously pissed off with his cryptic approach to whatever was going on. She began to move from the booth but was stopped by Butler, his hand snapping across and firmly pinning hers to the table.

"I said don't!"

"Take your hand the fuck off mine," she hissed angrily. Her body continued to move despite her hand being left behind, leaving her in the bizarre situation of leaning towards Butler while trying to get away from him. "I'm going to speak with those two assholes and find out what they want."

"Fine," Butler released his grip and let her walk two paces away before adding, "but they're going to kill you."

Swanson laughed but saw nothing in Butler's face to suggest that he was being anything but sincere. She looked outside. Her smile dropped slightly and she noticed that her movement had resulted in a readying of Chan and Smith. Their jackets had been opened and their handguns visible. The FBI standard issue weapon was a Glock. Years earlier it had been possible to use a personal weapon but those times had long since gone. Every FBI Agent who wished to remain one carried a Glock. From what Swanson could make out at the distance between herself and Smith and Chan, neither carried a Glock. Not good.

Noticing her hesitation, Butler went on. "They won't come in here, too many cameras. One above the till, one in the corner on the way through to the restroom and if I'm not mistaken, that smoke detector is a fish eye camera," he said without looking at any of them. "It's a twenty-four seven joint, lots of drunks and brawls. They'll have a direct alarm to the police and the cameras will be linked to the web. They can't simply steal the tapes. We're safe for now."

Swanson sat back down. She had a feeling Butler was finally revealing himself.

"Analyst?" she asked sarcastically.

Butler shrugged his shoulders. "I analyze situations," he offered with a smile.

"For who?"

"For whom," he corrected.

"Fuck, whatever!"

"Formerly the CIA."

"So you were downsized?"

"Hmm, I think fired would be more appropriate."

"That doesn't sound good," she said with some concern, wondering whether Chan and Smith really were the good guys.

Butler watched as she looked at Chan and Smith. "Trust me, I'm not your problem here."

"Are they CIA?" she asked watching the two become twitchier. Her sitting back down had unnerved them.

"I'm not sure. Hired assassins, probably," mused Butler, refusing to look at them.

"So they were going to kill you?"

"Right about the time you drove your car at them. Smith was about to pull the trigger when we had to brake."

"Holy fuck!" she exclaimed a little too loudly and caused a number of patrons to turn and look at them.

Butler threw a look towards the other patrons that resulted in them all suddenly finding whatever food lay before them far more interesting than anything else.

"I do therefore owe you a very heartfelt thank you," said Butler.

Swanson looked deep into the eyes of a man she had arrested the previous day, just spent the last hour with, and it seemed had just met in the last few seconds. The man before her bristled with confidence, sat straighter and sounded far more commanding than the man she had arrested.

"Who exactly the fuck are you?" she asked again.

"A great friend and a truly terrifying enemy," he replied while watching another Chrysler pull to a stop.

"And how should I view you?" she asked, her hand moving towards her Glock. She was going to have to choose sides. She had noticed the other car draw to a stop and three men had exited. It was five against two and Butler was unarmed.

"If your hand moves any closer to your gun, I'll be your killer but if you hand me the gun, I'm your only hope!"

"I thought you said they wouldn't come in?" she asked, the tension was palpable.

"I was wrong!" he replied simply. "But if we don't move now, a lot of innocent people are in danger!"

Swanson considered the threat and Butler's concern for the other diners and made an instant decision that she'd have to live with for the rest of her life, however long that would be.

"Run!" he said.

"What the fuck do you mean run?"

"Back door, hit it and run for our lives."

"You have got to be fucking kidding me," she said as they both stood up and Butler led the way towards the restrooms. They watched as the five men, as one, moved towards the diner's entrance. Chan raised his hand to his mouth. He was communicating with someone, whoever was covering the back, Swanson thought.

Before she had a chance to tell Butler, he swept past her, hit the emergency bar on the fire escape with his back and turning through one hundred and eighty degrees, raised his hand, and in one swift and seamless move, removed Swanson's Glock from her holster and shot the two men waiting for them in the alley to the rear. Swanson stood helpless; her backup weapon was in her Audi parked out front.

The noise of the Glock was followed quickly by the front door of the diner crashing open. All hell had broken loose.

Swanson was not unaccustomed to firefights but was used to a significantly larger force than the opposition and usually benefitted from having her own weapon.

Butler grabbed her free hand and catapulted her through the door with him. The two ambushers were down. Butler handed Swanson her weapon while retrieving one from the ground as they sprinted down the alley. The first shots rang out just as they cleared the corner.

"Fuck!" screamed Swanson, her adrenaline pumping to levels she had never before thought possible.

Butler just kept running. He wasn't kidding, she thought, his plan is exactly what he said, run.

"I'll call for backup!"

Butler shook his head. "You don't understand, we can't trust anyone!"

"We can trust the FBI," she replied indignantly.

"The same guys that handed me over to two killers!"

Swanson was about to reply but two bullets zipping past her head stopped any further discussion. Butler skidded to a stop, spun and dropped down to one knee, again all in one fluid motion. The shooting position allowed him to fire off four accurate shots that stopped the two pursuers in their tracks. They both slumped to the ground. From a distance, it was hard to tell how badly they were hurt but from the lack of screams, Swanson could only assume the hits were fatal.

"Who the fuck *are* you?" she asked in awe. He was fifty-four but ran faster and shot better than anyone she had ever trained with, and she had trained with some seriously tough guys.

"Let's go, and will you please lose that cell phone - they're tracking it!" he asked firmly but politely.

"Shit!" Swanson threw the phone towards the pursuers without a second thought. This shit was real.

After another ten minutes of running, Swanson was ready to drop. She could run a half marathon with ease but not at the pace at which Butler ran. He eased up, and she bent over, emptying the contents of her stomach onto the ground.

"Sorry about that," said Butler, "but I wanted to be sure we'd lost them. I assume two followed on foot while the others retrieved a car. We probably lost them when we ditched your phone."

Swanson looked up at him briefly. Her breath was slowly coming back and her stomach had relaxed.

"Now can you please tell me what the fuck is going on?" she struggled between breaths.

Butler looked around again. They were in the middle of a park under a bandstand; even from above they couldn't be seen. They were as safe as they were going to be anywhere.

"You've heard of America's Trust?"

"Of course, everyone has."

"Two years ago, when I was working a case, I stumbled across something. Two months later, I was fired. I've been looking into it ever since. America's Trust is a sham. America as we know it is on the brink of extinction."

**Please go to Amazon to continue reading America's Trust – available now.**

**Other books by Murray McDonald**

*Scion*

*Divide & Conquer*

*America's Trust*

**Young Adult – The Billionaire series**

*Kidnap*

*Assassin*

Printed in Great Britain
by Amazon

26365133R00223